After a
Brenda Cl
two childr
she has wr
of which w
name of B

Brenda Clarke lives with her husband in Keynsham, Bristol.

Also by Brenda Clarke

THREE WOMEN
WINTER LANDSCAPE
UNDER HEAVEN

and published by Corgi Books

AN EQUAL CHANCE

Brenda Clarke

CORGI BOOKS

AN EQUAL CHANCE

A CORGI BOOK 0 552 13230 6

Originally published in Great Britain by
Bantam Press, a division of Transworld Publishers Ltd.

PRINTING HISTORY
Bantam Press edition published 1989
Corgi edition published 1990

Copyright © Brenda Clarke 1989

Conditions of sale
1. This book is sold subject to the condition that it shall not, by way of trade *or otherwise*, be lent, re-sold, hired out or otherwise circulated in any form of binding or cover other than that in which it is published *and without a similar condition being imposed on the subsequent purchaser*.
2. This book is sold subject to the Standard Conditions of Sale of Net Books and may not be re-sold in the UK below the net price fixed by the publishers for the book.

This book is set in 10/11 pt English Times
by Colset Private Limited, Singapore.

Corgi Books are published by Transworld Publishers Ltd., 61–63 Uxbridge Road, Ealing, London W5 5SA, in Australia by Transworld Publishers (Australia) Pty. Ltd., 15–23 Helles Avenue, Moorebank, NSW 2170, and in New Zealand by Transworld Publishers (N.Z.) Ltd., Cnr. Moselle and Waipareira Avenues, Henderson, Auckland.

Printed and bound in Great Britain by
Cox & Wyman Ltd, Reading

I have never had a feeling ... that did not spring from the sentiments embodied in the Declaration of Independence ... which gave liberty not alone to the people of the country, but hope to all the world ... that all should have an equal chance.

ABRAHAM LINCOLN

PART ONE

1986

. . . to afford all an unfettered start and a fair chance in the race of life.

ABRAHAM LINCOLN

1

'Nineteen Twenty-six was a vintage year for girl babies,' Harriet Chance remarked, without turning her head. 'There was the Queen, Marilyn Monroe and . . . me!'

She did, now, glance fleetingly and provocatively over her shoulder at the man sitting on the deep chintz-covered sofa behind her, but almost immediately resumed her study of the view through the open window. Beyond the cream-painted railing of the balcony, with its deck-chairs and loungers and wide striped awning, the sun-baked scrub and hot white rock of the island of Agios Georgios stretched down to the sparkling sea. A mud road twisted between banks of juniper and sage towards the village – a huddle of houses, a kafenéion and a landing-strip – out of sight of the house which Spiros Georgiadis had built for himself on his private island, and which now belonged, until her death, to his widow, Harriet Chance.

Harriet Chance Canossa Contarini Cavendish Georgiadis Wingfield: she had been all those names at one time or another during her life, but it was by her maiden name that she was best-known to the millions of readers of the gossip columns of two continents. And today, Saturday, 28 June 1986, her sixtieth birthday, and in spite of a powerful counter-attraction in the forthcoming royal wedding – 'Is Fergie on a diet?' 'Is Andrew still in love with Koo?' – those same columns were full of speculation about the possibility of her marrying yet again.

'Will Harriet Chance, owner of the world-wide chain of Last Chance restaurants and arguably one of the richest women in the world, marry for a sixth time?' asked a well-known gossip columnist with unusual restraint. 'If so, who?' And then went on to rake over the ashes of her last divorce from film producer Rollo Wingfield; the latest scandal surrounding her third husband, formerly the Honourable Hallam Cavendish, now Viscount Carey and father of her younger son, Piers; and, finally, the unfortunate affair between her daughter, Elena Georgiadis, and an ageing Mexican film star nearly old enough to be her grandfather.

Other columnists dwelt on the private birthday celebration to be held today, and the lavish party being thrown tomorrow, when guests would be flown into Agios Georgios from all quarters of the globe: descriptions which managed to convey envy and disapproval in equal measure, with the inevitable harking back to Harriet's humble beginnings. 'Child of the vicarage', 'daughter of impoverished Cotswold Vicar' were two of their most hackneyed phrases.

'I see,' Edmund Howard observed in his soft Irish lilt, 'that the *Sun* has you earmarked for the Duke of Malmesbury, and the *Daily Mirror* for an American tycoon.' He patted the sofa beside him invitingly. 'Come and sit down, Harry, and for God's sake stop brooding. You've made up your mind that you're going to tell them this evening, so forget about it until then. Let's enjoy this special day together.' He held out a hand. 'Come and thank me properly for your present.'

Harriet turned away from the window into the cool of the airconditioned room, a smile replacing the frown which she had unconsciously been wearing for most of the morning. She glanced down at the sapphire and diamond ring which adorned her engagement finger, and which had replaced Rollo Wingfield's showy diamond, long since relegated to a London bank vault, along with Hallam's emerald. On her right hand, she still wore the cabochon ruby given to her by Spiros, and the little Victorian ring, set with garnets, which had belonged to Gus Contarini's grandmother. Dear Gus! She wished to God that she'd appreciated him more at the time. . . .

She crossed to the sofa and sat beside Edmund, lifting her face for his kiss. Then she snuggled into the crook of his arm, her right hand stroking the inside of his left thigh.

'Isn't it odd that not one English or American newspaper has nominated *you* as my future – my last! – husband? They must be blind.'

Edmund Howard laughed. He was a year older than Harriet: a handsome fine-boned man, whose thick mane of once-dark hair was now almost white. His body was still sleek and powerful, with the quiet strength that came from long years of training and handling horses. His movements were controlled, each gesture taking up the minimum of space. Only his eyes, a brilliant dark Irish blue, hinted at Celtic fire beneath the surface. All his life, he had cared passionately for the land which gave him birth, ardently believing that the whole of it should be free from British domination. The irony was, of course, that his other great motivation for existence had been, and still was, his love for an Englishwoman.

'Harriet Chance! Marry her racing manager!' he mocked gently. 'It would never cross their minds, girl dear! In their book, you must marry either someone immensely wealthy or someone titled. The days for you shacking up with a man who can only give you a sapphire the size of a pea are long gone, or so they're thinking.'

Harriet smiled. 'In that case, they're thinking wrong, my darling. All the same, is it quite dignified for two people of our age to be canoodling in this fashion?'

'Canoodling!' he grinned. 'Now, there's an expression that shows your age, acushla. You'll have to watch it. And you not looking a day over forty-five!'

'And that's a lie!' Harriet crowed delightedly. But she knew that the compliment was not undeserved. She did look much younger than her sixty years, in spite of the tell-tale wrinkles on neck and arms. She had spent so much of her life in the States that it had been second nature to watch her diet and figure, long before healthy eating and

11

exercising had become fashionable in Europe. It was years, too, since she had last seen the actual colour of her hair. She went regularly to the London and New York salons of Vidal Sassoon, and the once brown hair with its hint of chestnut was now a soft shade of blonde. The expensive make-up was equally discreet. Too many women tried to hide the ravages of time behind a mask of paint, which only emphasized their advancing years. A smudge of pale eye-shadow enhanced the blue of her eyes, and the brown mascara was thinly applied without the addition of liner. Carefully placed blusher showed up the fine bone-structure which she had inherited from her father.

In response to Harriet's half-hearted protest, Edmund took her in his arms and kissed her. He had loved her from the first moment of seeing her, nearly forty years ago, on a California beach. They had both been married to other people then, and had been married to yet other partners in the mean time. But through all the separations and mis-understandings which had come between them there had never been a day when he had not thought of her. They had been lovers, friends, enemies, employer and employee. Now, soon, they would be husband and wife.

For a moment, Harriet returned his kiss, her lips parting under his, holding him tightly. Then, abruptly, she pushed him away, twisted out of his arms and got up, pacing rest-lessly about the room. She looked drawn with worry.

'Harry,' Edmund pleaded, 'forget it. You've made up your mind what you're going to do. On the other hand, if it upsets you so much, don't go through with it. There's still time to change your mind before this evening.'

She shook her head. 'No. I must do what's right, whatever the consequences. I can't back away now. My conscience wouldn't let me.'

' "Child of the vicarage," ' he quoted softly.

A strong woman, Edmund reflected. A self-willed woman, a self-made woman, a powerful woman: she always had been. She was also a mass of contradictions,

12

like this room; like every room in every house she had ever furnished. He glanced around him.

The walls of this, the main salon, which ran the whole length of the first floor of the house, were painted white to capture the strong Aegean sunshine. Even the flowery English chintz of the sofa and armchairs was not entirely out of keeping. The Utrillo, a Montmartre street scene, which faced the balcony doors, was genuine, and had been moved some years ago to Agios Georgios from Spiros' Athens apartment. Also genuine, and adding to the mood of the room, was a Matthew Smith still life, which Edmund himself had bought for Harriet a few months previously. On the opposite wall, however, was a cluster of Atkinson Grimshaws – 'Moonlight, Glasgow Docks', 'Liverpool Docks', 'Where the Pale Moonbeams Linger' – dark, murky, cheap reproductions; aliens in that dazzling clarity of light. What had made Harriet hang them in this house, of all possible places?

One whole wall was taken up with stereo equipment and its attendant bank of records. Harriet moved towards it, selecting a disc apparently at random and placing it on the turntable. But when, instead of Mozart or Haydn, the soundtrack of *The Draughtsman's Contract* shattered the tranquillity of the morning Edmund realized that her choice had been no more haphazard than any of her other actions. The busy staccato chattering of the opening movement exactly suited her present disturbed, uncertain state of mind.

There was a knock on the door, and in response to Harriet's abstracted 'Come in!' her secretary, Bess Holland, entered the room, a sheaf of papers in her hand.

'Many happy returns of the day, Harriet,' she said, smiling broadly and handing over a gift-wrapped parcel. A few of Harriet's most favoured employees were permitted to call her by her first name. None of them, to Edmund's knowledge, had ever abused the privilege.

'Bess! How sweet of you! What is it?'

While she spoke, Harriet was busy tearing off the

13

wrappings, scattering paper and ribbons on the deep-piled carpet. She had never been able to resist the lure of presents; and even now, after years of being deluged with expensive, sometimes priceless, gifts, she retained the same excitement she had known as a child on Christmas morning.

'I hope you like it,' Bess Holland said anxiously. 'I'm sorry it's only one. I couldn't afford the set.'

It was a first edition of Jane Austen, beautifully bound.

'My favourite! *Emma!*' Harriet cried. 'Oh, thank you, Bess, darling! How did you know?'

'That it's your favourite? You told me once that you read it at least twice a year. More frequently sometimes, if you're feeling low. I remembered.'

Harriet blinked rapidly, her eyes full of tears. She kissed Bess's cheek. A moment later she was her usual brisk business-like self.

'Are those the lists for tomorrow's party? We'd better go through them. Have we enough room for all those guests who don't want to fly back to the mainland on Monday morning?'

'Yes, I think so. It doesn't amount to more than half a dozen. Most people are making arrangements to be collected immediately after the champagne breakfast.'

'You've checked with Air Traffic Control, Athens?'

'Twice. Three times. Don't worry. The arrival and departure times of both the private and chartered planes have all been cleared. The first guests will start arriving after lunch tomorrow.'

'You've asked Dick Norris to come as early as possible? I particularly want to have some time alone with him before the festivities get under way.'

'That's taken care of.' Bess glanced with veiled curiosity at her employer, before the blank secretarial mask descended once again. Dick Norris was one of Harriet's protégés. He was also a partner of Hutton, Taylor & Norris, her London solicitors. Bess went on: 'He and Mrs Norris are arriving in Athens today, and the yacht will pick

14

them up at Piraeus tonight. They'll be here by nine o'clock tomorrow morning.'

'Splendid.' Harriet smiled. 'You know, Bess, you're easily the most efficient secretary I've ever had.'

Bess Holland flushed with pleasure. She loved her job and her life. She was devoted to Harriet.

At forty-one, she was an extremely handsome woman with, as yet, almost no grey in the jet-black hair. Brown eyes which, during working hours, were partially hidden behind smart blue-rimmed spectacles, an excellent figure and beautiful legs were guaranteed to turn the head of any man in sight. She had married young, at eighteen, and been divorced by the time she was twenty, reverting to her maiden name. It was an experiment she had never repeated, preferring to be in charge of her own affairs. She had been to bed with a number of men over the years since she and Mark Skells split up, but not one of them had persuaded her that he was worth the career she had so painstakingly carved out for herself.

She said: 'I've also arranged to hire three more television sets from Sarantopolou's, that television firm near Omonia Square. The yacht can bring them across and return them on Monday morning.'

'Why?' Harriet asked, puzzled, while Edmund grinned understandingly. 'There are four sets in the house already, and surely no one's going to watch TV during the party?'

'Oh, yes, they are, my love,' Edmund said. 'Tomorrow's the final of the World Cup in Mexico. Argentina and West Germany. Well done, Bess. There's nothing worse than too many people crowded round one set. And they're certainly not invading our bedroom.'

'Football!' Harriet exclaimed disgustedly. Then she laughed. 'Yes, well done, Bess. But don't put a set in here. This room will be a refuge for all those unenlightened souls, like myself, who find the idea of eleven grown men trying to kick a ball between two posts, defended by eleven other grown men, a dead bore. I needn't ask you if the food and drink's all organized.'

'That's Dimitri's province,' Bess smiled. 'It would be more than my life's worth to interfere in the kitchen. Particularly since you decided that the buffet is to be made up of all Greek dishes. Dimitri is in his seventh heaven. Well, I must be getting on. There's still a load of things to see to.' She got up, paused and added shyly: 'I'm so glad you liked the book.'

When she had gone, Harriet sat staring in front of her for a moment or two, apparently lost in thought, while the first side of *The Draughtsman's Contract* drew to a close. She made no move to get up and turn the record over.

'A penny for them,' Edmund suggested lightly.

'What? Oh . . . nothing. My mind was a blank.'

And that was a lie, he thought. He saw her glance towards the table, where the remains of breakfast had not yet been cleared away.

Harriet consulted her wrist-watch and snapped irritably: 'Ten o'clock! You'd think they could come down to breakfast at a reasonable time on my birthday, wouldn't you?'

'Be fair, acushla,' he pleaded. 'Mike, Julia and the kids didn't arrive until late last night. They're probably suffering from jet-lag. New York to Agios Georgios is a hell of a way. And Piers never puts in an appearance until lunchtime when he's on holiday. You know that. And Elena's gone down to the beach. I saw her leave half an hour ago. She should be back soon.'

Harriet looked disapproving. 'It's so thoughtless. Maria and her daughter are most likely waiting to clear. They've such a lot to get through today.' She swung her sandalled feet over the edge of the sofa and stood up. 'You don't think Ellie's avoiding me, do you? Do you think she's really forgiven me?'

'For something that happened two years ago? I'm sure she has.' Edmund was instantly reassuring. 'She must have realized by now that it wouldn't have worked. A man more than old enough to be her father! An impoverished film star who was only after her for her money! Once the infatuation wore off, she was bound to see that you were right to put a stop to the affair.'

16

'I don't know,' Harriet said uneasily. 'Oh, the hatchet seems to be buried, all right. On the surface, at least, we appear to be as good friends as we were before. But there's a lot of me in her. She's inclined to be self-willed.'

Edmund chuckled richly. 'That, my love, must be the understatement of the century. "Inclined to be self-willed" doesn't begin to describe either you or your daughter. You're both as "headstrong as an allegory on the banks of the Nile", as Mrs Malaprop had it.'

Harriet moved towards the door, where she turned, her fingers on the handle.

'Personally, I've always agreed with that good lady's dictum that "all men are Bavarians"! And now, if you'll excuse me, I have things to do.'

She went out, leaving the door open behind her. The sound of Edmund's laughter followed her downstairs to the cool marble-tiled hall.

2

Elena had just entered the house, her long blonde hair tousled and damp from her swim.

Not yet twenty, she had matured early, and the sun-tanned body in the black bikini was fully developed. The breasts were deep and full, the legs long and slender; and the love-affair of two years ago had robbed her for ever of the innocence of childhood. The sapphire-blue eyes held an adult awareness.

'Mamma! Happy birthday! We'll be giving you our presents this evening, at dinner. Patience, as you told me once, is good for the soul.'

Had she ever said that? Harriet asked herself guiltily. Patience had never been one of her own abiding virtues.

'Ellie . . .' she began awkwardly, but hesitated, not sure how to continue. Beyond the open door, the sunlight lay in a bright flat wedge, with, in the distance, a gleam of brilliance which was the sea. A judas tree, lifting its cloudy head, cast a grateful patch of shade.

'It's OK, Mamma,' Elena said huskily, leaning forward to kiss Harriet lightly on the cheek. The honey-coloured skin smelt faintly of salt, and little tendrils of hair curled across the broad high forehead. 'I'm over it now. Really I am. What's more . . . I'm grateful.'

'Truly?' Harriet gripped her daughter's shoulders with painful intensity. 'You mean that? Promise!'

'I promise.' Elena smiled into the blue eyes so like her own. 'It was only my pride that was hurt. I knew it wasn't going to work before you came hot-footing it down to

18

Mexico. It was just the idea of "Mummy" having to come and bail me out of an impossible situation that I couldn't stomach. I thought I was able to take care of myself. I always was an arrogant little bitch.'

Harriet laughed with pure relief. 'Well, that makes two of us. I was far worse than you when I was seventeen. I didn't have a mother to pull on the reins when I got out of hand. My poor father! After your grandmother died, when I was ten, I don't think he knew what hit him. Now, come upstairs and have some breakfast.' She held out her left hand. 'And you can congratulate me.'

'Oh, Mamma! You've said "yes"! I can't tell you how thrilled I am, for both of you.' There was no doubting Elena's enthusiasm, or the warmth of the kiss which she planted, this time, full on Harriet's lips. 'Darling Eddie! Where is he? I must tell him how delighted I am, this minute!'

'He's in the main salon, reading the morning papers,' her mother said, following Elena up the stairs. 'And, for God's sake, put something on. That bikini is little short of indecent.'

'Afraid Eddie will decide to run off with *me* instead? Don't worry. He's waited too long for you to be interested in anyone else, however young and beautiful.'

'Conceited hussy!' Harriet watched with genuine pleasure as Edmund embraced his scantily clad future step-daughter.

But Elena was right. What was between herself and Edmund Howard was so old, so deep-rooted, that nothing and no one could threaten it any more. Harriet only wished that she could be as sure of her two sons' approval as she had been of her daughter's. Elena and Edmund had always been friends.

Elena sat down at the table and poured herself a cup of tepid coffee, grimacing as she drank it. She knew her mother's views on giving the servants extra work, so she refrained from pushing the bell to summon Maria. Punctuality at meal-times, or put up with the consequences, was one of Harriet's few domestic rules. Judging by the number of virgin place-settings, however, she was not the only one to be late for breakfast this morning. Even her half-nephews had not yet put in an appearance.

Recollecting the presence of the two boys in the house, Elena slipped on an outsize white T-shirt, which she had dropped over the back of her chair. Plain gold hoop ear-rings hung from the lobes of her ears, and a heavy gold bracelet weighted down one fragile wrist. She was, Harriet thought, watching her fondly, the best-looking of all her children: the child she had not expected, born when Harriet herself was over forty.

In fifteen months' time, at the age of twenty-one, Elena would become one of the wealthiest young women in the world, when she inherited the bulk of Spiros Georgiadis' fortune. She would become a prey to every fortune-hunter throughout Europe and America – a circumstance to which the affair with Ramón Perez had been merely a prelude. But from now on she would have Edmund to advise and guide her, standing legally in place of her father. And Elena loved and respected Edmund as much as she had despised and detested Rollo Wingfield. Harriet had wondered more than once during these past two years just how much the Mexican escapade had been her daughter's unspoken protest against her own marriage. Elena had had far more to do with Rollo than either of the boys, and had taken a violent dislike to him from the beginning.

Poor self-absorbed Rollo! Highly volatile himself, he had never had either the time or the inclination to understand the workings of other people's minds. From the start, it had been a marriage as doomed to failure as her first one to Gerry Canossa and her third to Hallam Cavendish; the only difference between the last two being that in the former instance she had made all the running, whereas in the second she had been blackmailed into marriage.

Which reminded her that Hallam was making trouble again – when was he not? – and her London solicitors had warned her only last week that he was negotiating the

20

male equivalent of a kiss-and-tell series of articles with one of the Sunday newspapers. She supposed with a sigh that she would have to make yet another substantial increase in his allowance. He knew too much, and although he no longer had proof – Spiros, bless him, had seen to that – he could still make potentially damaging allegations. And it wasn't good for Piers to have his parents publicly bickering. Ah, well! Now that Hallam had finally inherited the title, she supposed he did have a certain amount of added expense. There was that great white elephant, Carey Hall, to be maintained for a start. She didn't want it in a state of ruin by the time that Piers became Viscount Carey.

As though on cue, the door opened and the Honourable Piers Cavendish wandered in, sporting a dressing-gown which could only be described as flamboyant; an exotic shade of peacock blue, patterned with orange dragons breathing crimson flames. Edmund regarded it with disfavour.

'Who was it,' he enquired of no one in particular, 'who said that peacock blue was a great colour provided it was confined to peacocks?'

Piers ignored him. 'Mother, darling!' Gracefully he saluted Harriet's cheek, stooping from his six-foot height to do so. 'Many happy returns of the day. Presents are being given this evening, at dinner, or so I've been instructed. And you know what a good boy I am when it comes to doing as I'm told.'

Elena snorted and winked at Edmund. 'That's only because you know which side your bread is buttered,' she told her half-brother provocatively. 'You've probably exceeded your quarterly allowance again, and are hoping to borrow from Michael. It was Michael's idea,' she added for the benefit of her mother, 'that we should give the presents at dinner-time.'

Harriet's eyes went swiftly to her younger son. 'Is that true, Piers? Are you in debt again? You haven't been lending money to your father?'

'Good God, no! Wouldn't do anything so stupid.' Piers

21

refused the cup of cold coffee which his half-sister was offering him. He would go down to the kitchen presently and wheedle Maria into making him a fresh one. 'Not that he didn't try a quick touch when I saw him in Town last week. Been betting heavily on the gee-gees, I fancy. Probably has Joe Coral breathing down his neck.' Piers stretched full length on the sofa, which Edmund had recently vacated in favour of an armchair near the window. He eyed his mother from beneath half-closed lids. 'Mind you, he didn't let me go without a struggle. Appealed to the old school spirit. "Floreat Herga", and all that crap. But I stood firm, I do assure you, Mater.'

Piers knew that Edmund did not like him and, whenever they met, could never resist fuelling that dislike with an exaggerated performance of the upper-class public-school twit. In this he was helped by his looks. Tall and slender, with his father's slightly effeminate features, Harriet's blue eyes and straight brown hair, he would have been an instant choice for any stage or television play requiring a bumbling English aristocrat.

In actual fact, like many of his kind, Piers was a clever and shrewd manipulator of other people, devoted to his own interests. He had not been happy at either his prep school or Harrow, but the latter had hardened him and turned him into a survivor. Consequently, he had enjoyed his years up at Oxford, which had only just come to an end. He had done and tried most things during his time at Balliol, including snorting coke, but had always been careful never to over-step the mark. He had been an intelligent debater – listened to with respect, without ever setting the Isis on fire – and a lesser light of the OUDS. He had made friends, a few enemies and gained a sound second-class degree in English Literature. But, as with Harrow, he left behind no lasting impression. It was understood that, like his half-brother, Michael Contarini, before him, he would now be found employment in one capacity or another in the giant multi-national Chance Corporation.

Harriet was about to reply, when her two grandsons

burst into the room. Having slept off their jet-lag, they were ready and raring to go. Angelo, who was twelve, and Marco, two years younger, were attired in identical Bermuda shorts, bright green with a pattern of palm trees, and each carried a Sony Walkman and a quantity of very expensive underwater diving equipment. Both were short and stocky, dark-haired and brown-eyed, small clones of their father.

'Hi, Gran'ma!' Angelo reached up to plant a smacking kiss on Harriet's lips. 'Happy birthday! C'mon, Marc! Say "happy birthday" to Gran'ma.'

'Happy birthday Gran'ma. Hi, Aunt Ellie! Hi, Uncle Perce!'

Piers shut his eyes with an eloquent shudder. 'Dear child! The name is Piers. P-I-E-R-S! It's French.'

'Thought you were English,' Angelo objected. 'Seems kinda crazy t'me, having a French name if you're a limey.'

'It's Norman. Have you never heard of the Norman Conquest, or don't they teach you anything in the States prior to the Revolution?'

' "Prior to," ' repeated Angelo, with a wide toothy grin. 'I must remember that when I get back home. "Prior to the Revolution, you chaps!" ' He made a passable stab at Piers's upper-class English accent, and his brother dutifully fell about laughing. 'Anyway, it wasn't a revolution. We don't have revolutions in the States. It was the War of Independence. Gran'ma, can we go down to the beach? Mom says it's OK.'

'All right. But don't go too far out in the water. I'd rather you waited, really, until a grown-up can go with you.'

'Aw, Gran'ma, we're old enough to take care of ourselves now!' Angelo protested.

'Old enough to take care of ourselves,' Marco repeated, an obedient echo.

'Not underwater, you're not,' Harriet decreed firmly. 'Leave all that stuff behind, and we'll bring it down later. You can swim around on the surface for the time being. . . . Yes, all right, Maria,' she added to the woman hovering patiently in the doorway, 'you can clear away now.

23

It doesn't look as though Mr and Mrs Contarini are coming down to breakfast. What about you boys? Do you want anything to eat?'

'They already been down to the kitchen,' Maria said, coming forward with her tray. 'Dimitri, he give them cookies and milk.'

'And, Gran'ma, we'll be fine swimming underwater,' Angelo insisted. 'When we go to Palm Beach, Mom lets us do it all the time.'

'Not without supervision, I hope,' Harriet said austerely.

'I'll go with them.' Elena pushed back her chair and shepherded her half-nephews to the door. 'Come on, you two. Last one into the water's a cissy!'

The boys yelled and hurtled towards the door, almost colliding with Maria and her loaded tray as they did so. Still yelling, they clattered downstairs, Elena hard on their heels and contributing a series of Indian war-whoops to the general din. Piers raised his eyes to heaven.

'How long are they staying?' he demanded plaintively. 'No, for God's sake, don't tell me! I don't think my nerves could stand it. And if I were you, Mother dearest, I'd sue that extremely expensive finishing school of Ellie's under the Trade Descriptions Act. If she's finished, then I'm Margaret Thatcher.'

'Oh, go and get dressed,' Harriet said, half-amused, half-irritated. Piers always seemed to have that effect on her. There was too much about him that reminded her of Hallam.

'Very well.' Piers rose gracefully from the sofa. 'I can tell when I'm *de trop*. And don't think I haven't noticed the ring. I want you both to know that you have my blessing.' He smiled beatifically and drifted out of the room just as his half-brother and sister-in-law entered.

'Really, he's impossible!' Harriet exclaimed with an uncertain laugh. 'Michael! Julia! I hope you're feeling rested. I'm afraid,' she added guiltily, 'that Maria's just cleared away the breakfast things.'

'We had it in bed.' Julia kissed Harriet on both cheeks and

nodded vaguely at Edmund before sinking into the depths of the other armchair. 'Maria brought it up. I hope you don't mind.'

'Of course not.' She might have known, Harriet thought, that Maria would look after Michael. She smiled at her daughter-in-law, wishing that she could like her better.

At thirty-six, Julia was already running to fat: she loved eating and was inordinately lazy. When she was at home, in New York, her most strenuous occupation was her six-days-a-week bridge sessions with her friends. Every now and then, she would visit a health farm in the Catskills and be pummelled and dieted back into some sort of shape, but then she would go on another eating binge and the pounds would pile on once again. The black hair, knotted in a chignon at the nape of her neck, was as carefully tended as the creamy, skilfully made-up skin; but all the attention lavished on her by hairdresser and masseuse could not disguise the puffiness around the dark liquid eyes or the spreading figure spilling out of the designer T-shirt and shorts.

Michael Contarini, thirty-eight years old and vice-chairman of the Chance Corporation, was an inch shorter than his wife; a tough, bull-necked, square-set man, whose olive skin and black hair proclaimed his Italian ancestry at the expense of his English forebears. He frowned after the departing back of his half-brother, a look of veiled contempt in his brown eyes.

'You're not really thinking of bringing him into the business, are you, Momma?' he asked, when he had, in his turn, kissed Harriet and offered her congratulations on her birthday.

'Of course.' Harriet sat down on the sofa and invited Michael to sit beside her. 'Part of it will belong to him one day, as part of it will to you. You'll just have to learn to work together.'

Michael Contarini snorted. 'Work? A guy like Piers doesn't know the meaning of the word. All I want from him is for him to keep his nose clean and vote the way I tell him, *when* I tell him.'

'I don't think he'll be that easy to handle,' Edmund warned, looking up from his perusal of the *Financial Times* index. 'He has a stubborn streak. There's a very cunning brain ticking away behind that vacuous expression.'

Michael glowered. 'I think you're wrong; but, if not, we can hammer it out between us. At least there's only the two of us. I shan't have Ellie to lick into shape as well.'

It had been an understood thing from the time of Elena's birth that Spiros' money would go to his daughter – his only child – and Harriet's would be divided between her two sons. And Michael found it difficult to disguise his jealousy of his half-sister, who would come into her inheritance in a mere eighteen months' time. He made no secret of the fact that he thought his mother should retire, especially now that she was sixty, from active participation in the corporation's affairs. He could then have total power – for, unlike Edmund, he discounted Piers – even if he was only destined for half his mother's fortune.

Preoccupied with his own thoughts, Michael did not see the uneasy glance which Harriet gave Edmund. Nor did it strike him that, a few moments earlier, she had referred to his inheriting a *part* of her money, rather than a full half-share.

Harriet got to her feet, sounding and looking somewhat flustered.

'I really must get on,' she said. 'There are so many things still to see to. Elena has taken the boys down to the beach, but I do think someone else should be there, Michael, if they're going to swim underwater.' She clasped her hands together and then unclasped them. 'Do as you please all day. There will be a cold buffet lunch in the dining-room between twelve and two. We'll probably see one another around. But I want us all sitting down promptly to dinner at half-past seven. And afterwards . . . I have an important announcement to make.'

3

By mid-morning Agios Georgios was overpoweringly hot. In England it was raining.

The airport was crammed with holidaymakers, excited children riding up and down on the escalators, every coffee-bar jammed to capacity. The queues at the luggage check-ins seemed to stretch for ever. It was over half an hour before Dick Norris rejoined his wife, clutching their tickets.

'Not over the limit, were we?' she asked.

Melanie Norris was a pretty fluffy little blonde, a good many years her husband's junior. A lot of people wondered what a clever man like Dick had seen in her, a woman whose only interests were her clothes and her appearance. It might have surprised them to know how devoted to Melanie Dick really was. He found her a restful person. He was surrounded all day by sharp legal minds. Away from the offices of Hutton, Taylor & Norris, he needed to relax.

'No,' he said, tucking her arm in his. 'Just under. But why you need that much baggage for a short weekend beats me! Anyone would think we're off to outer Mongolia for an indefinite stay. Let's see if we can get a drink somewhere. We've quarter of an hour before boarding.'

'Why do you think Harriet wants us to arrive early?' Melanie enquired when, after a great deal of hassle, they had managed to find themselves a table in one of the upstairs lounges. Dick went to the self-service counter and fetched two cups of coffee.

27

'Something's cropped up, I dare say,' he answered vaguely. Not even with Melanie would he discuss his clients' business. But he knew perfectly well why Harriet wanted to see him before her other guests arrived. She intended to make a new will. He couldn't help being interested. And intrigued.

Harriet's will had always been a fairly straightforward affair; as straightforward, at any rate, as a vast and complex estate like hers could be. The bulk of her fortune, her shares and her controlling interest in the Chance Corporation were to be divided equally between the two sons of her second and third marriages. Not a very sophisticated arrangement; but, then, in many ways, Harriet Chance (as, after five husbands, it was easier to think of her) was not a very sophisticated woman. Deep down, she was still the young girl from the Cotswold vicarage, with simple middle-class attitudes towards life.

Not that Dick would ever hear a word said against her. He owed everything he had, and was, to Harriet. If it hadn't been for the Chance scholarship scheme, he would probably still be drudging away in some obscure Birmingham solicitor's office, an underpaid clerk. It was only the offer of financial assistance from the Chance Corporation which had seen him through university.

He couldn't believe, either, that it was totally fortuitous that he had afterwards been taken on by Harriet's own London firm of lawyers, Hutton & Taylor. Her surprisingly personal interest in some of the people she helped was never half-hearted. And two years ago, when, at the age of thirty-nine, he had been offered a partnership in the firm, whose name had been changed to incorporate his own, he had suspected that Harriet was behind that, also. She was a very powerful and determined lady.

The Athens plane was announced over the loudspeaker. Dick swallowed the dregs of his coffee, while Melanie powdered her nose. Then they gathered up their coats and went through to the departure lounge.

*   *   *

28

Piers bathed and dressed in his usual leisurely fashion, before putting through a call to his father at Carey Hall in Berkshire. The old man probably wouldn't be there, but it was worth a try.

To his surprise, he was connected with Hallam almost immediately.

'What the hell do you want?' the Viscount demanded with a deplorable lack of enthusiasm at hearing from his only child.

'I thought you'd like to know that Edmund Howard is to be Mother's number six. The "verray, parfit gentil knyght".'

Hallam's derisive snort almost split his son's ear-drum. 'If you knew what I know about that bastard . . . !'

'So you keep saying,' Piers interrupted smoothly. 'But, as you never get round to telling me what exactly it is you know, these hints and innuendoes are becoming rather a bore. What is far more important is that Mother is up to something.'

'What do you mean, "up to something"?'

'If I knew, I'd tell you, but at the moment it's no more than a sixth sense. Call it intuition.'

There was silence at the other end of the line. Presently Hallam said: 'You must have a reason for feeling that way.'

Piers stared thoughtfully out of the window at the long lovely line of the bay. The slopes surrounding it were studded with scrub and dwarf juniper. A trail of vapour hung in the brilliant blue vault of the sky.

'Well?' his father prompted impatiently.

'I told you. Nothing I can put my finger on. But she's nervous and jumpy. Not acting at all like a woman who's just got engaged.'

'It is her sixth time,' Hallam reminded Piers nastily. 'You can hardly expect her to behave like a bloody virgin.'

'Perhaps not. But it's more than that. She's making a great thing of this dinner tonight being a family occasion. No outsiders. Except, of course, dear Edmund. It's leading up to something. I can feel it in my bones.'

His father grunted. 'What about Michael? What does he think?'

'There'd be no point in discussing it with *him*. My poor dear half-brother is completely unable to appreciate the subtler nuances of human behaviour.' Piers was suddenly tired of the conversation. 'If anything develops, I'll let you know.' He hung up abruptly, without bothering to say goodbye.

Wandering downstairs, he at once found himself in the midst of all the bustle and preparation for tomorrow's party. There didn't seem to be a room in the house where something wasn't happening. With an inward groan, he decided he would have to go out. He lifted the interhouse telephone and buzzed the chauffeur's quarters over the garage.

'I'm going to the village. I'll take the Porsche. Have it round at the door in five minutes.'

Bill Brereton dropped the receiver back in its cradle and grimaced. Taking the Porsche for a five-minute walk into the village! It made him sick! Overprivileged lout! Piers Cavendish should have had the backstreet upbringing of Bill Brereton! Glasgow would soon have cured him of those airs and graces.

Bill descended the outside staircase. There were two double garages built on to the side of the house, and he let himself into the first one. The Porsche gleamed metallically beside the land-rover in the dark interior. He slipped into the driver's seat and started the engine.

'Hi, Bill!' He turned his head to see Elena silhouetted against the sunshine outside. 'Where are you going?'

His heart missed a beat, as it always did at the sight of her, but he said evenly: 'Mr Cavendish wants to go to the village.'

'By *car*?' Elena was scathing.

The chauffeur backed the Porsche out of the garage. 'It's very hot, Miss Elena. Mr Cavendish doesn't like getting his feathers ruffled.'

She grinned. 'His feathers. . . . He was wearing a peacock-blue dressing-gown this morning. I suppose that just about sums him up.'

But Bill Brereton had gone as far as he dared. He wasn't risking his job by discussing his employers with other members of the family behind their backs. And Piers, he reckoned, would be particularly unforgiving. The memory of childhood poverty made him discreet. He had no intention of going back to Glasgow and the conditions from which Mrs Wingfield – or Mrs Georgiadis, as she had been then – had rescued him.

In 1965 he had been working in the Clydeside shipyards, a raw, ill-educated, dissatisfied young man of twenty, when she had turned up one day at the tenement building where he lived with his parents and offered him a job as her chauffeur-cum-bodyguard. She was in Glasgow for the opening of one of her restaurants, and said she had seen him on the street and liked the look of him. That was all. No other explanation. When he had confessed that he couldn't drive, she had merely shrugged her shoulders.

'Presumably you can learn.'

And that had been that. Within weeks, he had been transplanted to a style of life he had previously only seen on television or in films. For a long time, he simply could not believe his luck.

He was used to it now, of course. Twenty-one years of travelling the world had made him blasé. But not ungrateful. And not foolhardy. He smiled briefly at Elena and drove the Porsche round to the front of the house, where Piers was waiting. He got out, and the younger man slipped behind the wheel.

'House is a blasted shambles,' Piers said peevishly. 'The Kafenéion will be quieter.' The car moved off, as smooth as silk.

Elena had by now caught up with Bill. She appeared to be wearing nothing but an enormous baggy white T-shirt, and her hair was wet. It hung down in long damp strands across her shoulders, and her beautiful honey-coloured skin glowed with health. Bill had known her since the day she was born, but it was only recently, after her return from Switzerland, that he had really begun to notice her.

She was one of the most dazzling young women he had ever seen.

She was a handful, of course. She had been kicking over the traces ever since her early teens. And two years ago there had been the scandal of her elopement with some elderly Mexican film actor who had been working for her then step-father, Rollo Wingfield. Bill remembered the fuss: Mrs Wingfield flying out from New York to Los Angeles, and then on to Mexico City, closely pursued by hordes of newspaper reporters. Elena had been brought home in disgrace and packed off to a finishing school in Berne. Six months ago she had returned for good to become a permanent part of her mother's travelling circus.

And it was then that Bill had taken his first long look at Elena Georgiadis, and realized with a shock how beautiful she had grown. Unfortunately, there was nothing he could do about his feelings for her. Apart from the twenty-year gap between their ages, she was his employer's daughter; but he fancied her and fantasized about her, living in hopes that one day she would cast her roving sapphire-blue eyes in his direction. He was definitely not one for books, but he had read *Lady Chatterley's Lover* from beginning to end.

His day dreams were not as impossible as they might at first have seemed. He had often heard himself described as a good-looking man, and his mirror confirmed that the statement was true. He had no trouble at all in pulling the birds: it was one of the reasons he had never bothered to marry. What would be the point of encumbering himself with a wife, when he had everything he wanted as a single man?

Well, perhaps not all. He watched Elena as she disappeared into the house. That was one conquest he would still like to make in due time.

Madge Shelton, Harriet's personal maid for the past twenty years, was sorting through Harriet's wardrobe, making sure that all was in order, and that none of the favourite evening dresses had been left behind. It was a difficult job, with so many different places of residence, locating exactly where all the various items of clothing were stored. It was Madge's responsibility to have them assembled where Harriet wanted them at the right time.

The navy Jean Muir was here. Ought she to have sent it to the cleaners? No, it looked all right, as did the dark-red and gold Gina Fratini. Madge's anxious fingers shunted the hangers along the rail. There was the classically draped, jade-green Roland Klein, but where were the Bruce Oldfield black velvet pants and jacket? Missing! Still in New York, where Harriet had last worn them. Damn!

Should Harriet decide to wear that particular outfit this evening, she would expect it to be there. She would be angry when it was not. She put great store by efficiency, and it was one of the items she had listed for bringing to the island. Madge would just have to hope that its absence would not be noticed and that Harriet would choose to wear something else, both tonight and tomorrow. She checked the row of evening shoes and closed the wardrobe door.

Turning, she caught sight of herself in the long tilting mirror which stood near the bedroom window. Thoughtfully, she stared at her reflection. Not a bad-looking woman for her age, and the early forties were a notoriously difficult time. No grey hair as yet, and that in itself was quite an achievement. She wondered if Frank Bryan would be here for the party tomorrow. As the London office's chief accountant, he would certainly have been invited. Whether or not he would accept was a different matter.

Madge sighed. She had been in love with Frank for a long while now, but he was wedded to his job. People referred to him as a confirmed bachelor. At forty-one, he still lived with his mother and had never married.

Frank Bryan was also a member of what Madge, in her own mind, always thought of as 'the class of '65': one of the group of Harriet's employees known to the others as the Protégés; or more scathingly referred to by Piers as

'Mother's lame ducks!' And Madge had once overheard somebody – she could not now remember who – call them the Main Chancers. She had thought the remark quite witty at the time, but had resented it, too.

The fact was that, round about the mid-sixties, Harriet had set up a trust which made provision for financial aid to be given to certain deserving young people who would not otherwise have had the means of getting on. The trust still operated today, but it was only in the first few years of its existence that Harriet had taken a personal interest in those selected. She had actually found jobs within her own household for Madge, Bill Brereton and Bess Holland. Madge had often wondered why.

She turned away from the mirror and left the bedroom. Elena was just coming upstairs.

'Hi, Madge,' she greeted the older woman, and went along the corridor to her own room. At the door, she paused.

'You know Mamma's engaged to Edmund? Isn't it great?'

'Great,' Madge agreed, and proceeded on her way down. As she reached the lower landing, Bess Holland emerged from the main salon, looking harassed.

'Hello, Madge. If anyone wants me, I've gone to the village. There's a plane-load of flowers arriving from Athens. I'm taking the land-rover.'

'OK. You've heard about Mrs Wingfield and Mr Howard?'

'Yes, and I'm absolutely delighted, aren't you?'

'It's about time, I'd say.'

Bess grinned. Madge was never enthusiastic about anything, on principle; although on precisely what principle Bess was never quite sure. They descended the second flight of stairs together.

The ground floor was a hive of activity, with Maria directing operations for the evening's celebration dinner, workmen from the village stringing coloured lights along the front of the house, and Julia Contarini getting in everybody's way, arranging the floral centrepiece for the table.

Madge withdrew strategically to the library at the back,

where she could use the telephone undisturbed. She would ring Frank Bryan in London and find out if he would be present at the party tomorrow.

Michael Contarini lay in the shade of some rocks on the beach. His sons were laughing and playing in the water. It was really getting too hot, and they all ought to be indoors, but it was quieter out here, and he wanted to think.

He was feeling edgy. He didn't know why, except that it was connected with his mother. What did she mean, she had an important announcement to make at dinner? She was up to something, and he had no idea what it was. That made him very uneasy. And he could do without this decision of hers to bring Piers into the company as an active partner. As he had remarked to Julia, coming over on the plane, Momma thought that she could control her younger son.

'But she wasn't able to control his father, was she?' he had demanded with acerbity. 'She had to rely on Spiros to do that.'

Julia, who had been busy polishing her fingernails, had placidly agreed. But Julia was too stupid to have any sense of danger.

Michael shifted his position on the blue-and-white-striped air-bed, and made sure that he could still see two heads bobbing above the water. It was too bad of Julia and Elena to leave him in charge like this. Looking after children was women's work. How often had he heard his father say so!

4

Harriet could see the distant waves, silky and dark, rolling
quietly in from the vast expanse of the Aegean; rising and
falling against rocks bleached silver-white by the noonday
sun. In the cooler light of evening, the smell of sage and
lavender and verbena filled the lambent air; and on the
balcony outside her bedroom window a píthoi was filled
to the brim with a mass of pink and red geraniums. This
time tomorrow, the house would be awash with people,
drinking, chattering, dancing; celebrating her birthday in
jet-setting style. The beautiful people. A scattering of titles
from the aristocracy of Europe. Names known throughout
the civilized world. Pop stars. Film stars. People who had
inherited wealth or who, like herself, were self-made.

Impossible, sometimes, to believe that she was the same
Harriet Chance who had grown up in Winterbourn Green
Vicarage, attended the village school, then travelled
twenty miles each day by bus to the grammar school in
Cheltenham. She had left at sixteen, against the wishes of
her father, to become a temporary clerk in the Gloucester
Employment Exchange.

And yet there were other occasions, like now, as she sat
staring into her dressing-table mirror, when that young
girl felt very close to her indeed. Sixty years! And the last
forty of them taken at such a breathless pace that they had
vanished into the past almost before she was aware that
they had begun. Sometimes, that young girl was the only
thing which seemed real to her any more: the Harriet who
had existed happily in her own adolescent world,

absorbed in her fantasies; before the war and before the American GIs had come. Because that had been the start of it, the first step on the road which had led, unbelievably, to a private Greek island, a New York penthouse, a villa at Cap Ferrat and her Cotswold home. That had been the beginning, that autumn day in 1943, when she had seen Gerry Canossa for the very first time, standing outside the White Swan in Stratford-upon-Avon. . . .

Edmund's reflection appeared in the mirror, and she felt the pressure of his hands on her shoulders.

'Nervous?'

'Terrified. I can't think how Michael and Piers are going to react.' She turned and raised her anxious face to his. 'Am I doing the right thing, darling? It isn't just the boys. There's someone else to be considered. Someone who's suddenly going to be presented with a whole new identity. Fresh prospects. A different way of life.' She laid her head against his chest. 'Am I really doing the right thing? Tell me.'

'I think so. You're correcting what you see to be a wrong, which happened many years ago. Perhaps you should have done it sooner. I don't know. But at least the person concerned is now mature enough to be able to cope with whatever pressures there will be.'

'But supposing I'm not right. Should I, after all this time, try to play God? Am I doing it simply for my own benefit? That's what worries me. Am I just easing my conscience at the expense of everyone else's comfort? You heard what Michael said this morning. He doesn't even relish the idea of having to share with Piers.'

'That's because they don't like each other. Chalk and cheese.'

Harriet sighed and turned back to the mirror, hands hovering aimlessly over the clutter of cut-glass jars, silver-backed brushes, gold lipstick-cases; picking up first one object and then another; putting them down unused. She glanced at her image in the triple glass, her make-up only half-applied, her hair a mess where she had unconsciously been running her fingers through it. This indecision was unlike her: she had always been such a positive person. Nothing and nobody had ever frightened her...

She was back in the village school at Winterbourn Green, a belligerent six-year-old who had just had a violent quarrel with one of her classmates. The other girl – a small plump redhead named, as she recalled, Dora Jenkins – had been tearful after receiving a shove which had landed her on the asphalt surface of the playground.

'You jus' wait, Harry Chance!' Dora Jenkins had threatened furiously. 'I'll tell my dad on you! My dad's a policeman!'

A nervous murmur had arisen from the group of children gathered around them. Harriet's supporters had imperceptibly edged away, dissociating themselves from what looked like big trouble. No one, at six years old, had been quite sure exactly how far a policeman's authority extended. There was a vague idea that he could march you off and lock you up in Gloucester gaol.

Harriet had been just as uncertain on the subject as her friends, but even at that age a hard streak of common sense and a refusal to be intimidated had made her reply scornfully: 'Go on, then! Tell your dad! He can't do anything to me!' A memory had stirred. 'He can't do anything without a warrant.'

' 'E'll get a warrant!' Dora Jenkins had screamed, her face bloated and shiny with crying.

There had been a further edging away of Harriet's supporters, which had infuriated her still more.

'Don't talk so daft!' she had shouted at the top of her voice, facing her adversary, hands on hips. She sensed that Dora had never before had her awe-inspiring threat flung back in her teeth and was preparing to retreat in disorder. Searching for the *coup de grâce*, Harriet recalled overhearing two of the bigger boys talking in a corner of the playground. 'Why don't you just fuck off?' she demanded.

Unfortunately, one of the teachers had been listening to the exchange, and then there really had been trouble. Her parents had been informed, and her father had had to deal with her because her mother was, as usual, ailing. She had been sent to bed supperless for her rudeness and loss of temper, not for using a word whose meaning she did not understand.

At the same time, the Reverend Hilary Chance had told his daughter: 'You were quite right, Harry, not to let yourself be scared by empty threats. I'm proud of you for that. I only wish I had the courage to be more like you.'

She had always treasured that admission of her father's; and, subsequently, had never allowed herself to be bullied out of making a decision if she thought it right. . .

Harriet sat up straighter on the dressing-table stool and applied a tawny lipstick. She slicked a comb through her hair, watching it fall effortlessly into place, the result of expert cutting.

Edmund, who was buttoning his evening shirt, smiled at her in the mirror.

'You've made up your mind to go through with it, I can tell.'

'I have. *I* think I'm doing the right thing, and that's what matters.' She stood up, slipping out of the silk Japanese kimono which served her as a dressing-gown. 'Oh dear! I was the one who decided we'd dress for dinner, so I suppose I'll have to abide by my own rule.' She pushed back the sliding door of the wardrobe, which ran the whole length of one wall. 'Now, what shall I wear?'

Edmund grinned at her and held out his arms. 'We've plenty of time. It's only a quarter to seven. Why get dressed until we have to?'

She looked at him in nothing but his shirt, and moved with alacrity to join him. They fell together on to the bed.

His body was still as hard and firm as it had been when a young man, when she had first slept with him at Hallam's parents' house, near Ascot. She remembered it as though it were yesterday. They had always been good in bed together, completely in tune with one another's desires, and there was still that vital spark between them. Their

39

bodies moved rhythmically, each anticipating the other one's needs.

When it was over, they lay contentedly side by side. Later, they finished dressing and went downstairs to dinner.

The dining-room was on the ground floor of the house, its long windows open to the cool evening air, filled now with the distant hushing of the sea and the pungent scent of roses. The latter came from a massive floral arrangement in the centre of the table.

'I fixed it, Momma,' Julia told her complacently. 'It took me all afternoon. I sacrificed my siesta to surprise you.'

'That was sweet of you, dear,' Harriet said, pecking her daughter-in-law's cheek and feeling like Judas. She had decided to save her bombshell until after the meal. She had no wish to spoil Dimitri's cooking.

Elena was looking beautiful in a pale-blue silk dress with a wide silver belt and silver sandals. Her only adornment was a pair of diamond ear-drops and a narrow diamond clip catching back her long blonde hair. She looked like a sleek thoroughbred greyhound.

Julia, on the other hand, was more of an overfed poodle, rounding out a pink Bruce Oldfield dress bought on her last trip to London. Succumbing to the prevailing fashion for very large earrings, she wore a huge pair of diamond and gold Cartier studs, which dragged at her ear-lobes.

Harriet had settled for the elegance of the Jean Muir silk, with a plain gold chain and bracelet. She took her place at the head of the table, Edmund facing her at the opposite end.

'It's not going to be Greek food as well *tonight*, is it?' Piers asked querulously. 'I don't think I could stand lamb and squid two evenings running.'

The others ignored him, something which he was used to. He continued to smile inanely round the table, fully aware how much his vague insouciance irritated Michael.

The dinner was excellent. In spite of his deeply held conviction that there was no such thing as English cuisine,

40

Dimitri had taken great care with the roast beef and Yorkshire pudding, in deference to the fact that it was Harriet's sixtieth birthday. In common with most of her employees, the Greek cook who presided on Agios Georgios was devoted to her; and he had, at least, been able to give his genius full rein with the lemon-flavoured soup and apricot soufflé.

When the meal was finally over, they all went upstairs to the salon for coffee. Angelo and Marco joined them for the present-giving ceremony. Harriet, who had all the English dislike of making unnecessary fuss, endured it for the sake of her family. Piers, who also disliked it, handed her a package with a laconic nod, and retired to stare out of the window.

The gifts were fairly predictable; a Van Cleef and Arpel brooch, in the shape of a ruby and emerald flower spray, from Elena; a Cartier diamond and platinum bracelet from Julia and Michael; a shocking-pink silk scarf from the boys.

'They chose it themselves, from Bendel's,' Julia told her proudly.

'It looks like it,' commented Piers.

Harriet frowned him down.

'It's beautiful, darlings. I love it,' she lied enthusiastically, embracing her grandsons.

The only present she had not accurately guessed beforehand was Piers's. He, like Bess Holland, had chosen a book, but there the similarity ended. It was a handsomely bound, fully illustrated copy of the *Kama Sutra*.

'I thought you and Edmund might find it useful,' he said. 'And, in view of the forthcoming wedding, it should be doubly welcome.'

Harriet's face flamed with embarrassment, which made her angry with herself as well as with Piers. How like him! How very like him! He had known that it would make her feel awkward, and had chosen the gift deliberately. It was exactly the sort of thing Hallam would have done. There was a sadistic tendency in both of them, although less pronounced in the son. Nevertheless, it was there.

41

She glanced up just in time to catch a grin on Michael's face. He, too, was enjoying his mother's momentary discomfiture; and, in a way, Harriet was glad. She could now say what she had to say with less compunction than she might otherwise have felt. She exchanged looks with Edmund, who was obviously thinking along the same lines.

Harriet pinned on the brooch, clasped the bracelet around one wrist and draped the scarf around her shoulders. Delighted that she liked their present, the boys trooped happily off to bed, sustained by promises that they should stay up for at least part of tomorrow night's celebration. Harriet placed the *Kama Sutra* on a small table, beside her empty coffee-cup, and invited them all to be seated.

'I have something very important to say.'

Piers strolled over from his station by the window, and perched on the arm of the sofa.

'Sounds serious,' he remarked lightly, extracting one of the little Egyptian cigarettes he always smoked from a gold Tiffany cigarette-case, and lighting it with a matching initialled lighter.

'It is,' Harriet answered shortly. 'Don't go to sleep, please, Julia. This concerns you, too, as Michael's wife. The only one it doesn't concern is Elena.'

Elena pouted, and Piers observed astutely: 'It has to do with business, then. *Your* business, Mother. Or your money. The fortune which will eventually come to Michael and myself.' He added flippantly: 'Don't tell me you've lost it!' But, in spite of the joking tone, his eyes were hard and wary.

Michael's head had jerked up on the bull-like neck. For one glorious moment, he had thought that she was going to announce her retirement, but one glance at her face had scotched that idea almost before it was formed. Now he was staring at Harriet like an animal scenting danger.

'What's happened?' he asked. 'You haven't done anything stupid, have you, Momma?'

'No, Michael, I have not,' she responded with asperity. 'I am not yet senile, whatever you and Piers might think. I'm fully aware that you want me to retire and leave the running

42

of the company to you, but I have no intention of doing so until I feel the time is right.'

'Bravo, Mater!' Piers applauded, in the glossy public-school tone which incensed his half-brother still further. 'Just remember, old chap, that when that day finally comes there will be two of us. Don't, I beg of you, entertain the hope that I shall be a sleeping partner.'

Harriet seized the opening she had been looking for and said quietly: 'In fact there will be *three* of you. I have another child, older than you both.'

There was a stunned silence. Eventually, Piers gave an uncertain little laugh.

'All right, Mother. You've had your joke. Now, what is it that you really want to tell us?'

'That's it,' Harriet answered flatly. 'I have a child older than you or Michael. The child of my first marriage, to Gerry Canossa. A child originally named Hilary, after my father.'

There was another silence, deeper than before. Harriet was sure of their attention now, even Julia's. Her daughter-in-law was sitting bolt upright in her chair, staring at Harriet open-mouthed.

'Then, why haven't we heard of him earlier?' Piers enquired, striving to keep his voice level. 'He must be over forty.'

'Hilary was adopted while still a small child,' Harriet said, holding her hands tightly together in her lap. She had not expected this to be easy, but now that the moment had finally arrived it was proving even more traumatic than she had anticipated. 'As you know, Gerry deserted me before I got to New York. He divorced me, and I married Gus. Things were very bad financially, and I didn't feel I could ask him to take on another man's child. Another mouth to feed. I'd left Hilary with my father, in England, but when Dad died unexpectedly I arranged for the child to be adopted.'

'So he isn't legally yours any more,' Piers cut in swiftly. 'He has no claim on you whatsoever.'

Michael, who had so far said nothing, nodded heavily. 'That's right. If he's pestering you, Momma, I'll soon deal with him. I'll get on to our lawyers first thing in the morning.'

Harriet breathed deeply. 'No, Michael dear, there's no question of my being pestered, blackmailed or anything of that sort. Hilary has no idea of being my child. The decision to make the acknowledgement is mine, and mine alone. I feel a great wrong was done and I want to put it right.'

Piers rose abruptly, stubbing out his half-smoked cigarette.

'What you really mean,' he said harshly, 'is that you want to salve your conscience at the expense of Michael and myself. You're feeling guilty; and because you're now a very rich woman you feel that dear little Hilary should have his fair share. Compensation! Bought affection! Instant gratitude!' Harriet winced. 'Where, by the way, is our half-brother at present?'

'By tomorrow evening, when I intend to make the relationship public, on this island. It's someone you all know.'

'Ah!' Piers smiled coldly. 'One of your precious lame ducks. That explains a lot about your activities over the years. God! He'll think it's all his birthdays and Christmases rolled into one.'

'Not everyone is as mercenary as you,' Harriet snapped. 'And don't think you'll persuade me to change my mind. That's why I've arranged for Dick Norris to arrive in advance of the other guests tomorrow. I intend to alter my will.'

'A three-way split instead of two!' Piers exclaimed bitterly.

'For pity's sake!' Harriet, too, was on her feet, glaring at her younger son. 'We're talking about millions here! Not somebody's Post Office savings! You couldn't begin to spend even a third of what I'll leave you, not if you live to be a hundred, so what the hell difference does it make? Hilary is my legitimate firstborn and has the right to an equal share and an equal chance, like Michael and yourself.'

'We'll contest it! We'll contest the new will!' Piers was shouting now, saliva crusting along his upper lip, anger making him shake uncontrollably. 'Michael! Don't just sit there like a stuffed gorilla. Back me up, for Christ's sake! She can't do this to us. Tell her!'

Michael directed a warning glance at his half-brother. He was too prudent to antagonize his mother until he knew exactly what he was up against. That didn't mean to say that he would ever forgive her for what she was doing.

'There's nothing to be gained by losing your cool,' he advised Piers bluntly. 'Sit down. You, too, please, Momma.' He slewed round to face Harriet as she resumed her seat, somewhat shamefaced, on the sofa beside Edmund. Piers flung away to stare furiously out of the window. 'Now, Momma, I think Piers and I are entitled to a fuller explanation. We want to know more about this half-brother we've never even heard of until tonight. We want details. All of them. Why, for instance, after forty years, have you suddenly decided to acknowledge him? What has made you come to that decision?'

Harriet smiled faintly. 'You're asking for the story of my life.'

'OK. If that's what it takes. Like I say, I think we're entitled.'

Harriet hesitated. She didn't know if she could stand reopening old wounds. On the other hand, Michael was right. If she was going to disrupt their lives, his and Piers's, they did have the right to know why.

She leaned back against Edmund's shoulder, and he put his arm about her. She felt comforted. As long as he was with her, she could face anything.

'Very well,' she agreed, glancing from Michael to Piers's uncompromising back. 'As you say, I guess you're entitled.'

PART TWO

1943–50

The chance of war . . .
WILLIAM SHAKESPEARE

5

Harriet first saw Gerry Canossa and Gus Contarini outside
the White Swan in Rother Street, Stratford-upon-Avon.
The White Swan had been taken over by the American
Red Cross for the duration of the war, and the Stars and
Stripes floated from a pole above the main entrance.

It was a beautiful September day, the leaves already
turning bronze on the distant trees. A sudden gust of wind
scurried some litter along the pavement. The two GIs were
standing outside the pub, lighting cigarettes, sheltering the
match-flame behind Gerry's cupped palm. Then they
stared around them, looking lost. Harriet and her friend,
Susan Wyatt, paused by the garage next door.

'I'm going to speak to them,' Harriet said, and Susan
giggled.

'We ought not. My mum'd kill me if she knew.'

'I haven't got a mum. I'll speak to them on my own, if
you're afraid.'

Susan sighed. It was all very well for Harriet, accountable only to her easy-going father, but Mr and Mrs Wyatt
had definite views where their American allies were
concerned.

'They're fed up and far from home, and they've got
more money than sense,' Susan's mother had warned her
on frequent occasions. 'They're after just one thing! You
remember that, my girl, if you feel tempted to get too
friendly.'

At seventeen, Susan was only vaguely aware what that
thing entailed, whereas Harriet had had her first sexual

49

adventure when she was only fifteen. Or said she had. Susan was never quite sure whether or not to believe her. But, as Mrs Wyatt and the other ladies of Winterbourn Green were fond of pointing out, chorus and solo, Harriet Chance had been allowed to run wild for the past seven years, ever since the death of her mother. A headstrong girl and a gentle ineffectual man like the Reverend Hilary Chance were a sure recipe for disaster.

And Harriet Chance was old for her age. Less than three months past her seventeenth birthday, she already had the figure of a much maturer woman, and was permitted by her father to choose her own clothes; or such clothes as strict rationing allowed. The result was that she looked at least twenty, sometimes more, and men could hardly be blamed, according to Mrs Wyatt, if they took advantage of her.

It had been expected, because of her early display of academic precocity, that Harriet would stay at school until she was at least eighteen, then go up to university. The Reverend Hilary Chance had certainly taken it for granted, and had therefore been completely unprepared for his daughter's demand that she be allowed to leave school as soon as she had passed her sixteenth birthday.

'I don't want to be shut up in some kind of intellectual nunnery,' she had argued fiercely. 'Especially not now, when the country's fighting for its very existence. Please, Dad! It would be like chickening out. And, anyway, as soon as I'm old enough I want to join up. I'm hoping they'll take me in the WAAFs. If you make me stay at school, I won't study. I'll fail all my exams. Oh, come on, Dad! You can't make me, if I don't want to. As soon as I'm eighteen, I'll volunteer, so what's the point? I might just as well leave now and get a temporary job. You know we could do with the extra money.'

The Reverend Chance, cursed by his ability to see both sides of any argument, had given in without too much of a struggle. Harriet's headmistress, balked of one of her brightest pupils, had told Hilary exactly what she thought of his craven submission, but was forced to admit that there was little he could do about it. She had done her own level best to change Harriet's mind, but had run up against the girl's streak of stubbornness: Harriet's iron-clad determination to get her own way.

Harriet had therefore left school at the end of July 1942 and gone to work as a clerk in the Gloucester Employment Exchange. She travelled the twenty-odd miles to Gloucester and back each day without complaining, and spent the journey reading. She had always loved books and was rarely bored. She had an enormous zest for living.

It was she who had persuaded Susan to meet her in Gloucester this Saturday afternoon and to hitch-hike the forty or so miles to Stratford-upon-Avon. Susan had wanted to take the train, but had eventually let herself be persuaded.

'Hitching's more fun,' Harriet had said. 'And cheaper.'

They had been fortunate in picking up an army lorry going to Tewkesbury, and from there a lady and gentleman had given them a lift for the rest of the way. But so far the afternoon had not been a success. They had wandered along by the river, bought ice cream at a shop in Sheep Street, and discovered that neither of them had any of the month's sweet coupons left to buy chocolate. It was chillier, too, than they had anticipated, and their summer dresses and woollen cardigans afforded them barely sufficient warmth.

By the time they found themselves in Rother Street, Harriet was uncomfortable and bad-tempered. She was just about to suggest that they make their way to the station to enquire about trains, when she spotted Gerry and Gus outside the White Swan.

They were not, of course, the first Americans she and Susan had seen that afternoon. Stratford, like almost every town and village in the British Isles, was swarming with GIs, but the majority of them already had English girls in tow. These two seemed providentially lonely and unattached.

Harriet, catching at Susan's arm, slowed their pace as they walked past the half-timbered façade of the pub. Her eyes flicked sideways in a thinly veiled glance of invitation.

'Hi there, Gorgeous!' It was the taller of the two men who spoke, his gaze raking Harriet appreciatively from head to foot. 'Where ya going?'

'Just for a walk,' she said. 'Want to come?'

She half-expected him to answer that they were already waiting for dates, but to her surprise he grinned and replied: 'Sure thing!'

As he moved forward out of the patch of shadow cast by the overhanging flag, she realized that he was one of the handsomest men she had ever seen. He was tall and rangy, moving with a peculiarly feline grace on feet that were long and narrow, like his hands. His skin was pale olive, and his eyes a deep velvet brown, fringed with thick dark lashes. The hair which was visible beneath his cap was black and shiny, the mouth full and sensual. Harriet did not even notice the second man. This one was hers. Susan could have his friend.

'I'm Harriet Chance,' she informed him, 'and that' – she nodded over her shoulder to where Susan was walking stiffly beside the other GI – 'is my friend, Susan Wyatt.'

'And I'm Private First Class Gerry Canossa, and that there's my buddy, Private First Class Gus Contarini. You from around these parts?'

'No. We're just up for the afternoon. We both live in Winterbourn Green. That's a village halfway between Gloucester and Oxford.'

'Hey!' Gerry Canossa beamed. 'We're stationed near Oxford. We got a ride here in a jeep. You girls got transport laid on? Or can we give you a lift home, later on?'

'Yes, please!' Harriet beamed delightedly. 'We'd be terribly grateful, wouldn't we, Sue? If you can possibly drop us in Oxford, we can get a bus from there.' She could sense Susan's uneasiness, but ignored it. She wanted to be with Gerry and, besides, it would save all the bother of a train.

'Sure thing.' Gerry was pressing close to her. She could

feel the warmth of his body through the thin material of her dress. 'Is there anywhere round here we can eat, or get a cup of coffee? I guess you could use it. Your hands are as cold as ice.'

They went to a café in Bridge Street and sat at a table near the window. Gerry ordered coffee for them all, and sandwiches and cakes for the girls.

'We've already eaten,' he explained. 'In the club.'

Harriet was now at leisure to scrutinize the other GI more closely. What had Gerry called him? Gus? He had the same olive skin, black hair and brown eyes as his friend, but there the likeness ended. Gus Contarini was nearly a head shorter, with a chunky compact frame that spoke of a brute strength entirely belied by the gentleness of his expression. Like Susan, he seemed ill at ease in the present situation.

Gerry sensed the tension. 'My buddy here,' he said, 'is a nice Catholic boy whose momma told him never to speak to strange women. You'll have to forgive him if he's a bit on the shy side.'

Gus blushed scarlet, a deep tide of red which started at the base of his throat and gradually suffused his whole face. Harriet suddenly felt sorry for him.

'Hello, Gus.' She held out her hand across the table. Gus took it in one of his, and she winced at the strength of his grip.

Susan began to thaw a little after this, relieved by the discovery that not every American soldier was after only one thing. She engaged Gus in a politely stilted conversation, leaving Harriet free to concentrate on Gerry.

'There's a dance next Tuesday evening,' she said, 'at the Winterbourn Green village hall. Do you think you and Gus could come?'

'Yeah, why not? I guess we might fiddle an evening pass, if you tell us how to get there. What's the local talent like in your neck of the woods?'

'The local . . .? Oh, you mean the girls.' A waitress brought the coffee and food, which she banged down

53

gracelessly in front of them. Harriet bit into a sandwich and answered coldly: '*I'm* the local talent as far as you're concerned. And don't you forget it.'

'Hey! Would I? A great-looking babe like you!' But, even as he spoke, she saw his eyes slide past her to fasten on a striking ATS sergeant sitting at a neighbouring table.

She became conscious of Gus watching her, and raised her eyes to meet his steady gaze. She had an uncomfortable feeling that he wasn't fooled by her act for a minute, and knew that she was legally under age. Certainly, as they emerged from the café into the chill of an autumn evening, he refused to take Gerry's hint that they split up into pairs.

'We promised Kincaid we'd meet him at half-seven,' he said, looking at his watch. 'It's nearly that now. If we leave it too late, he'll go without us and then we'll be late getting back to camp. It ain't worth the risk, Gerry. Let's go.'

'OK! OK! Let's not get screwed up about it. Either of you girls know how to get to Clopton Bridge?'

'Yes, of course.' Harriet tried to keep the disappointment out of her voice. 'Straight along this road.'

The driver of the jeep, Johnny Kincaid, proved to be a smiling fresh-faced young man with a pronounced Southern accent, who professed himself perfectly willing to drop the ladies in Oxford or any other place they'd care to name. If one of them would sit beside him and give directions, he would take them right to Winterbourn Green.

'You know the roads and lanes better than I do, Susan,' Harriet declared, climbing into the back of the vehicle with Gerry and Gus. 'I'm hopeless when it comes to directing people.'

Susan gasped at this blatant falsehood, but saw that she had left it too late to protest. With a bad grace, she got in beside Johnny Kincaid.

Gerry put his arm around Harriet, and she snuggled close, liking the faintly smoky aroma of his jacket. But she couldn't shake off the sense of Gus Contarini's disapproval.

Harriet had been aware of boys, as such, from an early

age, almost as soon as she was conscious of certain bodily urges. Living in a rural community, she had quickly connected the two. There were always plenty of farmyard animals about to suggest a likely explanation. She also had a father who believed in giving truthful replies to all her questions, on the theory that if she was old enough to ask she was old enough to be told the answers. So, in an age when most children were ill-informed regarding sex, Harriet had known more than the majority of them.

Nevertheless, she had not been above pretending that she understood more than she actually did – a circumstance which had led her to exaggerate the incident, two years previously, when she and Leslie Norman had got lost during one of the church's blackberrying rambles. There had been a good deal of scandalized comment when they had eventually turned up, late at night, muddy and dishevelled, having been missing for over four hours.

The truth was that they had spent most of that time finding their way back to Winterbourn Green after becoming thoroughly lost and missing the charabanc home. The fact that nobody had noticed their absence until the passengers had unloaded in front of the vicarage had been allowed as an extenuating circumstance by no one except the vicar. Harriet Chance was a wild girl, and young Leslie Norman probably no better than he should be. Such was the general consensus of opinion, and Harriet had played along with it, dropping hints and making innuendoes, until even her father was worried. Only to him did she admit the truth, that nothing had happened: she was still a virgin.

As the jeep rattled along the narrow Cotswold roads, those ancient tracks with their sudden clusters of cottages and drystone lichen-patterned walls, Gerry's hand crept up from her waist to cup her breast. Harriet experienced the most delicious sensation. Trying to describe it to herself afterwards, she could only say that it was as if her inside had melted. By the time that the jeep drew up at the vicarage door she knew that, whatever else happened, she must see Gerry Canossa again.

He lifted her down from the back of the jeep. It was dark now, and in the blackout Harriet could just discern the pale oval of his face, but not its expression.

'You *will* come to the village dance on Tuesday evening, won't you?' she enquired breathlessly. 'And Gus, of course,' she added as an afterthought. 'Johnny, too. If they want to. Seven till midnight. I'm afraid it's only the local combo. They're not very good, but at least you can recognize the tunes. It's in the village hall, over there, on the other side of the green. You can just make it out, next to the pub, the George and Dragon.'

'Yeah, sure. If we can.' Gerry kissed her quickly on the lips as Susan came round the side of the jeep.

'I'm off,' she said to Harriet. 'My mum'll kill me! She doesn't know where I am. She'll be in a right state! See you.' She vanished into the shadows.

'We must go, too,' Gus put in, touching Gerry's arm. 'Our passes run out at eleven. You wanna be posted AWOL or something?'

'OK. I'm coming. What's with you, Gus? There's plenty of time. You're as jittery as some old woman.'

'Come on! Shift yourself, darn it!'

'A' right! See you, babe.' Once again, Gerry bent his head and kissed her.

'You *will* try to make it, Tuesday?' Harriet clung to his arm.

'Sure, I've told you.' He heaved himself back into the jeep and shouted: 'OK, you guys! Let's go!'

The jeep's engine sprang to life as Johnny Kincaid, following Susan's careful directions, headed out of the village towards the main Oxford road. Harriet stood and waved until the Americans were out of sight. Then she turned and went indoors, letting herself in with her key.

The Reverend Hilary Chance came out of his study as Harriet appeared in the entrance hall.

'Harry! Where on earth have you been? I've been worried sick. It's nearly ten o'clock. I was expecting you home for tea.'

'I've been with Susan. We hitched up to Stratford.' Her tone was defensive, although she tried to sound as if it were the most normal thing in the world.

'Stratford? That's nearly forty miles!' The vicar looked horrified. 'I don't like you hitch-hiking, you know that. There are so many soldiers and foreigners about these days.'

'Oh, Dad!' Harriet flung her arms around him, laughing. 'Don't be such an old worry-guts! You know I can take care of myself. We didn't come to any harm, and here I am again, safe and sound. I always turn up like the proverbial bad penny.' She kissed him. 'I'm going to bed. I'm tired. I'll see you in the morning.'

6

Winterbourn Green vicarage had been built in a more leisurely and luxurious age, when the incumbent had been a man of standing and substance in the local community; a man, more often than not, with a private income to supplement his stipend from the Church. The rambling old building of grey Cotswold stone had accommodation for half a dozen servants, stabling for an equal number of horses, a coach-house and a gardener's cottage, now derelict, at the far end of the long overgrown garden. In 1943 it was home only to the vicar and his daughter, still had gas-light downstairs and was dependent on candle-light above. There had been suggestions of renovating it, of at least installing electricity, all through the thirties, but the war had put paid even to the talk. The Church Commissioners had decided with a sigh of relief that for the time being there was nothing to be done.

Mrs Wicks, who came in daily, kept it clean, but there was little she could do about the general air of shabbiness and decay. She fought a losing battle against peeling wall-paper, fraying carpets and flaking paint. The cheap furniture, bought when Hilary Chance and his wife had first married, badly needed replacing, but there was no money with which to buy it. As vicar, Hilary was expected to give a lead in all the charitable work of the parish, and what was left over when the bills were paid was barely sufficient to keep himself and Harriet in clothes. Harriet's weekly wage from the Ministry of Labour and National Service had made things marginally easier.

That was one good thing about the war, she reflected, as she hunted through her wardrobe on Tuesday evening, desperately searching for something to wear to the village dance: clothes rationing meant that everyone was having to make do – turning collars and cuffs, sewing underwear out of parachute silk, knitting gloves with darning wool and sporting felt 'jewellery'. At least nowadays she didn't stick out like a sore thumb.

But tonight, just when she wanted to look her very best, she seemed to have nothing to wear. She stared despairingly at the pile of dresses heaped on the bed. Who could look good in any of that lot? There was the brown-spotted cream rayon, which she had found in the church jumble-sale and inexpertly altered to fit her own, far slimmer figure; the blue wool, bought in the Bon Marché January sale in Gloucester; the green floral cotton she had worn last Saturday; and the pink silk party-dress which her father had given her on her sixteenth birthday, and which now appeared too fussy and childish. These were the only dresses she possessed. Two serviceable skirts, with an assortment of jumpers and blouses, served her for work, but were ineligible for the dance this evening.

In the end, she decided on the blue wool. She would be too hot in it, especially when the hall became crowded, but it was more sophisticated than the rest. It had a straight skirt and elbow-length sleeves and tiny beaded flowers on the collar. It was this unexpected bit of frippery on a wartime garment which had first attracted her, and the fact that the dress fitted her perfectly was an added bonus. In the flickering candle-light, she turned and twisted in front of the mirror, combing her hair and applying lipstick. The conditions in this house, she thought viciously, were positively medieval.

Satisfied at last with her appearance, she snuffed the candle and ran downstairs. Her father was sitting before a small fire in his study; for, apart from the dining-room and the kitchen, the other rooms on the ground floor were shut up. Fuel rationing, as well as financial considerations, made it impossible to use them. The place, as always, smelt musty, a combination of gas-lamps, permanent damp and old furniture.

Harriet dropped a kiss on the top of Hilary's head, where the brown hair was beginning to thin. The faded blue eyes which raised themselves to hers had a hopeless look. The Reverend Hilary Chance had fought too many losing battles.

'Don't be late,' he said. 'I suppose I might come over with you for half an hour.'

'You wouldn't like it at all, Dad,' Harriet answered swiftly. 'It'll be nothing but swing and jive. Unless, of course, you've learned to jitterbug on the quiet! If I were you, I'd sit here and have a nice read.' She patted his shoulder and could feel the jutting bones beneath the patched shirt and cardigan. 'Mrs Wicks has left you some supper in the kitchen. Mind you eat it. You're much too thin.'

'I hope it's enough for two. I may have a visitor later on, to give me a game of chess.'

'Oh? Who's that? Old Alfred Tooze?'

'No. A Major Dombrouski. He's the RC chaplain at that American base near Charlbury. I met him in Oxford a couple of days ago, at that coffee-stall in Cowley Place. We got chatting, and he mentioned how much he missed a really good game of chess, so I invited him over this evening. He's won tournaments in the States, but I fancy he'll find me a worthy opponent. I, too, had my moments of glory when I was up at Cambridge.'

'Yes, I know,' Harriet assured him absently. It could be awkward if her father were to get too friendly with this Major Dombrouski. Things might get back to him that, for the time being at least, she would rather keep concealed.

Oh, well! She couldn't think about that now. She took her best coat from the hall cupboard and let herself out of the front door. There were already sounds of revelry from across the green, and two faint chinks of light indicated places where the blackout shutters had not been properly fixed. The air-raid warden would be shouting in a minute. She could see dark shapes making their shadowy way towards the hall, but so far there was no American jeep parked on the gravel space outside.

There were no American GIs inside, either; just the usual crowd of assorted locals and a couple of RAF uniforms; Billy Thompson and Mike Sherborne, home on leave. The Winterbourn Green Combo was bashing out *'The White Cliffs of Dover'* with more enthusiasm than regard for the tune, sadly depleted by three of its number having been called up for National Service. A few couples were desultorily circling the floor. Harriet sat down beside Susan, on one of the chairs ranged along the walls.

'God! This is slow,' she said.

Mrs Tucker from the bakery gave her a look. It was disgraceful to hear the vicar's daughter blaspheme!

'I don't reckon they'll come, do you?' Susan asked, and Harriet glumly shook her head. She knew without explanation who 'they' referred to.

'No, I don't suppose so.'

An hour later, dancing a sedate foxtrot with Billy Thompson, she felt near to tears and ready to go home. She had had a hectic day at the office, and the double twenty-mile bus journey to and from work had tired her out. But in her heart of hearts she knew it wasn't really the reason. In spite of her words to Susan, she had been convinced that Gerry would come. Her disappointment was correspondingly intense. . . .

There were sounds of tyres tearing up the gravel and voices raised. Minutes later, the doors which linked the hall with the darkened vestibule clattered open and the room was invaded by Yanks. There were at least half a dozen GIs, including Gerry, Gus and Johnny Kincaid, with three or four girls in tow.

'Hi, everybody!' yelled Gerry, heading in Harriet's direction. 'Hey, you guys,' he demanded of the band, 'can't you play something a bit more lively? How about "Boogie-Woogie Bugle Boy from Company B"?'

The Winterbourn Green Combo were only too delighted to oblige, and no one seemed to notice if half the notes were wrong. Before anyone else had time to protest, the Americans and their partners commandeered the floor. The older locals and the two British servicemen watched sullenly from the sidelines.

'Hey, kid! This is more like it!' Gerry twirled Harriet around. 'Now the joint is really jumping. You're looking great.'

She was feeling great. Suddenly, she was no longer tired. Cheeks and eyes aglow, hair flying, she felt a million dollars, as Gerry would doubtless say. She didn't even notice that the blue woollen dress was making her hot.

She did notice, however, that Gerry's glance kept straying to one of the girls he and the others had brought with them: a tall girl with long legs and a striking figure sheathed in a tight red frock. It was the one misery in an otherwise happy evening, particularly as Gerry insisted on dancing with the girl from time to time.

'Who is she?' Harriet snapped at Gus, as he partnered her in a slow smoochy waltz. But, whereas the other couples, including Gerry and Red Dress, seemed welded together, Gus held her at a respectful distance.

'I don't know. Just some broad we picked up in an Oxford bar.' There was silence between them for a moment or two, then Gus added awkwardly: 'You don't wanna take too much notice of Gerry's nonsense, you know. He's swell company, a good buddy, but where women are concerned he can shoot a pretty fast line. It doesn't mean anything. I . . . I wouldn't want to see you get hurt, that's all.'

'You mean he's a womanizer,' Harriet said grandly. 'Good heavens! I knew that from the second I first clapped eyes on him. I don't believe a word he says. I'm not a fool.'

'You're not as old as you pretend to be, either,' Gus answered steadily. 'I reckon you're not much over seventeen.'

Harriet blushed. 'I'm seventeen and three months,' she admitted tartly. 'How did you guess?'

'Oh . . . little things give you away. I have a sister of my own. Now, Gerry – he's an only child.'

The music came to an end, the dimmed lights went up and everybody clapped.

'You won't tell him, will you?' Harriet begged.

'Not if you don't want me to.' They moved towards the refreshment-table at the back of the hall: a long trestle supporting a tea-urn, thick white crockery and plates of unappetizing-looking sandwiches and rock buns. Gerry was still with the girl in the red dress, laughing and whispering something in her ear. 'But, like I said,' Gus went on, 'don't take him too seriously. I've known him ever since we were kids. We grew up together, in neighbouring streets in New York. He's always been the same. He was chasing girls almost before he could walk.'

Harriet made no response, pushing her way to the front of the crowd and obtaining two cups of tea while it was hot and not too stewed. The food she wisely left alone.

Gus looked taken aback. 'Hey! I'd've done that. It's a man's job to look after the woman.'

'Not this woman,' she answered shortly, her eyes still on Gerry.

Gus's warning, far from deterring her, had only made her more resolute. Gerry Canossa was the handsomest, most exciting man she had ever met, and she had made up her mind. She was going to marry him.

December 23rd was very cold. Major Jan Dombrouski shivered uncontrollably as he surveyed the chessboard. A moment later, he murmured: 'Checkmate.'

'Damn!' said the Reverend Hilary Chance, then grinned apologetically. 'Sorry, Father.'

'Think nothing of it.' The Major smiled. 'We of the old faith are more liberal-minded even than you Anglicans. Another drop of Scotch to keep out the cold?'

He had brought the whisky himself, courtesy of the United States Army Stores. It was almost impossible to obtain spirits in the British shops, and his weekly visits to the Winterbourn Green vicarage over the past few months had taught him the necessity of additional warmth. What little coal the vicar was allowed was totally inadequate to heat even one room of that primitive barn of a place. When, the chaplain wondered to himself, were the inhabitants of this island going to break out of the Middle Ages and get some twentieth-century comforts into their lives?

Hilary sipped his whisky and lay back in his chair, staring at the flames of the fire.

'This is very pleasant. I especially appreciate you coming this evening, when the next few days are going to be so busy for you.'

'For us both,' Jan Dombrouski amended. 'I expect you'll have a pretty sizeable congregation yourself on Christmas morning.'

'Half of mine will probably go to sleep. And, anyway, they're not going to die tomorrow. My message doesn't have to be as carefully prepared as yours.'

The Major stared into his glass at the tepid whisky, silently deploring the lack of ice. After a pause, he said diffidently: 'The truth is, Hilary, my visit today isn't entirely disinterested. There's something I feel I ought to say.'

'Fire away,' the Vicar invited curiously. 'I'm all ears.'

'It's not that easy.' The Major raised his eyes to his friend's. He noted how ill and thin the other man was looking, after a bout of the recurring bronchitis which had kept Hilary out of the forces. 'It's about Harriet,' he explained.

'What's she up to now?' the Vicar asked resignedly.

'She's been seeing a lot of one of the men at the camp. Private First Class Gerry Canossa, a member of my flock.'

'Half the adult female population of Britain is going out with American servicemen,' Hilary argued defensively. 'There's not much you and I can do about that. It was the same in the last show. Morals and standards have gone into abeyance for the duration, just as they did then; just as they've done in every war since the beginning of time.'

'I know that.' The chaplain hesitated, unsure how to continue. 'But I gather from a close friend of Private Canossa that she's pretty smitten. Isn't that the word you English use? Apart from everything else' – Jan Dombrouski twisted his now empty glass between his square workman-like hands – 'we shall be leaving here soon. The whole outfit is moving on. I can't tell you more, even if I were certain of anything myself. But things are afoot.'

Hilary nodded understandingly. 'The Russians have been pressing Roosevelt and Churchill for a second front for some time.'

The American made no comment, but his silence said everything for him. After another pause, he added: 'Your daughter could get badly hurt, Hilary, and I wouldn't want that to happen. She's a nice girl and she's young. This Gerry Canossa's not the marrying kind. Thinks a lot of himself, and he's a "wow with the dames". That's how his friend describes him.'

The Vicar sighed, and the hunted look returned to his eyes. It couldn't be easy, Jan Dombrouski reflected sympathetically, for a man on his own to bring up a daughter; especially one as strong-willed as Harriet Chance. He wondered why Hilary had never remarried.

'I'll have a word with her,' the Vicar said. 'And thanks for telling me.' He grinned lopsidedly. 'I suppose I should be grateful.' The truth was, of course, that he'd rather not know; then he wouldn't have to do anything about it. 'Now, can you spare the time for one more game?'

'So I don't want you to see him again, Harry,' the Vicar said quietly, but with a note of finality in his voice. 'Have I made myself clear?'

He had waited up and caught her as she stealthily let herself into the house just before midnight. Harriet, assuming she was going to be lectured for staying out late, had prepared her alibi well in advance. Instead, she had gently but firmly been told that her father knew all about Gerry Canossa and that she was forbidden to see him ever again.

'It's that RC chaplain, isn't it, who's snitched on me? Interfering old woman! Why doesn't he mind his own business! Good heavens! I'm seventeen and a half, Dad!'

'And old enough to imagine yourself in love, is that it?' The Vicar sat down wearily in his chair. 'Harry, believe me, at seventeen you can't possibly know your own heart.'

'Juliet was only fourteen,' Harriet flung at him.

The Vicar smiled. 'And what do you think would have happened if she'd lived and they'd set up home together? The chances are that they would have bored one another to death inside a month. Romeo would have returned to chasing Rosaline and whooping it up with the lads every night, and Juliet would have gone running back to Mother.'

Harriet ignored his attempt to make her laugh. She said: 'I'm going to marry Gerry Canossa.'

The Vicar was startled, remembering Jan Dombrouski's words. 'He's asked you?'

'Not yet.' Harriet bit her lip. 'But he will. I want to go to America, Dad. I'm fed up with this country. We're so slow. We're too obsessed with *who* people are and not *what* they are. You remember what Abraham Lincoln said in one of his speeches, about all people having an equal chance? Well, I want that chance to make something of myself. I know I can.'

'Maybe.' The Vicar closed his eyes. The fire was almost out. 'But it's not the right reason for getting married.'

'I love Gerry. I really do. There would never be anyone else. He's a wonderful man.'

' "Methinks the lady doth protest too much," ' Hilary muttered softly, opening his eyes again.

Harriet raised her chin defiantly.

'I'm going to marry him, Dad, and nothing you can say will stop me. Besides, there's something else that I haven't told you. I'm going to have a baby.'

7

She had not planned to get pregnant, that afternoon six
weeks earlier, when she and Gerry had wandered hand in
hand through the ruins of Minster Lovell and made love by
the banks of the Windrush. She had not even anticipated
the moment; but when, without warning, Gerry had produced the packet of condoms from his pocket she had
seized it and thrown it into the bushes.

'Not those things,' she had whispered urgently. 'This
must be special.' And at the back of her mind had lurked
the almost unacknowledged thought that, if she had a
baby, Gerry would have to marry her. Her father and
Major Dombrouski would see to that.

It had been perfect November weather, crisp bright
sunshine and a cloudless sky. She had taken the day off
work because Gerry had a twelve-hour pass. They had met
outside Fuller's in Oxford, and wandered around for a
while, looking at the shops. Gerry, however, was quickly
bored, his attention distracted by the female under-
graduates as they cycled along the High, skirts hitched up,
displaying well-muscled calves and thighs. In fact his attention was very easily distracted these days. Harriet sensed
that their relationship, if it had ever really dignified that
name, was coming to an end. She had to pump new life
into it rapidly, if she wanted it to last. Gus was right about
Gerry: he would never be a one-woman man.

But she wanted him. Desperately. And not just because
she saw him as a means to an end. She loved him. He was
the handsomest man, outside the cinema, that she had

ever seen. The fact that he so obviously did not feel the same way about her only made him more of a challenge.

'What'll we do?' he asked after they had lunched upstairs at Stewart's. 'How about a movie? Any idea what's showing?'

'I've a better idea,' she said quickly. 'It's such a beautiful day, we'll go to Minster Lovell. It's a ruined fifteenth-century house on the banks of the River Windrush. There won't be many people around, this time of year.'

The suggestion had not really appealed to him, but when she had insisted he had given in. A bad sign, she realized: he was not even interested enough to argue with her. It was just something to while away the time.

They hitched a lift to Burford and walked the rest. Five miles in Gerry's company seemed like one. He, on the other hand, complained bitterly and said they would try to hitch a ride all the way back.

'That's if we see anyone on these goddam country roads.'

He was indifferent to Minster Lovell itself; to the ancient manor-house, roofless and falling into decay, set in the water meadows bordering the lovely River Windrush. Haunted and full of echoing ghosts, Gerry saw it only as a pile of old stones. It occurred fleetingly to Harriet that Gus would have been more appreciative, but she suppressed the thought. She did not want to believe that Gerry was less sensitive than his friend. She did not want to believe anything that was detrimental to him in any way.

She chattered on, telling him stories connected with the hall: the skeleton found locked in a hidden room; the young bride who had suffocated in an oak chest while playing hide-and-seek on her wedding day; the woman who had had her eyes put out – and there was a blood-stained Bible still in evidence to prove it.

'Sounds like a load of boloney to me,' was Gerry's only comment.

After that she was silent. There didn't seem to be anything else to say.

They wandered along by the river, watching the shadows run before the changing light. Reeds stood like sentinels in the rippling water, and a jagged tooth of ruin towered before them. Starlings pecked for food in the grass.

But something of the romance of the place must have worked its way into Gerry's consciousness, for he suddenly stopped, twisted her round and kissed her. His body pressed urgently against hers. He nibbled the lobe of her ear.

They had done some heavy petting in the back rows of cinemas and the rear of a jeep, but he had never tried to go all the way with her before. Harriet had been unsure of the reason. Was it because he didn't fancy her that much? Or because her father was a clergyman and a friend of Father Dombrouski? Now, suddenly, he wanted to make love to her, bearing her down in the long damp grass, tugging impatiently at the buttons of her coat.

'For Chrissake,' he mumbled, 'get this thing off. You're done up like you're heading for Alaska.'

It was while she was struggling to free herself from her layers of winter clothing that he produced the packet of condoms from his pocket and she grabbed them and threw them away. Later, she refused to admit, even to herself, that her action had any ulterior motive. This was her first time; the moment when she was about to lose her virginity; when she would at last discover exactly what it was that everyone believed she and Leslie Norman had done all those years ago. She didn't want it spoiled in any way. Besides, didn't all the girls in the office swear that it was well-nigh impossible to get pregnant at the first attempt?

Harriet had not expected it to be so painful. She had listened to the older women in the Exchange talking and giggling about their various experiences, and had supposed that it would be just as wonderful for her. Instead, she wanted to scream out loud because it hurt so badly. When Gerry finally rolled off her, her thighs were wet with blood. Nor did he seem in the best of tempers.

'Why the hell didn't you tell me you were a virgin, you

69

stupid little fool? I'd have taken it easy.' Or he wouldn't have done it at all. With so much talent available for an easy ride, who needed to be giving driving lessons?

Who was he kidding? Of course he had suspected that she was a virgin. That was the reason he had never tried to lay her before.

'Is it always like that?' Harriet asked breathlessly, sitting up and beginning to straighten her clothes.

'No. Only the first coupla times, and then only for women. After a while, you'll get to enjoy it.' Now that they'd done it once, he didn't see why they shouldn't do it again. He reckoned that, given time, Harriet could turn into something quite special. There was a sensual quality about her which he had recognized from the first. However, in future he'd make damn sure that they took precautions. No more histrionic gestures like hers this afternoon. He couldn't afford them. Private First Class Gerry Canossa had no intention of getting hitched and settling down.

He had proved the truth of his words to Harriet on several occasions since: she had indeed learned to enjoy sex, and he only wished he had initiated her sooner. And as he always used a condom there was nothing to worry about. The unit would be leaving Oxford soon and moving south. When he finally left, he would have nothing but pleasant memories to take with him.

Harriet Chance and Gerry Canossa were married by her father in Saint Aldhelm's Church, Winterbourn Green, at the beginning of February 1944. Gus Contarini was best man, Susan Wyatt the solitary attendant.

It was a very quiet wedding with no more than half a dozen guests. Major Dombrouski was not amongst them. The man who had worked so hard to bring about the wedding, and who had exerted all his influence to speed up the cumbrous process of American military permission and approval, was absent on account of illness. A bad cold, caught the week before, had rapidly descended to his chest; but in a way the affliction was providential. As a

Catholic priest, he could not give his formal blessing to a mixed marriage, nor to one solemnized in a Protestant church. He was glad to be out of it at the finish.

Gerry had fought long and hard to avoid the marriage, but outside pressures broke him. He was fond of Gus Contarini. They had grown up together, enlisted together, joined the same unit. He could not endure Gus's reproachful silences; nor, when he did speak, the note of contempt in his voice.

'She isn't a floozie, Gerry. She's a reverend's daughter. A real nice kid.' Gus wished to God it was him she was fond of, instead of his friend. 'It'll ruin her life, being the mother of an illegitimate child. Besides, do you really want your own kid to grow up a bastard? You shouldn't have fooled around with her, Gerry, if your intentions weren't honourable. There's plenty of loose women about, if that's what you need.'

Father Dombrouski had said much the same thing.

'She's a decent girl from a decent home. You have to marry her, Gerry, not just for her sake, but also for the sake of your unborn child. Its future welfare must be your prime concern. An innocent soul. Are you prepared to ruin its life before it has even begun?'

Gerry felt trapped, both by these people whom he respected and by the promptings of his conscience. But he also felt angry. Several times he seriously considered going AWOL, but could not bring himself to do it. There was a big show coming up. How could he leave his buddies in the lurch, even supposing he was able to get away with it? Anyway, he'd be on the run for the rest of his life. Nothing was worth that, surely?

Harriet was aware of Gerry's reluctance to marry her. How could she not be, when they scarcely exchanged a civil word these days? The news that she was pregnant had been a terrible shock to him, but he had never attempted to deny that he was the baby's father. He knew how crazy Harriet was about him, and that she had been a virgin when they first made love.

71

There were many moments when Harriet felt deeply ashamed of what she had done. She had set out with the hope of trapping Gerry into marriage, and she had succeeded. It was no use telling herself that it was a chance in a thousand that she had conceived the very first time she had had intercourse with a man: she had known it was an outside possibility, and she had gambled on it. Gerry would have taken precautions, and she had prevented him. She felt guilt and elation in equal proportions.

She told herself that he would come to accept the idea once she was his wife, and especially after the child was born. Weren't all Italians supposed to be besotted with children? He would be delighted when he was at last the proud father of a son.

She spent her remaining clothing coupons on a cream dress she had seen and liked in the Bon Marché in Gloucester, and bought a cream hat to wear with it. Her father gave her some of his coupons to get new underwear and a nightdress, but she could have saved herself the trouble. Gerry announced that he was returning to base as soon as the wedding was over.

The reception, held at the vicarage, was a gloomy occasion. The bridegroom was sullen and the best man uneasy. The bridesmaid had a fit of the giggles, and the handful of guests, who nibbled at the home-made sandwiches and cake, were embarrassed by the whole affair. There had been a lot of speculation in the village as to the probable reason for this hasty hole-in-the-corner marriage, and now the bridegroom's behaviour confirmed their worst suspicions.

'That isn't going to last five minutes,' the Verger's wife remarked to her husband, as they returned home late that afternoon. 'That was a shotgun wedding if ever I saw one.' And the Verger, much as he detested gossip, felt bound to agree.

The Vicar had similar misgivings.

'You're sure you've done the right thing, Harry?' he asked, as they sat together on the old horsehair sofa in his study after everyone, including Gerry, had gone. 'You didn't have to get married, you know that. I'd have stood by you.'

'I know, Dad, and I'm grateful.' Harriet squeezed his hand. 'Don't worry about Gerry. He'll come round.'

Hilary Chance stifled his many doubts and answered reassuringly: 'Yes, I'm certain he will, especially once the baby is born.' He glanced at his daughter, watching the firelight play across the strong well-marked features, so similar to his own. But in character Harriet was like neither himself nor his wife, both rather timid people: she was a throwback to his mother, a powerful domineering woman. He asked gently: 'You do love Gerry, my dear, don't you? You haven't married him as an easy way of getting to the States after the war?'

Harriet shook her head vehemently. 'I'm crazy about him, Dad.' And it was true. But it didn't mean that her father's suspicions were groundless, either.

For as long as she could remember, Harriet had entertained a burning ambition to go to America. It was the land of opportunity. She felt in tune with everything she had ever seen or read or heard about it. She was sure that only there could she realize her full potential.

Just what that potential was, Harriet had no very clear idea. She only knew that, fond as she was of her own country, she found much about England too hidebound by class and tradition. In the United States, she felt, she could truly be free. And the arrival of American troops in Britain had done nothing to dispel her illusions. Better-dressed, better-paid and with far more self-confidence than the average British non-commissioned serviceman, they had swept through the towns and villages like a breath of fresh air. British women had gone down before them like ninepins, bowled over by their vitality and charm. More than ever, Harriet was convinced that her destiny lay on the other side of the Atlantic.

She had not, however, married Gerry Canossa for that reason alone. He was so good-looking, Harriet was unable to see anyone else when he was around. He had an eye for other women, it was true, but he would settle down. They would make a good life together in the States. She would make him proud of her.

Harriet was conscious that in all these plans she was ignoring the welfare and feelings of her father. But the Vicar had brought her up to believe that parent and child were separate entities, with their own separate lives to lead. Hilary had taught his daughter independence from a very early age; and now, as he was only too well aware, he was reaping the consequences.

He consoled himself with the fact that the war was not yet over. A lot could happen between now and whenever that might be. He wondered if Harriet had faced up to the possibility that Gerry Canossa might not survive.

He put an arm round her, holding her tightly.

'If . . . anything should happen to Gerry, my dear, you know that you and the baby can always make your home with me, for as long as you want.'

'Thanks, Dad. But even if Gerry is killed I think I'd still try to get to the States. I mean, the baby ought to see his grandmother – Gerry's mother – don't you think? I'm only talking about a visit, you understand.'

'Of course.' He understood all too well.

An uneasy silence descended on the room, broken by the hissing and crackling of the flames on the hearth. They had not lit the gas, content to sit together in the firelight, reflecting on the events of that unsatisfactory day. Harriet had been crying, and hoped that her father had not noticed. Hilary had, of course, but was at pains not to let her know it. Father and daughter had always found it difficult to communicate about things that really mattered.

It had been arranged that Harriet would continue working for as long as possible, before taking maternity leave, then return to her job for whatever period was necessary until the end of the war. During the day, the baby would be left in the care of her father and Mrs Wicks. As an American army wife, Harriet would receive a generous allowance, but she had decided to save the money for the start of her new life with Gerry. He should see what a prudent and thrifty wife he had married!

Two weeks after the wedding, the American army base near Oxford was deserted. Gerry and his companions had moved south to join the other thousands upon thousands of troops assembling along the southern coast of England. And on 6 June 1944 the world learned of the D-Day landings.

Hilary Canossa was born almost three months later, on 31 August. Harriet had received no word from Gerry since he left the district. She had no idea where he was, nor if he were alive or dead.

8

'I'm sorry, Mrs Canossa, we had no idea you hadn't been informed. I just can't imagine how it happened.'

The United States Army colonel looked flustered and unhappy. Outside the windows, open against the warmth of the autumn afternoon, the London traffic rumbled by sedately. The colonel felt hot and uncomfortable in the unexpected heat: this time last week, it had been blowing a gale and raining. He was counting the days until he was demobbed. The war in Europe had been over for more than five months, and the two atomic bombs dropped on Japan in August had brought all hostilities to an end. He longed to get home to Wyoming, to his wife and the kids. Instead, he was stuck in austerity Britain, dealing with other people's problems.

He smiled placatingly at the angry young woman seated on the other side of his desk. These damn GI brides were proving to be a nuisance.

'Er . . . how did you find out that your husband was still alive?' he asked her, wishing to God that Corporal Wisbichi would hurry up and telephone from Records.

'His friend wrote to me from New York. Private Contarini was demobbed last month,' Harriet added by way of explanation.

'And . . . uh . . . he told you that . . . uh. . .'

'He told me that my husband was not only alive, but had also been released from the Army only a few weeks after his liberation from a German prison-camp, where, apparently, he had been held since shortly after the D-Day

76

landings. Gerry, it seems, was taken prisoner just north of Caen. I was never informed of that fact, either.'

'Dear me.' The colonel puffed out his cheeks helplessly. What the hell was Wisbichi up to? 'We certainly seem to have got our lines crossed somewhere.'

But, more to the point, why hadn't the husband himself let her know what was happening? Even if he had been unable to write from the prison-camp – and things were pretty chaotic during the final few months of the war – surely he ought to have written to her once he was free! As it was, he appeared to have returned home to New York without so much as a word. If it hadn't been for the friend, the wife would still be wondering. One of those wartime marry-in-haste-repent-at-leisure affairs, the colonel decided. For his money, there were going to be a helluva lot of Anglo-American divorces. Well, the United States Army had done its level best to dissuade its soldiers from marrying foreign brides, but that had still not prevented thousands of men from flocking to the altar.

The telephone on the colonel's desk rang, and he snatched up the receiver.

'Wisbichi? What kept you? What. . .? Yeah. . . Yeah. . . OK. . . I see. That must be the answer.' Carefully, he replaced the receiver on its cradle and leaned forward, hands linked together on the desk. 'It would appear, Mrs Canossa, that your husband omitted to change his mother's name for yours as his next of kin. Mrs Canossa senior was notified fully of events as they happened. I'm afraid you'll have to take the matter up with him.'

The colonel beamed with relief at this relatively happy outcome. Someone would have to be carpeted for inefficiency. Someone should have picked up the fact that Canossa was married. But the reprimand would be slight. Information was constantly getting misfiled or mislaid between different departments. And if this young woman foolishly insisted on following her obviously reluctant husband to the States, instead of immediately filing for divorce, then that was somebody else's headache. The

77

colonel rose from behind his desk and held out his hand in a farewell gesture of dismissal.

Harriet sat on a bench near the lake in St James's Park, watching the ducks and eating the sandwiches she had brought with her. For all the taste they had, they might have been sawdust.

Gus's letter, when it arrived a few days earlier, had been a terrible shock. In over a year of silence, waiting for news of Gerry that never came, all her enquiries parried or ignored by overworked officials, Harriet had gradually grown reconciled to the idea that her husband was dead. So many unidentifiable bodies had been left behind on the Normandy beaches, or washed out to sea, that it was not possible, she had been told, to account for every man who had gone ashore on D-Day.

Then on Friday evening, when she returned from work, her father had met her on the vicarage doorstep, holding on to the thirteen-month-old Hilary with one hand, and proffering a letter with a United States postmark and stamp with the other. Harriet had snatched the letter with trembling fingers, only to realize that the writing was not Gerry's.

'It must be from Gus,' she had whispered uncertainly, and her father had nodded.

'Take it up to your room and read it in peace. Mrs Wicks will give Hilary tea. She's agreed to stay late tonight, on account of my Parish Council Meeting.'

There was still enough of the October daylight left to see, without putting match to candle, and Harriet sat down by the window. She ripped open the envelope without even bothering to remove her coat.

The letter was short and to the point: Gus had never been a man to waste words. After a brief introductory paragraph, which informed her that he had survived the war and was now demobbed and at home in New York, he went straight to the heart of the matter.

*   *   *

I met Gerry the other day, coming out of a deli-
catessen on Mulberry Street. I guess he didn't want to
see me, because he went back inside, like he'd for-
gotten something. I couldn't believe my eyes. Ever
since he was captured by the Krauts on night patrol,
outside Lisieux, I'd never heard a word from him.

I went after him and, when I'd finished calling him
a misbegotten son of a you-know-what for not getting
in touch with me as soon as he'd gotten out of the
Army, I asked about you, and what arrangements
were being made to bring the war brides over.

Then, of course, the whole story came out; how
he'd never written to you; how you'd never been kept
in touch with what was going on; how he'd never
even found out about the kid. When I got my breath
back, I told him exactly what I thought of him, and
that I was going to write to you and give you his
address. He's pumping gas at a station on Canal
Street and living with his mother. Mrs Canossa isn't
well, and most of his cash goes on keeping her in
medication, so maybe there's some excuse for his
behaviour. Maybe.

I'll be in touch again. I'm living with my sister and
her husband at the above address, and chasing up
jobs in my spare time. No success so far. I'll expect to
hear of you through Gerry. I've told him to write you
straight away, or he'll have me to reckon with.

He had given her Gerry's address on Mott Street, and
signed himself her 'very good friend, Gus Contarini'.

And he *was* a good friend, Harriet reflected gratefully,
listening to the ducks' ecstatic quacking as she threw them
the remains of her sandwiches. He was also very literate,
something she had not suspected. Gerry, she knew, found
it extremely difficult to express himself on paper, and his
spelling was abysmal. Somehow, she had always assumed
that Gus was equally. . . Equally what? Ignorant? She felt
a stab of shame at thinking of her husband in those terms.

But, then, with a face and body like Gerry's, who needed education?

When her father read Gus's letter, he suggested that she go immediately to the United States Army headquarters in London.

'Don't wait for Gerry to write. Find out what has happened,' he urged. 'Little Hilary will be fine with Mrs Wicks and me.'

So here she was, and now she knew; knew what she had suspected all along: that Gerry did not want her or her child; had never wanted them, but had let his conscience be worked on by Gus and Father Dombrouski. Once at a safe distance from her, he had had second thoughts. He had never intended to keep in touch.

A starling skimmed low over the pond, intent on stealing a crust or two from the ducks, its iridescent plumage gleaming in the soft autumnal light. Harriet tossed the last few crumbs on to the path and watched the bird peck greedily at them. Some leaves drifted to the ground from a nearby tree, thin wafers of beaten gold.

She knew what she ought to do; what her father desperately hoped she would do. She should give Gerry his freedom and settle down to make a life for herself and Hilary. But the old ambition to go to America burned as brightly as ever. It was her Jerusalem, her Mecca, her Delphic shrine. It was the land of opportunity, and Gerry was the passport which would get her there. There were so many British wives of American servicemen that, sooner or later, the United States Government would have to do something about transporting them across the Atlantic. Stories appeared daily in the British press concerning angry ex-GIs lobbying Senators and Congressmen to reunite them with their families.

Harriet stood up resolutely, the light of determination in her eyes. She was going to ignore the dictates of common sense and her feelings of guilt at leaving her father. If she failed to seize this opportunity, she would probably never have another. She would become trapped in the everyday business of living, of making ends meet, always short of money. Or she would marry again, tired of struggling on her own, and find herself caught in yet another snare. This was her big chance, and she had to take it or regret it for the rest of her days.

It occurred to her, as she walked briskly towards the park gates, that the word 'love' had not recently crossed her mind. Were her feelings for Gerry on the wane? Was she, as she had wondered once before, using him? Nonsense! Of course she cared about him! She *did!*

'Blimey! It isn't 'alf cold in this bleedin' place!' The girl in the next bed to Harriet's shivered dramatically. 'An' all these soddin' tests they're puttin' us through, you'd think we were a load of bleedin' cattle.'

'I know,' Harriet agreed. 'It's awful.'

She and hundreds of other war brides were being held at an abandoned British army camp on Salisbury Plain, while a team of American doctors and nurses went over their medical histories with a fine-tooth comb. Now that legislation had been passed to allow the GI brides into America, the authorities were taking no chances on importing disease along with them. Mental health, too, was being rigorously checked.

Although it was May, an icy wind still whipped across the open spaces of primeval grassland, bringing with it days of cold spring showers. Some of the hut roofs leaked, washing facilities were primitive, and sullen German prisoners of war were slack in their duty of cleaning the latrines. The dingy buildings seemed permanently to echo with the screeching of babies and toddlers; the women themselves were cold, bored and frustrated. Only the anticipation of their transfer to Southampton and the waiting liners kept them from going insane. The primal conditions were only made tolerable by the thought of seeing their husbands again at the end of the long transatlantic voyage.

The evenings were the worst. By nine o'clock, most of them had exhausted the common-room pleasures of table-tennis, reading or listening to the wireless, and retired to their beds to keep warm. Harriet had gone to the hut she shared with three other women as early as eight-thirty, hoping for half an hour's peace with Nancy Mitford's latest book, *The Pursuit of Love*. But she had barely settled herself, when the girl who slept in the neighbouring bed arrived and began to undress.

Kathleen Mason had attached herself to Harriet from the moment she had established that they were both from the same part of the world. Kathy was a Gloucester girl, a year younger than Harriet, being only eighteen. She was already homesick, but determined not to show it, hiding her youth and uncertainty behind a barrage of swearing, which she apparently felt conferred instant adult status.

She removed dress, shoes, cardigan, and rolled into bed in her underwear. She started talking almost immediately, and Harriet closed her book with a sigh.

'I wonder what it'll be like,' Kathy said, after a brief moment of silence. 'Livin' in soddin' America, I mean. My bloke's a coal miner in Pennsylvania.'

'Yes, you told me.' Harriet refrained from adding: 'At least half a dozen times.'

'Be funny, won' it, seein' them without their bleedin' uniforms? Wonder 'ow they'll look. Won' be the same, really, will it?'

'No, I suppose not.' Privately, Harriet considered that Gerry would look good in or out of uniform, but she did not say so. A child in the next hut started to scream.

'You were bloody wise, leavin' your kiddie behind with your ol' man. I'm glad I 'aven't got 'ny. Fuckin' nuisance, that's what kids are.'

'It's only temporary,' Harriet said quickly. 'I'm going to send for Hilary as soon as I can. It's just that Gerry's a bit pushed for money at the moment. I told you, he's supporting his mother, who's sick. I shall have to get a job – at least, for a while.'

But there was more to her decision to leave Hilary behind than she would admit to Kathy; indeed, to anyone, including, most of the time, herself. In her more honest moments, however, Harriet knew that her marriage was on shaky ground. It probably would not last. And if she tried to make it on her own in America she would be in no position to support a child.

'Leave Hilary with me for the time being,' her father had begged. 'At least until you find your feet over there.'

She had given in without much of a struggle. The three letters she had received from Gerry during the past eight months had not been reassuring. Almost illegible and frequently misspelled, they had grudgingly accepted the fact that she was intent on coming to New York, and informed her that he had been in touch with the relevant authorities. The documents which would ensure her a passage were duly delivered; but reading between the lines of Gerry's sparse missives Harriet suspected that it was Gus who had kept his friend up to the mark, steering him through the bureaucratic labyrinths and filling in the necessary documents; in short, doing everything but sign them. It was a suspicion which filled her with serious misgivings, and persuaded her to submit to her father's wishes. But she was already riddled with guilt, and certainly had no intention of discussing her affairs with Kathleen Mason.

'Do you know anything about where you'll be living?' she asked, although she knew the answer. Kathy had told her on at least three previous occasions.

'Some mining village north of Pittsburgh. I forget its bleedin' name.' Kathy sniffed glumly. ' "Township", Gene calls it.' She reverted to her earlier theme. ' 'E were lovely in 'is uniform. 'S a pity, really, war 'ad to end.'

'Why are you going to America if you're so unsure of your feelings?' Harriet asked curiously, aware that she was the last person who should be putting such a question.

'Oo says I don' wanna go?' Kathy was defensive. 'Besides, what's there to stay 'ere for? There ain't no future in England. My dad says so. Bleedin 'Ugh Dalton and 'is austerity Britain! I want t' see some life!'

The land overflowing with milk and honey, Harriet thought, sitting up in bed and clasping her knees. But milk and honey cost dollars. How much of either commodity were she and Kathy likely to get?

She must not think like that! She must hold on to her conviction that America was the land of opportunity. Once she abandoned that dream, there would be nothing else left. . .

She realized with a start that she had at last shed all her illusions about Gerry. If she could keep the marriage together long enough for her to get on her feet, that would be the most she could hope for; the most, probably, that she deserved.

'You manipulate people, Harry,' her father had once said to her. 'You're unscrupulous, my dear girl. You manipulate everyone for your own ruthless ends.'

The accusation had been made half in jest, and at the time Harriet had laughed it off. Lately, however, she had begun to suspect that her father might have been right.

The hut door banged open, and the two other women who shared the hut came in, grinning all over their faces.

'Here you are!' the taller one with the Manchester accent exclaimed. 'Talk about early birds! But you both went to bed too soon tonight. You missed the announcement.'

'What announcement?' Harriet and Kathleen Mason demanded, almost in unison.

'We're off on Monday. To Southampton,' the other woman said, forestalling her friend. 'We embark Monday evening and sail on Tuesday morning. Now! Isn't that a piece of news worth having?'

9

There was no sign of Gerry anywhere. In the excited, cheering, milling throng of men beyond the Customs sheds, Harriet looked in vain for her husband. Her heart sank, and there was a queasy feeling in the pit of her stomach, dispelling the euphoria of the morning.

Like most of her travelling companions of the past few weeks, Harriet had been up at dawn to watch the fairy-tale towers of Manhattan rise out of the mist, a floating island on the edge of the world. The Statue of Liberty, familiarized by dozens of newsreels and Hollywood films, was both a tried and trusted friend and a stranger; an affirmation that they were foreigners in a foreign land.

During their time at sea, the women had been subjected to a number of pep talks and endless good advice.

'Rid yourselves of the notion, ladies, that you are going to a home from home. The United States of America is not England-over-the-water. Don't think you can carry on exactly as you would at home.'

'Remember that you are guests in someone else's country. Don't keep saying: "We do things this way in England, Ireland, Scotland, Wales." You will only put up the backs of people.'

As the ship had reached the halfway point in the voyage – the point of no return – an atmosphere of uneasiness had hung like a pall over the crowded decks. One or two women had been in tears, wishing they had not come, as the realization gripped them that they were thousands of miles from all that was most familiar and dear.

But this morning, with the city emerging over the sky-line, and faced by the prospect of seeing once again the husbands from whom they had been parted for so many months, even years, the mood of depression had lifted. They crowded the ship's rails, nervous excitement finding an outlet in a volley of high-pitched giggles and shrieks.

Docking had proved a long and frustrating process. The women, packed and anxious to disembark, had tried to pick out their men, kept at a safe distance from the quayside. A few had been successful, holding up their children to show how much the latter had grown. But at last they were on dry land again, flash-bulbs popping and cameras whirring as the emotional reunions were recorded by waiting pressmen and television reporters. Microphones were thrust at embracing couples by radio journalists, concerned to catch a few happy words for the evening programmes.

The Customs search had been carried out aboard ship, so there was nothing for Harriet to do except identify her two cases when they were finally brought ashore, and wait uneasily for Gerry to appear. He was late, that was all, she assured herself. However reluctantly, he would turn up some time. Even Gerry would not leave her to fend for herself. Would he?

After an hour of chaos, the crowds were beginning to thin. Only one or two women, like herself, were left standing alone, being eyed askance by the social service volunteers and party organizers. Harriet tried to ignore their muttered asides to one another and their glances of compassion.

Kathleen Mason had been one of the first to leave. She had attached herself to Harriet throughout the voyage, and when they disembarked she had still been tailing her like a shadow.

'Bleedin' 'ell!' Kathy had muttered as they descended the gangway. 'Suppose the sod doesn't turn up. Don' leave me until 'e does, 'Arry, there's a mate. An' if 'e don't can I come 'ome with you?'

But in the event it was Harriet who had to watch as Kathy was borne off by a huge bear-like man with bushy fair hair and beetling eyebrows. They made an incongruous couple, one so large, the other so small and thin.

Kathy waved and called goodbye. 'Don' suppose we'll be meetin' again!'

The same thought had occurred to Harriet, and she suddenly felt desolate. She hadn't particularly liked Kathleen Mason, but now she was alone it needed an enormous effort of will not to panic.

But of course she was not alone! Gerry would come! He must!

A hand touched her elbow, and a voice said: 'Hi, Harriet!' Her head jerked round. She had neither seen nor heard him approach.

'Gerry –' she began, then stopped.

It was not her husband. It was Gus Contarini.

Harriet cradled the cup of hot coffee between her hands, trying to draw warmth from it to stop herself shivering. When at last she spoke, to her surprise her voice sounded perfectly normal.

'Where has he gone?' she asked.

Gus shrugged, avoiding her eyes. 'No one knows. He cleared out the day after his mother's funeral. Like I told you, Mrs Canossa's death was very unexpected.'

'She'd been ill.' Harriet struggled to keep at bay the moment when she must face, fairly and squarely, the fact of Gerry's defection.

'Yeah. But nobody'd thought she was dying.'

'What finally killed her?' And did it matter, the death of this mother-in-law she had never known?

'Doc Bartoldi said her heart just gave out, while she was asleep. She couldn't have known anything about it.'

'I'm glad.'

The meaningless words were lost in the hubbub all around them. Gus had taken her to a café not far from the dock, a long narrow building with a central uncarpeted aisle and separate booths, with seats like high-backed pews down both sides of the room. The tables were covered with red check cloths and, at the far end, there was a counter supporting a coffee-urn, with a row of hot cupboards behind it. The walls, a stained and faded blue, sported advertising posters, among which was one for Laurence Olivier's Broadway appearance in the double bill of *Oedipus Rex* and Sheridan's *The Critic*, and another for his film of *Henry V* showing at the City Center. They gave Harriet a sudden pang of nostalgia which was almost too great to bear. She was overwhelmed by homesickness for Cotswold hills and their ever-changing light; for long grey walls, jewelled with cress and lichen; for blue-grey distances and flights of rooks beating upwards on great, ragged, shiny wings; for sturdy four-square Cotswold sheep. . .

'. . . so I'm taking you home with me until you can get things sorted out.' She became aware that Gus was speaking.

'I'm sorry, what were you saying?' She smiled lop-sidedly. 'I'm still a bit shell-shocked.'

'That's natural.' Gus returned the smile. 'I said I'm taking you back to my sister's place. You can have my bed, and Sophia will fix me up on the couch in the living-room.'

'I couldn't do that!' Harriet's reaction was instinctive. 'I couldn't impose.'

'For Chrissake don't be so goddam British!' he answered impatiently. 'What the hell else are you going to do?'

'I don't know.' She felt unutterably weary and extremely frightened. Gus was the only person she knew in the whole of this vast teeming city. 'No, of course you're right. And I do have some money that Gerry sent me. I'd . . . I'd prefer to pay my way until I can sort out what to do.' And to herself she thought: Thank God I didn't bring Hilary! Out loud, she added: 'What a stinking mess!'

Gus reached out clumsily towards her, knocking the spoon from a bowl of sugar as he did so.

'Harriet, I'm sorry. I wouldn't have had this happen for the world.'

88

'Dear Gus.' Shakily she set down the cup of coffee in its saucer and took his hand. 'It's not your fault.' Hot tears stung her eyelids. 'I always knew that Gerry didn't care for me really.'

'He's a stupid no-good bastard!' Gus said vehemently. 'And I hope he rots in hell.' He squeezed her fingers. 'C'mon. Finish your coffee and I'll take you home.'

Gus's sister and brother-in-law were a childless couple living in a two-bedroom apartment in that area of Manhattan nicknamed Little Italy: a gridiron of streets centred on Mulberry and bordering on Chinatown, with Canal Street as the symbolic divider.

Sophia and Carlo Geraldino's greeting was muted. Neither could hide the fact that Harriet's indefinite presence was an added difficulty they could well have done without. Throughout the war, Carlo had worked in a munitions factory, earning more money than he had ever seen in his life before, which was probably the reason why he and Sophia had spent it so fecklessly. Now the good times were over with nothing saved, and the factory had reverted once more to the manufacture of tin cans. And, to add to their problems, Gus was living with them, and was unemployed.

But that, at least, he had been able to remedy. Over supper, he told them: 'I've got Gerry's old job at the gas station. I saw the manager this morning and convinced him that Gerry wasn't coming back. The pay isn't great, but it's a living.'

'Hey! That's really good news!' Sophia's expression brightened a little, and Carlo nodded. He glanced at Harriet.

'That Canossa sure is a shit. What you going to do, Harriet? You going to try tracing him?'

'How can she?' his wife demanded. 'Who knows where he's gone? He's got the whole of the United States to hide in. . . Sorry! I didn't mean . . .'

'That's all right.' Harriet was too numb even to be upset.

She pushed her spaghetti around her plate with the back of her fork. 'I'll go to the British consulate tomorrow, if some-one will tell me how to get there, and see what's to be done. I don't have enough money for the return trip. Maybe,' she added, without much hope, 'they'll advance me some.'

'Look, don't be in too much of a hurry,' Gus advised her, ignoring the consternation on his sister's face. 'Wait a bit. Maybe you can get a job or something. Gerry might come back.'

Harriet glanced at her reluctant hosts.

'Yeah... Yeah, sure.' Sophia forced a smile. 'Wait a coupla weeks, why not? If Gus thinks you ought to.'

It had soon become obvious that Sophia adored the baby brother who looked so much like her. Square, stocky, with the same dark hair and eyes, she was an older version of Gus. How old, Harriet was not quite certain. Sophia had the appearance of a woman in her forties, but she could be younger than that. Apart from the war years, it was clear that her life had not been easy.

Sophia gathered up the dirty dishes, frowning at the wasted food on Harriet's plate.

'I got ice cream in the refrigerator,' she said. 'Pistachio. Anyone want some?'

Harriet shook her head. 'Would you all excuse me, please? I think I'd just like to go to bed.'

'Of course.' Gus was on his feet at once, ready to hold her chair. 'You have a good night's sleep. We'll talk things over some more in the morning.'

But once in the little bedroom, which still bore traces of Gus – his old baseball bat and catcher's mitt on the shelf over the radiator and a blotched photograph of him in the school basketball team beside the bed – Harriet made no attempt to undress or unpack her cases. Instead, she sat down on a chair near the window and rested her elbows on the sill, listening to the nocturnal noises of this alien city. This was what she had dreamed about; what she had schemed for. She had flouted common sense and her father's advice and come by her deserts. She knew the cold comfort of having no one to blame but herself.

Land of milk and honey... Land of opportunity... The words spun like a broken record, round and round inside her head. After a while, she buried her face in her hands and burst into tears.

The next few weeks passed like a dream, and in retrospect Harriet could remember very little about them.

Gus scrounged an hour or two from his work at the gas station in order to contact City Hall and make whatever arrangements were necessary on her behalf. He lied vigorously, swearing that Gerry was coming back and explaining his absence by the sudden offer of another job, upstate. On Sundays he showed her around New York: Broadway with its theatres, Fifth Avenue with its shops, Wall Street, Times Square and the Empire State Building – all places and names made familiar to her by the cinema, but so much more magical when actually seen. The city began to lay its spell on her; a potent spell, which the passage of time would never quite erode. Homesickness receded. After three weeks, Harriet knew that she wanted to stay. She prayed each night that Gerry would return.

'What you gonna do about the child?' Gus asked one Sunday afternoon, as they walked together up the gentle slope of East Drive in Central Park. To their left, the land shelved to the soft glimmer of the Pond; ahead, trees and statues were aligned in a formal row. There were people everywhere, sitting or lying on the grass, enjoying the fine July weather. Gus had bought a newspaper and was carrying it under his arm. The headlines, thick and black, trumpeted the blowing up of the King David Hotel in Jerusalem, with a devastating loss of British life. It all seemed impossibly remote and unimportant.

'Hilary's OK.' Harriet watched enviously as a young girl swung past in a tight-bodiced full-skirted frock of bright orange cotton. Her hair fell in a shining curtain across one eye, a fashion made popular by the Hollywood film actress

Veronica Lake, and one slender ankle was circled by a gold identity-bracelet. She wore very high-heeled, open-toed sandals, and by comparison Harriet felt dowdy and forlorn. She went on: 'My father likes the company. Besides, what can I do? Carlo and Sophia wouldn't welcome another mouth to feed; and, until I know if Gerry's ever coming back, Hilary's better off at home.'

Gus nodded. He knew she was right. Money was scarce and getting scarcer with the threatened closure of the factory where Carlo worked. And Harriet's own supply of money was dwindling. Sophia was already throwing out hints that Harriet should be looking for a job and somewhere of her own to live.

Only last night, when Harriet had gone to bed, she had asked her brother: 'Why should we keep her? She isn't our responsibility. She ought to be shipped back to England.'

But Gus wouldn't hear of it. 'We can manage,' he had answered stubbornly. And, as it was partly his money which put what food there was on the table, Sophia had refrained from further comment.

That evening, however, at supper, Sophia remarked casually: 'Mrs Petrucci says there's a vacancy for a waitress at Muldoon's place, in the Village. The Last Chance Saloon.'

Gus's head jerked up, and he glared at his sister.

'If you're suggesting that Harriet should apply for it, forget it! She wasn't raised to be a waitress.'

'Oh, pardon my mistake.' Sophia was angrily sarcastic. 'I didn't realize we were entertaining the Queen of England.'

'Of course I'll apply for the job,' Harriet put in quickly, frowning at Gus, 'if you think there's any likelihood that I'll get it.'

'I don't want you working in a joint like that,' Gus retorted fiercely. 'It's rough. It isn't any sort of place for a lady.'

'For God's sake . . .' Harriet was beginning dismissively, when Carlo interrupted with a timely reminder.

'She ain't your wife, Gus. What Harriet does is her own business.'

'Except that you've made it ours,' Sophia pointed out,

turning once again to her brother. 'We need the dough if Harriet's going to go on lodging here. Carlo and I can't support her.'

'I don't want anyone to support me.' Harriet's voice was determined in the face of Gus's continued look of disapproval. 'If you'll give me directions how to get there, Sophia, I'll go round and see Mr Muldoon tomorrow morning.'

Harvey Muldoon wiped his hands on a greasy cloth and scrutinized Harriet thoughtfully.

'Yeah, you heard right, kiddo, I do want a chick to wait at table. But you ain't the usual sort I get applying. For a start, you talk kinda fancy.' An idea struck the amiable Mr Muldoon. 'Hey, you ain't one of these GI brides they're talkin' so much about, are you?'

'Yes, as a matter of fact I am.' Harriet smiled winningly. 'I really do need this job. I'll work hard. You won't regret it if you take me on.'

'Finding things tough, huh, you and your husband? That's the trouble with these here wartime marriages. They're fine until peace breaks out.' The tiny piercing blue eyes, set in rolls of sagging flesh, twinkled at her, inviting her to share his amusement. He lifted one podgy hand to tug at his sparse goatee beard. 'Look, I'll be frank with you, kid, we get all sorts in the Last Chance Saloon. Being in the Village, it's kind of a mixed clientele.' He pursed his small red lips. 'The way I figure it, you're a bit too classy for a joint like this. That fancy accent could get some of my customers reaching for their hats. No disrespect intended.'

'None taken,' Harriet assured him. 'But won't you at least give me a trial, Mr Muldoon?'

He wavered slightly. 'What's your name?'

'Harriet Canossa. But my single name,' she added with sudden inspiration, 'was Harriet Chance.'

'Hey, really?' Harvey Muldoon was tickled. 'That's kinda cute. Harriet Chance of the Last Chance Saloon. I like it, I like it.' He clicked his teeth consideringly. 'OK,' he agreed, after a moment's silence, 'I'll give you a try. Ten dollars a week and anything you can pick up at table. But, if the customers don't take to you, you're out. Go see Josie in the back office. You don't need no work permit or nothing, do you? You really are an American citizen?'

Harriet nodded. 'By marriage. And thanks, Mr Muldoon. I promise you won't regret it.'

10

Far from resenting her English accent, the customers of the
Last Chance Saloon seemed to like it. Within six months,
Harriet was the restaurant's most popular waitress, and
there was an outcry when Harvey moved her into the cash-
desk after Josie left to have a baby. The protest was so great
that he was forced to resite the pay-kiosk nearer the door,
where the regulars could stop to chat on their way in and
out. Harvey raised her pay to fifteen dollars a week and consoled himself that it was cheap at the price in terms of extra
business. Harriet had a flare for accountancy which surprised herself much more than him. She discovered that she
liked figures and dealing with money.

She also liked Greenwich Village. She loved the population with its mixture of businessmen and artists, the clustered rows of houses with their neat little gardens, the tree-
shaded streets. The tangle of shops with their displays of
exotic fruit and vegetables, dozens of different kinds of
bread, exciting tangy cheeses and delicious-smelling herbs
never failed to fascinate her and slow her feet. At the heart
of the Village, at the end of Fifth Avenue, lay Washington
Square, for a brief period in New York's history its most
fashionable venue, before the tide of change swept people
on to build elsewhere. The 'handsome, modern, wide-
fronted houses' mentioned by Henry James still decorated
the north side of the Square, although seven years previously numbers seven to thirteen had been gutted behind
their Greek Revival façades and turned into one big
apartment-house.

95

The memory of Winterbourn Green was receding in the interest of Harriet's new life. Her father wrote regularly and cheerfully of himself and Hilary, but his descriptions of church jumble sales, the Women's Institute Annual Fair, Harvest Home and Mr Protheroe's new cow seemed tame by comparison with New York. The September Festival of San Gennaro, when Little Italy took to the streets around Mulberry and Grand, to honour the patron saint of agnostics, presented Harriet with a tempo of life she had never experienced in England. Then there was Thanksgiving Day and, looming on the horizon, Christmas.

Occasionally, she felt a pang of guilt that she was not missing her father and child more than she did, and worried that they would be all right without her; but events crowded in on her too thick and fast for her to sustain her anxiety for long.

She was still living with Gus and the Geraldinos in their apartment, and Gus was still bedding each night on the living-room floor. But the atmosphere was more relaxed. The closure of the tin-can factory had been postponed, and the money Harriet brought in every week made a big difference to them all. It promised to be a moderately affluent Christmas. . .

On 21 December, Harriet received official notification that Gerry had obtained a divorce in Reno. Her marriage was over before ever it had begun.

'Is . . . is this legal?' she demanded incredulously of Gus. 'Can he do this to me, without my consent?'

'You probably could contest it,' Gus conceded unhappily. 'But it would cost.' He put his arm about her. 'Anyway, what's the point in hanging on to a man who doesn't want you? There are plenty who do.'

'Oh, yes?' She laughed shakily. 'Harvey Muldoon, for example?'

Harvey had said more than once: 'I'd marry you like a shot, kiddo, if there wasn't a Mrs Muldoon. God knows where she is now, but we've never gotten around to getting unhitched. I must see about it one of these days, when the sun shines.'

96

Of course, he never would, but it didn't stop him lusting after Harriet in his own lazy way, and some days she had her work cut out to keep her employer at a decorous distance.

'No, not Harvey,' Gus answered quietly. 'Someone much closer to you than he is.'

She knew at once that he was referring to himself, and took refuge in pretending not to understand him. Harriet supposed that she had known for a long time now how Gus felt about her. The trouble was, she had no idea how she felt about Gus. She liked him, felt enormous gratitude towards him, knew him to be solid, kind and dependable. But that wasn't love.

Somewhat to her surprise, Gus let the subject drop, and as the weeks went by, and 1946 slid into 1947, he did not mention it again. She had intended, after that first hint, to hold him at arm's length by throwing as much reserve into her manner as was possible in the circumstances. Lulled, however, by his silence into a false sense of security, Harriet soon forgot her resolution. In February she accompanied him to Chinatown to see the parades and carnivals which welcomed in the Chinese New Year.

They walked the few blocks to Mott Street, and took up a position on the corner of Worth, across from Chatham Square. Already, the streets were crowded with excited adults and children, exploding firecrackers and huge 'lions' and 'unicorns' and 'dragons', on the prowl to keep away evil spirits. People were dancing and yelling out, 'Kung hay fat choy!' which Gus told her meant 'Prosperity and a Happy New Year!' Shopkeepers were standing at their doors offering heads of lettuce, which were already 'sprouting' leaves of green dollars, afterwards to be distributed among the poor.

A great fire-breathing 'dragon' heralded the start of the procession proper, and the night was starred with the lights from a hundred Chinese lanterns.

'It's like fairyland,' Harriet breathed in wonder, thinking, but not saying, that for her the spectacle outrivalled even that of San Gennaro. She was carried away on a tide of euphoria: a feeling that until this moment she had never really lived. She was in a mood to be kind to everyone; to love the whole world.

So when Gus slipped his arm around her waist and whispered: 'Will you marry me?' she answered, 'Yes,' without any hesitation.

The following morning, she was having second thoughts, but by then it was too late. Gus had insisted on telling Sophia and Carlo the news as soon as they returned home the previous evening.

Harriet had been prepared for – had she hoped for? – their opposition, but instead Sophia and Carlo had seemed pleased: pleased to be getting their living-room floor back at nights, now that Gus would be moving in with Harriet; pleased to think that the couple might eventually look for a place of their own; pleased that they need no longer feel total responsibility for Sophia's baby brother. Two things disturbed them: the fact that Harriet was not a Catholic and expressed no intention of converting, and that she was divorced. But when Gus assured them that any children of the marriage would naturally be brought up in the faith they were happy again.

'You might have had the courtesy to consult me first before making such a promise,' Harriet complained bitterly, during the course of their first, very one-sided quarrel.

For the truth was, as she was soon to discover, it was almost impossible to fight with Gus. He never answered back when she shouted at him, but simply listened with an expressionless face while he mulled over what she was saying. Then, if he thought she was right, he would admit it straight away; otherwise, he remained intractable. In the end, Harriet, equally stubborn, found that there was only one way to deal with him, and that was to go her own road in defiance of his wishes. And she realized early in their marriage that she held all the cards, because Gus was in love with her. She was merely fond of him.

They were married at the beginning of March in a civil ceremony, attended only by Sophia and Carlo. Three months later Harriet was pregnant, but a great deal had happened by then.

'You're late, kiddo!' Harvey Muldoon turned from wiping over the counter as the restaurant door slammed shut behind Harriet. Outside it was raining and there was sleet in the air. It was still very cold for mid-March. 'Here,' he added, 'get some coffee inside you. You need it on a morning like this.'

Harriet took off her coat and shook it, sending a shower of raindrops hissing across the lid of the black iron stove. She ignored the coffee and went into the pay-kiosk, shifting her ledgers on to the desk from the shelf beneath. She could hear the waitresses giggling in the back room as they put on their aprons and powdered their noses, ready for the day ahead.

'Hey!' Harvey lumbered across and leaned his elbows on the ledge of the kiosk, staring at Harriet through the glass partition. 'You look like you had a rough night. If that's what marriage does for you, I'm thankful I've done with all that crap.'

'It's not that, Mr Muldoon. . .'

'Harvey! Call me Harvey for Chrissake! I've told you often enough.'

She ignored his entreaty, as she had ignored it previously. Harriet had strong views on the relationship between employer and employee. She hesitated, then said flatly: 'Gus has lost his job.'

'Shit!' Harvey Muldoon was genuinely concerned. 'That's tough. How come?'

'The boss's nephew is back from Germany. He was discharged from the Army last week and needs a job. Mr Costa was very sorry, but he said family comes first. He only told Gus last night, when he went to collect his pay. He got a month's wages in lieu of notice.'

The girls were beginning to line up with their trays, and

99

the breakfast customers were gathering outside the door, shivering in the cold. Harvey reached through the opening in the glass and squeezed Harriet's hand.

'D'you feel like working today? I can manage if you want to go home.'

Harriet shook her head. She and Gus had talked all night and, for the time being, there was nothing more to be said. He had left the apartment before she had that morning, to begin the search for work. One of the things they had frequently discussed in the weeks since their marriage had been the possibility of bringing Hilary over. Now there was no chance of that.

But worse was to come during that bitter spring. Two days after Gus lost his job, the tin-can factory manager decamped with the petty cash and the police moved in. The company's finances were found to be in total disarray, and the company itself went into immediate liquidation. Carlo, too, was on the bread-line. When one of the waitresses got married and moved to Ohio, Harriet persuaded Harvey to take on Sophia in her place; but Sophia resented her sister-in-law's superior position in the restaurant and tension mounted at home. Everyone's temper was short, and the little apartment echoed to constant rows and recriminations.

'The place is getting claustrophobic,' Harriet said, as she and Gus sat outside on the apartment-house steps one Friday morning. It was the first fine day for several weeks, and Harvey had given her the day off. The soft blue of an April sky showed above the roof-tops, and at the corner of the street a tree was fuzzed with green. All the same, it wasn't really warm enough to sit out of doors, but Harriet had been desperate for air. She felt that if she didn't get some elbow room she would break down and scream.

Gus said nothing. He had drawn into himself since losing his job, and Harriet knew that he hated her being the breadwinner. It hurt his masculine Italian pride. To him, there were clearly defined demarcation-lines between the roles of the sexes: men went out to work and earned the

100

money to support their families, women stayed home, cleaned and cooked, and had children.

It wasn't at all the way Harriet saw the world as being run. As she sat there on the steps, watching the sun riding higher in the sky and the chimney-line lighten from blue to amber, she knew that she should never have married Gus Contarini. Her affection for him was sisterly, and when he made love to her she felt absolutely nothing. She had learned in the eight weeks of their marriage to fake a climax, something she had never had to do with Gerry. She would not be twenty-one for another two months, but she had been forced to grow up fast since leaving England.

The woman who lived in what Harriet was learning to call the first-floor, rather than the ground-floor, apartment came out on to the steps and called: 'Are you Mrs Contarini?'

Harriet glanced up. 'Yes. That's me.'

'There's a call for you,' the woman informed her, jerking her head towards the hallway. 'Phone's been ringing for minutes. Wonder you didn't hear it. You must be deaf.'

Harriet got up and ascended the steps. 'Sorry. I didn't hear anything, did you, Gus? For me, you say? Did they say who's calling?'

The woman shrugged. 'Didn't ask. But it's transatlantic, I'll tell you that for free.' There was a spark of curiosity in the faded blue eyes. 'English, ain't ya? Guess it must be someone calling from your home.'

Dad, Harriet thought joyfully. Hilary had telephoned her once or twice in the past, and she had called him with the news that she was getting married again. Other than that, communication had been by letter.

She grabbed the swinging receiver. 'Hello? Pops?' she asked breathlessly, reverting for the first time in years to her favourite childhood diminutive for him.

'Is that Mrs Contarini?' a strange male voice enquired. 'Mrs Harriet Contarini? Née Chance?'

'Yes, speaking.' A sudden presentiment of disaster almost strangled the sound in her throat.

'This is Athelstan Phipps of Gardiner, Son and Phipps,

101

your father's solicitors. I'm afraid I have some very bad news for you, Mrs Contarini.'

The Reverend Hilary Chance had died suddenly in his sleep the previous evening. Mrs Wicks had found him when she arrived at the vicarage that morning, still sitting in his armchair by the cold ashes of the study fire.

'The doctor said he'd been dead at least twelve hours,' Mr Phipps informed Harriet as gently as he could. 'He obviously hadn't suffered. His expression, I understand, was peaceful.'

Little Hilary had been sitting up in bed, crying, a circumstance which had first alerted Mrs Wicks to the fact that something was wrong. The child was usually dressed and running about at that hour.

Harriet was devastated by grief and by the realization that she could not possibly go home for the funeral. Her father was only forty-seven; she had expected him to live for years yet. The knowledge that he was there – the stable rock, the permanent base to which she could always return – had made her feel secure. Now he was gone and she was alone, except for her child.

Her child! Whatever was to become of little Hilary?

'Have you no relations at all, Mrs Contarini?' Athelstan Phipps had enquired accusingly, as though it was somehow her fault; as though she had carelessly lost or mislaid them. 'Mrs Wicks has taken the child for the time being, but it can, of course, be only a temporary arrangement.'

'Yes, I understand that. But there truly isn't anyone. Both my parents were an only child. There may be distant cousins but, if so, I'm ignorant of them.'

'Dear me! Dear me!' The solicitor had not been encouraging.

The weeks that followed that dreadful day were a nightmare, during which Harriet discovered, not for the first time, that Gus was a tower of strength. He comforted her at nights and left her alone by day, fending off the well-meant attentions of Sophia and Carlo. He kept her job warm for her at the Last Chance Saloon, then stepped aside grace-fully when she felt able to return. Knowing how he felt about her working, and his own unemployed state, Harriet appreciated this particular gesture even more than all the others. Gus might well have taken advantage of her absence to persuade Harvey Muldoon into giving him the job, but he was far too honourable to do anything of that kind.

Halfway through May, Harriet discovered that she was pregnant again.

She was ill with worry, and when Mr Phipps, who kept in constant touch by telephone and airmail letter, made his suggestion she felt that it was the only answer.

'Have your own child *adopted*?' Gus was horrified. Although Sophia and Carlo were all he had, his Italian sense of family was highly developed.

The four of them were seated at table, drinking coffee after Sunday dinner. Before Harriet could reply, Sophia cut in.

'It seems like a sensible idea to me,' she observed tartly. 'It's going to be overcrowded here, as it is, now that *you've* been foolish enough to start a child.' There was more than a hint of jealousy in her tone. It was the greatest tragedy of Sophia's life that she and Carlo had been unable to have a baby.

Harriet pushed the hair out of her eyes. The weather had turned warm. She felt hot and exhausted.

'Sophia's right, Gus, so please don't argue. It isn't as though little Hilary knows me any more. I can't be any-thing but a dim memory, if that. Mr Phipps has offered to take care of all the arrangements. He'll make certain that the child goes to a good home. All I'll have to do is sign the necessary papers. The legal expenses will come out of my father's estate.'

'It doesn't seem right,' Gus persisted stubbornly. 'There must be some other way.' But his voice lacked conviction.

'There isn't any other way!' Harriet was suddenly at the end of her tether. She pushed back her chair and stood up, clutching at the edge of the table with shaking hands. 'Do you think, if there were, I wouldn't have thought of it by now? I've been over and over it in my mind. I haven't been sleeping. I'll harm this baby – *your* baby! – if I go on like this.' She started to cry. 'For God's sake, Gus, there's nothing else I can do! Nothing! Nothing! *Nothing!* I've made up my mind, so please don't try to change it!'

She ran into their bedroom and slammed the door.

11

The last customer had gone. Harvey Muldoon closed and locked the main door of the Last Chance Saloon, and the three girls who had been waiting at table all day finally allowed their shoulders to slump and kicked off their high-heeled shoes. From the kitchen came the clatter of crockery and the chink of cutlery as the late shift of washers-up got into their stride. Outside, the streets of the Village were dusty and hot. New York was sweltering in a heatwave.

Harriet closed the grille of the pay-kiosk and switched on the overhead light. Although it only needed half an hour until midnight, she still had to check the books.

Harvey opened the little door at the back of the kiosk and looked in.

'Leave that,' he ordered. 'I said leave it!' He leaned over and twitched the pen from Harriet's fingers. 'You look all in.'

'I have to make sure that everything's been properly entered,' Harriet protested. She was tired, desperately; but, even so, she had no desire to go home. Sophia and Carlo might still be up, keeping Gus company while he waited for her to return, and the tension would be like a palpable presence as soon as she opened the door.

Sophia had been involved in a stand-up row with Harvey Muldoon, over something quite trivial, and been dismissed. Harriet had made matters worse by siding with Harvey: Sophia had been so rude, she honestly didn't see what else she could have done. But Harriet felt guilty, too, knowing

105

that her sister-in-law's bad temper was largely due to the crowded conditions in which they were living, and Gus and Carlo's failure to find new jobs.

'I'll see to the goddam books after you've gone,' Harvey told her. 'I don't sleep well anyhow, and if you don't watch it, kiddo, you're going to harm that baby. But, before you go, come into the office and have a nightcap. I wanna talk to you.'

She followed him meekly into the cubby-hole of a room that was grandly referred to as 'the office' and sat down on a chair facing the dilapidated desk. A green-painted filing cabinet, a corner cupboard and a coat-stand completed the furnishings.

Harvey produced a bottle of whisky, soda and a couple of glasses and proceeded to pour them both a drink. Then he wedged himself into the swivel chair, which no longer swivelled, on the other side of the desk. He was doing quite nicely with the business, Harriet reflected, but if only he would smarten the place up a bit he could be doing a lot better than that. The restaurant was a potential gold-mine.

For a moment there was silence between them. In the kitchen someone was whistling a tune from the latest Broadway hit musical, *Brigadoon*. One of the girls was giggling. Harriet sipped her whisky gratefully and eased her neck muscles, trying to rid herself of the long day's aches and pains. Harvey regarded her with concerned shrewd eyes. The little goatee beard waggled thoughtfully.

'I've grown very fond of you, kiddo,' he observed unexpectedly. 'I shall be sorry to see you go.'

'Go?' Harriet glanced up in astonishment. 'I'm not going anywhere.' She patted her stomach. 'At least, not for a while. The baby's not due until February.'

'And then what?' Harvey swirled his whisky round in his glass. 'Four of you and a screaming kid in a two-bedroom apartment, three storeys up, day in, day out. All together.'

'I was hoping you'd take me back as soon as I could manage it,' she told him anxiously.

'Leaving the baby with Sophia?' The little eyes peered

106

sharply at her from between the ever increasing rolls of flesh. Harvey was far too fond of eating. 'And whose kid do you think it would be after a few months of that? That woman's starving for a child.'

Harriet was jolted. She had not considered that aspect of her problem. But now that Harvey had stated it so bluntly she could see that there was a very real danger there. She had been forced to abandon one child to the mercy of other people. Could she afford to make the same mistake again?

'But what the hell can I do?' she demanded explosively, angry with Harvey for adding yet another to her burden of worries.

'Get out of there. Get out of New York.'

'What on?' Her tone was abrasive. 'It takes money to move, or had you forgotten? Gus and I can't possibly afford it.'

'You can if the Government pays.'

She stared at him. 'What on earth do you mean?'

Harvey took another swig of whisky and grinned at her over the rim of his glass.

'Y'know, you're cute when you get all ruffled up. You come over terribly, terribly British.' He gave a passable imitation of her English accent. Then he grew serious and leaned forward in his chair. 'Listen, kiddo, I've been making some enquiries from a friend of mine. You ever heard of the GI Study Scheme for ex-servicemen?' Harriet shook her head. 'Well, it's something your husband should have been told about before he got his army discharge. Probably was. May have forgotten it.'

'More than likely,' Harriet agreed bitterly. It was just the kind of information Gus would forget. 'What does it do, this scheme?'

'It provides financial aid for ex-GIs and their families while they train for a profession. It also helps get them places at the various institutes and universities.'

Harriet's heart sank. 'Gus doesn't seem to have any particular ambitions, that's the trouble. He's never known

107

what he wants to do, except work hard at whatever job happens to come along.'

Two of the waitresses put their heads round the door to say goodnight. In the kitchen, plates were still rattling. Through the grimy windows of Harvey's office, Harriet could see the trees in the square, and a pale sliver of moon netted in the topmost branches.

Harvey said: 'When he was here, filling in for you, after your father died, the cook was off a coupla days, sick. Gus deputized for him. That husband of yours is a damn fine cook. If Pietro wasn't elderly, with a wife who's always ill, I'd have sacked him and taken on Gus instead. The customers loved his food.'

'Gus? Cooking?' Harriet could hardly believe her ears. At home, he never went near the kitchen. Sophia wouldn't let him.

'Yup.' Harvey finished his whisky in one final noisy gulp. 'If he trained to be a chef, got diplomas and things, he could earn good money.' Harvey rose to his feet and rested his jutting paunch on the top of the desk. 'And now I'm going to walk you home. Tell Gus what I've said, and get him to make enquiries. If he doesn't, he's a bigger fool than I take him for. But I'm pinning my faith on you.'

The Riverdale Domestic Science Academy lay some miles south of Santa Barbara, and west of the Los Angeles–San Bernardino freeway. It must, thought Harriet, be one of the most beautiful places in the world.

Gus had taken a great deal of persuading to apply for help under the GI Study Scheme, but in the end he had done it, his natural disinclination overborne by the combined weight of opinion marshalled against him. Sophia and Carlo had backed Harriet one hundred per cent from the moment she had told them about her conversation with Harvey.

'Can't you see that they want to be rid of us?' she had asked Gus impatiently, when still he had jibbed. 'And, frankly, I don't blame them. They want their home to

108

themselves again. And what else are you going to do? Tell me that! Bum around all your life, grabbing at any old job that comes your way? Or live off the State? Where's your precious independence then, I'd like to know? Harvey says you're a good cook. That you like cooking! So learn the trade properly. At the end of two years, you'll be in a position to earn a decent living.'

'Cooking's a woman's job. I only did it to help Harvey out.' Gus had been sullen and resentful.

'For God's sake! All the world's greatest chefs are men. Including Italians!'

The force of her arguments and his own common sense had eventually worn Gus down. He had reluctantly applied, half-hoping that he would prove to be ineligible; but not only was his application successful, he was also informed that a place was available at Riverdale Academy in California for the term beginning in the early fall. An allowance would be paid for the two years of his training, and accommodation would be provided for himself and his wife in one of the campus bungalows. There was no possible excuse for him not to accept the offer, and by the end of August he and Harriet had packed up and gone.

Harriet had taken an emotional farewell of Harvey and the girls at the Last Chance Saloon.

'I don't know how to thank you,' she had said, kissing Harvey's sagging cheeks.

'Yeah, I must be nuts,' he had answered, blinking away the tears. 'Getting rid of the best cashier the Last Chance ever had! Who but a schmuck would want to do that?' He had returned her kiss, surreptitiously squeezing her hand. 'Know what, kiddo? I shall miss you and your funny little limey ways. The old place sure ain't going to be the same without you. And to think I only hired you in the first place because you said your single name was Chance! Well, just keep on taking chances, kiddo. Chance by name and chancy by nature, eh? Don't let this vale of tears get you down.'

Harriet's leave-taking of Sophia and Carlo was more restrained. Nevertheless, she was equally grateful to them.

'I don't know what I should have done without both of you,' she said. 'You've been wonderful to me.'

'Hell, it was nothing,' Carlo demurred. He was so relieved to see them go that all the aggravation and dissension of the past fourteen months seemed suddenly unimportant.

The flight to Los Angeles had been spent by Harriet largely in sleep. This pregnancy, like her previous one, was making her very tired.

The college bus had collected them at Los Angeles airport and driven them upstate to Riverdale. It was the first time in her life that Harriet had seen lemon groves.

'Isn't it ridiculous,' she said to Gus, 'but it still surprises me to see lemons growing on trees?' She glanced at his closed expressionless face and tucked her hand in his arm. 'You're not regretting it, are you?'

After a moment or two, he forced a smile. 'No. I suppose not.' He added more cheerfully: 'At least it's stopped you working. I never liked you having to go to that awful place.'

'The Last Chance?' Harriet laughed. 'It was a bit of a dump, wasn't it? But it had – has – a lot of loyal customers. Harvey could really make something of that place if he tried.'

There was another silence, while the bus with its complement of students, most of them much younger then Gus, sped past the shining expanse of the Pacific Ocean to their left and the flat-topped forests of lemon trees on the opposite side.

Abruptly, Gus asked: 'Do you have any regrets? Like marrying me, for example?'

'What?' Harriet was caught off guard. 'No. No, of course not.'

'I wonder. . . I mean, I wonder sometimes . . . if you don't still hanker after Gerry.'

'I haven't thought of him in ages. Does that answer your question?'

And, to her surprise, she discovered that she was speaking the truth. She couldn't remember the last time she had really thought of Gerry Canossa, not even in connection with Hilary ... But her child was really someone she didn't want to consider. If she did, she would start wondering what the adoptive parents were like, if Hilary was happy, if ... if ... if. ...

But as far as Gerry was concerned, she could honestly swear that he meant nothing to her any more, and she found it difficult to believe that he ever had. She couldn't even recall his darkly handsome good looks: on the few occasions she had tried to summon up his face, it had obstinately remained a blur. Had she ever truly loved him? She thought she had, but it wasn't easy to stay fond of someone who had treated her so badly.

'What made you ask?' she enquired of Gus.

'Dunno.' He found and held one of her hands. 'I'm jealous, I guess. I love you so much. I always have.'

'Yes, I know.' Harriet returned the pressure of his fingers.

She wanted desperately to assure him that she loved him, too, but it wouldn't be the truth, and it wasn't easy to deceive her husband. Gus always knew when she was lying. She did, however, have a very deep affection for him, and had every intention of making him happy. She owed Gus a lot; more than she could ever hope to repay.

The next two years passed unbelievably swiftly for both of them, even though Harriet enjoyed herself less than she had anticipated; probably because Gus enjoyed himself more.

Once he got over his initial resistance to the course and conquered his innate shyness, he found that he liked the life of a student, particularly a mature one. Far from making fun of his advanced years, the other trainees deferred and looked up to him, impressed by the fact that he had fought in the war and taken part in the D-Day landings. Gus also discovered that he did indeed have a flair for cooking and, as time passed, became more and more absorbed in his studies, his exams and the day-to-day life of the campus.

Harriet, on the other hand, was increasingly isolated as

the months progressed, especially after the birth of their son, Michael. There were no other wives tagging along on this particular course, and she had not yet sufficiently overcome her inbred English reserve to mix freely with the rest of the students.

During their first few weeks, Gus bought an old second-hand Ford convertible from one of the instructors. It was prewar vintage and had seen better days. The leather upholstery was rubbed and faded, and it blew a gasket the very first time they took it on the road. But to Harriet it was the height of luxury and independence – her father had never owned a car – and she would not have exchanged it for all the Cadillacs in the United States. They spent happy weekends exploring the locality: Santa Barbara, with its fascinating Spanish-style houses, built from local adobe clay, climbing from the harbour up the beautiful mountain slopes; Pismo Beach, home of giant clams; and Santa Paula, surrounded by lemon groves. The lemons were picked every five or six weeks, and in a single year one tree could produce as many as three thousand lemons. The reason for lopping the trees to a flat-topped uniform height was to increase the yield.

After a while, however, these expeditions became less frequent. Gus was increasingly absorbed in his work, and once the baby was born Harriet had less time to herself and felt constantly tired. She breast-fed Michael for as long as she could, until recurring bouts of milk fever forced her to stop. She began to resent Gus's preoccupations outside the home and the way she was expected singlehandedly to look after the baby.

'It's your job, honey,' Gus would point out gently whenever she complained. 'It's my job to train as hard as I can in order to support you and Michael. And you swore, if I took this course, you'd back me all the way.'

There was no answer to that, because it was precisely what she had promised, and Gus deserved her whole-hearted collaboration. But she was lonely and bored, and most of her good resolutions were in tatters.

Since Michael's birth, her sexual drive had temporarily diminished, and at nights she often pushed Gus away. He had never been a man to force himself on her, but as weeks then months went by, and still she rejected him, he began to feel resentful. It never occurred to him to find consolation elsewhere, so he got rid of his frustration by working harder than ever. By the time Michael was one year old, and Harriet ready, even eager, to have sex with him again, Gus was far too busy studying for his final exams in the summer. He was the one now too exhausted at nights to do more than kiss her a chaste 'sweet dreams' before immediately falling asleep. It was Harriet's turn to feel frustrated and resentful.

On the morning of Gus's first practical final, he was more abstracted than usual.

'I won't be home to lunch,' he said, cramming textbooks and copious notes into a bulging canvas bag, and arranging a row of pens and pencils in the pocket of his shirt. He hitched up his jeans. 'I'll eat in hall with the rest of the guys. We'll want to exchange notes on how things went.'

'OK.' Harriet shrugged resignedly. 'I'll take Mickey to the beach.' She glanced towards her son, who was busy stuffing his mouth with boiled egg and pieces of toast. At eighteen months, Michael Contarini was already showing signs of a sturdy self-reliance.

'Yeah! You do that. Do you both good. You ought to get out more when I'm not here.' Gus dropped a kiss on the top of her head. 'See you.'

'Good luck,' she called, recollecting what day it was just in time.

'Thanks, honey.' He vanished through the door, leaving her alone with Michael.

12

With nearly thirty miles of unspoilt beaches to choose from, Harriet was used to picking her spots without fear of crowds. There was one place in particular, south of Riverdale, which she regarded as peculiarly her own.

She packed sandwiches and fruit, a flask of coffee for herself and fresh orange juice for Michael, strapped her son into the back seat of the Ford and drove slowly off the campus. In the distance, she could see the hurrying figures of the second-year students as they made their way to the main block of buildings which housed the kitchens, where they would take the first of their practical exams. Tomorrow would come the first theoretical paper: Gus would probably be up until the small hours, studying.

Once on the freeway, she turned south for some miles, then swung to her right and bucketed down a narrow track to the sea. Learning to drive had been the most sensible decision she had made during the past two years, and something which had received Gus's blessing. People rarely walked in the States if they could ride and, since coming to America, Harriet had been forced to readjust her notion of distance. A hundred miles were soon covered on the vast network of interstate highways; whereas the narrow twisting roads and lanes of the English countryside strung them out to a four-hour journey.

She parked the car on a patch of wind-stunted grass, unstrapped Michael and picked up the picnic-basket. Slowly, shortening her steps to keep pace with her son's, Harriet made for the cluster of rocks where they always

sat. But this morning, to her profound annoyance, someone was there before her.

The young man, about her own age, she guessed, was
stretched full length on an air-bed, a bottle of sun lotion
and a towel at his side. She was unable to see the colour of
his eyes because they were shut, but the two half-moons of
thick lashes, which lay against his sun-bronzed skin, were
as dark as the thatch of hair above them. He wore a pair of
black swimming-shorts and an identity-disc on a thin gold
chain around his neck. Other than that, he was naked.

Harriet's first thought was that he was rather ugly, her
second that he was not so bad, her third that he was hog-
ging all the shade. Ignoring his presence as best she could,
she set down the basket, helped Michael off with his sandals
and flopped on the towel which she had spread. The man
turned his head and opened his eyes, which she could now
see were a very deep blue.

'Isn't the beach big enough for you,' he demanded
irritably, 'that you have to sit right on top of me?' He spoke
with a pronounced southern Irish accent.

Harriet raised her eyebrows haughtily. 'May I point out
that you have the only patch of shade for miles around? I
have no intention of eating my lunch in all the glare of the
midday sun.'

His look of annoyance became more pronounced.

'Jesus! That's all I need! An Englishwoman. I might have
known it. Only the English have such damn bad manners.'

'This beach is not your private property,' Harriet
snapped. 'Michael! Leave that alone!' For her son, escaping
momentarily from his mother's vigilance, had removed
the cap from the sun-lotion bottle and was busily pouring
its contents into the sand.

The man swore and sat up, reaching out a hand.

'Don't you dare touch my child!' Harriet told him
furiously. 'Oh, Michael.' She stared helplessly at the now
empty container which her son was holding out to her.
'That was a very naughty thing to do.' She glanced at
her irate companion. 'I'm sorry,' she apologized stiffly.

115

'Perhaps, as compensation, you would care to share our picnic. You don't seem to have any food.'

'I usually go to the San José Eating House, back along the freeway, and have a taco.' The man's irritation was gradually disappearing, and he smiled at her. 'But, yes, sure I'll eat with you. Thank you.' He rolled Michael over in the sand and gently tickled his ribs. 'You're a very destructive young man. What's your name? How old are you? Old enough, anyhow, to be deep in sin.'

Harriet supplied the information as she unpacked the basket, arranging the fruit and sandwiches on disposable plates. 'I'm afraid it's only ham, salad and fruit,' she said. 'If you'd rather have that taco. . .'

'This'll do fine,' he grinned. 'Now that I actually see food, I realize just how hungry I am.'

While they ate, and jointly controlled Michael's determination to wander off and explore, they exchanged names and histories. A few hundred yards away, the blue-green Pacific hissed gently against the long rolling sands, and further out a crowd of boys rode the breakers, laughing and calling to one another from their surfboards. On the rock, a jewel-eyed lizard searched for shade, and as the afternoon sun became fiercer a water mirage hung across the track leading from the shore.

Harriet learned that the young man's name was Edmund Howard; that he came, as she had suspected, from southern Ireland; that he had been in the States for over five years, having left his home in Waterford at the age of eighteen; that he was married to an American girl from whom he was in the process of getting a divorce; and that he earned his living as a horse handler and trainer for Twentieth Century-Fox.

Sensing Harriet's disappointment, he grinned.

'Confess now,' he said, selecting a peach from the plate she was offering him, 'when I mentioned the film studios, you thought I was an actor, at least.'

'A star,' she corrected, smiling. 'They have some very odd-looking people in films these days.'

'Thank you.' His eyes twinkled. 'I take it this is your revenge for me robbing you of all your shade.' Although he had in fact moved over, so that there was plenty of shelter for all three of them in the lee of the rock. 'I've often been told that I look rather like Ronald Reagan. Would you agree?'

Harriet regarded him. 'Perhaps there is a faint resemblance. He's much handsomer of course. But you both have Irish faces, and presumably Irish charm.'

'I like you, too,' he said in growing amusement. 'Now it's your turn to tell me what brings you to this part of the world.'

So she told him her story, expurgating where she felt it to be necessary, although she had an uneasy feeling he could read between the lines. When she had finished, there was silence for a while, surprisingly companionable for two people who were almost strangers.

Presently, she said: 'It upset you when you found out that I'm English. Why?'

'Why?' Edmund Howard shifted his weight so that he was looking straight at her, and she could see the sudden anger blazing in his eyes. Michael, replete with food, had curled up on the towel, thumb in mouth, and was sound asleep. Now and again, he snorted.

'Yes, why?' Harriet would not let herself be intimidated by his renewed antagonism. 'You're surely not going to give me all that crap about Cromwell and the Drogheda massacre! That was centuries ago, for Pete's sake.'

He leaned forward, his eyes burning so fiercely that, for a moment, she knew a spasm of fear. He gripped her arm.

'Why should I talk to you about Cromwell? Why, when there are so many more recent betrayals and treacheries and atrocities I could mention?' His voice was low and furious. 'Easter nineteen sixteen, for example. All seven men who signed the Proclamation of the Republic were shot. One was so badly wounded he had to be carried out to his execution in a chair. What about Sir Roger Casement, hanged for high treason, and when there were

117

calls for clemency the British government circulated alleged passages from his diary to prove that he was a homosexual. That soon put a stop to the great British public's demand for a reprieve! And then there's Lloyd George, God rot him! He promised independence, and what did we get? The Irish Free State within the British Empire, with the six counties of Ulster still a part of the United Kingdom.'

'It was Ulster's choice,' Harriet retorted with spirit, trying to reconcile this tense fanatic with the relaxed ironical young man of a few moments earlier. 'And, anyway, aren't you the Republic of Ireland now? Didn't I read something about that earlier this year?'

'Yes. On Easter Monday, an appropriate day, we were formally acknowledged a republic. Thirty-three years late.' Edmund withdrew his hand from her arm and leaned back against the rock, some of the fire dying out of his eyes. 'We've finally severed all remaining constitutional ties with Great Britain. But it hasn't solved the problem of the six counties. We're still a divided nation.'

No longer nervous, Harriet asked curiously: 'You're not a member of the – what d'you call it – Irish Republican Army? Isn't that the name?'

Edmund Howard closed his eyes and raised his face to the sun.

'No, I'm not. You're forgetting, I've been over here for the past five years. Not that there isn't plenty of support for the IRA in America. There are a hell of a lot of Irish in the States.'

'Would you ever join?' Harriet asked curiously.

He smiled enigmatically. 'Ah, girl dear, that would be telling.'

Harriet contemplated the possibility for him. Like the majority of English people, she knew very little of Irish affairs, and tended to regard any outlawed organization in a romantic light. The war, and the European underground movement against Hitler, had lent a glamour to all such subversive activities. But after a few minutes the heat and

118

the silence dulled her senses and she, too, drifted off to sleep.

She woke an hour later, unrefreshed, to find Edmund Howard trying to build a sandcastle, and her son watching his every move with determined concentration. The Irishman looked across at her and grinned.

'He's likes to learn, doesn't he? There's not much that'll escape him as he gets older. Is he your only one?'

'Yes. . . Yes, he's our only child so far.' Harriet stood up, brushing the sand from her dress. The birth of Hilary and the child's adoption were two of the things she hadn't mentioned when telling her story. 'We'll have to be going,' she added. 'My husband will be home soon. His exam is due to end at three-thirty.'

Michael began to whine as she put on his shoes.

'Stay! Stay!' he insisted.

'We can't, darling. Daddy will wonder where we are.' Harriet addressed Edmund, trying to sound casual. 'Do you come up this way often?'

'At least once a week,' he lied, 'when I'm not working.'

He consigned Malibu and Long Beach to limbo. There was something about this young woman which powerfully attracted him, and made the chance of seeing her again irresistible. He wasn't sure what it was; there were hundreds of beautiful women in California: bronzed long-limbed creatures with clear-cut features and incomparable American dental work to lend brilliance to their smiles. His wife – his nearly ex-wife – was one of them, a minor starlet attached to one of the major studios: gorgeous, perfectly proportioned, shining with health and vigour. Perhaps that was it. Harriet Contarini was the first woman he had met in a very long time who didn't look as though she had been gift-wrapped at Neiman Marcus. She was an individual; a delicate intelligent face under a mop of untidy hair. Her suntan was uneven, the backs of her legs almost white. Her green cotton dress was unfashionably skimpy and short in this era of Dior's New Look.

She was also English, and he hated the whole goddam race!

'Perhaps. . . Perhaps we could meet again, then,' she suggested tentatively.

He smiled. 'I'd like that. Next week, same day, same time? I'm always off on Tuesdays.'

'All right.' Gus would be tied up with exams for the next three weeks. Not, she told herself, that that had anything to do with it. She just wanted the young Irishman as a friend. And, in any case, the friendship would be short-lived. As soon as Gus knew he had qualified, they would be flying back to New York.

She shook Edmund's hand matter-of-factly, to establish the nature of their relationship, but could not suppress the feeling that he was secretly laughing at her.

'Same time next Tuesday, then,' she said. 'We'll see you then.'

'I shouldn't be here,' she said nervously, looking round the empty beach-house. 'I can only stay for an hour. One of the students is babysitting for me. Mickey frets when I'm not there, and I don't know how long he will sleep.'

As she spoke, Harriet was twisting her cheap imitation-crocodile bag between her hands. Edmund closed the door and came to stand behind her. She leaned against him, and he folded her in his arms.

A surge of love swept through her; a depth of emotion which she had never felt for Gerry Canossa and certainly never experienced with Gus. This, then, was what people meant when they talked about falling in love; what poets had written about from time immemorial; what women like the Brontës had dreamed of. But she had never envisaged it happening to her.

It was impossible to believe that this was only the fifth time she and Edmund had met. And on the previous four occasions there had been Michael to keep amused. So how was it that they had come to feel this way about one another?

On their second meeting, Edmund had taken her and Michael to the San José Eating House for lunch, and they had fed the sandwiches she had brought with her to the gulls. They sat on a shaded terrace, facing the sea, strings of coloured lightbulbs bobbing above their heads, eating clam chowder and shrimps, and picking from a bowl of freshly gathered dates and figs. They had talked a lot, discovering that they had a lot in common.

'Why is it,' she had asked him, 'that the Irish can always make the English laugh? Sheridan and Wilde and Shaw. We've always loved them.'

'It's because they poke fun at the English,' he had answered. 'The English love laughing at themselves. They're the most insensitive nation on earth.'

'Or the most stable,' she had retorted.

Politics had not been mentioned. They had carefully steered clear of the subject.

When she went home that evening, she felt as though she were treading on air.

Gus was too busy swatting to ask her where she'd been or even if she had had a good day. But when they went to bed that night he kissed her and clung to her, finally making love to her, like a child in need of reassurance. She realized that he was frightened he was going to let her down by failing his exams. She felt ashamed.

But it didn't stop her going to meet Edmund the following Tuesday, and again last week. And it was then, sitting together in their favourite place, in the shadow of the rocks, while Michael played happily in the sand, that he had told her about his friend's beach-house.

'It's a bit further up the coast and it belongs to this guy I know, who works in the sound department at MGM. Laurie – my wife – and I used to go there sometimes at weekends. I've asked Chuck if he'll let me have use of it next Tuesday. Do you think you could get a babysitter for Mick?'

Her heart had begun to beat unnaturally fast. 'I'll try,' she had promised breathlessly.

She wanted him. She wanted him so badly it couldn't

possibly be wrong. She had never felt like this about anyone before, and she doubted if she ever would again.

Harriet told Gus that she was going to meet a friend at Santa Barbara, and asked him if he thought Shirlene McCarthy would be available to look after Michael on Tuesday. She hadn't lied, but now that she was actually here, in the beach-house, with Edmund's arms around her, she found it no consolation. She kept seeing her husband's gentle trusting smile.

She had driven the Ford to the San José Eating House and parked it round the back. Edmund had picked her up in his ancient Buick a hundred yards further up the road. Somehow, remembering, it smacked of conspiracy; of deliberate intent to deceive. Gus didn't deserve that. She owed him too much.

Edmund turned her round to face him and slowly began unbuttoning her blouse. She started to tremble and go weak at the knees. All the romantic clichés were true, it seemed. There was no other way to describe how she felt; as if her very bones were melting. . .

Edmund's mouth was on hers, and she could see the beads of perspiration standing out along his forehead. They were all the lovers the world had ever known rolled into one. They had a right to a life together. . .

They had no right to anything! Not as long as Gus needed her. And there was Michael, too! She could not abnegate her responsibilities for a second time. She pushed Edmund away with such force that he staggered and nearly fell.

'No!' she cried. 'We can't! Take me back, please. At once!'

She expected him to be angry, perhaps to lash out, and for a moment he did look murderous. But the anger quickly drained from his face and he held out his hands.

'I'm sorry, acushla. It's my fault. I should never have suggested it. I can't quite fathom what's between you and that husband of yours but, whatever it is, it must be pretty special.'

122

She was in his arms again, holding him tightly and crying as though her heart would break.

'I love you,' she whispered. 'I'll always love you, but I can't do this to Gus. He trusts me, and I can't betray him.'

Edmund nodded silently. He had looked forward to their love-making with such painful intensity that somewhere, deep down, he had known that something would happen to prevent it.

He could feel every curve of her body pressed against his. If he insisted, she would probably give in – and hate him after! He couldn't risk that; he loved her too much. He wondered vaguely whatever he had seen in Laurie; in any woman except this one.

After a while, Harriet raised her head from his chest and looked at him enquiringly. Her eyes were full of tears and her cheeks blotched with crying. She was not even pretty at this moment, but strangely it didn't seem to matter to a man, who, until now, had never liked his women less than perfect.

He kissed her again, but this time very gently.

'Come on,' he whispered, 'let's get out of here.'

13

They returned to New York in September. Sophia and
Carlo met them at the airport.

'Why the hell d'ya wanna come back to this dump?'
Carlo asked as they piled into a taxi. 'We felt sure you'd
decide to stay in sunny California.'

'I'm a New Yorker. Why'd I want to live any place else?'
Gus demanded, while Carlo grinned in total agreement.
'But I'd have stayed out west if Harry had really wanted it.
As it was, she couldn't wait to leave.'

'Is it true?' Sophia looked incredulous. 'Catch me passing
up the chance of all that sun.'

Harriet smiled weakly and stared out of the yellow cab's
windows at the passing skyscrapers. Michael, thumb in
mouth, was dozing on her lap, worn out by the journey.
Fortunately, Sophia didn't seem to expect an answer to
her question and had turned once again to her brother.
Harriet was glad not to speak, or her voice might have
betrayed her pent-up emotion.

She and Edmund had not met again since the day at the
beachhouse. It had been her decision, and he had
respected it. He was a good man, like Gus. Harriet grimaced to herself. Perhaps women were better off, after all,
with men such as Gerry Canossa: selfish, self-centred,
unfeeling. Goodness was much more difficult to cope with:
it imposed on other people the penance of obligation. Gus,
she sometimes thought, was a greater burden than Gerry
would ever have been.

She must not think like that. But why, oh, why had Fate

not permitted her to meet Edmund Howard sooner? Two years in California, and they had only known each other right at the end. Yet, if she couldn't bring herself to betray Gus, wasn't it better that the time had been short? Wasn't that the reason she had opted for a quick return to New York as soon as Gus knew the result of his exams? She couldn't trust herself to be near Edmund, because eventually she would have gone to bed with him. She wouldn't have been able to help herself, their mutual attraction was so strong.

How absurd, how unbelievable, that she should suddenly fall in love with one man to the exclusion of all others. And on such a brief acquaintance! It didn't make sense! But she knew with absolute certainty that Edmund Howard was locked inside her heart for ever.

Yet she was going to have to live without him, because of her debt to Gus. The one good thing about the affair was that it had put her feelings for Gerry Canossa in their true perspective. She knew now that she had never loved Hilary's father.

'Hey, Harry, I'm speaking to you,' protested Carlo, leaning forward to tap her knee. 'Where were you? You looked like you were a million miles away.'

This time, they stayed only a couple of weeks with Sophia and Carlo while settling themselves and their affairs. By the end of October, Gus, with his new diploma and glowing references from the Academy, had obtained a post as assistant chef in the kitchens of the Algonquin on West 44th Street. Two weeks later, he, Harriet and Michael moved into a three-bedroom apartment just off Mulberry, a block away from Sophia and Carlo.

During the past year, Carlo had found fresh employment with a radio and television company as a door-to-door salesman, and was consequently away from home a good deal. Sophia, with time on her hands, was delighted to have her sister-in-law so close, and was always ready to look after Michael if Harriet wished it.

Harriet began to get bored with having nothing to do. It hadn't seemed to matter so much in California, where life went at a slower pace. But here, in bustling New York, things were different. Besides, working would help her to bury the memory of Edmund.

She broached the subject to Gus, but he wouldn't hear of it. He hoped that they would have another baby.

They were certainly trying hard enough, Harriet thought, looking at herself in the long bathroom mirror. Only nothing was happening. Could that possibly be because she was willing it not to? Nonsense, of course; but none the less, she felt guilty.

She began to dress slowly after a long leisurely bath, her second that day. Bathing broke the monotony. Michael was with Sophia, who had fetched him early on the pretext of showing him off to members of the Ladies' Catholic Guild, whom she was entertaining to lunch. In reality, she just adored looking after the child, and Harriet hadn't the heart to deny her.

When she had finished dressing, Harriet wandered into the living-room, hoping to find something to do, but she had cleaned the apartment only that morning. Gus was on late shift and would eat at the hotel, so there was no evening meal that needed preparing.

Damn! If she didn't do something, she would start thinking of Edmund; fighting the overwhelming urge to phone him long-distance. She must not contact him. *She must not!* If she once heard his voice, she would be tempted to pack her bags and fly out to California on the very next plane. She couldn't do that to Gus and Michael. She had deserted her father and Hilary, and for the sake of her own sanity she dared not put herself in that situation again.

She picked up her discarded novel, *The Loved One*, but for once Evelyn Waugh's account of Californian burial rites failed to make her laugh. She put it down again. She simply had to find something to do. . .

Of course! Harvey! Harvey Muldoon. Harriet was ashamed to realize that she had not once called at the Last

126

Chance Saloon in the two months since her return. She hurried into the bedroom, where she wrapped up warmly in her thickest coat and long woollen scarf, for after two years in California she felt the cold of a New York winter. Five minutes later, dragging on a pair of fur-lined mittens, she let herself out of the apartment building and headed in the direction of the Village.

'Hi, kiddo! I heard you were back. You're looking great.'

Harriet wished she could return the compliment. Harvey's appearance shocked her. His already bulky figure seemed to have doubled in weight since she had last seen him, and his skin was an unhealthy putty colour. He moved and breathed with increasing difficulty, chain-smoking his own particular brand of Turkish cigarettes. The restaurant, too, had a seedy air about it. The table-cloths were soiled, and there were stains on the carpet. In the old days the place had been immaculate.

'Gus is a chef, I understand, at the Algonquin. Ain't you glad you took my advice and made him apply for that grant?'

Harriet kissed his cheek, which was cold and clammy.

'It was the best thing I ever did. I owe you, Harvey.'

'You don't owe me nothing, kiddo. I'm just happy it all worked out. Now you're here, wanna stay for an early dinner?'

She was about to refuse, then thought: Why not? She was only going home to an empty apartment and a slice of yesterday's pizza. Michael could be collected on her way home. Sophia wouldn't care how long he stayed.

'Fine. I'd like to,' she said, 'if you'll eat with me.'

They sat at a table near the pay-kiosk where she used to preside, and which was now occupied by a drab elderly female of uncertain years. The waitresses, too, were different girls. All the old crowd had gone.

'How are things, Harvey?' she enquired, eyeing with distaste the plate of tepid liquid passing itself off as soup.

'OK! OK! The old place is doin' great. A bit slack this time

127

of year, but we're serving our special Thanksgiving dinner next Thursday. Turkey, corn and sweet potatoes. All the trimmings. It'll be packed.' He caught her eye and slumped in his chair, dropping his spoon back in his dish. 'Who do I think I'm kidding?' He wheezed heavily. 'Truth is, kiddo, the joint's falling to pieces. I don't feel so good these days. Can't keep my eye on things the way I used to. All the decent girls have left, and they're not so easy to replace now the economy's picking up. Everyone wants higher wages. And the cook's lousy.' He gave her an apologetic grin. 'Wouldn't like to come back and run things for me?'

Harriet sighed. 'There's nothing I'd like better, Harvey. I'm fond of the good old Last Chance Saloon. But Gus wouldn't approve. He thinks, now that I'm a mother, my place is at home.'

'That's Italians for you! Never moved out of the Stone Age where their womenfolk are concerned. Did you mean what you said just now? Are you really fond of this dump?'

Harriet nodded. 'It was like a second home to me in the old days. I used to tell Gus: "Harvey's got a gold-mine in that place." '

'Yeah, only the seam's run dry. Or it was fool's gold all the time. That's enough of my affairs. Tell me about California.'

It was the last thing Harriet wanted to do, but by shutting out all memories of Edmund she was able to keep Harvey amused, and his mind off his troubles, right through the overcooked steak and too sweet chocolate pudding. The poor quality of the food, however, didn't put Harvey off: he had two helpings of everything. It was no wonder he was badly overweight. There were a few other customers in, besides herself, but he was the only one who was eating heartily.

When the meal was finished, Harriet said she must be going, and Harvey escorted her to the door. It was seven o'clock and raining. The trees on the street-corner rattled their skeletal branches, and he insisted on summoning, and paying for, a taxi.

'You gotta take care of yourself, kiddo,' Harvey said,

when Harriet protested. 'You don't wanna go roamin' the streets after dark.' She climbed in and gave the driver Sophia's address. 'Be seein' ya! Don't lose touch.'

'Promise,' she laughed, lowering the window and leaning out. 'If Gus is working late again next week, I'll be round on Thursday for Thanksgiving dinner.'

'Give that woman a medal!' The pendulous cheeks quivered in a silent spasm of laughter. 'You have Thanksgiving with the family, kiddo. I'll accept that you're with me in spirit.'

She grinned and raised the window again, waving to him through the rain-spattered glass. His vast shape was still silhouetted against the lighted doorway as the cab cruised round the corner and he was lost to sight.

That was the last time Harriet was ever to set eyes on Harvey Muldoon. Four days later, he was dead of a massive heart-attack.

'He's *what*? Harvey Muldoon's done *what*?' Gus was staring at her as though she had taken leave of her senses.

Harriet removed her hat and coat, glad to be home. It was bitterly cold outside; and now, a week before Christmas, New York had had its first fall of snow.

'He's left me the restaurant,' Harriet said numbly. 'He made a new will apparently, the day after I went to see him.'

The letter from Arthur Weston, attorney-at-law, requesting the pleasure of a visit from her, had come as something of a shock when it arrived at the apartment that morning. As it was one of Gus's weekly rest-days, he had suggested that she ring the lawyer's office at once and make an appointment, if possible, for that same afternoon.

'I'll look after Mickey. It isn't good for the boy always to be palmed off on Sophia.' Gus's tone had been reproachful. 'It's not doing her any kindness, either.'

Harriet took his advice. She hated suspense; and, although her initial fear that the matter had something to do with Gerry had been partly assuaged by the words 'hear

129

something to your advantage', she remained uneasy. Fortunately, the lawyer was able to see her almost immediately.

Travelling uptown on the subway, all Harriet's misgivings returned, to be reinforced by Arthur Weston's Fifth Avenue suite of offices. She knew no one who could possibly be connected with such opulence. But there she was wrong. The lawyer, it appeared, had his roots in the Bowery, and had known Harvey Muldoon since they were children together. As a favour, he had continued to handle Harvey's affairs long after he had moved out of his old friend's price-bracket.

'So you see, Mrs Contarini,' Arthur Weston had told her with a condescending smile, 'you are now the sole owner of the Last Chance – er – Saloon. My recommendation is to sell it. Properties in the Village are beginning to command very good figures, but as a going concern I'm afraid the restaurant is no longer viable. And Harvey's savings, such as they are, have been left to his wife. That is, if we can trace her.'

'He's right, of course,' Gus told Harriet. 'The old Saloon should fetch a fair price.'

Harriet said thoughtfully: 'If I sell it.'

'What do you mean?' Gus was bewildered. 'What else can you possibly do with the place?'

'Make a go of it.' She put her arms round his neck. 'With you doing the cooking, it really could become a gold-mine, just like I've always predicted.'

'But I have a job. A good one.'

'You can leave. Give in your notice. There are living-quarters over the restaurant. Think of the rent we could save. Oh, Gus, please! It would give me something to do, running the Last Chance, and we should be working as a team.' Her embrace tightened. 'We wouldn't have to be apart all day. And Sophia and Carlo could move in with us. There are an awful lot of rooms upstairs, which could easily be turned into two separate apartments. Sophia could look after Mickey, and Carlo could be our advertising manager. Sophia says he's made quite a success as a salesman.'

'No!' Gus shouted, horrified. 'Positively no!'

They argued all evening and most of the night. The next day, Harriet went to see Sophia to enlist her support, rightly guessing that her sister-in-law would be enthusiastic. Anything which brought her in closer contact with Michael would be all right by Sophia.

'It's a great idea, Harry, and Carlo'll think so, too. Just leave him to me.'

As it turned out, Carlo needed very little persuading. He was tired of door-to-door selling and being out in all weathers. He liked the idea of more static employment.

They worked on Gus all over Christmas and into the New Year.

'It'll soon be nineteen fifty. A new decade, a new life,' Sophia coaxed her brother, as they waited together in the Contarinis' apartment for midnight on New Year's Eve. 'A family business, Gus. Think of it! Momma and Poppa would have been so proud.'

'We can make a go of it,' Carlo urged. 'I'm darn sure we can! It's like Harry was saying just now, there's a hell of a lot of goodwill goes with that place. It used to be one of the most popular eating-houses in the Village.'

'Used to be,' Gus demurred, frowning.

'And can be again,' Harriet wheedled, kissing him gently on the cheek. 'With your cooking, the place will be famous. It'll be something of our own to leave Michael.'

Sophia opened her mouth once more, but Harriet gave her a quick warning shake of the head. Gus was beginning to weaken, she could tell. A moment or two's quiet reflection was all that he needed.

'A small family restaurant,' he said at last, and Harriet nodded, holding her breath. 'We'd have to alter the name to Contarini's. That has a bit more class.'

Harriet was conscious of a great feeling of relief. 'You agree, then?' She exchanged triumphant glances with the other two.

131

Gus sighed. 'Yes, I agree. With reservations. I pray to God I shan't live to regret it.'

'You won't,' Harriet assured him eagerly. 'But . . . about the name. I think we ought to stick to the original. Perhaps not the "Saloon" bit. The Last Chance Restaurant. How does that sound? You see,' she went on rapidly, to forestall any argument, 'Last Chance is the name people in the Village associate with the place; the name which carries all the goodwill. And there are so many Italian restaurants in this part of New York that "Contarini's" isn't going to stand out from the crowd.'

She didn't want to admit the truth; that she was almost paranoid about keeping her own name in the restaurant's title. It was her inheritance, her idea, her project. Her baby! Therefore, it had to have her name.

She hoped that none of the other three would make the connection. It was doubtful if Sophia and Carlo even knew what she was called before her marriage to Gerry, and Gus's mind was far too unsubtle.

'Harry's right,' Sophia agreed. 'The Last Chance is how people round here will always think of it. It would be foolish to call it anything else.'

Carlo nodded; and, finding himself once more outvoted, Gus merely shrugged and gave in.

'The place will need redecorating,' he pointed out. 'And that'll cost. Carlo and I had better go see the bank manager just as soon as we can.'

Harriet was busy recharging the glasses. As the hands of the clock showed midnight, she rose to her feet.

'A toast,' she said. The others got up with her. 'To us! As Sophia remarked earlier, to a new decade! To a new venture! To the Last Chance Restaurant! May it prosper and thrive. And, finally, to the memory of the man who made it possible. To the late Mr Harvey Muldoon!'

PART THREE

1957–61

*Times go by turns, and chances
change by course,
From foul to fair, from better hap
to worse.*

ROBERT SOUTHWELL

14

'Well, thirteen may be unlucky for some, but certainly not
for us.' Harriet dropped her fur jacket over the back of a
chair and went to tidy her hair in the mirror. 'The opening
in Philadelphia went like a dream, and the restaurant is
already doing marvellous business.' She turned to smile at
Gus, who was sitting on the couch, his left leg, encased in a
plaster cast, propped on a stool in front of him. 'I wish you
could have been with me, darling.'

'Yeah, that would've been great,' Gus said without much
enthusiasm. He reached up to kiss her as she bent her head,
and reflected, as he reflected every day of his life, on
where marriage with Harriet had brought him.

For a start, it had brought him to this plush Fifth Avenue
apartment, with its magnificent views over Central Park;
and every summer it took him to their house on Long Island.
It had made him a wealthy man before he was even forty
and given him a son, who, nowadays, he hardly ever saw
because, during term-time, the boy was away at a prep
school in New England. It had brought him the sort of
success he had never wanted.

It was ironic in a way; and sometimes, when his sense of
humour was not too impaired, Gus could see how funny it
all really was. He, a New Yorker born and bred, had never
had any ambition to fulfil the Great American Dream. He
would have been more than content with a small family
business in Greenwich Village, living cosily on the premises with his wife and son. He recalled with nostalgia the
early days of the renovated Last Chance Restaurant. Were

they only seven years ago? They seemed impossibly remote, so much had happened in the mean time. It had been fun, building up the business, coaxing back the clients, working alongside Harriet and Carlo. Every evening, when he had gone upstairs, he had peeped in at the form of his sleeping son; and every night, before they went to bed, he and Harriet, Carlo and Sophia had met together for supper, and to discuss how the venture was shaping.

It had taken a little while to get the restaurant back on its feet, but by the end of the first year the Last Chance was pulling in the crowds and they had almost paid back their bank loan. For this, three things were mainly responsible. The first was Gus's undoubted flair as a cook, the second was Carlo's ability to organize the necessary publicity, and the third was Harriet's drive and determination to make the enterprise succeed, coupled with her sound business instincts. Sophia as happy to contribute by looking after Michael and cleaning the two apartments.

This time round, there was very little friction between the two families. In their few off-duty hours, they could see one another or not, as the fancy took them, and each was happily immersed in a job which he or she liked doing.

On New Year's Eve 1951 as they toasted the second year of financial success, Gus squeezed Harriet's waist and whispered: 'I reckon we could take things a bit easier now, don't you, honey? It's high time Michael had a baby brother or sister. I don't really care which.'

Harriet said nothing. She had no intention of having another child just at the moment. She could see, if the others could not, that, gratifying though the success of the Last Chance was, that success could be even bigger. By this time next year, they could have a second, maybe a third restaurant in New York. By the year after that, they could have moved even further afield. Their bank manager had recently expressed his company's willingness to finance them in any future schemes.

'You have a sound and very thriving business there, Mrs

136

Contarini. I shall certainly recommend to my directors that we assist you in any way we can.'

After that, the pace of their expansion had quickened. Harriet, backed by Sophia and Carlo, who found themselves for the first time in their lives not merely well off, but growing richer by the day, had again bullied and coaxed Gus into compliance with their wishes. The first Last Chance restaurant outside New York was opened in Washington in the January of 1953, just in time for President Eisenhower's Inauguration. It was an immediate success, pulling in the crowds on the evening of the Inaugural Ball, and staying open all night to accommodate the demand, going smoothly from serving supper to dishing up breakfast.

'And that's what we'll do in future in all our restaurants,' Harriet had told the board of the newly formed company, consisting of herself, Gus, Sophia and Carlo. 'We'll stay open longer than any other quality restaurant; all night if we have to. Wherever they are, the Last Chances will live up to their name: the last chance of getting a first-class meal.'

It was the bank which had advised the setting up of a company, with shareholders and a board of directors to administer their rapidly growing concerns. How Harriet came to be elected chairman of the board, the other three were never quite certain, but it had seemed a perfectly natural choice at the time, just as it had seemed common sense to call the company Chance Enterprises. No one but Harriet recognized the personal connotations of the name, and she smiled secretly to herself when Gus proposed it.

By the end of the Korean War, in July of that same year, nothing could stop the company's onward march. Another three restaurants opened their doors, two in California, the other in Maine. The money rolled in, in a relentless tide, altering the Contarinis' and Geraldinos' way of life for ever. Suddenly, there were secretaries and accountants and a magnificent new suite of offices near the Dakota building on West 72nd Street.

137

Gus hated every minute of it. More and more, he found himself caught up in the administrative side of the business, responsible for vetting and appointing the head chef at every restaurant, because, as Harriet pointed out, quality of cooking was the mainstay of the Last Chance reputation. At first, he had tried to carry out his new duties while still maintaining his position as chef at the restaurant in the Village. But this became impossible once they ceased to live on the premises.

In the autumn of 1955, while Wall Street reeled under the news of President Eisenhower's first heart-attack, Harriet and Sophia had made the decision to move uptown. Chance Enterprises seemed to suffer no ill effects from the head of state's suddenly questionable health, yet another proof of the young company's stability. Gus and Carlo found themselves wrenched from the dilapidated cosiness of Harvey's old living-quarters and transplanted to the bleak pretentiousness of a Fifth Avenue apartment-block.

Harriet was ruthless in accomplishing the move.

'We shall probably have to do a lot of entertaining. We can't do it in Harvey's shabby old rooms.'

She had seen the look on Gus's face, and for a moment her resolution had wavered. But only for a moment. This was what she had dreamed about when she came to America: the 'equal chance' to prove herself that Abraham Lincoln had once so powerfully advocated.

The following year, she acquired a house on Long Island for a ridiculously low sum, while Britain and France's actions at Suez once again threw the stock market into a panic. A few weeks later, after Eisenhower's re-election for a second term of office, things steadied once more, and property prices rose to pre-panic levels. Gus congratulated Harriet on her acuity and felt more miserable than ever. Even when she took the decision to send Michael away to prep school, he stood by and said nothing. Sometimes he wondered what the hell was the matter with him.

The truth was, of course, as Harriet had long ago recognized, she held the whip hand because she was not in love with him; whereas he, poor fool, had been hopelessly besotted from the moment of first seeing her, outside the White Swan in Stratford. Why he loved her so much he would never wholly understand, because she was everything he least desired in a woman. He had known from the beginning that she was self-willed, ruthless and determined to get her own way. She had wanted Gerry, she had got him. She had been set on coming to America; here she was. She had needed to prove herself; she was a success. She had left her father, her child, her country, and he had no doubt that she would abandon him with an equal disregard for his feelings if he tried to hold her back.

So what was it about her, Gus wondered, lying there on the couch with his leg in plaster, looking up into her flushed triumphant face, that made him love her as he did? Her courage, her humour, her sudden spurts of British self-deprecation; all those things perhaps. But most of all it was the instinctive knowledge that underneath her hard outer coating she was vulnerable; that in their marriage he was the rock on which she depended, not, as she and everyone else imagined, the other way round.

It wasn't the whole explanation, and sometimes he despised himself for giving in to her so tamely, but he could not risk losing her, so there was no alternative. They needed one another too much.

The thirteenth Last Chance restaurant had opened its doors in Philadelphia two days earlier, and Gus had been all ready to accompany Harriet to the gala opening night, when he had slipped getting out of the elevator and fractured the shin bone of his left leg. He had told Harriet that he had tripped and fallen awkwardly, but in fact he could remember nothing between the moment when he had gone to step outside and the moment when he had found himself lying in the corridor, writhing in agony. He could only conclude that, for some mysterious reason, he had lost consciousness for a second or two.

'How's the leg?' Harriet enquired, sitting beside him and lighting a cigarette. She took a few puffs before stubbing it out. She disliked the smell of smoke – it reminded her too vividly of incendiary attacks during the worst period of the Blitz – but smoking was an almost universal social habit, and she was not the woman to be out of the swim.

'Itchy,' Gus smiled. 'I'll be glad when the plaster's off. I gather the celebrations went OK.'

'Perfect. They couldn't have been better. Anyone who's anybody was there. I danced with the Governor twice.' She giggled self-consciously. 'He told me I'm a very attractive woman.'

'So you are,' said Gus. And, indeed, it was true. At thirty-one, she had a patina of beauty which the younger Harriet had lacked. Maturity had brought a confidence which, in its turn, had given her an inner glow. She looked good: slender, trim, well dressed, with a knack of knowing what suited her, rather than slavishly following fashion. The brown hair, with its glossy hint of chestnut, was waved away from her face, revealing the fine bone structure inherited from her father.

She accepted the compliment, but drew down the corners of her mouth in an amused grimace. She was still English enough to be embarrassed by overt admiration.

After a moment, she jumped to her feet. 'I'm hungry. Is there anything in the place fit to eat? I'd better fix dinner. I'd forgotten it was Jeanette's night off.'

Jeanette and Edward Baynton were the pleasant Canadian couple who ran the Fifth Avenue apartment. Having servants, however privileged their status, was another circumstance which made Gus uncomfortable.

'I'm not really hungry,' he said apologetically. 'Why don't you go out and eat? I'll be fine. There's one of those quizzes I want to watch on TV.'

This particular form of entertainment had made its début on American television three years earlier, and the mania for it was now so great that almost every channel was clogged with game shows.

'You haven't got that pain again, have you?' Harriet asked quickly. 'The one you've been complaining about for ages?'

'I have not been complaining for ages!' Gus protested indignantly. 'I get a little indigestion from time to time, that's all. And I haven't got it now,' he added, trying to sound convincing. 'I'm simply not hungry. Jeanette gave me an outsize luncheon.'

'OK! OK!' Harriet took one of his hands and held it in hers, feeling relieved, happy to persuade herself that he wasn't lying. Sometimes, when the bouts of indigestion were particularly bad, she felt a pang of conscience, wondering if Gus were getting an ulcer, and feeling to blame. And now she was going to suggest something which would upset him even further, but it was a project she had been mulling over for a long time, and she had set her heart on it.

'I want to open a Last Chance restaurant in London,' she said. 'I think it's time we expanded overseas. I'm going to put it to the vote at the next board meeting.'

A silence settled over the room, so brittle that she could hear it cracking. It was growing dusk, and beyond the window the lights were beginning to blossom. The homeward rush of traffic was gathering momentum as the queue of cars built up along Fifth Avenue.

'Haven't you got enough, Harry?' Gus asked eventually. He sounded tired. 'What do you want? To own the whole world?'

'Oh, Gus!' she exclaimed impatiently. 'Why do you have to pour cold water on everything I do? I thought every American wanted to be rich.'

He leaned his head against the soft leather of the couch and carefully adjusted a cushion in the small of his back.

'That's like saying every Englishman wants to wear a bowler hat and be something in the City. Besides, we *are* rich. Richer than I ever dreamed of.'

'Well, then! What's wrong with being even richer?'

He turned his head and looked at her eager face, at the parted lips and shining eyes, fringed with their thick spiky lashes. It wasn't the money itself that attracted Harriet, but what it represented: success and power. Her driving force

141

was phenomenal. He wondered if anyone had really touched her heart. What would she be like if she fell in love? She hadn't loved Gerry Canossa, he could see that now. If he had understood Harriet then as well as he did today, he would never have pressured Gerry into marrying her. But in that case she would not have come to America and he wouldn't have known her, so perhaps it was all for the best.

'If that's what you want, then that's what you must do,' he said. He felt too weary to argue. She knew his opinions, so there was no point in labouring them. And the pain in his chest was growing. 'I'm sure Carlo and Sophia will back you.'

He reflected that they didn't see much of his sister and her husband these days, except in the line of business, even though they lived in the same block of apartments. Since Michael went away to school – a move with which Sophia had strongly disagreed – the two couples had, socially, drifted apart. But Sophia and Carlo always sided with Harriet in company matters and, like her, they resented Gus's attempts to slow down the rate of expansion. They had grown up with nothing and experienced hard times, except briefly during the war; and now that Fate had unexpectedly boosted their fortunes they were intent on giving her every assistance.

'Well, if it's agreed,' Harriet said, 'I want you to come to London with me. When everything's settled, we can have a second honeymoon in the Cotswolds. I'd like to see Winterbourn Green and the vicarage again.'

'We never had a first honeymoon,' Gus remarked quietly. 'And, no, I won't come with you, Harry. You're more than capable of managing on your own.'

'But you must approve the chef! You've done that for all our restaurants.'

'Offer enough money and you'll get the right applicant.' He sounded unlike himself, bitter and cynical. 'It shouldn't be too difficult.'

She moved abruptly across the room to pick up her coat.

142

Then her annoyance abated. The prospect of a trip to England on her own was quite alluring. It gave her a sense of freedom she hadn't experienced for years. Her affection for Gus, her sense of debt and gratitude were emotionally very wearing. It would be good to have a break, to be out of his company for a little while.

'I'll go eat,' she said. 'Are you sure you're OK? You're not just saying that to make me feel better? I shouldn't be deserting you again the minute I get home. It makes me feel so guilty.'

'No. I told you. I want to watch the quiz game on TV. I'm quite expert at hobbling around on these crutches.'

But as the door closed behind her he could feel the stupid tears welling up at the back of his eyes.

15

Harriet drove herself to the Last Chance restaurant in Times Square, through the glittering heart of New York's threatreland, the November sky blazing with neon lights. People hurried along the pavements, cars jammed the streets. She suddenly felt at peace. The girl from Winterbourn Green, Gloucestershire, had become part of the great bustling city: it seemed far less alien to her now than the quiet fields and sunken lanes which, for the first two-thirds of her life, had been her home. She loved the sense of urgency about New York, its air of thriving independence, its thrusting self-importance. It reflected so much of her own personality that she sometimes felt it to be a living entity, its concrete canyons made of flesh and bone. . .

She smiled at her fancies and stopped to buy an evening paper. The headlines naturally concentrated on President Eisenhower's recent stroke, but running the story a close second was the continuing saga of the Russian Sputnik II, with the dog, Laika, aboard. Tucked away on an inside page were two brief paragraphs about trouble in Northern Ireland, with armed IRA raids over the border. Harriet caught the word 'Ireland' with the tail of her eye and automatically skipped the item. It was eight years now since she had seen Edmund Howard, and she had at last managed to expunge his memory. His face no longer returned in the night to haunt her dreams, and she avoided everything that might remind her of him.

She parked at the back of the restaurant and went in by the staff entrance, taking the elevator up to the manager's office. Francis Derham, a bright young man who had been personally selected by Harriet, was delighted to see her.

'Mrs Contarini! How nice.' He rose from behind the big walnut desk in the centre of the room and hurried round to relieve her of her coat. 'How did things go in Philadelphia?'

'Superbly, naturally.' Harriet slid out of her fur and watched while Francis laid it reverently across the back of a chair. 'Everything OK here? Anyone interesting in tonight?'

'Mr Sinatra. I made sure he had his usual table. Stephen Sondheim's in with a party. Oh, and there's a Viscount and Viscountess Carey who were asking about you. Appears they know an old friend of yours.'

'Really?' Harriet was indifferent. People were always claiming acquaintance with her. 'Who's that?'

Francis Derham shrugged. 'They didn't say. They're at table twelve, if you're interested.'

'I suppose I might stop and have a word with them later on. Just at the moment, I'm starving. Could you ask Luigi to send whatever he most recommends to my usual table?'

'Of course. At once.' The young man picked up the telephone and asked for the kitchens.

Harriet had a table permanently reserved for her at all the New York restaurants, usually in a strategic corner where she could observe, without being observed too much in return.

It had been her decision, carried for once in the teeth of Carlo's and Sophia's, as well as Gus's, opposition, that the interior decoration of all Last Chance restaurants should be subdued; more in the nature of an English gentleman's club, rather than the brasher décor which the name suggested. In the early days of the Village restaurant, they had experimented with various ideas, from check cloths and Chianti bottles to Wild West memorabilia plastered all over the walls. But as the venture grew and the clientele became steadily more sophisticated Harriet had insisted on more elegant surroundings.

'What goes in the Village won't suit Times Square and

145

Broadway,' she had argued. And it was after their Washington début, and her decision that the Last Chance restaurants should stay open as late as possible, that she had bullied the others into accepting her point of view. 'People want something quiet and decorous in the wee small hours of the morning, when they're just beginning to feel the effects of a long hard night. There are plenty of nightclubs where they can whoop it up to their heart's content. They come to a Last Chance for the food, and the peace in which to appreciate it. They don't want any distractions.'

The Times Square establishment, in the wedge-shaped shadow of the Tower, was a little more vulgarly self-assertive than its sister restaurants, but not by very much. The red of its upholstery and curtains was garnet rather than crimson, and the walls were panelled in dark pine. The lighting was indirect, giving an illusion of cosy intimacy to a very large room.

Harriet ate a leisurely meal, keeping an eye on what was going on; registering people's expressions of contented repletion, or not, as the case might be, particularly vigilant of any hint of dissatisfaction. From her corner, she could not see all the room, but knew that those customers within her line of vision were a sufficiently representative cross-section. Presently, when she had finished her coffee, she would circulate amongst the tables, introducing herself where necessary.

It was almost eleven o'clock, and late-night suppers were taking the place of dinner, by the time she made her way to table twelve. Viscount Carey and his wife were still lingering over their brandy. Harriet smiled and held out her hand.

'Lady Carey! Lord Carey! How do you do? I hope you enjoyed your meal. I'm Harriet Chance.'

It was about a year ago that Harriet had started using her maiden name again when introducing herself to customers. She had discovered that the name Contarini meant nothing to many people, and she was forced to explain who she was. One night, in the Village, the name Harriet Chance had slipped out without her thinking, and immediately the man to whom she was speaking had made the connection. After that, it seemed sensible to use it for business purposes most of the time.

Viscount Carey was a tall man in his early sixties, with grey hair plastered flat to a skull-like head, and a hairline moustache adorning his upper lip. His eyes were a pale watery grey, cold and distant, his mouth almost colourless. But the most immediately striking thing about him was a thinness close to emaciation. He was what Mrs Wicks would have called 'a rasher of wind'; and as the recollection rose unbidden to the surface of her mind Harriet had to stifle a giggle. The hand which the Viscount extended in response to hers was skeletal and clammy.

Viscountess Carey was equally thin and faded, with an air of martyred resignation. She managed to convey, within the space of a few seconds, that life had used her ill, but that she was bearing up bravely. Harriet took one look at her and decided that she did not like her.

In response to her query about the meal, Lady Carey said, in a voice as thin and faded as her general appearance: 'It was very good, wasn't it, Guy? A touch more mace in the béchamel sauce, perhaps, wouldn't have come amiss, but one can't have everything. If life has taught me anything, Mrs Chance, it's taught me that.'

'I'm sorry. I'll speak to the chef,' Harriet answered lightly, having no intention of doing any such thing. If she so much as hinted that Luigi was unable to make a perfect béchamel sauce, he would, quite rightly, throw one of his famous tantrums. Luigi was simply the best, in his own and everyone else's opinion.

'It's not Mrs Chance, my dear,' the Viscount rebuked his wife. 'It's Mrs Contarini. You remember, Howard told us.'

'Oh, yes, of course.' Lady Carey looked confused. 'I'm sorry, Mrs – er – Contarini. I have a perfectly dreadful memory, as Guy will tell you.'

147

'Howard?' Harriet spoke sharply, her heartbeats quickening.

'Edmund Howard, my trainer. I race horses,' the Viscount added, as though it should be a fact sufficiently well known on both sides of the Atlantic to obviate any explanation.

'Do you?' Harriet asked stupidly, her customary *savoir-faire* momentarily deserting her. 'I mean... Yes, of course... Of course...' Her voice tailed away while she desperately tried to ignore the mention of Edmund's name and cudgelled her brains for some recent report on the Viscount in the English press. She made it her business to read as many American and foreign newspapers as she could make time for each day, concentrating particularly on the society and gossip columns. It was a habit which frequently paid off, as now, when memory stirred. 'You had a Derby winner a couple of years ago.'

'Dry Ice. Your friend Edmund Howard trained him.'

Harriet knew what she ought to do; say something polite and move on quickly to the next table. There was nothing she wanted to know about Edmund. He was of no possible interest to her...

'May I join you for a few moments?' she asked; and almost before a gracious permission had been granted she had beckoned to a passing waiter to bring her a chair. She ordered more coffee and brandy on the house.

'I had no idea Edmund was in England,' she said. 'Last time I saw him, he was working for Twentieth Century-Fox, out in California.'

'Ah! Yes... He did mention something about the pictures, didn't he, dearest?' The Viscountess was vague.

'It was all in his references,' her husband answered shortly. 'He came to me three years ago, Mrs Contarini, after working on a stud farm in southern Ireland.'

'When exactly did he leave America?' she enquired.

The Viscount hunched his shoulders, and his dinner-jacket rode up with them. As he poked his head forward on the stringy wrinkled neck, he looked for all the world like a

148

tortoise peering out of its shell. Once again, Harriet had a hysterical urge to giggle.

'He'd been with the stud farm for about eighteen months when he applied for the position I was offering.' Lord Carey pursed his lips. 'So, by my reckoning, he must have left the United States some time in nineteen fifty-two. You, I believe, knew him a year or two earlier than that?'

'Nineteen forty-nine.' July 1949; it was a date indelibly etched on her memory, however hard she had tried to forget it. 'How did he . . .? How did he come to mention me?'

'When he knew we were coming to New York, he advised us to visit one of your restaurants. We'd never heard of them.' The Viscount smiled condescendingly. 'But Howard seemed to have all the gen. Said they were famous in America for the quality of their cuisine. Or words to that effect. Must have kept tabs on you. Knew what you were doing. So here we are, and I must say that, for once, we were not misled. The food is excellent.'

'And Mr Howard wished to be remembered to you,' Lady Carey added. ' "If you get a chance to speak to Mrs Contarini," he said, "give her my best regards." '

'I see. . . Yes. Thank you. It's most kind of you to have taken the trouble.' The banal message was like a slap in the face. But what else could he possibly have said? 'Has he . . .? Has he married again? When I knew him, he was on the brink of getting a divorce.'

The Viscount raised his eyebrows at his wife. Obviously affairs of the heart were a female concern, unworthy of male attention.

'Oh, he's not married, no. But I believe he is . . . well, courting.' Lady Carey glanced at her husband. 'You know, dear, Isabelle Hutton. Her father's a solicitor; senior partner of Hutton and Taylor.'

The Viscount nodded. 'Fine-looking girl. Rides to hounds. Good seat.'

Harriet sipped her coffee. She felt as though there were a lead weight in the pit of her stomach.

149

'What else did Edmund tell you about me?'

'That you're English. War bride. Father was a vicar.' Lord Carey gave a short bark of laughter, as if he found the information slightly amusing.

'He was the vicar of Winterbourn Green, in the Cotswolds,' Harriet murmured, not really aware of what she was saying; just talking while she coped with a variety of conflicting emotions – excitement, disappointment, elation, depression, hope, fear – all her memories of Edmund, suppressed for so long, jostling sharply and painfully into focus. She gave a meaningless smile. 'You said, Lord Carey, that you had never heard of the Last Chance restaurants until Edmund Howard told you about them. We have thirteen now, by the way, nationwide. And another opens in San Francisco next month. But we're hoping to start up in London as soon as possible. I shall be putting out feelers very shortly, regarding properties and so forth. I hope to be in England by mid-summer.'

'Then, you must come and stay with us, mustn't she, Guy?' Lady Carey demanded, with more animation than she had shown hitherto. 'At Carey Hall,' she added for Harriet's benefit. 'It's in Berkshire. Between Ascot and Windsor. The village is Carey Wanstead.'

Harriet was as taken aback as the Viscount seemed to be. To his credit, he recovered faster.

'Of course.' He smiled his death's-head smile. 'We should be delighted to have you.'

'I . . . I don't know what to say,' Harriet stuttered. 'I really wasn't angling for an invitation.'

'Shouldn't have asked you if I'd thought you were.' The Viscountess sounded faintly insulted.

Harriet was swift to retrieve the situation.

'In that case, thank you. I should be very pleased to be your guest. It's most kind of you to offer.'

It was two in the morning before Harriet finally got home, after doing the remainder of her rounds and inspecting Francis Derham's books.

Guiltily, she peeped into the guest room, where Gus had banished himself until his leg was mended. He was lying flat on his back, snoring loudly, and as she tiptoed closer she could smell the whisky on his breath. He had been drinking heavily, and she wondered why. Although still in some discomfort, he had sworn that the leg was no longer painful. Perhaps he had been lonely. She shouldn't have stayed so long at the restaurant, but she had been enjoying herself, discussing possible improvements with Francis, menus with Luigi, and making the acquaintance of new members of the staff. She had lost all sense of time.

Once in the bedroom she normally shared with Gus, the pleasant tiredness which she had experienced during the drive home was replaced by a feeling of tension. Her nerves were suddenly as taut as piano wires.

What the hell was she doing, letting Edmund Howard back into her life? She should have refused Lady Carey's invitation. She should never have lingered with them in the first place. The moment she heard Edmund's name, she should have cut and run. Gus commanded all her loyalty and whatever love she had to give. She should not be laying herself open to temptation.

Harriet undressed slowly and put on her nightdress. Then she sat down at the dressing-table and began absent-mindedly to brush her hair. It had been the mention of that other woman which had made up her mind for her, when Lady Carey had voiced her invitation; Isabelle Hutton, who was fine-looking, rode to hounds and had a good seat on a horse.

Harriet slapped down the hairbrush and got into bed, switching off the overhead light. The darkness was stuffy and oppressive, and she felt as though she were never going to get to sleep. All right, she said to herself, supposing you do meet Edmund Howard again, what then? Supposing he's in love with this Isabelle Hutton? Or supposing he isn't? What difference can it possibly make to you, one way or the other? You're not free, any more than you were eight years ago.

She thumped her pillows and turned on her side. She would write first thing tomorrow morning and refuse Lord and Lady Carey's kind invitation – except that she had no idea where they were staying in New York. She could find out, couldn't she? Her secretary could ring round all the main hotels. It wouldn't take that long to locate them. Or she could write direct to Carey Hall in Berkshire. Better still, she could abandon the whole scheme of opening a restaurant in London.

But she knew she would do none of those things. Once her mind was made up, it was as though her will had a life of its own. It didn't matter what her heart prompted her to do, or what her head told her was the common-sense course to adopt, she still drove relentlessly forward along her chosen path.

As she at last drifted over the borderline of sleep, she heard her father's half-forgotten voice.

'You're unscrupulous, my dear girl! You manipulate everyone for your own ruthless ends.'

16

It was odd to be in England again; to drive on the left-hand side of the road along narrow country lanes, flanked by hedges. It was odder still to feel herself a foreigner in her own country.

The sense of alienation had begun at the airport, where Harriet had found herself herded into a queue of people holding non-British passports, and had continued during the hire-car drive to London. Only now, a month later, as she approached Carey Hall, seen through the haze of a July afternoon, was she beginning to lose the sensation of strangeness.

It had been Harriet's decision to stay in London while she broke the back of her business dealings. The realization that Carey Hall lay not only twenty-two miles outside the capital, but also well off the beaten track, convinced her that it would be far more convenient to stay at Claridges during the early, and vital, part of the negotiations. She had written to Lord and Lady Carey explaining the situation, and taking them up on their offer for the beginning of July.

Before leaving New York, at the end of May, she had tried once again to persuade Gus to accompany her, but he had been adamant in his refusal.

'I'll stay and keep my eye on things over here. If you want support, take my advice and ask Carlo. He'll go like a shot.'

Gus had been right. It was Carlo's first trip abroad, and he was entranced by everything he saw.

'It's all so old,' he kept saying, until Harriet wanted to scream. 'So old and so . . . well, sorta *cramped*!'

Nothing Harriet could say, not all her lists of British scientific and technological achievements during the past three hundred years, could alter his initial impression that England was a kind of living museum.

But in spite of the way they managed, almost daily, to get on one another's nerves she soon realized that her brother-in-law was the best man to have brought along. His business acumen was more acute than Gus's, and he stood no nonsense from bankers, lawyers, estate agents or prospective staff. He treated them all the same: they were there for *his* pleasure, *his* convenience. In dealing with the slightly stand-offish attitudes of the British, Harriet found Carlo invaluable.

She had forgotten how condescending many of her countrymen could be, particularly towards Americans. There was a tendency to treat them as country cousins, hicks. Carlo was adept at disabusing their minds of all such notions.

They found exactly the right premises in the Haymarket, not far from Fribourg & Treyer, and Harriet immediately clinched the deal, even though the rent was far higher than she had anticipated. Carlo jibbed a little, particularly at the prohibitive cost of the rates, but Harriet knew what she wanted and was prepared to invest a good deal of capital in her first British venture.

And all the time she was negotiating with estate agents and lawyers the thought that she would soon be seeing Edmund again persisted at the back of her mind. It had been a conscious decision to choose Hutton & Taylor as her solicitors from the moment she had established that they were a London firm. She introduced herself to Ronald Hutton as a friend of Edmund Howard's.

'Ah! Isabelle's fiancé! How nice! How nice!' He had beamed at her across the cluttered desk. 'You know Lord and Lady Carey, too, I understand!'

'Fiancé?' Harriet clasped her hands together in her lap,

kneading her fingers painfully. 'Lady Carey didn't mention that Edmund and your daughter were engaged.'

'For about a year now.' Ronald Hutton laughed heartily, inviting her to share his amusement. 'Don't seem in any hurry to tie the knot. Both too damned independent, if you ask me. But that's how you younger people are these days.'

There were moments during the next few weeks when Harriet nearly changed her mind about going to Carey Hall. Edmund was engaged; probably happy and contented, genuinely in love with Isabelle Hutton. Harriet didn't know if she could bear to see him that way, but in the end curiosity and the yearning to meet him once more got the better of her good resolutions.

At the beginning of July, therefore, she left Carlo to deal with any outstanding business, telephoned the Careys and packed some clothes into the boot of the hired Volkswagen.

'I don't know when I shall be back,' she told her brother-in-law, as he stood beside the car, waiting to see her off. 'Maybe two weeks, maybe two days. I shall see how it goes and how welcome I really am. The domestic agency knows our requirements, and there is a shortlist of three for the position of head chef. If any problems arise where you feel you need a second opinion, call me on this number and I'll come up for the day, or longer.'

'OK,' said Carlo. 'Have a good trip.' He added with a grin: 'Sounds boring to me, though. I'd rather stick around here and sample the strip joints of Soho.'

'You behave yourself,' Harriet admonished him, 'or news'll get back to Sophia, and then you'll be for it!'

'Yeah!' Carlo made a rueful grimace. 'That broad's got built-in radar.'

Harriet laughed and slammed the car door. A few minutes later, she was threading her way through the early-afternoon traffic of Brook Street, and within half an hour was on the Ascot road. Just before entering the town, she turned off along a sleepy rural lane leading to the village of Carey Wanstead.

*　　*　　*

Carey Hall was built on the traditional plan of the English manor-house: kitchen and serving quarters to the north, hall and principal rooms to the south. Begun in the second half of the sixteenth century by Sir Nicholas Cavendish, and added to by succeeding generations of the family, it now presented a rambling, rather haphazard appearance, its chief beauty being the honey-coloured stone of the original structure, brought by the cartload from Ham Hill quarry in Somerset.

'The poor man's Montacute,' the Viscount said with his thin-lipped smile.

Lady Carey, showing Harriet to her room, was flustered and apologetic.

'Rather a chilly house, I'm afraid, especially after all that American central heating. What a good job it's so warm today. July can so often be an unpleasant month, when it chooses. Ah, well! One mustn't grumble about the weather, I suppose. One simply has to grin and bear it.'

She pushed open the door of a room gloomily furnished with several large Georgian mahogany pieces. A particularly fine marble-topped washstand, with retractable mirror, stood near the window, while the centre of the room was taken up with a four-poster bed, with cluster foot columns and a painted six-foot-wide cornice.

'My husband says it's Chinese Chippendale,' the Viscountess murmured, 'but I say not. Only a near relation.' She cast her eyes anxiously around the room to assure herself that all was in order. Domestic staff were so slack these days; that was, when one could get them. She added: 'I hope you don't mind, Mrs Contarini, but I've asked Miss Hutton and Mr Howard to join us for dinner this evening. I thought it would be nice for you and Mr Howard to renew your acquaintance as soon as possible. But don't worry. We shan't sit down an odd number. My son, Hallam, is living at home just at present.'

Harriet barely registered the fact of Hallam Cavendish's presence in the house. With the mention of Edmund's name, everything else became of secondary importance.

156

She could feel the blood pulsing in her throat, and the tell-tale colour crept up under her skin. Hastily, she turned away, to stare out of the window.

A sweep of lawn set with trees led down to a small meandering stream fringed by willows. Through the lush green of the branches, Harriet caught a distant glimpse of paddocks and stables and several red-brick outbuildings.

She was going to see Edmund this evening! In a very few hours from now, she would be in his company. The intervening years dropped away as though they had never been. She was back in the beach-house near Santa Barbara, his arms around her, his body pressed close to hers. The palms of her hands were damp, and she could feel the old familiar churning sensation in the pit of her stomach. . . She also became aware of Lady Carey's politely curious silence.

She turned and forced her lips to smile. 'I was just admiring the grounds. Are those the stables I can see from this window?'

'Yes.' The Viscountess sniffed in disapproval. 'Guy's pride and joy, those racehorses. Of course, we don't own all of them, only Dry Ice and Shepherd's Lad; but, even so, they eat up an awful lot of money. I can think of a hundred better ways of using that sort of cash expenditure, as you'll appreciate, being a woman, Mrs Contarini —'

'Please! Call me Harriet.'

'Very well, Harriet. But, as I am told so often, my opinions don't count. They're only those of a woman.' Lady Carey thinned her lips in an unconscious parody of her husband's smile.

Harriet, being shown over the remainder of the house by the Viscount later in the day, could see what she meant. Though full of antique furnishings, some of them no doubt extremely valuable, there was an air of shabbiness – even, in places, seediness – about the interior of Carey Hall. In many ways, the place reminded Harriet forcibly of the vicarage at Winterbourn Green.

But she shied away from thoughts of Winterbourn

Green. She felt that she should be using her spare time in England to visit her father's grave, not in pursuing a man whom she could not, in any case, have. The memory of her old home irritated her, because it made her feel guilty, and she seemed to have spent a large part of her thirty-two years trying to exorcize guilt about someone or another: her father, Gerry, little Hilary, Gus, and nowadays Michael for having sent him away to school. She supposed it was the dilemma which had faced Woman throughout the centuries; the battle between being someone, and doing something, in her own right, and her traditional role as daughter, wife and mother.

The Honourable Hallam Cavendish had not been home to tea, but when Harriet entered the drawing-room just before dinner that evening he was standing with his back to the empty hearth, talking in a loud drawling voice to his parents, who were seated on the couch sipping sherry.

Harriet thought that she would have recognized him anywhere as the Careys' son. He had a little more flesh on his bones than the Viscount, enough to make him handsome in an aquiline aristocratic sort of way; of which fact, Harriet deduced from his supercilious manner, he was obviously well aware. She guessed him to be about her own age, and later learned that he was in fact only four months older. He had dark brown hair, blue eyes, and copied his father's hairline moustache. He reminded her in some ways of Gerry.

The Viscount rose to his feet as she entered and made the necessary introductions. The Honourable Hallam Cavendish took her hand in the bony, slightly damp grip which seemed to be a family peculiarity. He looked her up and down.

'I'm delighted to make your acquaintance, Mrs Contarini. You're not at all what I imagined an American lady tycoon to be.'

'I'm English,' Harriet answered shortly, sitting beside her hostess and accepting the Viscount's offer of sherry, as that seemed to be all there was. Curiosity, however, prompted her to ask: 'What exactly were you expecting?'

'A peroxide blonde, loud voice, pushy manners, appalling clothes. Certainly not a vision in a Paris frock.'

'How little you know of American women, Mr Cavendish. They are neither pushy nor strident and are probably far more clothes-conscious than the average Englishwoman. This dress, incidentally, is not French. I bought it at Bonwit Teller's.' Harriet tried not to let her eyes stray towards Lady Carey, who wore a very old lace dress, undoubtedly nineteen twenties vintage, which had once been black but was now turning green.

Hallam Cavendish was not in the least offended by this rebuke.

'Fierce in your defence of your adopted country, Mrs Contarini! Or may I call you Harriet? And you must call me Hallam.' He seated himself beside her, at the other end of the couch, and immediately Harriet felt the urge to move away from him. There was an indefinable something about all three of them, mother, father, son, which made her flesh crawl. 'You know,' he went on, 'I've always wanted to meet someone who'd actually made one of those Hollywood rags-to-riches stories come true. And now I have. Isn't that splendid?'

'Oh, hardly rags to riches, Hallam darling,' Lady Carey expostulated. 'Harriet's father was a vicar.'

'Indeed?' He smiled his slightly wolfish smile. 'I didn't know that. It makes her even more interesting. Obviously she doesn't have any childhood inhibitions about the eyes of needles or anything of that sort. Or do you, Harriet? I'd be most intrigued to know. You and I must have a little talk about it some time.'

Thankfully, before Harriet was forced into an answer, the maid, whom Lady Carey slightingly referred to as 'that girl, Harrison', and who had replaced the prewar butler, opened the drawing-room door and announced: 'Miss Hutton and Mr Howard, ma'am.'

She was seated directly opposite him throughout a

surprisingly excellent meal. The Careys, in spite of appearance to the contrary, were clearly fond of their food.

But it was only much later that Harriet was able to recall what she had eaten. At the time, it was all she could do not to sit and stare at Edmund. Nine years had wrought hardly any change in him. The hair was as thick and dark, the eyes the same deep Irish blue, the body as well muscled and as powerful as ever. He had the same quiet contained strength that had thrilled her then, and continued to weave its spell now. She felt the pull of the same old magic. . .

Edmund, however, seemed unaware of her except as an old friend. His manner was pleasant and open, but he paid as much attention to Lady Carey as he did to her. He asked after Michael, and uttered the usual platitudes about how fast children grew up and was he really ten years old and how time flew! There was no hint that they might ever have meant more to one another than just the beach acquaintances they professed to be. Harriet, who had been expecting some indication, however small, of his former feelings towards her – some pressure of the hand, perhaps, or a look – was met instead with a wall of blank indifference. By the end of the meal, she was beginning to wonder if she hadn't, over the years, exaggerated in her own mind what had been between them – at least, on his part. She was quite clear about her feelings for him, both then and now. She loved him.

She couldn't quite make out his relationship with Isabelle Hutton. They were certainly engaged, and Isabelle wore a large solitaire diamond ring on the third finger of her left hand to prove it. But there was nothing lover-like in their attitude, and they might, at times, almost have been brother and sister in the dispassionate way they criticized and argued with one another.

Isabelle Hutton deserved the Viscount's description of her as a fine-looking woman. She was tall, blonde, handsome in a horsey sort of way, rather severely dressed in a plain blue frock, with a string of very good pearls and imitation diamond earrings. Not Edmund's type at all, Harriet decided; definitely not the bronzed Californian beach girls he had professed to admire in the past. Isabelle was so very English, and Harriet remembered Edmund's dislike of her countrymen.

But it was quite possible that his ideas had changed over the years. The better relationship between the British and Irish governments, the growing prosperity in Ulster and Eire, and the suppression on both sides of the border of the militants of either persuasion had probably dampened his ardour for the Republican cause. Harriet had read a newspaper article, only the other day, which claimed that it was becoming almost impossible to recruit young men to the ranks of the IRA, and that the recent armed campaign had been a total failure. Only yesterday, an attempt by two Irishmen to break into an MP's home, near Oxford, had been leaked beforehand to the British police. One man had been caught red-handed, the other was on the run. Sectarian attitudes were beginning to break down, and an IRA spokesman had volunteered the information that they were selling off their caches of weapons. The future struggle would be political, not military. The Carol Reed film *Odd Man Out*, made twelve years earlier and starring James Mason, had romanticized the Irish Republican Army with a tear-jerking finale. Harriet had seen it twice, once in the cinema and again, within the past two months, on late-night television. She, who shed few tears over real-life disasters, had cried copiously each time.

'A penny for them,' Hallam Cavendish breathed in her ear, and Harriet jumped.

'I'm sorry! What did you say?'

'I said a penny for them. You were miles away.'

She turned her head to meet his mocking smile. 'How rude of me. I don't know what I could have been thinking of.'

'Don't you?' Hallam's smile deepened. His eyes flicked towards Edmund on the other side of the table. 'Did you and Eddie know one another well, out in California?' There

161

was a leering emphasis on the word 'well' which infuriated Harriet.

'We were friends, that was all,' she answered coolly. 'We knew each other for a very short time. Only a matter of weeks.'

'Really?' His hand brushed her arm. 'But, then, time's relative, isn't it? One can live a whole lifetime in a couple of weeks.'

17

It seemed as though Edmund was deliberately avoiding her. In the days that followed, Harriet saw him only twice, once when the Viscount took her round the stables, and again on the open Downs, where the horses trained. Harriet, whose knowledge of horses was confined to the fact that they had a leg at each corner, a tail and a mane, feigned an interest she was far from feeling. Her one object was to see Edmund; but when they met he was as friendly – no more and no less – as he had been that first evening at dinner.

On the second occasion, Isabelle put in an appearance, mounted on a magnificent bay, looking imposing in jodhpurs and open-necked shirt. Even Edmund managed to seem impressed, and Harriet was shocked by the strength of her jealousy.

But, if she saw too little of Edmund, she saw all too much of Hallam Cavendish. Wherever she went, he was there, ready to show her over the estate, take her driving or to the races, teach her croquet, partner her at tennis. She didn't like him, but he was the son of her hosts and she couldn't refuse. In the end, she demanded irritably: 'Don't you ever work?'

'When I feel like it,' he answered. 'I'm a junior partner in a brokerage firm in the City. The senior partner's a friend of the old man and doesn't really care if I'm there or not. I'm my own boss. Have I offended your Puritan work ethic? I'm really far better at spending money than at earning it. I'm made that way. One should never interfere with nature.'

'And where do you propose to get this money, if you don't do any work?' Harriet asked.

They were walking aimlessly in the direction of the stables, the July morning hot and still all about them. Faintly, on the breeze, was borne the scent of newly scythed grass and the more pungent aroma of horses. Somewhere a pigeon called. The path skirting the paddock was white with dust and, in the distance, the edge of the Downs glimmered in the haze.

Hallam Cavendish tut-tutted gently. 'What terribly bourgeois attitudes you have, my dear. Only fools work for money. The rest of us either inherit or marry it. You wouldn't care to divorce your husband, I suppose, and marry me instead? I'm sure I'd be more entertaining.'

Harriet turned to look at him. 'If I thought for one moment you were serious —' she began angrily, but he interrupted her.

'Oh, but I am. Deadly serious.'

'Then, you ought to be ashamed of yourself,' she snapped.

It was a trite thing to say, but she was so furious, she could think of nothing better. No doubt later all sorts of clever and cutting remarks would occur to her, but for now all she could do to convey her anger was to quicken her pace in an effort to outstrip him. It was, of course, impossible: he simply lengthened his stride to match hers.

They were in the stable-yard before Harriet registered where she was. One of the lads was coming towards them carrying a pail of oats, and he raised a hand in half-hearted greeting. Harriet got the impression that most of the stable-boys disliked Hallam Cavendish, and treated him with veiled disrespect.

No one else seemed to be about. A horse whinnied from a nearby stall. Further along the row, another beast moved restlessly and there was the dull thud of a hoof striking wood. Isabelle Hutton's bay was eyeing Harriet over a stable-door, and she went up to pat its nose.

Hallam followed her, trapping her between himself and the front of the stall.

'You're very attractive when you're angry,' he said,

smiling down at her. He laid both his hands flat against the wall, imprisoning her between his outstretched arms.

'Oh, for heaven's sake!' Harriet exclaimed impatiently. 'Do you always talk in clichés? Besides, I'm a married woman.'

If he resented her snub, he didn't show it, except for the tightening of a muscle in his left cheek. His voice was as suave as ever.

'Now who's talking in clichés? And I wonder if that line worked with Edmund Howard? Somehow, I doubt it.'

Harriet felt herself blush and cursed inwardly.

'I don't know what you mean,' she said. 'There was nothing between Edmund and me. He was just a friend. Someone I met on the beach.'

Hallam made no reply, but just stood there, looking down at her, enjoying her discomfort.

After a while, he murmured gently: 'I'm not a fool, you know. I've seen the way you both look at each other when you think the other one isn't watching.' She raised her eyes swiftly to his face, and Hallam saw the glint of disbelief change to excitement. 'Ah! That's got your attention, hasn't it? You hadn't realized that he still feels the same way about you as you do about him. Does Mr Contarini know about you and Eddie?'

'There's nothing to know,' she answered sharply. 'I've already told you that.' She grew calmer. She was speaking the truth. Nothing had happened in the beach-house.

She had been foolish to come here, putting temptation in her own way. The mention of Gus in connection with Edmund increased her feeling of guilt.

'Now, what's going on in that head of yours?' Hallam asked softly. His body pressed closer, and Harriet felt a momentary panic. She didn't want to call the stable-lad for assistance. A grown woman of thirty-two unable to deal with a man like Hallam Cavendish? It was absurd. And yet there was something menacing about him which made her uneasy. She tried unsuccessfully to push him away.

'Don't you think we should be getting back to the house? It's nearly lunch-time.'

'In a minute,' Hallam said. She could feel his breath on her face. He was going to kiss her.

The thought of his lips on hers made her lose her self-control. She started to shove frantically against him, trying to break out of the cage made by his arms, but Hallam was much stronger than he looked. She felt the beginnings of hysteria.

'Let me go! Let me go!' she sobbed and hammered at his chest.

The violence of her reaction annoyed him – an annoyance which rapidly turned to anger as he grasped the fact that she actually found him repulsive. What had started out as a casual piece of flirtation became deadly serious as he determined to teach her a lesson. He put one hand under her chin and forced back her head, still holding her prisoner with his other arm. Savagely, he brought his mouth down on hers. . .

'Were you looking for me, Mr Cavendish?' Edmund enquired politely.

Neither of them had heard him approach, and Hallam jumped and swore.

'What the bloody hell do you mean by creeping up on us like that? No, I don't want you! I'd have come up to the house if I had.'

But he let go of Harriet, who slumped against the front of the stall, wishing the earth would open and swallow her up. What a mess she'd made of that! If she had responded to Hallam's advances in the way he had obviously expected, she wouldn't have antagonized him, nor been caught in such a compromising situation by Edmund. She wondered desperately how it must look to him.

'Well, now you're here, sir,' Edmund continued smoothly, 'perhaps you'd be good enough to take a message to your father. I've been hoping to see him, but he hasn't been down this morning. It's that grey of Mrs Whitson's. She has a touch of colic. The vet's been, and everything's well in

166

hand, but I thought Lord Carey ought to know.'

'Sod Mrs Whitson's mare!' Hallam swung on his heel and went back along the path leading to the Hall.

Edmund looked at Harriet. 'Are you all right?'

She nodded. 'Yes. Perfectly OK now, thank you.' She took a deep breath and managed to smile. 'Stupid to behave like that. I don't know what got into me. I imagine he tries that sort of thing on with most women that he meets. It doesn't mean anything.'

'It means he's a typical English establishment shit!' Edmund exclaimed with such cold fury that Harriet was startled.

He hadn't changed, after all, then. Under the pleasant deferential exterior he still hated the English. So what was he doing here, working for Lord Carey? Then she saw the look in his eyes and forgot everything else. The next moment, he had pulled her into the narrow alleyway between the stable-block and the tack-room. His arms were round her, his mouth hungrily locked on hers.

Presently, he raised his head. Harriet could feel him trembling.

'Dear God,' he breathed. 'I've been dreaming about that for nine long years.'

'Me, too.' She rested her cheek against the rough tweed of his coat and let out a sigh. 'I thought you didn't care about me any more. I thought you were in love with Isabelle Hutton.'

He laughed. 'She's a good woman and will make me an excellent wife if we ever get round to being married. But I've only ever loved one woman, and that's you, God help me.' He kissed her again, but this time when they separated he asked: 'Nothing's really changed, acushla, has it? You're still married to Gus.'

She nodded silently, unable to speak. He was right: she still owed Gus too much ever to hurt him. As long as her husband needed her, she would have to remain with him. And Gus was comparatively young. There wasn't much hope for her and Edmund.

He smiled wryly, reading her thoughts. 'It's no good, is it? If I asked you to run away with me this minute, you wouldn't come.' Harriet shook her head, tears filling her eyes. 'That's it, then.' He moved back from her, not angry, merely resigned. 'I don't know how long you're staying up at the Hall, but we'll probably run into each other around the place. If you need me, you know where I live.' He jerked his head in the general direction of the red-brick house, standing in its own patch of garden, which adjoined the stables and went with the job. Then he began to walk away.

'Wait!' Harriet called hoarsely. She couldn't let him go, not again, without showing him how much she loved him. And she owed him an explanation about Gus, however belated. 'I must see you alone. Will you be home tonight? I mean . . . Miss Hutton . . . Isabelle . . . won't be there if I call?'

He hesitated, then said. 'No. She never comes round unless I invite her.' He realized how that must sound and shrugged. 'It's not a very passionate relationship, as you may have gathered. We respect one another. We're very good friends. That's all.'

'A very sound basis for marriage,' Harriet answered, forcing a laugh which broke in the middle. 'Do you want me to come, if I can get away after dinner?'

'What will you tell them? Lord and Lady Carey, I mean.'

She thought for a moment, then shrugged. 'The truth. Or part of it. That you've asked me for supper in order to talk about old times. I . . . I shan't say Isabelle won't be there. In fact,' she ended in a rush, 'I shall probably give them the impression that she will be.'

He nodded slowly, his eyes never leaving her face. He walked back and kissed her once again.

'Until this evening, then,' he whispered.

'Did you have much trouble getting away?' he asked, as he welcomed her inside and closed the door behind her.

'No. Lord and Lady Carey seemed to think the invitation perfectly natural, although I think Hallam may have been slightly suspicious.'

168

'I shouldn't take any notice of that one,' Edmund said, pulling her into his arms. 'The Honourable Hallam has a naturally suspicious nature.'

'In this case, justified,' Harriet grinned a few minutes later, when she was at last able to speak.

There was no answering smile from Edmund, as he smoothed the hair back from her forehead.

'You're looking beautiful tonight,' he said.

'Don't I always?' She tried to sound flippant, fending off his second attempt at an embrace, still unsure just how far she was prepared to go. She needed to talk to him first.

He stepped back immediately and opened the sitting-room door. Although it was still fairly light, only half-past nine, he had already drawn the cream linen curtains across the windows. The remaining daylight filtered through the loosely woven fabric. He switched on a table-lamp with a heavy orange shade, and the room was suffused in a warm amber glow.

'Won't you sit down?' he asked formally, indicating a couch like a squashed brown sausage, but surprisingly comfortable. 'Can I get you a drink? Martini? Whisky?'

Harriet chose whisky with water.

'It's Irish,' he warned her, pouring two measures into a couple of Waterford tumblers and adding Evian water from a bottle. He came across and sat beside her, handing her one of the glasses.

'Well!' he said, suddenly mocking. 'Who could have guessed that the little beach girl would have made it so big?' He looked at the green silk-chiffon evening dress, with its crusting of rhinestones round neck and sleeves, at her immaculately cut and styled brown hair and at the gleam of diamonds in her ears. It was all a far cry from the cotton frocks and rope-soled sandals she used to wear, when he knew her first. She could guess what he was thinking.

Harriet was nettled. 'I wish everyone would stop talking as though I'm a multi-millionaire!' she exclaimed irritably. 'There's still a long way to go. Our present success is really quite modest.'

The blue Irish eyes glazed over, leaving Edmund's face devoid of expression. 'It depends what you're comparing it with, I suppose.'

She hesitated for a moment, tempted to recant, but knew it wouldn't do. This was one relationship she wanted to be entirely honest. She shifted her position on the couch, so that she was facing him squarely.

'All right,' she said, 'I am ambitious. Very. Ruthlessly so, my father used to tell me. But that's me. I'm made that way, and I should be lying if I pretended otherwise. If you love me, you'll have to take me, like Oliver Cromwell, "warts and all".'

He returned her gaze unblinkingly for what seemed an eternity, then his mouth crumpled into a grin.

'You've got a damn cheek, mentioning that man's name in my house,' was all he said, but his defences were down again, disarmed by her candour. There was a glint of admiration in his eyes. He moved his free hand and placed it over one of hers.

They linked fingers. Harriet sipped her drink.

'I want to explain about Gus and me,' she said quietly. 'There are a lot of things I didn't tell you about myself, back in California, and I'd like to tell you now, if you'll listen. After that, you may feel differently towards me.'

'I doubt it.' His grip tightened. 'Go on, then. Shoot!'

So she recounted, as briefly and as matter-of-factly as she could, the story of her life up to the present. As her voice died away into silence, she waited for his verdict.

'OK,' he said finally, 'so your first husband was a shit, and you couldn't foist your child on to your second without causing more hardship than there was already. What's so terrible about that?'

'In a way, I used Gerry, although I didn't see it so clearly then as I do now. I thought I was in love with him. And I used Gus to stay in the States. I ought to have gone home to Dad and Hilary.'

'You were young and, as you said, ambitious.' Edmund

smiled. 'I agreed to accept you "warts and all", remember?'

She looked at him again. 'Aren't you afraid I might use you?'

He shook his head. 'You love me. Why should I be afraid?'

'Are you sure I love you?' she teased.

'Positive.' He put down his glass and removed hers from her hand, putting both his arms around her. 'You love me the same way I love you. Entirely. Without strings. Tomorrow, I'm going to tell Isabelle that our engagement's over. She won't be too upset. I think she's seen it coming. I've no more idea than you have what the future holds for us, and I accept that you won't leave Gus. But *I* want to be free if *you* should ever be so. And, if you're not, we'll work something out between us that won't hurt your husband. But right now we're going to bed. No. Don't argue.' He placed a finger against her lips, stifling her half-hearted protest. 'You've been faithful to him for eleven years. I've had to wait for you almost as long. He can't grudge me just this one evening.'

Edmund rose to his feet, drawing her up with him. One arm encircled her waist as they moved together towards the stairs. . .

The front doorbell rang.

18

Harriet didn't know who she had expected to see; probably Isabelle Hutton or Hallam Cavendish; certainly not the frightened young man with dark circles under his eyes and the appearance of having been sleeping rough, who pushed his way through the front door as soon as Edmund opened it.

The man said in a low urgent voice: 'They told me to come here if things got desperate. I've got to get to London, but the police have been on my tail for forty-eight hours now. I can't seem to give the buggers the slip for very long.' He spoke with an Irish accent, but Harriet was unable to place it exactly. She guessed it was somewhere south of the border: it wasn't an Ulster intonation. The young man's eyes wandered aimlessly around the hall before suddenly taking in her presence. 'Mother of God! I thought you were alone. I did, honest. I've been watching the house fer ages, and I'll swear I didn't see a soul come in.'

'For God's sake!' Edmund rasped. 'Shut your noise! Jesus! They must be getting short of recruits if they're down to using amateurs like you. Go in there a minute' – he indicated the sitting-room – 'and don't utter another bloody word.'

The man went obediently, and Edmund pulled the door closed behind him. He looked at Harriet.

'Well, now you know,' he said. 'I'm sorry, my darling. I had no intention of involving you.'

'He's a member of the IRA, isn't he?' she asked slowly. 'He's the man who escaped after an attempt to break into

172

an MP's house near Oxford. I was reading about it in the papers. Where exactly do you fit in, Edmund?'

'I made contact with the Army after I returned from the States, while I was working on the stud farm in County Westmeath. I'm not a serving member, but when I knew I was coming to England I offered to help if ever I was needed. The men who come over here are given this address as a "safe" house.'

'Very convenient. No one would think of searching Lord Carey's property.'

'True.' Edmund's voice was steady.

'Dear God!' Harriet put a hand to her head, still not quite able to take it all in. 'Do you know the risks you're running?'

'Yes, I think so.'

'Don't tell me Isabelle knows about this. She couldn't possibly approve. I don't myself. Some of these men are murderers.'

'Isabelle knows nothing. No one does but you. And you need never have known if that idiot hadn't come blundering in.' He assumed a flat, slightly defensive tone. 'As for your accusation that members of the Army are murderers, yes, some of them have killed. But they live in a partially occupied country. No one called the European Resistance fighters murderers during the war. On the contrary, they were heroes. The IRA will disband as soon as Britain renounces all claim to the six counties.'

Harriet felt confused. She felt there ought to be a flaw in Edmund's argument somewhere, but for the moment she was unable to find one. She recalled her father's view that the English record in Ireland over the past eight hundred years was a bad one. And on top of everything else she loved Edmund Howard with a passion that suspended criticism. Her horror stemmed from the fact that he might be caught and imprisoned, rather than from what he was doing. Moreover, she had just demanded that he accept her 'warts and all'. Surely he had every right to ask the same of her. She thought once again of the film *Odd Man Out*: the excitement, the romance, the drama. The present

173

situation began to slide over the border of reality into the shadowy world of the theatre. She felt a little bit like an actress in a play. Real life became temporarily suspended.

'Would you . . . would you ever have told me about it?' she faltered.

Edmund shook his head. 'It's too dangerous. I have no right to involve innocent bystanders. Now, unhappily, because of that crass fool in there, you are involved. Unless you go straight to the police, you're an accessory.'

Harriet blinked rapidly several times, then hunched her shoulders. The aura of unreality persisted.

'An accessory after the fact,' she murmured. 'It sounds very Agatha Christie. Well' – she drew a deep breath – 'as I have no intention of being the means of sending you to prison, you might as well let me help you. Your friend said something about wanting to get to London. I could be of assistance there. Let's go and talk to him. He looks as though he could do with a good hot meal.'

Carlo was sitting up in bed, working his way through a pile of facts and figures on the new restaurant, occasionally pausing to sip his Scotch on the rocks or take a bite from a chicken sandwich. Everything was coming along just fine, and costs were well down. The limeys weren't so difficult to handle, once you had them rumbled. You just didn't have to let them intimidate you with their frosty manners.

The bedside telephone rang, and he stretched out his hand.

'Yeah? This is Carlo Geraldino.'

'Carlo!' Harriet's voice sounded from the other end of the wire. 'I want you to do me a favour.'

'Sure. And things are going pretty good here. Thanks for asking.'

'Sorry.' She was contrite. 'We'll discuss the restaurant in a minute.'

'Hey, you must be having some great vacation! It's not like you to postpone talking about business.'

'Yes . . . Yes, I am having a good time. A lovely time.

174

Lord and Lady Carey are being extremely kind. That's the problem. They keep arranging things for me to do every day, and I'm finding it difficult to keep saying "no" without being rude. I want to come up to Town tomorrow, just to see how things are going, but they've organized me a day at the races. So would you telephone me first thing tomorrow morning and say that you have to see me? Say there's an urgent problem. Something you need to consult me on. It's only for the day.'

Carlo grunted. 'That sounds more like you. You had me worried there for a minute. But there's no call for you to break into your holiday. Everything is under control.'

'Please don't argue, Carlo. Just do as I say. It's important!' Harriet sounded edgy. Perhaps she wasn't enjoying herself as much as he thought. But, in that case, why the hell didn't she just give this Lord what's-his-name the elbow and come on back? He supposed it wasn't etiquette, or something equally stupid. He'd never really understand the people of this country, not if pigs grew wings.

'OK! OK!' he said. 'If that's what you want, I'll buzz you nine o'clock sharp tomorrow morning.'

'Make it eight-thirty. Thanks, Carlo. I owe you. I'll see you tomorrow some time.' The line went dead.

In Edmund's sitting-room, Harriet replaced the receiver. 'That's fixed,' she said. She looked at the young man whose name she now knew to be Seamus Hogan, and who was wolfing down the plate of bacon, eggs and sausages which Edmund had cooked for him. 'I suppose he really has got contacts in London. I'm not going to be stuck with him, am I?'

Seamus raised his eyes briefly from the business of eating.

'Do you mind, lady, not talking about me as if I'm not here?' He tapped his head. 'This isn't a turnip, you know. If I say I've got friends in London, I've got friends. You just get me to the address I've given you. After that, you can forget you ever saw me.'

'You didn't exactly make a great job of watching this

house,' Harriet retorted, nettled. 'You didn't even see me arrive. Do you wonder that I'm worried?'

'I may have dozed off fer a moment. I haven't been getting much sleep.'

Edmund muttered something blasphemous about the unbelievable stupidity of ringing front doorbells, then banged his fist down on the table, making Seamus Hogan jump.

'You just keep your senses alert tomorrow,' he warned, 'or I'll have your guts for garters. This lady's risking her freedom to help you, and if anything happens to her you'll have me to reckon with, you bungling idiot!'

The young man made no reply, but he looked venomous. However, he was in no position to argue, and he knew it. He continued eating his meal in sullen silence.

Harriet said: 'Carlo's phoning me at eight-thirty. I'll pick Mr Hogan up at nine. He'll have to lie on the floor in the back of the car, covered with a rug.'

Edmund rubbed his hand across his forehead. 'I ought not to be letting you do this, but I just can't get away tomorrow, and it's difficult for the rest of the week. And in the circumstances it would be too dangerous to keep him here for more than a couple of nights.' He turned back to Seamus. 'You're sure, absolutely sure, that you gave that policeman in Windsor the slip?'

Seamus laid down his knife and fork and lit a cigarette.

'I'm positive. The dozy bastard fell for one of the oldest tricks in the book. I went into a shop, and when no one was looking I slipped out the back way and shinned over a wall. That's an English copper for you!'

'How did he recognize you in the first place?' Harriet asked.

Seamus puffed a smoke ring. 'From me picture in the paper, I suppose.' He saw Harriet's look of horror and laughed. 'It wasn't a photograph. Nothing like that. A "likeness" they called it, from a description given by one of the rozzers who nearly nabbed me.' His face darkened.

'They got poor old Petey. Someone blew the whistle on

us, and I'd like to know who. I reckon it was an inside job. The whole organization's rotten to the core. Bloody demoralized, that's what we are. They're talkin' about doing things *politically*, and crap like that. Don't they know by now that they can go on arguin' with the Brits until their stupid heads fall off, but things'll never change until they make them? Violence. That's the only language politicians understand.'

'How good was this likeness?' Edmund demanded, ignoring the rest of Seamus's speech.

'Not bad.' The youth was grudging. 'Good enough for me to make unnecessary detours. Otherwise, I'd've been in London days ago. But only one newspaper carried the picture. And that's another sign that the rot's set in. They don't take us seriously any longer.'

'They'd take it seriously enough if they found you in this lady's car,' Edmund answered harshly. 'So just keep your head down tomorrow and no funny business.'

'Surely. Surely.' Seamus Hogan lit another cigarette from the stub of the first. Harriet noted the nicotine stains on the long and surprisingly beautiful fingers.

Half an hour later, when Seamus had fallen almost instantly asleep, curled up on the spare bed, Harriet and Edmund made their final arrangements. She handed him one of the diamond earrings she was wearing.

'I've dropped this here tonight. It will give me an excuse, just supposing that anyone's interested, for calling here on my way to Town tomorrow morning. I'll bring the Volkswagen round to the back, and you can smuggle him in without anyone seeing.'

Edmund put his arms around her and held her close.

'I'm sorry,' he whispered against her hair. 'This wasn't at all the evening that I'd planned. I shouldn't be letting you do this. It's wrong of me, I know.'

'Nonsense!' She lifted her head from his shoulder, smiling. 'I'm thoroughly enjoying myself, if the truth be told.'

His conscience pricked him harder than ever. Her initial fear had receded, and she had persuaded herself that it was all a game. But if she were caught with Seamus Hogan in her car it could mean years in prison. He went cold at the thought; but in his own way he was every bit as ruthless as she was. He needed to get Seamus to London as quickly as possible, and Harriet's offer to take him had seemed like a gift from the gods. He would have managed, as he had managed on three previous occasions, had she not been there this evening, but it would have been nowhere near as simple.

If the worst came to the worst, he told himself, he would think of some way to exonerate her; and, in any case, he was probably being over-sensitive. Seamus's presence in the Volkswagen was very unlikely to be discovered. . .

Harriet pulled herself out of his arms.

'Heavens! Look at the time! It's nearly twelve-thirty. The Careys will be wondering what has happened to me.'

Everything went so smoothly, it was almost an anticlimax. Harriet found herself feeling disappointed and let down.

As soon as she received Carlo's telephone call, she sought out her hosts and explained the situation. Lord and Lady Carey were early risers and, for once, Hallam was up as well. The day before, he had received a sharp reminder from the senior partner that it was high time he put in an appearance at the office.

'You might as well travel up to Town with me,' he said. 'There's no point taking both cars, is there?'

It was the only sticky moment of the whole affair.

'Thank you, but I don't know when I shall be coming back,' Harriet answered serenely. 'I may have to stay overnight. It depends on why Carlo wants to see me.'

'You must do as you please, of course.'

Hallam touched his lips with his napkin and rose from the breakfast table. He had had very little to say to Harriet since the scene in the stable-yard. Lunch and dinner yesterday had passed in a frosty silence on his part. Now, it seemed, all was forgiven. Harriet was vaguely surprised. She had marked him down as a man who bore a grudge, particularly when his pride had been wounded.

She did not even need the excuse of the lost earring to call at Edmund's house. No one was sufficiently interested in her movements. She decided that, at the end of the week, she would leave Carey Hall. She had an uneasy suspicion that she had already outstayed her welcome.

Edmund was waiting anxiously for her. They bundled Seamus Hogan into the narrow space between the front and back seats and covered him with a rug of Edmund's providing.

'You can still pull out, if you want to,' Edmund said, his conscience making one final bid to be heard above the clamour of expediency.

'I don't.' She could hear the stable-boys clattering around the yard, and didn't dare kiss him in case one of them appeared. She slipped the unneeded earring into her handbag and seated herself behind the steering-wheel. 'I'll be back this evening. If you don't hear from me, you can assume everything went OK. It might arouse suspicions of a different sort if I came to visit you again tonight.'

She grinned at him as she let in the clutch. He had a sudden vision of her as she must have been as a girl, and realized why, as she had once informed him, her father had found her such a handful. At thirty-two, she was the same person who had hitch-hiked around the countryside in wartime; who had refused to submit to bullying when she was six; who had deliberately got lost on a church outing with a boy called Leslie Norman in order to shock people; who had followed Gerry Canossa all the way to America and a strange new life on the off-chance of making her fortune. Life was not so much a game to Harriet as a challenge, and so far she had won against all the odds. He could only pray that she would go on winning and that this occasion would not be the exception which proved the rule.

She waved and moved off. Within half an hour she was making her way along the main street of Staines, all her concentration centred on driving with due care and not involving herself in an accident. She was still unaccustomed to driving on the left-hand side of the road. She didn't even notice Hallam's pale blue sports-car as it pulled out of a side-street, where he had stopped to buy a morning paper.

Hallam recognized the cream Volkswagen immediately, but made no effort to attract her attention. He was still smarting from her rejection of him the preceding morning. The traffic was heavy, and there was no possibility of overtaking her, even though his was the faster car. She was still one or two places ahead of him by the time they reached Knightsbridge, and was still unaware of his presence in the queue. Then, at Hyde Park Corner, Harriet turned right, down Grosvenor Place, moving away from the city centre and Claridges, where Hallam knew her brother-in-law was staying.

On a sudden impulse, he followed her, braking hard and swerving right, to the vociferous fury of the driver immediately behind him. He was still tailing her when she crossed Vauxhall Bridge and threaded her way through the maze of little streets behind the Albert Embankment. A few moments later, the Volkswagen slowed to a halt in front of a terraced house and Harriet got out. So did a man who had hitherto been invisible – concealed, apparently, in the back of the car.

The man glanced furtively up and down the street as Hallam cruised past. Harriet once more failed to see him. In his rear-view mirror, Hallam saw the man ring the door-bell and, after a second or two, be admitted inside. Harriet returned to the Volkswagen, and Hallam accelerated. By the time she turned left into Black Prince Road, he was already heading back across the river, via Lambeth Bridge, looking extremely thoughtful.

19

Harriet drove to Claridges feeling deflated. The excitement of the early morning had gone stale. Nothing had happened; there had been no road-blocks, no battle of wits with suspicious policemen, no car chase during which she had given her pursuers the slip. It had been an uneventful journey, an even tamer ending; no high adventure. And now that she had more time to think about it objectively she felt less proud of her part in the affair. Unlike Edmund, she was English by birth: his war was not hers, and she should never have allowed herself to be drawn into it. She wouldn't have betrayed him, of course, because she loved him, and because people should always come before causes. She could also accept that he had a point of view. But her silence would have been sufficient; she should never have offered active help. She was old enough and responsible enough to stop confusing real life with the cinema. Seamus Hogan wasn't James Mason: he really was a member of the IRA.

She went up in the lift to the first-floor suite she was sharing with Carlo, to find her brother-in-law pacing the sitting-room floor, his face creased with anxiety.

'Where the hell have you been?' he burst out as soon as he saw her. 'That Carey fella said you left there at a quarter before nine. He said you ought to be here in an hour. It's ten-thirty already!'

'Hold on!' Harriet tossed her handbag on to a chair and went across to the mirror to tidy her hair. 'This is only make-believe, you know. You don't really want to see me.'

Carlo gripped her arm.

'Sophia telephoned over an hour ago. Gus has been taken to hospital.'

Harriet's stomach turned over, but she was not too concerned as yet.

'What's the matter with him?' she asked. 'He seemed OK when we left New York.'

'You'd better sit down.' Carlo was displaying a compassion which turned her bones to water. 'Gus was taken bad a coupla days after we arrived in England, but he didn't want us told. Thought you had enough to do setting things up over here.' Harriet heard the note of reproach in her brother-in-law's voice, chiding her for her desertion, and deeply resented it. But before she could register a protest Carlo went on: 'They've run a lot of tests on him, according to Sophia. It's cancer.'

'Oh, no!' Harriet's hand crept up to her mouth. Her face drained of colour. 'How . . . how bad is he? Did Sophia say?'

'No, but she didn't sound too chirpy. The head medic won't say anything until he's seen you. Sophia thinks you should go home at once. So I've made you a reservation on the afternoon plane and got one of the chambermaids to pack your clothes. What about the stuff you took away with you?'

'What . . .? Oh . . . I don't know.' Harriet took a deep breath, trying to steady her nerves; trying to make herself think concisely and clearly. The news that Gus was seriously ill had knocked her sideways. Until this moment, she hadn't realized just how fond she was of him. 'I'll . . . I'll ring Lady Carey. Someone can send the rest of my clothes on here and you can bring them back with you. Will you stay on a while longer and wind things up?'

'Yeah. Sure. I was planning to, anyway. It won't take more than a week at the outside. Look, kid, I don't want to hustle you, but you'd better get moving if you're gonna catch that plane.'

Harriet nodded grimly and reached for the telephone. Both lines at Carey Hall were engaged. She tried Edmund's number, but there was no reply. Then she recollected that Hallam was in the City today, and spent five frantic minutes trying to recall the name of the brokerage firm he worked for. When she finally remembered, she prayed hard that he would be there. Somehow or other, she had to get a farewell message to Edmund.

She was connected with Hallam almost immediately and gave him her news. After his expressions of polite concern and her request about her clothes, she added: 'And, if you see Edmund Howard, would you give him a message from me? He . . . he asked me to deliver a . . . a package to someone on my way into London. Would you tell him . . . tell him it was delivered OK?'

'Yes, of course,' Hallam murmured dulcetly. 'The package was delivered OK.' The Americanism sat awkwardly on his tongue, and the slight stressing of the word 'package' made it sound odd and faintly sinister.

Harriet decided that she was being over-sensitive. There was absolutely no reason why Hallam should suspect that the message had any ulterior meaning. And she had too much to do to let it worry her. Even her love for Edmund had faded into the background, taking second place to her anxiety for Gus. Everything else seemed unimportant. She said her goodbyes and hung up.

'Ring down for a taxi for me, would you?' she said to Carlo, and went into her bedroom to collect her cases.

She went from one doctor to another, from one eminent specialist to another, but they all, after examinations and tests, gave her the same answer. There was no hope. Gus was dying. The only point of disagreement amongst them was exactly how long he had to live. Estimates varied from six months to two years.

'The cancer has spread throughout the body,' Harriet was told by the last specialist she saw, sitting in his luxurious consulting-room overlooking the Hudson river. 'There is every possibility that the disease could go into recession for a period, but don't let that build up your hopes.'

183

'I want him home,' Harriet said. 'He'll have the best attention, day and night, whenever he needs it. However long it takes, I intend to be there when . . . when he dies.' She forced herself to utter the word for which there were so many euphemisms; euphemisms which never altered the inevitable final fact. 'Does Gus know he's dying?'

The consultant sucked in his thin sallow cheeks.

'We haven't told him, but I suspect he guesses. He's an intelligent man.' There was an echo of surprise in the well-modulated tones which annoyed Harriet.

'Of course he is!' she retorted. 'He'd hardly be in the position he's in today if he weren't. Chance Enterprises is very big business.'

The consultant permitted himself the flicker of a smile.

'Take him home, Mrs Contarini,' he said in a gentler voice than he had used so far. 'Take him home and make him as comfortable as you can. If he wants to work, if he feels able to work for a little while longer, let him. It can do no harm. Don't fuss him until it's necessary. Help him to die with dignity.'

Harriet warmed towards the man seated behind the desk. 'I fully intend to,' she said, rising to her feet.

The consultant looked at her appreciatively; at the white silk suit and little black hat, at the fine-boned face and strongly marked chin. A formidable woman, he thought. But there was a compassionate streak there as well; a soft inner core, which could lure her into doing rash and foolish things.

Gus came home to the Fifth Avenue apartment, but he was not happy there. He showed no inclination to do anything but sit and watch the quiz shows which were now deluging the television channels. Five new ones had been introduced in one day alone. Harriet tried her best to interest him in other things. She booked seats for the Broadway hit musical *Flower Drum Song* and for a piano recital, given by the twenty-one-year-old Russian, Vladimir Ashkenazy, who had won the Queen Elizabeth Prize in Brussels two years earlier, and who was at present touring the United States. But when the time came she had to give the tickets away because Gus refused to go. He could not be bothered to make the effort.

In that late fall of 1958 the cancer had, as the consultant had predicted, gone into temporary recession, but it seemed to make no difference as far as Gus was concerned. Harriet had no idea if he knew how ultimately serious his condition was, and did not have the courage to ask him; but she hated to see him behaving as if he were dead already. She was a fighter, and she desperately wanted Gus to be one, too.

Michael, now nearly eleven years old, came home for the school vacations, but he had never been close to his father and was too wrapped up in his own concerns to provide much of a diversion. Even at that age, he liked accompanying his mother to the office and learning as much as he could about the business.

As Christmas approached, Harriet and Carlo were deep in negotiations to open their first two European restaurants outside London; one in Brussels, the other in Amsterdam. Sophia had retired from any very active participation in the company's affairs, and it was Carlo who flew to Belgium and Holland.

Harriet, who did not entirely trust Carlo's judgement in the choice of venue and décor, chafed at the bit, but could not bring herself to leave Gus for more than a few hours at a time. It was obvious that he needed her. Now and then, in unguarded moments, she thought of Edmund, then firmly suppressed all memories of him. She had written him one letter since her return to New York, telling him that she loved him, but that from now until his death she belonged to Gus. She had received a reply to say that he had broken his engagement to Isabelle Hutton. He loved her, and only her, and would wait for as long as it took. She stored the precious words away in her mind, shredded the notepaper into the trash-can and devoted herself to Gus.

On Christmas Eve she drove home through the rush-hour traffic, through carol-singers and white-bearded

Father Christmases ringing their bells, through canyons of shop-windows, brilliantly lit and lavishly decorated, each one a glittering Aladdin's cave of consumer goods, announcing that this was one of the wealthiest societies in the richest country in the world. And she, the little English girl from the Cotswold vicarage, had made it in that society; had done what she set out to do. Here, in this vigorous, forward-looking, essentially young-minded country, Abraham Lincoln's equal chance still held good for anyone who was prepared to take it.

But there was still a lot she could achieve. Money made money: it was a well-known fact. Harriet wanted to expand the company even further. She was only thirty-two and she wanted to spread her wings. When Gus died, she would become the major shareholder. As well as being the chairman, she would be the board member with the biggest say. . .

She pulled herself up short, disgust sweeping through her. Gus was still alive, and yet here she was planning how she could use the power that his death would bring her.

She parked the Plymouth coupé in the basement and took the elevator up to the fourth floor. When she let herself into the apartment, she could hear gales of raucous laughter emanating from the television set in Gus's bedroom.

Jeanette Baynton came through to the hallway from the dining-room to relieve Harriet of her hat and coat.

'Hi, Mrs Contarini. How are you this evening?' The Canadian accent was soothing after a hectic day.

'Hello, Jeanette.' She slipped out of the heavy fur coat and removed her hat. 'I thought you and Ted would be gone by now. It's Christmas Eve, remember?'

The housekeeper laughed. 'Sure. But we stayed on to keep Mr Contarini company until you came in. We don't like leaving him alone. Thank you for our presents, by the way. Mr Contarini gave them to us earlier this afternoon. The jacket fits like a dream, and Ted's thrilled with that beautiful decanter. But it's too much. You really shouldn't.'

'Rubbish!' Harriet, as always, was embarrassed by gratitude. 'I don't know what we'd do without you!' She nodded in the direction of the bedroom. 'I gather my husband hasn't got up.'

'No.' Jeanette Baynton grimaced ruefully. 'We couldn't persuade him.'

Harriet went into Gus's room. He was still in his pyjamas, lying on top of the big double bed which they no longer shared. She needed her sleep, and since Gus's return from hospital she had moved into one of the other rooms.

'How is it, my darling?' She bent to kiss her husband's forehead. It was cold and clammy, and his eyes had the slightly glazed appearance of someone constantly on drugs. The noise from the television set was deafening. 'Can't you turn that thing down?' she asked, but he only shrugged.

She went outside again and found Jeanette still waiting for her in the hallway.

'Could ... could we have a word together, Mrs Contarini?'

'Yes, of course.' Harriet, faintly puzzled, led the way into the dining-room. 'What is it, Jeanette? Has he been bad today?'

The housekeeper shrugged. 'It hasn't been one of his better days, but I've known him worse. It isn't that. I don't know quite how to put this, but ... there's something bothering him. I know that sounds kinda foolish in the circumstances, but I don't think he realizes how ill he is. On the other hand, maybe he does. Maybe he's bottling the knowledge up inside of him because he thinks he's protecting you from finding out. I think perhaps all this pretence is ... well, separating you at a time when you ought to be drawing closer together. I know it's not my place to say so, but I do think maybe you should talk to him. Find out what's bothering him, because something surely is.' The plain good-natured features broke into a smile. 'Doctors don't always know best, Mrs Contarini. After all, they're only men.'

187

Harriet felt guilty. She was the one who should have noticed that there was something troubling Gus. But how could she? She was out all day.

After dinner, when the Bayntons had at last departed and they had the apartment to themselves, Harriet persuaded Gus to put on a robe, shut off the television and sit quietly with her on the couch in the living-room. Michael had gone to a Christmas Eve party in one of the neighbouring apartments and would not be home until midnight. It was the first time he had been allowed to stay out late, and he was very excited.

'Tom Stroud will bring him back when it's over,' Harriet said, 'but I guess Mickey'll be too tired to sleep. God knows what he'll be like tomorrow. "Obstreperous" is probably a good word to choose.'

Gus chuckled, and, encouraged, she stretched out a hand. After a moment, he took it and held it in one of his.

They were sitting side by side on the long couch which faced the window. Beyond it, Central Park, with its crowding trees, was transformed by the darkness and the sparkling necklaces of lights into some enchanted forest from Hans Andersen or Grimm. Harriet had switched off the room's main supply of power, leaving them in the jewelled glow from the Christmas tree; amber and ruby, sapphire, lilac and green. The double glazing shut out all exterior sound, and the only noise was the occasional seep of water through the central heating pipes. Outside, it was bitterly cold; indoors, the warmth was tropical.

Harriet thought unexpectedly of the vicarage; of inadequate coal fires and jigsaws of frost on the window-panes; of the gloom of a winter's evening and breath hanging in the air like clouds of steam.

Just as though he could read her thoughts, Gus asked abruptly: 'Remember Stratford-upon-Avon?' He pronounced it the American way, giving equal weight to every syllable. 'Outside the American Red Cross. That was the first time I saw you. I can recall each detail as though it were yesterday.'

Harriet could, too, but it was not Gus she remembered, but Gerry, self-consciously handsome in his uniform, his cap pushed forward at a rakish angle against the dark hair. Gus was a shadowy figure, somewhere in the background, already made over in her mind to Susan Wyatt. . . . Dear heaven! She hadn't thought of Susan in God knew how many years! Suddenly, it was all so vivid, like travelling in reverse through time. But she didn't want to go back into the past; it contained too many unhappy and disturbing memories. She had to go forward, towards the future. That was where she belonged.

Gus's voice came out of the darkness, once more uncannily echoing her thoughts.

'I don't have a future, do I? I'm dying.'

20

Harriet did not answer immediately, wondering what he wanted her to say. Then the almost telepathic communication which seemed to exist between them that evening told her that he wanted the truth.

'Yes,' she said quietly. 'You're dying.'

He stared straight ahead of him, at the trees silhouetted against the night sky, and Harriet wondered what he was thinking. She was no longer in tune with his mind. It was as though he had deliberately switched himself off.

'How long?' he asked finally but, before she could reply, went on: 'It's cancer, isn't it? I've known for a long time, really, but I've tried to shut the knowledge out.'

The television, of course, had helped. Harriet suddenly understood his passion for the frenetic hilarity of the quiz shows, the inane laughter, the hosts' endless mindless chatter. It had all helped to stop him thinking, providing him with his own little world, where nothing mattered except who would win the next gigantic sum of money. Now that he had at last stopped pretending he would get better, he would need all the love and support of which she was capable.

He repeated, 'How long?' and she gripped his hand tighter.

'Six months. A year. Two years. The doctors aren't certain. You'll get periods of recession, like the one you're going through now. Times when you feel much better.'

'But they won't last?'

'No.' There was a catch in her voice which she tried to conceal. 'No, they won't, I'm afraid.'

'*You're* afraid!' He gave an ironic smile, and she moved closer to him, taking him in her arms, cradling his head against her shoulder as if he were a child. Presently, he added: 'I want to get away from Manhattan. I love the place, but everyone's so busy, so involved. It makes me feel isolated. So alone. Let's go to Long Island. Just you and me, and Michael in the holidays. Strange, isn't it, but we've been man and wife all these years, and I don't feel I've really gotten to know you. We've always been too busy, rushing around.'

Harriet's heart sank. Long Island was by no means the end of the world: she could travel to work daily. But she knew that that was not the sort of life Gus had in mind. He wanted her to be with him night and day. He wanted the domestic existence he had planned for them when they first got married. He didn't intend that she should go haring off to the office each day, while a succession of nurses looked after him at home.

He was using his illness as a kind of moral blackmail, and there was nothing she could do but agree. She owed him that, however much it put paid to all her immediate plans. She had no excuses to put forward. Carlo was more than capable of deputizing for her and of running Chance Enterprises affairs. It was just that he didn't have her flair; her nose for business. As a subordinate, he was fine – although she was careful never to let Carlo know that that was how she regarded him – but she would have preferred not to leave him in charge. Because that was what Gus was asking for, a hundred per cent of her time. She would be kept informed of what was going on, of course, but it would not be the same as being in the office every day, her finger on the company's pulse. But she had to do it: she had no choice. She felt weighed down by the emotional responsibility, the nervous strain.

She said: 'Of course we'll go to Long Island, if that's what you want. We'll close up this apartment. Sell it, if you like.'

'And you'll stay with me? You won't leave me? You'll be there all the time? I don't want a lot of strangers round me. I just want you.'

'I'll be there,' she promised, leaning over to kiss him and tasting the salt sweat along his upper lip. 'I'll be there, so now you don't have to be afraid.'

Gus died just over two years later, on 8 January 1961.

They were two years in which Harriet nursed him devotedly; in which she grew to appreciate his gentleness, steadfastness and courage; in which she came to loathe and detest the house over-looking Long Island Sound. She learned, if she had ever needed teaching, that she was not cut out to be simply a wife and mother. The challenge of the commercial world was vital to her if she was not to wilt and die of boredom.

They were also two years during which the fortunes of Chance Enterprises stagnated. After the opening of the restaurants in Brussels and Amsterdam, Carlo, as deputy chairman, seemed content to let the company rest on its laurels and reap the rewards which he considered already great enough. He could not understand Harriet's desire for further expansion.

'It's not just the restaurant business,' she had said to him once, when he and Sophia were visiting, and Sophia was keeping Gus entertained. 'We could diversify. We're sufficiently strong, sufficiently big to put in a bid for the Coleman chain's bankrupt stock. We'd get it, and the premises, dirt cheap.'

'But they make radio components,' Carlo had protested, bewildered. 'We know nothing about that sort of business. And, besides, if the Colemans couldn't make a go of it, why should we?'

'We find and pay people who do know something about it. Oh, not radio components. I'm talking about computers. They're the coming thing. I was reading about them only the other day. They're big unwieldy things at present. But the writer of the article reckons that in fifteen, twenty

192

years' time they'll be small enough and cheap enough for use in the home.'

But Carlo had been adamant in his refusal to put the proposition before the board.

'What's wrong with consolidating what we've got?' he had demanded truculently. 'We're rich, Harry! Rich! What drives you, huh?' And later, driving home, he had said to Sophia: 'She sure is one crazy dame! What we know is the restaurant business, and I'm sure as hell not going to risk everything we've built up for some goddam stupid notion that would probably land us in the bankruptcy courts as well.'

Sophia had agreed. She had grown fat and complacent, her hands heavily beringed. She spent her days shopping for unsuitable clothes, going to matinées of all the successful Broadway shows, and playing bridge with friends. Her one aim in life was to hang on to what she had, terrified that she might wake up one morning and find that it had melted away. It was the fear of someone who had known poverty. It made her neurotic, causing her to pour thousands of dollars into the pocket of her psychiatrist.

'Of course it could. Sometimes, I think Harriet's just plumb crazy.' She added spitefully: 'I wish the board would make you chairman, instead of her.'

'I'm working on it,' Carlo replied.

At her first board meeting after Gus's funeral, Harriet sensed hostility in the air. Not only was Sophia present, in itself a highly unusual occurrence, but the three other directors, who had been recruited over the years – Ken Lambert, the company's chief accountant, Pete Zanardi and Jack Colia – were less enthusiastic about her return than she might have expected. And her move to get Francis Derham elected to the directorship left vacant by Gus's death was openly opposed.

'He's nothing but a restaurant manager,' Carlo objected. 'What the hell does he know about running a company?'

'What the hell did we know, when we started out?' Harriet countered.

She glanced round the table at the faces of Sophia and the other three men and knew that she would be outvoted. In her absence, Carlo had succeeded in undermining her authority all too well.

She returned home that night in a thoughtful mood, and watched a recording of President Kennedy's inaugural address to the nation on television. She had rented an apartment in the same building where she and Gus used to live and had thankfully closed up the house on Long Island. This was where she was happiest, in the bustling heart of Manhattan; but, at the same time, she was lonely in a way she had never been before. She hadn't realized how necessary Gus had been to her; how much confidence his calm stable presence had given her. Now she was completely on her own.

The previous evening, she had gone, unescorted, to the Majestic on West 44th Street, to see Richard Burton and Julie Andrews in *Camelot*. The music, the subject had made her nostalgic for England, and had inevitably summoned up memories of Edmund. It was the first time in two and a half years that she had let herself think of him freely, and the strength of her desire for him had shaken her. She couldn't exist much longer without seeing him, and she had already written to him to tell him of Gus's death. So far, she had resisted using the phone. To talk to him, actually to hear his voice, seemed, obscurely, to be betraying Gus. Later, it would be all right. Now was too soon.

President Kennedy had finished speaking, and she switched channels. A heavily made-up woman, with incredibly long false eye-lashes, was holding forth to another, equally heavily made-up woman, who was hung about with innumerable gold chains and bracelets that rattled each time she moved. The first woman was saying that everybody – but *everybody!* – would be wearing the new Dacron and Lycra synthetic fabrics this season, and hot pinks and purples were absolutely *the* colours to be seen in. The second woman agreed, and predicted that the bouffant hairstyle, created by Mr Kenneth at Lilly Daché for Jacqueline Kennedy, would be more popular even than the shingle had been in the twenties. Harriet spent a few moments contemplating this woman of the sixties, in her purple Dacron and bouffant hairdo, then turned off the set. She had more to occupy her mind just at the moment than fashion.

First thing the following morning, she made an appointment to see her bank manager and spent a useful forty-five minutes in his company.

'I'm offering to buy you out. You and Sophia.'

Harriet leaned back in her chair and looked at Carlo across the desk. She had decided that the formality of her office, rather than inviting her sister- and brother-in-law to her apartment, would give her proposal added weight.

'Buy us out?' Carlo was incredulous. 'Both of us?' He sneered. 'You couldn't afford it.'

'It'll take some doing,' Harriet admitted, 'but the bank is willing to back me and extend me the necessary credit.'

'Why?' Carlo asked bluntly. He stared at a reproduction Modigliani on the wall behind Harriet's chair. He had once heard her say that she wouldn't be satisfied until the copy was replaced by the original. For him, the remark encapsulated her insatiable ambition.

Harriet was equally blunt. 'Because I want to be in charge of this company, and I shan't be as long as you're around to subvert the other members of the board. And don't bother to pretend that isn't what you've been doing,' she added as she saw Carlo's lips open in denial. 'I realized what I was up against the other day, and I don't intend it shall happen a second time. Ken Lambert and the other two will be perfectly tractable once you and Sophia are out of the way. I'm offering you half as much again as your shares are worth on the open market. You and Sophia won't have to worry about money again for the rest of your lives. Well? What do you say?'

Carlo passed his tongue between his lips.

195

'I'll have to talk it over with Sophia,' he said, but Harriet knew that he had already made up his mind to accept. A bird in the hand was always worth two in the bush to Carlo, just as it had been to Gus. Carlo had been more enthusiastic than his brother-in-law in the early days of the venture, but he still hadn't thought big enough for Harriet, and he never would. He was rich, and that was enough for him. He didn't have her relentless driving force, and with the amount of money she was offering he could take it easy for the rest of his life. He and Sophia could go on that round-the-world cruise they had always promised themselves.

Sophia agreed with her husband. 'You'll have nothing but trouble with her, if you stay. Fight, fight, fight! That's all it'll be, now that Gus isn't there to restrain her. Look at her now, putting herself and the company in hock to the tune of five million dollars, just to buy us out. The woman's a lunatic! But why should we worry, if it benefits us? Poor old Gus must be turning in his grave.'

'Yeah!' Carlo grinned, stretching luxuriously as he made ready for bed. 'Start packing your bags, kid! Look out, world, here we come!'

Three weeks after Carlo and Sophia's resignation, Harriet saw Francis Derham and two other directors of her own choosing elected to the board. She was in debt, but for the very first time she was in complete control of her own destiny and that of Chance Enterprises. She was also free of the burden of obligation which had beset her ever since Gus had married her and given her the protection of his home and his name. She might never have been able to remain in America but for him.

She started to expand the restaurant business, opening two new Last Chances, one in Winnipeg, one in Toronto, and persuaded the bank to lend her even more money to buy up a failing hamburger chain. The Take-a-Chance eating houses opened in the fall amidst a fanfare of nation-wide publicity, which promised the identical high quality of food as was available in the bigger and better-known restaurants. The menu might be different, but the standard of excellence would remain the same.

By the time Russia's Major Yuri Gagarin had orbited the earth, and America's Commander Alan Shepard had travelled a hundred and fifteen miles into space, the Take-a-Chance eating houses were beginning to break even; and long before the Berlin Wall was begun, on 13 August, they had started to show a small profit. And when Francis Derham proposed that Chance Enterprises make a take-over bid for a network of fast-food takeaway bistros Harriet and the rest of the board agreed, always with the same reservation.

'Fast or not, the food must be *good*,' Harriet emphasized. 'That's our hallmark. I'm leaving this up to you, Frank. The whole shebang. I'm going to be away for a while, in England.'

But, first, she drove up-country, to Maine, where Michael was now at college, in Portland. She booked into a hotel overlooking Casco Bay and telephoned the college principal, requesting that her son might join her.

'Just for one night, Dr Rutherford. There's an important family matter I have to discuss with Michael.'

When Michael arrived at the hotel two hours later, Harriet was surprised all over again at how little there was of herself in her son's physical make-up. He was so like his father that she was able to see exactly how Gus must have looked at the age of thirteen; dark, stocky and tough, with eyes which resembled deep brown velvet. But there the similarity ended. In all other respects, Michael was her son; and over dinner he wanted to know all about the business. Harriet was a little disturbed that his questions should be so well informed and probing. A boy of his age should surely be more interested in base-ball, basketball, football than in the current price of Chance Enterprises shares or the present state of the Dow-Jones Index.

She replied to his questions, however, to the best of her ability, recalling her father's old maxim that if a child were old enough to ask he was also old enough to be told the answer. After dinner, she suggested that they go for a walk along the harbour.

The air was clear and fresh, heavy with the scent of pines,

197

reminding her of long-ago holidays in Devon. They walked for some way in silence, listening to the grieving cries of the gulls as the birds foraged along the sea-shore for food.

'OK,' Michael prompted at last, bored with communing with nature. 'What is it you want to see me about? Doc Rutherford said it was a family matter.'

Harriet was slightly disconcerted by this direct attack. She had been planning to lead up to the subject gradually.

'Mickey,' she asked, 'how fond were you of your father?'

She supposed, on reflection, that it was an odd question to have to ask, but she had never been quite sure what Michael's feelings had been towards Gus. She did know that Gus had resented her decision to send the boy away to school, and had blamed her for Michael's seeming lack of affection.

'He was OK,' Michael said. 'Bit of a stick-in-the-mud.'

'He loved you very much,' Harriet said gently.

'Yeah. Well, he would, wouldn't he? I was his only child.'

The clinical approach depressed her. The old sense of guilt returned; the same old price which always had to be paid.

'The thing is,' she went on, 'I'm thinking of marrying again. Someone I've known for ages. I'm flying over to England to see him next month. I just wanted you to know in advance. I wanted to explain that I'm not being disloyal to your father.'

Michael shrugged, regarding her with bright shrewd eyes.

'I guess you don't have to ask my permission.'

'No, but I'd like your blessing, all the same. This man will be your step-father.'

Again there was the slight dismissive movement of the shoulders.

'Sure. But I don't suppose we'll see that much of one another. If you're certain you want to marry this guy, go ahead and do it. Just as long as he understands what's what, and doesn't try to muscle in on the business.'

21

'I hope you told the little blighter that I don't give a damn about the business, or your money. All I want is you.'

Edmund was propped on one elbow, in bed, looking down into her face. Outside, the September day was fading in a blaze of glory. Streamers of light threaded the racing clouds; banners and pennants; scarlet and gold.

' "Crystal tresses in the sky," ' Harriet murmured irrelevantly.

'*Henry VI, Part One*, Act One.' Edmund grinned like a schoolboy, pleased that, having followed her eyes, he had also been able to follow her train of thought, and that he knew the quotation. 'Right at the very beginning, when all the English lords are moaning on and on about Henry V having snuffed it. "Hung be the heavens in black", etc., etc.'

'Ten out of ten,' Harriet said, winding her arms around his neck and drawing him down once more into the bed beside her. 'You're good for me, darling, do you know that? When I'm with you, I'm still Harriet Chance of Winterbourn Green. People need to hang on to their roots, otherwise they lose touch with reality.'

'Very profound,' Edmund mocked gently.

'Yes, I know. Seriously, you don't have to worry what Mickey thinks about you. I'd like you to like each other, of course, but I'd never let him influence me against you. He says he remembers you vaguely. He recalls a man playing with him somewhere, on a beach.'

After returning her son to college, the morning after their somewhat one-sided conversation, Harriet had gone back to New York and booked herself on to the first available flight to London. Once there, she had hired a car and driven directly to Carey Wanstead and Edmund's house near the Downs.

'As we're going to be married,' she had said, 'I see no reason at all to put up at the village pub. The sooner everyone is aware of our intentions, the better.'

'I haven't actually asked you to marry me yet,' Edmund had pointed out, laughing, but Harriet had brushed his protest aside as a mere formality.

'This is nineteen sixty-one. I'm asking you.'

She had telephoned the house from the airport to announce that she was on her way, and had found supper waiting for her on her arrival. Afterwards, before she had even bothered to unpack, they had gone to bed.

'Third time lucky,' he had said, drawing her into his arms and kissing her eyes and mouth.

Loving him, giving him all she had to give, had been the most beautiful, the most satisfying experience of her life. Not Gerry, and certainly not Gus, had aroused such passion in her. She wanted the moment to go on for ever, but even after it was all over, and she and Edmund lay quietly side by side, there was no feeling of loss; just a great welling up of contentment and a pleasurable anticipation of the times to come. She told him about her visit to Michael and what he had said.

'You'll have to give in your notice to Lord Carey,' she remarked, after a pause, 'now that you'll be living in America with me.'

A tiny frown appeared between Edmund's brows.

'I haven't really thought about what's going to happen after we're married.'

'But you can't stay here.' Harriet turned her head on the pillow. 'Darling, the hub of my business is in New York. I have to be there. You must have realized that. And Lord Carey can always get another trainer.'

Edmund's frown deepened. 'I like working with horses. It's the only thing I know how to do well. I told you just now. I don't give a damn about your business.'

'Well, I do! Darling, be reasonable!' She rolled on her side and stroked his bare chest. 'There are plenty of racing stables in America, God knows! If that's what you really want to do, I'll buy you one of your own. But I was hoping you'd let me recruit you to the board. Whatever Mickey says, I want you as part of Chance Enterprises, alongside me.'

Edmund felt a surge of anger, more with himself than with her, for not having thought this thing through. When Harrriet had written to him in January, to tell him that Gus was dead, he had been able to think of nothing except the fact that at last they could be married. What that marriage would entail had not even occurred to him until this moment; and her calm assumption that he would naturally give up his present way of life to be with her in the States had come as a jolt. Yet he should have known that it would have to be so.

He supposed, if the truth were told, he didn't much mind. He liked America and he had lived there before. There was very little nowadays to keep him on this side of the Atlantic. His ties with the IRA had dwindled to almost nothing, as the Army's activities had been voluntarily curtailed. In Ireland itself, caches of weapons had been sold, and it was generally acknowledged that the campaign against partition had failed. The extreme activists had gone into hiding – some into exile in America – and the rest were reluctantly coming to terms with the idea of a divided country. In Ulster, as well as in Eire, moderate opinion was gaining ground.

There had been only two men after Seamus Hogan, seeking temporary refuge at the house, and the second of them had been over eighteen months ago. Edmund's own views, too, had undergone certain modifications. He had found it impossible to live in England all these years and not to grow fond of some of its people. He had come to like even Lord Carey in an odd detached kind of way, although he detested Hallam Cavendish as much as ever. Hallam personified everything he most hated about the English: arrogance, class-consciousness, contempt for foreigners and those he considered to be his inferiors. But, unfortunately, England wasn't populated by Hallams: it would have made things so much simpler if it were.

Of late, Edmund had found himself wondering what he would do if another member of the IRA turned up, asking for asylum. He supposed he would comply, because, deep down, his beliefs were still the same as they had always been. But he wouldn't be proud of himself, abusing his employer's trust, and he was thankful when nobody came. Not that he was surprised: it was extremely doubtful that the Army would ever mount campaigns in England again.

So what was to keep him here? Why was he suddenly turning churlish at the prospect of living in America with Harriet? He had known for a long time that she was a businesswoman, but the implications hadn't really hit him until this minute. To him, she had remained the girl on the beach; the girl in the cheap cotton frock, with a small son, and a husband in college, struggling to survive financially. Her money had never seemed real until now, but her offer to buy him his own racing stables, frivolously meant or not, had been like a blind lifting in a darkened room. Suddenly, he wasn't sure if he could cope with that sort of wealth.

Harriet's hand stopped caressing his ribs and came up behind his head, forcing him to turn and meet her eyes. She wriggled into a sitting position, revealing the long lovely line of her breasts.

'I know what you're thinking,' she said, 'that it's wrong for men to take financially from women. For heaven's sake, why? There's this ridiculous ingrained belief that man has to be the provider. That was all very fine and necessary when we were living in swamps and forests, and a dinosaur had to be knocked on the head before you could get any dinner. But nowadays why should anyone care?'

'But people do care,' he argued. 'You know that they do. They'll say that I married you for your money.'

'If they say that,' she answered warmly, 'they don't

know what they're talking about. Right now, I'm in hock to the bank up to my eyeballs. And, anyway, I don't care what other people think. It's what *we* both know to be the truth that matters.'

Edmund felt ashamed of himself, but a persistent little doubt niggled at the back of his mind. He loved her too much, however, to let her go again. Fate had given them a second chance, and only a fool would let it slip through his fingers.

He raised his hand and stroked her hair, letting it drop to her shoulder and then on down to her waist. Her skin was smooth and cool

'I love you,' he whispered.

'And I love you,' she responded fiercely, as their eager bodies once more locked together in a kiss.

Edmund lifted his head briefly.

'I'll see Lord Carey in the morning.'

'The announcement of your engagement was quite a surprise to us,' Lord Carey said. 'Wasn't it, my dear?'

Thus appealed to, the Viscountess smiled vaguely.

'Oh, absolutely. We were astounded.' She appealed, in her turn, to her son. 'Weren't we, dearest?'

'Knocked over by the proverbial feather.'

The affected drawl grated on Harriet's nerves, and she noted that Hallam Cavendish's smile failed to reach his eyes. She could have done without this dinner-party which Lady Carey had kindly arranged: it would have been so much more rewarding to have spent the evening in bed with Edmund. He had been out all day, in the stables and up on the Downs with the horses, and she would have liked some time to be alone with him again. However, she thought philosophically, it was only a few hours out of all the rest of their lives.

'I hope this doesn't mean you're taking Edmund away from us immediately,' Lord Carey said to Harriet, as he escorted her in to dinner. 'Good trainers aren't that easy to find.'

His tone was almost jocular, and Harriet reflected that the Viscount had mellowed somewhat since she had seen him last. He still looked as cadaverous as ever, but his manner was less distant. A little of the starchy formality seemed to have gone. Perhaps it was because she was more relaxed with him. Happiness had broken down many of her restraints and inhibitions.

She was conscious, throughout the meal, of Hallam watching her from the other side of the table. No one had been invited to make up the number, and he therefore had no partner to claim his attention. Nevertheless, his scrutiny seemed excessive. Harriet felt as though he were assessing, down to the last penny, the value of everything she had on.

'When's the happy day to be, then?' he asked dulcetly, as soon as they were all seated.

'We haven't made any plans yet,' Edmund said. 'I haven't even bought Harry a ring.'

Hallam laughed and raised his thinly marked eyebrows. He made no comment, but his meaning was crystal clear. Whatever Edmund could afford, it would be unable to compete with the diamonds Harriet was already wearing.

Harriet cursed Hallam silently and held her breath, willing Edmund not to rise to the bait. To her relief, he turned to Lord Carey with some remark about one of the horses.

The meal progressed. Lady Carey engaged Harriet in conversation about events which were currently taking place in the southern states of America. What exactly were Freedom Riders? Why were they being pulled off buses and beaten up? Why wasn't President Kennedy doing something about it?

'You can't beat people up, even if they are black,' she kept saying.

It was a point of view so loaded that Harriet hardly felt it worthwhile trying to explain the Negro protests in Alabama and South Carolina. The feeling of euphoria, which had gripped her for the past twenty-four hours, began to evaporate. She felt menaced and hemmed in.

Edmund was right: people would talk about him behind his back; so many were entrenched in age-old prejudice. Black people were inferior; men shouldn't live off women. Their marriage was not going to be easy, because of their reversal of roles.

He turned his head to smile at her, and her doubts vanished like snow in the sun. As long as they loved one another, they could afford to ignore the gossip and the backbiting. Nothing was important except themselves.

The following day, she found herself once again on her own. Lord Carey had a horse running at Exeter; and Edmund, who had some reservations about the animal's staying power, wanted to be present to see for himself how Ice Diamond performed.

'I'm sorry, acushla,' he said, kissing her goodbye, 'but I'm still working for his Lordship until my notice expires. I've got the day off tomorrow, so we'll see then about buying you a ring.'

'Don't worry,' she answered, returning his embrace. 'I want to go to Town today, anyway, to visit the Haymarket restaurant. Business there has been a bit slack lately, and that's not good for the Last Chance reputation. I like my restaurants full every night. If they're not, I want to know why.'

Once more, Edmund felt the stirrings of unease. One moment she was the woman he loved, soft, vulnerable, melting; the next she was the hard imperious tycoon, running a highly successful and profitable business, light-years away from him in thought and feeling. Would he be able to cope with these changes of mood, of being relegated suddenly to the periphery of her life, of hearing himself referred to – as he undoubtedly would – as 'Mr Harriet Chance'? He wondered how Gus Contarini had coped.

But the difference between Gus and himself, of course, was that Gus had been an integral part of Chance Enterprises; a co-founder of the firm. He, Edmund, on the other hand, was an outsider, who, against his natural inclinations, was being drawn in. He worried about the situation all the way to Exeter, and was thankful that Lord Carey had decided to drive, or his lack of concentration might have caused a serious accident.

Once at the racecourse, however, set on the top of Haldon Hill, with panoramic views of the Devon countryside in all directions, Irish optimism reasserted itself. The wind, which blew constantly at that height, seemed to blow away the doubts which were clogging his mind. He was whistling cheerfully to himself as he went in search of Nick Carew, the Viscount's jockey.

Harriet spent a frustrating morning.

Richard Pace was an affable young man with excellent references, who had taken over the management of the Haymarket restaurant six months earlier, since when attendances had fallen. Harriet's demands to know why had met with the kind of stonewalling at which the English excelled. Her inspection of the books convinced her that a great deal of fiddling was going on. The quantities of food being ordered and delivered to the kitchens were not justified by the amount and quality of the meals being served. She was not surprised. Poor management invariably led to a lowering of standards among the staff. She disliked sacking employees. It gave her a sense of failure. But there was no doubt that Richard Pace would have to go.

She told him so, gave him a month's notice and found herself involved in an ugly little scene. By the time she emerged from the restaurant, she was suffering from an unusually bad headache and her hands were shaking. She needed food. It had been her intention to eat on the premises, but now she couldn't face staying there a moment longer. It worried Harriet slightly. Being in love was making her soft: she was losing her nerve.

She didn't even see Hallam Cavendish until he was standing immediately in front of her, blocking her path.

'My dear Harriet, this is a delightful surprise. I'd imagined you at home, counting the minutes until Eddie's return this evening.' He glanced at his watch. 'One o'clock.

Let me take you to lunch. Or have you already eaten?' He indicated the frontage of the Last Chance restaurant.

'No. No, I haven't.' Harriet conjured up a smile, aware that she was looking grim-faced and not wishing to give Hallam any opening for speculation. Hallam was capable of jumping to any number of wrong conclusions.

Under normal circumstances, she would have refused his invitation. She disliked him and preferred to be in his company as little as possible. But just at that moment she needed someone to talk to, so she accepted before allowing herself time to think.

'Thank you,' she said. 'That would be very nice.'

'Good! Good!' He put a hand under her elbow and began steering her along the crowded pavement. 'There's a little Italian place just round the corner that I often patronize when I'm in Town. I think it would appeal to you as an obvious connoisseur of Italian food and wine.'

Harriet made no demur, although just at the moment she would have preferred a good thick steak, followed by that most English of panaceas, a nice cup of tea.

The restaurant was in a basement, with a number of small tables islanded in a Stygian gloom. The lighting came from red-shaded table-lamps, and Harriet was acutely conscious of the intimate atmosphere of the place.

As Hallam seated himself opposite her at the secluded corner table he had chosen, he smiled.

'Now, isn't this cosy?' he asked. 'I'm so glad you agreed to come. I've been wanting to talk to you, you see.'

22

She finished the last mouthful of raspberry sorbet as the waiter put the coffee on the table. Hallam nodded, indicating that was all for the present.

The conversation during lunch had been spasmodic. Harriet had told him of her encounter with Richard Pace, and Hallam had been both amused and incredulous at her personal involvement. Chairmen of companies as big as Chance Enterprises, he pointed out, did not usually go around hiring and firing employees. That was a job left to subordinates.

'We only have the one restaurant in this country at the moment,' Harriet had replied defensively, 'and there's no British management team and offices. The Haymarket Last Chance is run from New York. And, anyway, what's wrong with the personal touch? I like to know what's going on in all my restaurants, first-hand if possible.'

'Such a terribly bourgeois attitude,' Hallam had deprecated mournfully. 'No, no! Don't fly out at me, my dear. I meant it in the nicest possible way, I do assure you.'

After that, the talk had flagged again. Now, as the waiter deftly removed her empty dish, Harriet remarked coldly: 'You said earlier that you've been wanting to speak to me. I can't really believe that any topic we've discussed so far is of burning importance to you.'

Hallam smiled and stirred his coffee. The reddish glow from the table-lamp gave him a saturnine look.

'No. The fact of the matter is, my dear Harriet, I feel the time has come for me to think of settling down. Carry on the family name, and all that rot. My parents have been hinting at it more and more frequently of late, and I'd like to oblige them. They'd like a grandchild, you see. A grandson, to be more precise. They'd like to know the inheritance is safe. There's been a Cavendish at Carey Hall for generations, and they don't care for the idea of the family dying out.' He went on stirring his coffee, making patterns in the cream with the back of his spoon.

Harriet said politely, 'Oh, yes?' and wondered why he was bothering to tell her all this. It really was none of her business.

'The thing is,' Hallam continued, raising his eyes to hers, 'that if I do marry I shall need a rich wife. I have very expensive tastes and I like the odd flutter on the gee-gees. Well, more than the odd flutter, if I'm honest. It can lead, every now and then, to some rather embarrassing debts. The poor old Pater's had to bail me out on more than one occasion, and the last time he was quite unnecessarily touchy about it. Went so far as to intimate that I was on my own in future, and would have to put up with the consequences. That could be nasty, you know. Some bookies just won't see reason, and have quite physical ways of collecting their money.'

'I'm sure.' Harriet was growing impatient. 'But I still don't see what all this has to do with me.'

'I was coming to that.' Hallam sipped his coffee. 'Unattached rich women aren't that easy to find, and until your husband died I didn't number any among my acquaintance. Now, however, here you are, widowed and wealthy. So I'm asking you, my dear Harriet, to marry me. And before you refuse me out of hand,' he added, 'let me point out the advantages. In due time you'll be Viscountess Carey, and that can't be bad for business, either here or in the States. Odd, isn't it, how republicans love a title? In this country, of course, it's always good for a bit of bow and scrape. Furthermore, I don't have any inhibitions about how much money you might make. Give me a nice fat annual allowance, and I shan't bother you all that much.

Naturally, as I said, there have to be children. Or child, if the first one's a boy. No need to overdo things. And then there's the Hall. A bit run down at present, but you'll enjoy doing it up. So what do you say? Give the worthy Edmund his cards and become the Honourable Mrs Hallam Cavendish instead.'

'You are joking, I presume?' Harriet asked coldly. 'Because, if you're not, the answer is an emphatic "no"! I wouldn't marry you if you were the last man on earth.'

'Ah.' Hallam looked thoughtful. 'You know, I was afraid you'd say that. Or something of the sort. What a pity. I was hoping that everything could be settled in a civilized fashion without my having to resort to blackmail. What a very unpleasant word that is, don't you think?'

Harriet, for no accountable reason, suddenly felt frightened, but she maintained a cool outward appearance.

'What do you mean, "blackmail"? What could you possibly blackmail me about?' The little restaurant was extremely hot and stuffy. She could feel the prickle of sweat across her skin.

Hallam lowered his voice and murmured gently: 'I'm sure you haven't forgotten a gentleman – and I use the term loosely – called Seamus Hogan. A member, I believe, of the IRA and still wanted by the police in connection with a break-in at an MP's home three years ago. The "packet" that you delivered to a house near the Albert Embankment. No, please don't deny it. I saw the delivery, you see. I'd followed you – oh, quite by accident, I do assure you, in the beginning – all the way from Staines. Unlucky for you. Fortuitous for me.'

Harriet took a deep breath and endeavoured to remain calm. Don't panic, she told herself. He can't prove a thing. Aloud, she said: 'You were mistaken. And if you did see this . . . Seamus Hogan, did you say? If you thought you'd seen a wanted criminal, why didn't you go straight to the police?'

The waiter was hovering with the bill. Hallam poured more coffee and waved him away.

'That would have been foolish, wouldn't it? Know-ledge of that kind should always be stored against a rainy day. Besides, I didn't recognize him at once. I thought the face was vaguely familiar, but it was only after you'd telephoned with your message that the penny dropped. I have a friend who works on the *Daily Telegraph*, and I got him to dig out the picture of the man who'd escaped. It was only a drawing, but nevertheless it was a very close likeness. I'd always had a suspicion that Eddie had Irish Republican sympathies, although until that moment it had never occurred to me that he might be foolish enough to let himself be used by the IRA. I suppose they recruited him during that year he worked in Eire, before coming to us. So stupid. These handsome men have more brawn than brain. He's definitely not the right partner for you.'

Harriet's fingers were clenched tightly round her cup, but she still refused to let herself be flustered.

'You can't possibly prove anything,' she said. 'It's my word against yours, and it's a long time ago. The police would only ask why you hadn't told them earlier.'

'Oh, quite.' Hallam settled himself more comfortably in his seat. Some people having a late lunch at the table next to theirs were talking and laughing. They obviously hadn't a care in the world, and Harriet regarded them enviously. Hallam went on: 'But it put me on the scent, you see. One of the advantages of having a viscount as a father is that one knows all sorts and conditions of people. I have friends and acquaintances in all kinds of privileged and influential places. People who can find things out for me. And greasing the odd palm never comes amiss. The result is that I now have quite a little dossier on Eddie. He was definitely recruited by the IRA and came to England with the sole intention of providing shelter for his colleagues who were on the run. And in case you're interested, yes, I do have evidence. Written testimonies. As I say, you can buy most things if you're prepared to pay.'

'Where . . . where is this evidence?' For the first time,

the catch in Harriet's voice betrayed her nervousness. Hallam heard it and smiled.

'In a safe deposit, in my bank. You surely don't think I'd keep it anywhere else?'

'How do I know what you're saying is true? I only have your word for it.'

'That's very true. But you can't afford not to believe me, can you? Eddie could go to prison for a very long time.'

'He'd be out of this country before you could get him arrested,' she answered.

'Oh, I don't think so.' Hallam rested his elbows on the table and laced his fingers together, regarding her over the top of them. 'He's in Exeter and he won't be back until late tonight. I could have my evidence in the hands of the police long before then. And, in addition to poor Eddie going to prison, I'm afraid you might, too, for aiding and abetting. Not a very long sentence, perhaps. Mitigating circumstances. But not good publicity for your business.'

'There's a lot of sympathy for the IRA in America,' she told him, clutching at straws.

Hallam considered her statement, his head tilted judiciously to one side.

'Mmm. Amongst certain persons, maybe. Not amongst others. And you couldn't rely on the publicity running in your favour. I've checked up on you, too, during the past few months, since your husband died. I thought it wise. Since you bought out your sister-in-law and her husband, you owe the bank a great deal of money. Far too much for you to be able to risk any falling off of business. And you've other irons in the fire that everyone knows about. The Take-a-Chance hamburger chain and the fast-food shops you've recently acquired. You really are in debt right up to the top of your handsome head. You can't afford the slightest loss of business. Added to which, I've been nosing around Winterbourn Green.'

'Winterbourn Green? What are you talking about?' Harriet was confused. 'That's got nothing to do with Edmund.'

'I didn't say it had. But they remember you very well in your old home village. Very well indeed. Especially how you left your father and child and went to America. And later, after your father died, how you had your child adopted.' Hallam flung up a hand as Harriet attempted to speak. 'Oh, I can guess that you had no choice, but in the wrong hands – one of the more sensational Sunday newspapers, for example – the story could create quite an adverse impression. Callous daughter. Hard-hearted mother. Do I have to go on?'

'You're despicable!' Harriet exclaimed bitterly. 'God, how I loathe you! Do you want to be married to a woman who hates your guts?'

Hallam clicked his tongue reprovingly and said: 'Don't let's descend to the language of the gutter. It's not you I'm marrying, my dear girl. It's your money.' But she had seen the tightening of the skin across his temples and the thinning of his lips. Hallam Cavendish had a very high opinion of himself and found personal abuse hard to take. Harriet hoarded the knowledge against the future.

But she was trapped and she knew it. She did not make the mistake of underestimating Hallam's strength of purpose. If he did indeed have the evidence he claimed to possess, he would not hesitate to use it. He was not an impulsive man: he was a plotter, a planner, who garnered information and stored it away, just on the off-chance that one day it would come in useful. He was cold-blooded, and such a man would carry out his threats. Edmund would be arrested and go to prison. She might go to prison. Chance Enterprises could well be ruined. . .

She guessed that there was no hope of telling Edmund the truth; and, as if in answer to her thought, Hallam leaned across the table and whispered viciously: 'Breathe one word of explanation to that treacherous Irish bastard, and my dossier on him goes straight to the police. I'm not living in constant fear of him, or one of his friends, beating me up.'

'You could be in trouble for suppressing evidence,'

Harriet said. Her voice shook, but this time she did not even try to disguise the fact. There was no point. Hallam must know that she had realized all the cards were stacked against her.

'Maybe. Maybe not.' He leaned back in his chair, urbane once more. 'That's a risk I'm prepared to take.'

He smiled the self-satisfied smile of a man who had managed to kill two birds with one stone. He had found a way to solve his financial problems and, at the same time, revenge himself on two people against whom he had harboured a grudge ever since that humiliating scene three years ago in the stable-yard.

Harriet raised her chin defiantly.

'You say I'm not to tell Edmund. But won't he suspect something – smell a rat,' she added with a sneer which brought an angry flush to Hallam's thin cheeks, 'if I suddenly announce that I've changed my mind since this morning? That I'm going to marry you, who he knows I can't bear!'

The colour receded from Hallam's face, leaving it paler than before. He grinned.

'You won't have to say anything, my dear. You won't even have to leave him. He'll leave you.'

'What do you mean?' Harriet's voice was edged with fear.

'Tonight, when the worthy Edmund returns from Exeter, he'll find us in bed together. In his house. Now, isn't that a simple, but most effective, idea?'

She drove back to Carey Wanstead, caught up in a nightmare of emotions; fear, hatred, self-contempt all struggled for paramount position. But she saw no way out of the dilemma which faced her. She would have to agree to marry Hallam.

'I'll see you after dinner, about half-past eight,' he had said, as they stood together on the pavement outside the Italian restaurant. He might have been making the most mundane of arrangements. Only the feverish glitter in his eyes had betrayed his excitement. 'And don't think of running away, my dear. Such a move would have the same dire consequences for you and Eddie.'

'For God's sake, stop talking in that damn theatrical way!' she had spat at him, anger momentarily washing through her like a cleansing balm. 'And do stop calling him Eddie!'

The house was very quiet when Harriet let herself in; quiet and empty. Yet Edmund's presence was all-pervasive. His old mackintosh hung on a peg in the hallway, his Wellington boots, still dirty from the mud and rain of the day before, lying where they had been tossed, in a corner. Upstairs, in the bedroom which they had shared since her arrival, his pyjamas were stuffed in a badly folded heap beneath his pillow, the blue and white cotton counterpane drawn anyhow over the top. Everything was exactly as it had been that morning when she had left for London, happy and counting the weeks to her wedding. But in the mean time she felt as though she had aged a hundred years.

She sat down on the edge of the bed and thought hard. Surely there must be something she could do, someone to whom she could turn? But the answers were always the same. Nothing. Nobody. Anger welled up in her again, this time against Edmund. It was his fault that they were in this mess; it was his stupid idealism, devotion to a cause, which had made him ready to flout the law and drag her with him. Why on earth couldn't men grow up and leave those sorts of cloak-and-dagger games behind them in the nursery? But then, she supposed, women wouldn't love them so much. Some part of every woman's feelings for a man was maternal.

She went down again to the hall and looked at the telephone. Edmund would not have left the Haldon racecourse yet. She could still warn him. She reached out a hand to pick up the receiver, then dropped it back again to her side. Hallam had meant every word he had said. Long years in business, learning the hard way, had taught her to know when someone was bluffing. And she knew Edmund

215

as well. Instead of heading straight for the nearest ferry terminal and Ireland, he would come raging back here, demanding, perhaps literally, Hallam's blood. She turned and went slowly back upstairs.

What a stupid fool she'd been! Her anger veered towards herself. She had set herself above the law by helping Seamus Hogan and now she was reaping the consequences. Her father, who had sincerely believed that no one could change anything by violence or subversion, would have told her that it was divine retribution.

'Nemesis, Harry. Nemesis!' His voice echoed across the years.

The thought of her father made her think of that other Hilary, and she felt a sudden agonizing longing for her child. She couldn't let Hallam give that story to the press, whatever else happened. Little Hilary – who was little no longer, but sixteen years old – had another life, another name, other parents, hopefully settled and thriving. There was no reporter worth his salt who would not manage to sniff out the child's whereabouts if Hallam ever made her desertion public. She could see the screaming headlines, the distorted interpretations, the loaded angles which would rip apart the precious anonymity of a sensitive teenager.

Harriet sat down at the dressing-table and stared at herself in the mirror. Her head ached dully, and a lead weight seemed to have settled over her mind. Her business, her lover, her child – was the order in which she listed them significant? – could all be used against her to bring her world crashing about her ears.

'You've no option, my girl,' she told her reflection grimly. 'You'll have to marry Hallam Cavendish and lump it.'

And if that were so, then Hallam's swift and brutal solution to the problem of informing Edmund without arousing his suspicions was by far the best way.

The doorbell rang promptly at half-past eight, and she went downstairs again to let Hallam in. He smiled at her as he stepped over the threshold.

216

'The old man phoned,' he said, 'while Mother and I were having dinner. They expect to be back around nine-thirty.' The smile deepened to a sadistic grin. 'That gives us an hour.' He stroked her hair, and Harriet had to exert all her powers of self-control to stop herself shuddering. 'I'm going to enjoy this. I do so hope you are, my dear.'

Harriet had not thought about them actually making love, and the idea revolted her. She undressed and got into bed in a sort of daze. When Hallam forced himself on top of her, she detached her mind and tried to pretend that it wasn't happening. She felt him climax and sink back on to the pillows, exhausted. There was a savagery about his lovemaking which she realized she should have expected. Behind the urbane façade lurked a primitive animal.

It was dark, and she switched on the bedside lamp to look at Edmund's alarm-clock. The hands showed twenty minutes to ten when she heard the rattle of his key in the lock. The front door opened and closed, and his eager footsteps sounded on the stairs.

'Acushla! I'm back!'

He turned the handle of the bedroom door and came in.

PART FOUR

1964–9

*Chance is perhaps the pseudonym
of God when He did not want to
sign.*

ANATOLE FRANCE

23

Harriet indicated the chair on the opposite side of her desk.

'Sit down, Ken,' she said. 'I think I know what you're going to say.'

Ken Lambert was looking older. There was a lot of grey in the once brown hair, and his skin had the unhealthy greyish tinge indicative of a duodenal ulcer. He had been Chance Enterprises' chief accountant for some ten years now, and had steered the company safely through the shoals and sandbanks of expansion, until today, three years after his employer had become the Honourable Mrs Hallam Cavendish, it was steadily growing into one of the biggest concerns in the United States. The past twelve months alone had seen it swallow up four new companies which had nothing to do with the catering business. Chance Enterprises itself was now merely a part of the Chance Corporation, whose interests, among other things, embraced a television rental chain, a record company and a string of dress shops, catering exclusively, and lucratively, for the new pop-crazed generation spawned by the phenomenal success of the Beatles.

It was good, Ken Lambert reflected, to be part of an organization which could weather the Kennedy assassination, the previous November, without so much as a hiccup in the value of its shares; but the workload was punishing and had taken its toll. Every now and then he felt like quitting, and today was one of those days. But looking at the determined woman on the other side of the desk he knew he would not be allowed to go without a struggle. Harriet Cavendish gave one hundred per cent of her time and energy to the firm, and expected the same sort of dedication from her employees. Ken recognized that the Chance Corporation would grow bigger yet. Harriet had the Midas touch. Everything she handled seemed to prosper.

The same, however, could not be said for her private life. It was small wonder she devoted herself to work, married to a husband like Hallam Cavendish. Ken had only met Hallam on half a dozen occasions, but he had taken an instant dislike to the Englishman. Fortunately, Hallam spent very little time in New York with his wife and baby son, preferring to live and play in London. And how he played! He was forever demanding huge sums of money over and above the more than generous allowance which Harriet made him; and it was a constant bone of contention between Harriet and her chief accountant that she always paid them. Only this morning, Ken had been instructed to transfer another half-million dollars into Hallam's account, and it was the main reason he was now sitting in Harriet's office. He was feeling unwell but, more than that, he was feeling thoroughly pissed off!

Involuntarily, he uttered the last two words aloud. They sounded loudly in the hushed air-conditioned silence. For a moment, Harriet looked as startled as he did. Then she began to laugh.

'OK, Ken. You're pissed off. So what else is new?'

'It's time I retired,' he said, avoiding her eyes. 'I'm fifty-three, I have a family I hardly ever get to see, I've a pain in my gut from this goddam ulcer, and' – he switched his gaze suddenly to meet hers squarely – 'a pain in the butt from the Honourable Hallam Charles Guy Frederick Cavendish. Ain't that the truth!' And now, he thought triumphantly, you can fire me.

'My husband,' Harriet replied, 'is a pain in the butt to everyone.' She leaned forward across the desk, her voice low and urgent. 'I need you, Ken. I can't afford to let you go. I don't know what I'd do without you. Fifty-three! What sort of an age is that? I intend to go on until I'm carried out of here, feet first, in a box. I know we haven't always seen eye to eye, but that was a few years ago now, and I blamed Carlo for most of our misunderstandings. We've worked together well since he went. I'm fully aware that your workload is heavy. And increasing. All right! You don't have to say it! But you have marvellous back-up, Ken. A wonderful team, all trained specially by you. They'd feel let down if you quit.'

'I don't see enough of my family,' he repeated doggedly. 'Aileen complains that she has to make an appointment before she can see me, and is making noises about a divorce. My boy, Jack, has got in with the wrong set at college. He's burned his draft card and joined the "We Won't Go" brigade against this rumpus in Vietnam. And if that should escalate into a full-scale war he could be in serious trouble. I ought to be around.'

'Ken, you know you can have extended leave of absence whenever you wish, just so long as you come back to me at the end of it.' Harriet smiled her most winning smile. 'As for these payments to Hallam, let me worry about them. I just want him off my back. Just keep him happy, so he'll stay in England and leave me and Piers alone.'

'He's rooking you, Harriet!' The family man abruptly became the accountant once more. Ken Lambert pounded the desk-top for emphasis. 'He's robbing you right, left and centre. God knows what he's doing with all this money, but he sure as hell isn't giving it to charity! My guess is that he's up to his neck in shady deals, and he's doing it with our money!'

Harriet's smile grew broader. When Ken began referring to the corporation as though he owned it, she knew that thoughts of retirement had, if only temporarily, receded. She had him hooked again. He wasn't yet ready to leave her.

'Look, Ken, Hallam's my husband, my responsibility. Just keep the payments flowing until I say otherwise. And don't be so disapproving. Hallam's a luxury; but one, thank God, that I can afford. I think it's time you had a raise in salary. So how about a Scotch and soda to celebrate?'

Fifteen minutes later, Ken Lambert walked out of Harriet's office uneasily aware that he had once again been bribed and conned into staying. His ulcer was sending out warning signals from the region of his large intestine, but he would stay on, he supposed with a sigh, as long as Harriet needed him. The Chance Corporation was in his blood: he had grown addicted to it over the years and, if the truth were told, its welfare meant more to him than that of his wife and family.

Once Ken had left the office, Harriet's smile faded. She sat, staring into space, her lips thin with hatred. Damn Hallam! God damn his soul to hell! *How* she loathed him! She got up, as though jerked by an unseen hand, and began to prowl restlessly up and down the room. The mention of her husband always had that unsettling effect on her.

She detested Hallam with an intensity which could, on occasions, make her physically ill. She had no doubt that Ken Lambert was right: Hallam was up to his neck in shady dealing. But there was nothing she could do about it. She had no proof and dared make no move to get any. Hallam could still make things unpleasant for her and Edmund with his revelations.

Edmund was respectably married now to Isabelle Hutton, and running his own stud farm in southern Ireland. It could damage his growing reputation as a breeder to be linked with the IRA, and would prevent his ever returning to England. But the greater damage would be to herself. She was now an internationally recognized figure; that still rare phenomenon, a woman who had made it all the way to the top in the essentially male-dominated commercial world. There were a lot of people who would be delighted to see her pilloried; caught in a net of her own weaving. Harriet had no doubt that the press, on both sides of the Atlantic, would have a field-day. On one hand she would be represented as ruthless, hard-hearted and callous, and on the other foolish and doting to the point of breaking the law. Hallam still had the power to hurt her and damage the Chance Corporation, although he could no longer send either of them under. Nowadays, they were both too big and too well entrenched for that. All the same, Harriet shrank from the kind of adverse publicity he was able to inflict.

She walked over to the window and stood looking down into West 72nd Street. Opposite was the prestigious Dakota apartment-block with its Victorian Gothic façade; gables, arches and oriel windows, ornamental stonework and romantic balconies. It always made her think of Europe. And Europe made her think of Edmund. . . She closed her eyes and leaned against the window-jamb, letting the hot July sun seep into her bones.

Any memories of Edmund led straight to the terrible scene in the bedroom, when he had found her, that night, with Hallam. At first, Edmund had refused to believe it, not trusting the evidence of his eyes. He had punched Hallam, accusing him of rape, and she had been forced to prevent a further assault by telling him the truth; that she was going to marry Hallam. She would never forget Edmund's look of searing contempt, when finally she had convinced him that she meant it.

'I see,' he had said slowly. 'You can't resist the lure of a title. That's it, isn't it, acushla?' And this time the endearment had been like a red-hot brand laid against her skin. 'The future Viscountess Carey. It'll do your precious business a world of good! Well, you warned me yourself, years ago, and I was foolish enough not to listen. You told me your father accused you of using people, and the poor old devil was right. You use them and then cast them aside, like a pair of old shoes.' He had laughed, but without any warmth. 'Oh, I believe you came over here intending to marry me, all right. Any man was better than no man, and you need a father for your boy. You need a male presence in your life, to make you feel safe. But now you've got a better offer from a member of the British aristocracy, no

225

less. The Honourable Mrs Hallam Cavendish, the future Lady Carey, sounds a damn sight better than Mrs Edmund Howard.'

He had paused, waiting for her to deny his accusations; and then, when she had not, he had started bundling her clothes anyhow into her cases. Hallam, grinning, had got dressed.

'Edmund —' she began, but he had turned on her in a frenzy of rage, striking her across the face and sending her reeling on to the bed.

'Get out of here!' he had shouted. 'Get out of here, you whore, and never come back! I never want to set eyes on you again!'

She had hurriedly thrown on slacks and a sweater and gone. Hallam had taken her up to the Hall and announced their engagement to his parents. The Viscount and his wife were genuinely delighted. Like their son, they saw her as an infusion, not of new blood, but of new money; the rich provider of an even richer heir. Carey Hall would be restored to its former glory. A few days later, she had heard that Edmund was once again engaged to Isabelle Hutton, and that they were to be married almost at once by special licence. He had not withdrawn his notice to Lord Carey, and had left, with his new wife, at the end of the month, to go home to southern Ireland. She had neither seen nor heard from him since.

She did, however, hear of him through her London solicitors, Hutton & Taylor. Ronald Hutton, who knew nothing of her part in the erratic course of his daughter's engagement, spoke affectionately of his son-in-law from time to time, and Harriet knew that Edmund was doing well, rapidly establishing a reputation for himself as one of the top breeders in both the Republic and in Britain. She was pleased for him, but sad for herself. Occasionally, she thought that perhaps it had all turned out for the best: Edmund was his own man, respected in his own field, not simply another adjunct of the growing Chance empire. And the press, and the world at large, had loved her marriage to Hallam. The Americans were enchanted, if a little confused, by her designation as the Honourable Mrs Hallam Cavendish and her future status as a viscountess; while the British were pleased by what they saw as the prodigal's return to the fold. She might have done the unforgivable thing by making her fortune on the other side of the Atlantic, but she had made amends at last by marrying an Englishman, and a member of the aristocracy at that. Whenever she was in England, there was always a call for pictures of herself with her husband, baby son and parents-in-law in the historic surroundings of Carey Hall; one big happy family.

If they only knew! Harriet thought savagely. She hadn't shared a bed with Hallam since Piers was born, ten months previously. She had kept her part of the bargain, allowing Hallam his conjugal rights until she had given him a son. And, in fairness to Hallam, she had to admit that he had made no attempt to inflict himself on her. He seemed to have been as relieved as she was when the baby turned out to be a boy. Harriet suspected that, having achieved his two main objects of unlimited money and an heir for the title, her husband had quickly grown bored with her. He preferred a succession of dolly-birds and call-girls, who kept him entertained during their long separations. Harriet had heard rumours that Hallam had been involved, in some minor way, in the Profumo scandal of the preceding year; a scandal which had rocked the world and led to the resignation of the then Prime Minister, Harold Macmillan. But, whatever Hallam's part in the affair, it had been hushed up, no doubt aided by some generous backhanders of her hard-earned money. . .

The sun, streaming in through the window, was hurting her eyes. Harriet pulled down the blind and returned to her desk. She had a board meeting in half an hour, and she must get herself in the right frame of mind. She must forget both Hallam and Edmund and concentrate on her current pet project of opening a chain of Last Chance restaurants throughout the British Isles. For some reason, the

Haymarket had remained her only venture in her native land. Now, at long last, she intended to remedy that omission. Eventually, there would be a Last Chance restaurant in every major city in the kingdom, with administrative offices based in London. It was a project which would take precedence over all others.

When she let herself into her apartment late that evening, Harriet was greeted by an unaccustomed silence. For almost the first time in months, Piers was not crying. His fretful wail was usually the first sound to assail her ears as she opened the front door. Tonight, however, all was quiet.

Jeanette Baynton, who had recently returned to Harriet's employ after the early, and unexpected, death of her husband, came into the hall to greet her.

'The new nanny's here,' she said. 'Moved in this afternoon, just after Nanny Cartwright moved out. And I think, this time, the agency has sent us a winner. There's been hardly a peep out of my-lad-o since she arrived.'

'Thank God for that,' Harriet breathed devoutly. 'Cartwright was an unmitigated disaster from the start. Mind you, in her defence, I will admit that Piers is a difficult baby.'

Harriet had tried hard to feel normal maternal affection for Hallam's son, but she had not found it easy. Piers Hallam Guy Julian Cavendish was a peevish child from the moment he was born. Even at the tender age of ten months, he quite definitely resembled his father and the Viscount. His slip of a face, beneath its wing of dark hair, and seemingly undernourished little body disguised a voracious appetite and a quite remarkable determination to get his own way. Constantly wakeful and fractious, he had been the despair of two nannies and three nursemaids, all of whom had either resigned or politely been asked to leave within a matter of months. Michael, now a sturdy sixteen-year-old, whose hero was the Louisville Lip himself, Cassius Clay, found his baby brother not only a noisy addition to his tight little world, but also an embarrassment.

'Gee, Mom,' he had protested indignantly, 'how many guys of my age have a kid brother still in his cradle?'

The implication was that Harriet, at thirty-eight and with one foot already in the grave, should have conducted herself with greater propriety. His attitude had annoyed her, and it had been with even more alacrity than usual that she had helped him pack to return to school.

'Perhaps I'm devoid of natural maternal feeling,' she had told herself despairingly. Now she asked Jeanette: 'What's the new nanny's name? I've forgotten. I recollect you saying that she was English.'

The housekeeper, who had done the interviewing, nodded. 'She's English all right, even though her name is Tettenburg. She was a war bride. Married a miner called Eugene Tettenburg from near Pittsburgh. Divorced him years ago and trained to be a nurse, then a children's nanny. A highly successful one, I should guess, by the way she handles young Piers. I'll call her out to meet you.'

Jeanette disappeared into the nursery, while Harriet frowned, wondering why certain details of Nanny Tettenburg's story seemed familiar to her. Then, suddenly, she remembered. As the new nanny, neat in her crisp blue and white uniform, walked into the hall, Harriet's face broke into a grin. She held out both hands.

'I'm right,' she said. 'It *is* you. You're Kathleen Mason..'

24

Kathleen Tettenburg, née Mason, no longer swore with every other word, and she had learned to speak grammatically, although she still retained her Gloucestershire accent. She and Harriet laughed about it together, that first evening: nearly twenty years in the States, a painful and laborious re-education of speech patterns, and yet she continued to speak with the hard *r* and flat vowels of her native county. By contrast, Harriet's mid-Atlantic pronunciation sounded strongly American.

'It's wonderful to see you again,' Harriet said as they shared an evening meal cooked by Jeanette. She could never have believed that she would be so pleased to see Kathleen again. It was like a voice from the past, and for once Harriet broke with her rule of being friendly with employees but, at the same time, keeping them at a respectful distance. Nevertheless, when Kathleen unreservedly poured out her life's history since the day of their arrival in the United States, Harriet was careful not to do the same.

In fact there was very little in Kathleen's version of events which had not already been summarized by Jeanette Baynton; a mere fleshing out of the bones. She had hated the rough-and-ready mining community in which she had found herself; and Eugene Tettenburg, miner, under the dominating influence of his mother, had been very different from Gene Tettenburg, Private Second Class, United States Army, hellraiser and general good-time guy. After seven childless years, with Kathleen being

230

blamed by the entire Tettenburg family for her and Eugene's lack of children, she upped and left for New York, where she did a number of jobs before enrolling as a nurse. And it was nursing, particularly children's nursing, that Kathleen had found was her true vocation. It was now her life.

'I've finished with men for good,' she said in answer to Harriet's query about any future marriage plans. She wrinkled her nose. 'I had enough with Gene.'

By the time Harriet left for England in November, Kathleen was an indispensable member of her household. She was the only person who could do anything with Piers, who was rarely fretful or bad-tempered when she was around.

'I've just got a knack with babies,' was her only explanation of this phenomenon.

Now and then, she had a lapse and reverted to her former self. The first occasion on which she found herself in Claridges, a hotel whose name was as familiar to her as her own, but whose august portals she had never thought to enter, she uttered a breathless: 'Bloody hell!'

She apologized at once. 'Sorry, Mrs Cavendish.' She had quickly learned that her past friendship with Harriet did not put them on first-name terms, except in very exceptional circumstances. 'It's just that if my parents could see me now they'd have a fit. I can't wait to write to them on Claridges notepaper. The letter'll be shown to everyone in the street.'

'I didn't realize your parents were still alive,' Harriet said, surprised.

'Oh, yes. Mum, Dad and my older sister, Ingrid, still live in Gloucester. And my brother, Bernard, works on a farm near Stroud.'

'Have you ever been back to see them?'

'Once. Couldn't manage any more visits because of the fare. But we write regularly to one another. I shouldn't feel comfortable if I lost touch.' Kathleen was busy changing Piers, her fingers expertly busy with talcum powder, safety-pins and nappy. Without raising her eyes, she asked hesitantly: 'You never said . . . I mean . . . what happened to the kiddie you left behind?'

Harriet had forgotten that, of course, Kathleen knew all about Hilary, and the question hit her like an unexpected blow in the solar plexus. She felt winded and more shaken than she cared to admit. The word 'kiddie' jarred on her nerves.

'The child was adopted,' she answered stiffly, and was glad of the sudden ringing of the nursery telephone.

It was her highly efficient secretary, June Grazini, to inform her that tea had been sent up to the sitting-room, that Mr Ronald Hutton of Hutton & Taylor was waiting downstairs to see her, that Ken Lambert was on his way up in the elevator – or should she say 'lift'? When in Rome, etc. – from his suite on the floor below, and that the manager of Coutts Bank was on the other line, asking to speak to Harriet personally. Life was back to its normal tempo, and the past receded.

But, for some reason, its intrusion could not be so easily shaken off as on previous occasions. For the rest of the day, memories of her father and lost child kept on surfacing.

And kept on surfacing.

All through the next few hectic weeks, while Chance Enterprises (UK) Ltd, a subsidiary of the Chance Corporation, gradually took shape; while plans were made to open Last Chance restaurants in Birmingham and Glasgow by the end of 1965, and in Cardiff by the following spring, Harriet found her mind dwelling on Winterbourn Green more often than she liked. Faces from the past kept coming between her and her work. She would lose the thread of her discourse at critical and inopportune moments, until even Ken Lambert expressed his concern.

'You need a break, Harriet. Everything's under control here. Why don't you go chase up that husband of yours and give him a piece of your mind?'

Harriet laughed. 'Blow off a great head of steam, do you mean? Maybe I will.'

'Is he in London?'

'Oh, sure he's in London, but so far he hasn't had the decency to call in and say "hello"!' They were lunching at the Last Chance restaurant in the Haymarket, now back on form after the enforced departure of Richard Pace three years ago. 'I understand he's been snooping around the nursery on a couple of occasions, when he's been sure I wouldn't be there. Not that I've a yen for his company, but, as you say, there might be one or two things I'd like to discuss. Anyway, Nanny and the baby are going down to Carey Hall tomorrow. Perhaps I'll join them for a few days at the end of the week.'

'You do that. Like I say, there's nothing further to keep you here. Have a break before we go back to New York. Are they fond of the kid, his grandparents?'

'Dote on him. He's their future.' Harriet turned the conversation. 'What did you think of the result of the election?'

Ken Lambert shrugged. He was indifferent to politics outside those of the Chance Corporation Boardroom.

'Foregone conclusion. The black vote was bound to swing it.'

Lyndon Johnson had just been re-elected President of the United States, beating his Republican rival, the ultra-right Senator Barry Goldwater. There had been Negro riots and demonstrations throughout the southern states all year, and near-chaos following the murder of three black youths in Philadelphia, Mississippi. Malcolm X had recently urged black students to 'stay radical'. It was the only way, he told them, to get their freedom.

It occurred to Harriet that she had never heard Ken Lambert express an opinion about anything other than his work and his family, and sometimes she worried that she, too, was treading the same all-excluding road. She must not let the Chance Corporation become her whole life. She must broaden her horizons.

'I'll take your advice and have that break,' she said. 'I

233

won't wait until the end of the week, after all. I'll go tomorrow, with Piers and his nanny.'

She was driving Lord Carey's battered old Rover, because she had let Kathleen borrow the hired Aston Martin to go to Gloucester to see her parents and sister.

'No, go on, take it,' she had insisted, when Kathleen had demurred. 'You'll get there that much quicker.'

'We-ell, if you're sure . . .' Kathleen had pocketed the keys and issued last-minute instructions concerning her charge. She was in the process of potty-training the one-year-old Piers, and was reluctant to leave him just at present. But it seemed foolish to be within a two-hour drive of Gloucester and not go home to see her parents.

Harriet had smiled. 'Yes, quite sure. Enjoy yourself, and don't worry about Piers. His adoring grandmother is looking after him for the day, so he'll be OK. I'm taking a leaf out of your book, and visiting my old home at Winterbourn Green.'

Kathleen regarded her oddly. 'Haven't you ever been back before?'

Harriet shook her head. 'Not once in eighteen years.' She had tried to keep her voice light. 'Dreadful, isn't it? But since my father died there's been no one I really wanted to see.'

She had not mentioned her child, but the thought of that younger Hilary was there, in both their minds. She had not discussed the subject further with Kathleen, after that one brief conversation four weeks earlier, but she could sense the other woman's curiosity. She could also sense her disapproval. Once or twice, Harriet had been tempted to reopen the matter and explain the circumstances, but obstinacy and pride had held her silent. She did not have to make excuses to an employee; or to anyone. She was Harriet Chance of the Chance Corporation. She need account to no one for her actions.

Why, then, was she driving through Oxford on a cold December morning, on her way to Winterbourn Green?

Why had she allowed Kathleen's silent condemnation to get under her guard? Enough, at any rate, to send her scurrying off on this sentimental pilgrimage. Why, after nearly two decades, had she allowed her guilt about her firstborn child to get out of control? It had always been there, but she had managed to suppress it for most of the time, buried deep beneath layers of consciousness, so that, over the years, it had troubled her less and less.

She passed the turning to Minster Lovell and the ghosts came crowding all about her. A mile or so further on, she left the main road and plunged into the maze of country lanes which had once been as familiar to her as the back of her own hand. The trees were not yet completely bare of leaves, but a raw wind was busily stripping the branches. She drove across a small hump-backed bridge which straddled a willow-fringed stream and, almost without warning, found herself in the centre of the village.

She had forgotten how abruptly the clustering houses drew back to reveal the green itself. It was exactly as she remembered it, with the church and vicarage on one side, the pub and the village hall opposite; the same as on that morning in 1946 when she had piled herself and her cheap cases into a taxi and started out on the first leg of a journey which would end in New York. She parked the Rover in the lane, which ran alongside the churchyard, and got out.

There were changes, of course, but she didn't notice them all at once. She pushed open the little gate in the grey stone wall and went into the churchyard, wandering along the path between the tipsy tombstones with their curiously rolled tops, so typical of that part of the world. St Aldhelm's, too, was essentially Cotswold; neat, small and plain, the spire gleaming whitely against its background tracery of trees. Harriet passed under the Norman arch, with its dog's-tooth carving, and entered the church.

The recognizably musty smell of a building too little opened to air and light mingled with the smells of damp and cold. Austerely lettered eighteenth-century memorial tablets let into the flags contrasted sharply with florid

Victorian monuments and brasses cluttering the walls. Parts of the stonework dated back to the early twelfth century and the reign of Henry I.

Harriet sat down in one of the pews and stared around her. It was all so achingly familiar. She recalled countless Sunday mornings, when she was either too cold or too hot, and always bored, listening to her father's sermons, but too embarrassed to look in his direction. The vicar's daughter: she had never been cut out for that role. She had been expected to set an example of good behaviour, to help in the parish, to assist her father, after her mother's death. But she could not do it. She had insisted on going her own way, and people had not liked it. They had called her selfish, self-centred. Only her father had tried to understand.

A door opened, and someone came through from the vestry. Harriet saw from his clerical collar that he must be the vicar. He noticed her and smiled.

'Are you admiring our little church? Not one of the more imposing examples of Cotswold architecture, I'm afraid. Burford is much finer.' He held out his hand. 'I'm Philip Gresham, by the way. The present incumbent.'

Harriet got up and shook hands. 'I'm Harriet Cavendish. My name used to be Chance. My father was vicar here during the thirties and forties.'

She could see that he knew at once who she was. A wary look came into his eyes, and there was the faintest flicker of disapproval in their cool grey depths. He took in the suppleness of her red leather coat, the high-heeled boots and the expensive tan leather handbag.

'Ah! Yes.' He evidently could think of nothing else to say.

Harriet laughed. 'My goodness! I didn't realize I was quite so notorious. The scarlet woman returns. Well, at least I'm appropriately dressed.'

The vicar blushed up to the roots of his curly fair hair, and she saw for the first time how young he was. What was the old axiom? When policemen – and, presumably, vicars – started looking like babes-in-arms, you were feeling your age. What nonsense! She was only thirty-eight, and she liked to kid herself that she didn't look a day over thirty.

'Do you have electric light in the vicarage these days?' she asked, to break a silence which was growing uncomfortable.

'Electric light?' The vicar looked puzzled for a moment, then his chubby face cleared. 'You're talking about the old vicarage, of course! No, no! I have a nice little semi nowadays, on the new estate at the end of Vicarage Lane. The original vicarage is almost derelict. The property's been up for sale for quite some time now, but the Church Commissioners are having a job getting rid of it. Developers won't touch it because it's so close to the church, and the Town and Country Planning bods won't allow the site to be used for housing. What it really needs,' he added innocently, 'is for someone with money to salvage the old place and put it to rights. Oh! I didn't mean ... I honestly had no intention. . .'

'That's OK,' Harriet said, hardly conscious of his apologies. Her old home was in danger of falling down. She could not let it happen. She couldn't!

'I'd like to see it,' she said to the vicar.

They walked through the churchyard. Part of the roof had fallen in, and the walls were crumbling. The garden was lost beneath a tangle of overgrown weeds and rioting briars. The front door hung loose on a solitary rusty hinge, and was creaking dismally in the rising wind. Harriet pushed it aside, regardless of possible damage to her clothes.

The empty rooms were thick with dust, and she could hear the scamper of mice as soon as she went inside. Two of the stair-treads were broken, and part of the banister was missing.

'I don't think it's safe to go upstairs,' Philip Gresham warned her. He had followed her in and was staring round him in awe. 'What a barracks of a place! It must have cost a fortune in coal and gas.'

'It did,' Harriet answered drily. Her voice echoed queerly in the silence. 'How long since anyone lived here?'

'Let me see. . . Ten years, I should think. At least. My predecessor was the last person in the house, and he must have moved out a good five or six years before he retired in nineteen sixty.'

'Ten years,' Harriet repeated slowly. Nineteen fifty four. Only seven years after her father's death, the Church Commissioners had finally rejected this costly dinosaur. They had done what they should have done a decade or so before, moving the vicar and his family to a small, easy-to-run, easy-to-warm house, near enough to St Aldehelm's for comfort, but not so close that people could ring the doorbell at all hours of the day and night. How her father would have enjoyed a cosy little semi!

An unexpected rush of affection for her old home, such as had seized her in the church, filled Harriet's eyes with tears. So many childhood memories came flooding back, and not all of them bad. Some of them, in fact, very good indeed.

She realized suddenly that she needed a home of her own in England. Carey Hall was nothing to do with her. She hated the place. She had spent some of the unhappiest moments of her life there. She would go on spending money on it for her son's sake, but she could never live there for any length of time. A few days, as at present, were as much as she could manage. She turned to the young man standing at her side.

'Do you know who the estate agents are for this place? I've decided to buy it.'

25

She went back to Carey Hall, packed her cases and installed herself in the George and Dragon at Winterbourn Green. When she finally left to return to Claridges, two weeks later, the derelict vicarage and its garden were hers. The village had not had so much to gossip about in years.

'The appearance of the Prodigal in their midst certainly put the cat among the pigeons,' Harriet said with a grin. 'Or am I mixing metaphors?'

She was watching Kathleen get Piers ready for bed. In another four days they would all be returning to New York in time for Christmas.

'You're glad you went now, aren't you?' Kathleen asked, lifting Piers out of the bath and enveloping him in a big fluffy towel. 'Did you see anyone you knew?'

'Mrs Wicks, who used to keep house for Dad and me. Two old friends, Susan Wyatt and Leslie Norman. They're married now, to each other. But I don't think anyone was really pleased to see me. People didn't like me intruding.'

'Jealous, most like,' Kathleen answered briskly, rubbing Piers dry. 'Understandable, I suppose. You make them feel like failures.'

'Oh, no!' Harriet was shocked by the notion, then realized that of course Kathleen was right. English people in general did not care for success; they thought it brash and offensive. The villagers would resent the money she was going to spend on making the vicarage habitable again, and, even more, the fact that she would not be there

239

all that often. It would not matter what she did for the village, or how much cash she poured into the Church Restoration Fund; even while they accepted her money and put it to good use, they would ostracize her. She shrugged. She could not let it worry her. The Old Vicarage, as it was now to be known, was her home, and she would not let anyone drive her away.

She spent the next two days interviewing some of the best interior decorators and builders in London, telling them exactly what she wanted done, and it was not until twenty-four hours before she was due to leave for New York that she went to see Hallam. It was a visit she had been putting off ever since her arrival but, as she had told Ken Lambert, there were things she needed to discuss with him. The previous day, Ken had informed her that another large sum of money had been transferred to her husband's private account.

'I didn't prevent it,' the accountant said woodenly, 'because you made it perfectly clear that Mr Cavendish can take what he wants, and no questions asked.' But Ken's whole attitude intimated that it was high time she did something about it.

'All right,' she agreed wearily, 'I'll go and see Hallam tomorrow. That's a promise.'

Hallam, when he was in London, lived in Cheyne Walk, Chelsea. The row of elegantly proportioned eighteenth-century houses was built on the site of Henry VIII's old manor, overlooking the river. Rossetti had lived there, and so had George Eliot under her real name of Mary Ann Evans. It looked a peaceful backwater, out of the main-stream of London life. Just the place, Harriet thought grimly, for Hallam to pursue his nefarious dealings.

She drove there the following morning in the hired Aston Martin. Ronald Hutton, stuffily English, deplored this habit of chauffeuring herself everywhere she went.

'Apart from the fact that it's slightly *infra dig* for a woman in your position,' he had once dared to point out to

240

her, 'it's also rather risky. You're a very rich woman, my dear. You need some protection.'

She had laughed at his well-meant concern for her safety; but today, visiting her husband, she felt she might have been more comfortable with a man waiting outside for her in the car.

It was a feeling reinforced by the sight of an American-style limousine drawn up in front of Hallam's house and the two men getting into it. Harriet thought she had rarely seen two uglier-looking customers. One had obviously done some boxing in his time, having a broken nose and a cauliflower ear. Both were big and burly and could have been mistaken for nightclub bouncers, except that they were far too well dressed. The older one sported a flashy diamond tie-pin, and the gleam of gold at their wrists proclaimed very large and very expensive watches. Their similarity of feature suggested they were brothers, and Harriet found their moon-shaped faces disturbingly familiar.

Hallam was standing on the pavement, talking to them, and as the men got into the back of the chauffeur-driven car he bent down to the open window for a final word. There was a burst of laughter from all three; and as Harriet locked the door of the Aston Martin it suddenly came to her where she had seen her husband's visitors before. Although she no longer made the rounds of her New York restaurants as frequently as she had once done, she nevertheless retained her habit of reading the British and American morning papers. In recent months, the British press had been full of the shady dealings of the King brothers: Albie and Charlie, as they were known to their friends. And those friends included quite a number of well-known people: small-time actors and actresses, would-be television personalities and society hangers-on. There were even one or two more established names on the list, although the truly famous tended to avoid them.

No one knew for certain what Albie and Charlie King did for a living, but everyone agreed it had to be crooked. For the sons of a Smithfield meat porter without visible means of support, they had done extremely well for themselves. Their names had been linked with nearly all of London's major crimes of the past few years, but the police had been unable to proceed against them for lack of evidence. Witnesses, when they could be found, mysteriously disappeared or, more often, simply changed their testimony. It was generally accepted that the King brothers made the bulk of their fortune from the extortion racket but, again, nothing could be proved.

Harriet had parked a little way down the road, and Hallam did not see her until she was abreast of him. He was looking in the opposite direction, watching the brothers' car as it disappeared in the direction of Chelsea Embankment.

'Hello, Hallam,' she said, and he jumped. When he first turned his head, he looked put out and annoyed. He recovered rapidly, however, smiling and dutifully pecking her cheek.

'My dear! What an unexpected pleasure! To what do I owe the honour of this visit?'

'You haven't changed,' she told him bluntly. 'You still talk like a bad thirties play.'

He flushed angrily, but continued to smile. 'Such compliments,' he murmured. 'Shall we go inside?'

Indoors, Hallam showed her into what was obviously his study, on the ground floor. Harriet glanced around her. She knew enough of furniture and paintings by now to be sure of recognizing the genuine article when she saw it. The desk was Sheraton, as was the corner cupboard, containing books. The oil painting on the wall above the desk was a James Henry Crossland. There had been a couple of cheap reproductions of his Lake District landscapes in her father's bedroom at the vicarage, but Harriet had no doubt that this was an original.

Hallam waved her into a dark-green leather-upholstered armchair by the window.

'Coffee?' he suggested. 'Sherry? Or is it too early in the

day for you to drink? I really know so very little about you, my dear. We've spent such a short time together.'

'Nothing for me, thank you,' Harriet answered shortly.

'Then, I trust you won't object if I do.' Hallam crossed to a tambour-topped table, where a whisky-decanter and glasses were already set out. Three of the tumblers were dirty. He selected a clean one and poured himself a generous whisky and soda. 'I hear you took the boy down to the Hall recently. The parents were delighted. I understand he's a credit to both of us.'

'If you came to see him more often, you might be able to judge for yourself,' Harriet retorted acidly, but she did not press the point. The last thing she wanted was for Piers to fall under his father's influence. Instead, she demanded: 'What were those two crooks doing here?'

'You recognized them?' Hallam perched on the edge of the desk, sipping his whisky. 'Albie and Charlie would be gratified. But, on second thoughts, perhaps not. They wouldn't like you to call them crooks. Neither has ever been convicted of so much as a traffic offence.'

'Only because they've either bought off, or bumped off, the witnesses.'

'You know, that's slander,' Hallam pointed out gently. 'Albie and Charlie would be most upset.'

'*I'm* upset,' Harriet retorted angrily. 'You're bleeding me white with your insatiable demands for money.' Both knew this to be a wild exaggeration, but accepted it in the spirit in which it had been meant. 'I make you a more than generous allowance! There's no need for you to overspend! And I will not have company money used to finance thugs like the King brothers!'

There was a sadistic gleam in Hallam's blue eyes.

'You, my dear, have no say at all in the matter, unless you want to be involved in a nasty little scandal. I still have my dossier on your friend Edmund Howard tucked away in a bank vault somewhere. You probably wouldn't go to prison after all this time, but it could still stir up some very muddy water. Eddie's a successful horse-breeder nowa-

243

days, I hear. It wouldn't do him much good in this country to be branded a friend of the IRA. It wouldn't do you any good, either, just as you're about to open all these new restaurants over here. You note, I hope, that I keep up to date with all your doings. So I'd leave me and my friends well alone, if I were you. Was that all you came to see me about?'

Harriet clenched her hands over the clasp of her handbag.

'I want a divorce. You have your heir and I'll see you're well provided for. But I want to be shot of you.'

Hallam swallowed the last of his drink and got up to fetch himself another. Slowly, and with a look of spurious regret, he shook his head.

'I'm sorry, my dear, but I have absolutely no intention of letting you go.' The decanter chinked against the rim of his glass as he poured the whisky. 'Where would be the point? This way, I know you'll look after me for the rest of my life. It would be foolish to throw that away for however large a lump settlement. And our son needs both his parents.'

'Don't give me that pious crap! What have you ever done for him?'

Hallam contrived to look hurt. 'I saw to it that he's entered for my own old house at Harrow. Could any father do more?'

'It wasn't your influence that got him in,' Harriet snapped. 'It was your father's.' She steadied her voice. 'Please, Hallam, let me go. I've told you, I'll make it worth your while.'

He came back to her chair and stood smiling down at her.

'And I've told you, my dear, I just can't afford it.'

Something about the smile, half leer, half triumphant grin, broke what remained of her self-control. She jumped to her feet.

'We'll see about that!' she said furiously. 'It's time you were taught a lesson!'

She had just time enough to hear him say: 'And it's time

you were taught one as well,' before she was winded by his knee jabbing into her stomach. Then he hit her and kept on hitting her.

At first, she felt nothing but fear. The blows which sent her sprawling on the floor registered no hurt to begin with. All she could think about was the blaze of lunatic rage in Hallam's eyes. He was mad, she thought, terrified. Temporarily insane. Then her terror gave way to dozens of darting, shooting pains. She could taste blood on her tongue from a split lip, which was rapidly swelling, and a kick in the groin had her doubled up in agony. An arm flung up to protect her face received a blow from his fist which made her scream. For a moment, she wondered if the bone were broken, but found that she could still use it to defend herself, so assumed that it was not. She curled up into a ball, her hands locked behind her neck.

The onslaught ended abruptly. When, at last, she dared to raise her head, Hallam was leaning against the desk, breathing fast; but, as she watched, the blood-lust died out of his eyes, and his livid features assumed their normal, rather bland expression.

'Don't. . .' he was still panting a little. 'Don't ever threaten me again.'

Anger began to replace Harriet's fear. Slowly, she tried to get up, dragging herself on to the seat of the armchair. She hurt all over, and the left side of her face felt as big as a football. There was a persistent throbbing ache in her stomach, and she was afraid she was going to be sick. Little things began to assume a ridiculous importance. Her stockings were laddered, and the lapel of her coat was ripped. Her handbag had fallen open when she dropped it, and its contents were spilled all over the floor. Carefully, painfully, as though her very life depended on it, she started to pick them up and tidy them away. Hallam made no move to help her.

She felt debased and degraded; physically dirty. Everything she was wearing would have to be burned. The only thing she wanted at the moment was to immerse her

245

bruised and battered body in a long soothing bath. But, first, she had something to say to Hallam.

She pulled herself upright, using the edge of the desk as a lever. Because Hallam was slumped against it, he had momentarily lost the advantage of height. Their eyes were on a level with one another's.

Harriet found it difficult to speak out of her cracked and swollen mouth, but she forced herself to ignore the pain.

'I won't forget this,' she said, as calmly as she could. 'You may hold the whip hand now, but I'll do anything to get rid of you, so be warned. Because when there's no one to pay your debts and support your extravagant way of life, you could well find yourself in Carey Street.' She began to laugh on a rising tide of hysteria. 'That's funny! That's really funny! Not Carey Hall, but Carey Street!' She made an enormous effort and managed, at last, to control herself. 'You'll regret today.'

She wasn't sure how much of this speech her husband had understood: however hard she tried, her broken lips had refused to form some of the words. But Hallam's look of unease suggested that he had grasped the gist of it. He shot out a hand and gripped her left wrist, making her yelp with pain.

'Don't try anything, Harriet, or you'll regret it. One sign of trouble from you, and that file on Edmund Howard goes straight to the police.'

But he continued to look worried, as well he might, she thought. Perhaps he realized that he had overplayed his hand.

He released her. After a moment's hesitation, he said: 'I'm sorry that things went a bit over the top. But I've the devil of a temper, as you know, and I can't always control it. You shouldn't threaten me. It's asking for trouble.'

'And I got it, didn't I?' In the face of his growing agitation, she suddenly felt calm. She nodded towards the telephone on his desk. 'Will you call me a taxi, please? I'd do it myself, but I'm not sure they'd understand what I'm saying. I'll send someone round to collect my car after I get back to the hotel.'

He did as she asked, a measure of the guilt that he was feeling.

They waited for its arrival in total silence. Refusing his offer of support, Harriet made her way to the hall and sat on an upright Regency chair, until she heard the taxi draw up outside.

'Harriet!' Hallam said, watching her from the study doorway.

She ignored him. She also ignored the appalled exclamation of the taxi-driver, when she opened the front door to him.

'Bleedin' 'ell, missus! 'Oo's bin doin' you over?' His glance sought out Hallam. 'Was it 'im? D'you want me to get the police?'

'No, thank you,' Harriet said firmly. 'Just drive me to Claridges.' She glanced back at her husband. Their eyes met briefly. Then she turned away.

26

'What you need is a holiday.' June Grazini had been taking dictation. Now she flipped her notebook shut and stuck her pencil behind her ear. 'You haven't been well since ... since before Christmas.'

Harriet frowned. Was she looking that bad? She had never known her secretary to pass a comment before on her state of health. They usually both took it for granted that Harriet was blooming. For a woman only a few months short of her thirty-ninth birthday, she kept remarkably fit. She couldn't recall the last time she had so much as caught a cold.

It was true, however, that since that morning in early December when Hallam had beaten her up she had suffered from recurring headaches, slept badly and felt generally under the weather. But she disliked the idea of cosseting herself, of taking a holiday. What would she do on a holiday? She would be bored to tears by the end of a week. She had never forgotten those endless months when Gus was dying; how heavily the time had hung on her hands. She had known then that she needed a constant diet of work to keep her going. Nevertheless, there was no escaping the fact that she did not feel completely well.

It was part of the conspiracy of silence amongst all her staff that June Grazini did not refer specifically to the incident with Hallam. When Harriet had returned to Claridges, she had called everyone together, told them in as few words as possible what had happened, and then forbidden them to mention the incident ever again.

To begin with, no one had paid any attention to her wishes. During the first horrified reaction to her injuries, there had been a general clamour to notify the police. Ken Lambert had been with difficulty restrained from going round to Cheyne Walk and beating up Hallam in his turn. Kathleen Tettenburg had forgotten years of careful training and declared that 'the fuckin' bastard wouldn't half feel it if I got me bleedin' 'ands on 'im!' June Grazini had been all in favour of hiring a bed in a private clinic, so that Harriet's injuries could receive professional attention.

'We go home tomorrow, as planned,' Harriet had snapped through bruised lips. 'And I mean what I say! I don't want to hear another word about this affair from any of you. I shall deal with it in my own time and in my own way.'

Brave words! But she had no more idea now than she had then what she could do about it. As long as Hallam held – or said he held – information relating to herself and Edmund, she was powerless to proceed against him. He could get away with anything, including drawing ever larger sums of money each month from company funds. And some of that money was undoubtedly financing the King brothers. British press reports suggested that Albie and Charlie were as active as ever. And they were confident enough to have been prominent, last month, among the crowds filing past Sir Winston Churchill's catafalque in Westminster Hall during the lying in state. They had lingered ostentatiously in silent prayer beside the coffin.

Harriet drummed her fingers on the desk-top, lost in thought, but when she realized her secretary was watching her curiously she pulled herself together.

'That's all for today, June. When you've finished typing those letters, you can go home. Looks like it might snow.'

June Grazini nodded and got up; a tall thin girl with dark hair and eyes, always elegant and fashion-conscious. Her tailored grey skirt, Harriet noticed, was already an inch above the knee, in accordance with current trends on both sides of the Atlantic.

'Thanks. And don't stay too late yourself. I think you could be right about the snow. It's bitter, even for February.' She hesitated before adding: 'I wish you'd think about what I said. About taking a vacation, I mean.'

'I'll consider it, I promise,' Harriet said, not mentioning that it was all she intended to do.

Later, however, driving home through the first pale flurries of snow, reading the depressing headlines on the news-vendors' stands – the latest update on the assassination of Malcolm X – feeling the all too familiar symptoms of yet another headache, she thought that perhaps she ought to get away for a while. The apartment felt lonely, now that Michael had returned to school after the holidays, and Kathleen had taken Piers to the newly acquired farm in Connecticut. Kathleen had never really liked New York and considered it an unhealthy place to raise a child. So there were just Harriet and Jeanette Baynton rattling around in the twelve-room penthouse. And tonight was Jeanette's evening off.

After a solitary dinner, eaten in front of the television set, Harriet settled down to read some of the reports she had brought home with her. But she could not concentrate. The words straggled across the page in an endless procession of meaningless dots and squiggles. The pain in her head grew steadily worse. Just after the New Year, Harriet had reluctantly consulted a doctor, haunted by the fear that Hallam had done her a permanent injury. To her intense relief, she was assured that what she was experiencing was a bad bout of delayed shock, which would pass in time. She recollected that the doctor, too, had urged her to take a holiday.

She pushed the reports aside and picked up *Harper's Magazine*, lying with other periodicals on a table beside her armchair. She flicked impatiently through the pages, waiting for the headache to ease, now that she was not concentrating so fiercely. Suddenly, her attention was caught by a full-page photograph of the Acropolis, and she let the magazine fall open on her lap. The white sunlit columns of the Parthenon rose against the impossibly brilliant blue of a cloudless sky. Opposite was a smaller but no less compelling picture of the monastery at Daphni.

The glory that was Greece... Who had written that? Milton? No. *Athens, the eye of Greece, mother of arts/ And eloquence...* That was Milton. Wasn't it someone unexpected, like Edgar Allan Poe? Edmund would have known at once, but she mustn't think of that. She suddenly found her eyes were full of tears. She began to sob, loud rasping intakes of breath, rocking herself backwards and forwards in the chair, beating her fists impotently against its arms. There seemed to be two of her: one, the grief-racked pitiable creature in the pool of amber light cast by the table-lamp; the other, her real self, standing in the shadows, unable to help and more than a little frightened. She thought desperately: I have to stop this! Stop it! Stop it! Stop it! But the woman in the chair refused to obey her. She just went on rocking more and more frenziedly.

The telephone rang, its shrill clamorous bell tearing up the silence of the room and jerking her back to normality. She was a whole person once again, but her knees buckled as she rose to her feet and staggered across the room to answer it. She managed to save herself by clutching at the back of the couch.

'Hello?'

'Hello, Harriet? Francis Derham here.'

'Francis Derham? Oh . . . oh, yes. How are you, Frank?'

'No different than when you saw me this afternoon. Are you OK? You sound kinda weird.'

'Do I?' Harriet clenched the receiver tightly and drew a deep steadying breath. 'No, I'm fine. I was asleep,' she lied. 'I was dozing over some reports I brought home to read.'

'As a matter of fact, that's what I'm calling about. The report on the proposal to open a Last Chance in Athens. I originally said I was against the idea, but I've changed my mind. I've been giving it a lot of thought, and I've decided it might be a good thing to branch out into eastern Europe. It doesn't always do to play safe.'

Athens! Was there a project to open a restaurant in Athens? Harriet broke into a cold sweat. She really was losing her grip.

'I – er – I haven't read that particular report yet, Frank, but thanks for letting me know you've changed your mind. That's useful. It'll help me when I make my final decision.'

'Yeah. I figured you'd want to know. I must dash now. We've tickets for *Man of La Mancha*, and I can hear Judy hollerin' that we're going to be late.'

'Right. Enjoy yourselves. 'Bye.'

Harriet hung up and went into the kitchen to make coffee. She was shivering and felt weak, as though recovering from a long and debilitating illness. In the end, she rejected the coffee for that great British panacea, a nice cup of tea. Why was a cup of tea always referred to as 'nice'? she wondered. Wasn't there such a thing as a nasty cup of tea? By keeping her thoughts firmly fixed on such trivialities, she managed to shut out whatever demons had been possessing her, and went back to her chair in a calmer frame of mind. The tea, hot and very sweet, soothed her frayed nerves still further, and she searched through the pile of reports for the one on Athens. How odd that she should have been looking at that photograph of the Acropolis earlier. It was one of those coincidences which almost seemed like fate.

The headache had gone, released by her hysteria, but in its place was a terrible lethargy. She would have a really early night, Harriet decided. She would finish reading the reports, including the one on Athens, before she went to the office in the morning. She smiled to herself. She had not been in bed before nine o'clock in the evening since she was a child.

But, although she fell asleep as soon as her head touched the pillow, she was troubled by dreams. In one particularly vivid one, she and Leslie Norman were trekking through an endless expanse of woods near Winterbourn Green, looking for something. She was weeping silently: she could feel the tears running down her face. Leslie Norman, as she

252

remembered him from their youth, not as she had last seen him, a staid married man, kept asking her what it was that they were searching for. But she didn't know, and that seemed to make it so much worse. . .

Harriet woke with a start. The hands of her illuminated bedside-clock pointed to three-thirty in the morning. She really had been crying: her cheeks were wet. And suddenly she knew what she had been looking for so hopelessly in her dream. She had been looking for her and Gerry's child.

She switched on the overhead light and sat up. This simply would not do! She had to get a hold of herself; put the past behind her, including the beating she had taken from Hallam. Perhaps June was right. She needed a holiday. Somewhere different. Not America. Not England. Of course! Greece.

The answer was so simple, she couldn't think why she had not thought of it at once. She would go to Athens. If they were thinking of opening a restaurant there, she would do the preliminary survey. Alone. Well, perhaps not entirely alone. She'd take June and Ken Lambert with her. They would be company for one another when she decided to go off by herself. Ken's marriage was on the rocks anyway. Everyone knew that. June Grazini might be just what he needed.

Harriet switched out the light and snuggled down in bed again. She felt peaceful and relaxed, as though a huge burden had been lifted from her shoulders, like Christian at the end of *The Pilgrim's Progress*. A few moments later, she was deeply and dreamlessly asleep.

She fell in love with Athens from the moment she first saw it. Not with the brash tourist-infested hotels and their terrible food; not even with the Acropolis and the Parthenon, crowded as they were with hundreds of other eager, loud-voiced, sweating and pushing sightseers; but with the old town below the Acropolis, the Plaka.

Harriet loved everything about it; the maze of narrow streets with the press of shops, selling jewellery and sponges, ironwork, pottery and goods beautifully tooled in delicately coloured leathers. Roast-chestnut vendors plied their wares on almost every corner; and lottery-ticket salesmen, carrying sticks festooned with slips of paper, appeared, seemingly from nowhere, in the midst of any crowd, however small. And at night the whitewashed roof-top cafés throbbed to the rhythms of the bouzouki players.

By the end of her first week, Harriet had become the possessor of three pairs of sandals, made to measure while she waited, half a dozen 'evil eye' charms, two strings of 'worry' beads and innumerable belts, shoe-laces and other souvenirs, bought from the roadside kiosks. None of which, apart from the sandals, she either wanted or had any use for. She simply could not resist the charm of the Greek shopkeepers.

She left Ken Lambert, ably assisted by the competent June, to make the necessary contacts, approach the correct officials and grease any palms that needed greasing.

'I trust you,' she told Ken blithely, and went off to see the monastery at Daphni, with its collection of Byzantine mosaics, including the superb Christ Pantocrator in the dome. Greece was having an odd effect on her: she felt like a child who had escaped its leading-strings for the very first time. The beautiful April weather contributed to her general state of euphoria. She had needed this holiday!

The mood lasted precisely a week. On the Sunday morning after their arrival in Athens, Harriet woke up in her hotel bedroom, the old sense of boredom gnawing away inside her. She had had enough of her own company, of sightseeing, of behaving like a tourist. All she wanted now was to get back to work. Ken Lambert, who had promised himself a well-deserved day off, was justifiably incensed to be summoned to a working breakfast in Harriet's sitting-room, to report on his progress. His answers to her questions were terse.

Harriet frowned. She did not take kindly to mutiny among her subordinates, but her sense of fair play whispered that Ken had every right to be annoyed. She had left him to get on with things for the past seven days, and now, suddenly, she was back in charge, demanding to be put in the picture, messing up his day.

'Ken, I'm sorry,' she said contritely. 'Why don't you just tell me to go to hell?'

He grinned, his bad temper vanishing. 'Because I like my work and I don't want to find myself out of a job.'

'OK. Point taken. But is there anything I can do to make up for a week of neglect?'

He hesitated, then shrugged, helping himself to toast and marmalade; English marmalade, Harriet's favourite sort. It must be June who had organized that.

'I've been invited to a party this evening by Andreas Papidopolou, who owns the site we want to rent. It's at his apartment in Omonia Square. It's mainly a social thing, but there are sure to be some useful people present. I was going because I thought you didn't want to be involved. Not for the present, at any rate. But I'd really like to take June for a meal. There's a restaurant just round the corner where they do the most wonderful souvlaki, or so I've been told.'

'And you'd like me to go along to this Mr Papidopolou's in your place?'

'Would you? I've ordered a hire car for nine o'clock, if that's OK.'

'Of course I'll go. Give me the full address. I'll get June to telephone and say that I'm going instead.' Harriet eyed him thoughtfully. 'You and June seem to be hitting it off very well. Anything in it?'

Ken Lambert was taken aback. 'Hell, no! That is. . . Sure, I like the girl. But I'm not even divorced yet. My lawyers and Aileen's are still fighting over the settlement. I don't know if I'll be able to afford even to look at another woman.'

'OK! OK! But, if you do ever glance in June's direction in a serious way, let me know well in advance. Secretaries like her don't grow on trees.'

'If it ever happens, you'll be the first to know,' he promised.

They returned to discussing plans for the Athens Last Chance restaurant. When they had finished breakfast, Ken took himself off to his own suite, while Harriet pressed the bell for room service and a waiter to clear the table. Then she went to run her bath and to look through her wardrobe for something to wear that night. She stared at a choice of gowns by Hartnell, Balmain, Jacques Griffe, and remembered a young girl in a candle-lit vicarage bedroom, desperately trying to find something to wear to the village dance. She had wanted to impress Gerry Canossa. Dear God, how she had wanted to impress him! In the end, she had worn a blue wool dress, bought in the Bon Marché sale in Gloucester, and had been too hot for the rest of the evening.

She went back to the bathroom and turned off the taps. She had promised herself that she would not think about the past, and for a whole week she had avoided the subject. But, no matter how hard she tried, it would intrude. She kept thinking about Hilary, her lost child, now grown up. Twenty years old.

27

The main salon of the Papidopolou apartment in Omonia Square was so crowded that it was impossible to see from one end to the other. Within five minutes of her arrival, Harriet had recognized two film stars, one Greek and one American, the members of an English pop group, a well-known thriller-writer and various generals from the prevailing Greek military junta.

The women were showily gowned and dripping with jewels, making Harriet wish that she had taken a little more trouble with her appearance. At the last moment, feeling bored by the prospect of an evening of small talk with people she neither knew nor cared about, she had chosen at random the plain black Balmain dress, the pearl earrings which Gus had given her many Christmases ago and a diamond Tiffany brooch which she had bought for herself. On the third finger of her left hand she still wore Gus's wedding ring and the Victorian garnet which had originally belonged to his grandmother. The platinum band given her by Hallam was locked away in her New York safe, together with the square-cut emerald he had bought for her when they had first announced their engagement.

Mr Papidopolou, small and thin, and his large, fat, jolly wife were delighted and gratified to see her, overwhelming her with Greek hospitality. Unfortunately, with other people still arriving, they could do little more for the moment than express their warmest thanks to her for coming and usher her forward into the already overcrowded salon. A waiter offered her a tray of drinks, and she took one. After a minute or two, she made her way to a corner which seemed less heavily populated than the rest of the room. All the furniture had been pushed back against the walls, and here a couch stood at right angles to a deep armchair, a small table, supporting an enormous bronze-based lamp, between them. Harriet sank down into a corner of the couch and wondered what on earth had possessed her to come.

The noise was deafening. She sipped her drink, grateful to find that it was neither retsina nor ouzo, but a pleasantly light, non-resinated wine which she had tasted before, and which she had a vague idea came from the Peloponnese. She should have insisted on Ken escorting her; then at least she would have had someone to talk to. She had forgotten the indignity of being a wallflower. She wished to God she could see someone she knew, and thought suddenly of Mrs Allen in *Northanger Abbey*, always wishing for 'a large acquaintance'. She smiled, mocking herself gently.

'It amuses you, the human race?'

The voice, with its precisely spoken, slightly accented English, startled her. She had not noticed that the armchair was occupied, but now, turning her head, she became aware of someone watching her closely.

In the glow of the lamp, she saw a man considerably older than herself – sixty, sixty-one, maybe? – with thick grey hair waving back from a high forehead. Bushy grey eyebrows above a pair of very dark eyes and a prominent nose completed the picture. It was, Harriet decided, a Hellenic face, so often depicted on the sides of Greek urns and vases. The body belonging to it, immaculately dressed in a suit of dark blue worsted, was short and compact, with surprisingly long, narrow hands and feet.

In answer to the question, she said: 'Yes. Yes, I suppose it does. Always remembering, of course, that I'm part of it.'

'Ah, yes,' he agreed and smiled. The action transformed his rather sour appearance, lighting him up from within. It was a real smile, of a kind which Harriet seemed not to have encountered for a very long time, and which contrasted vividly with the politely insincere grimaces all around them. 'It is a great mistake to take oneself too seriously. That is what I admire most about you British; the ability to laugh at yourselves, even in the most disadvantageous situations.'

'How do you know I'm British?' she asked curiously. 'I might be American. In fact, I've lived in New York for almost twenty years.'

She expected some quick and facile answer about her still having an English accent, but her companion paused, considering, his head tilted to one side.

'Europeans,' he said after a moment, carefully searching for the words to express himself correctly, 'have much older faces than their transatlantic cousins. You can still recognize medieval features. You can still see what their ancestors looked like. Americans, because of the ... the blending of so many different nationalities, have lost those racial characteristics. Except, perhaps, in the remoter, more isolated parts of the country, where groups exist who have not intermarried and become part of the greater whole.'

'How extraordinary!' Harriet exclaimed. 'You must be a thought-reader. Only a moment ago, I was thinking what a very Greek face you have. It reminds me of something on an urn.' She set down her empty glass and held out her hand. 'My name's Harriet Cavendish.'

He responded with 'Spiros Georgiadis', and paused fractionally, as though expecting some reaction from her. When none came, he went on: 'I know who you are, of course. You own the Chance Corporation.'

'You're very well informed. I didn't think my name was that well known.'

'You underestimate your importance in the financial world.'

'Do I? Yes, perhaps.' She looked into the brown eyes, so steadily regarding her, and said impulsively: 'My father

259

was the vicar of a small rural parish, and I had a conventional middle-class English upbringing. Maybe that doesn't mean much to you as a . . . as a. . .'

'Foreigner?' He cocked an amused eyebrow at her. 'I lived in England for many years, so I was able to study the species at first hand.'

That made her laugh. 'Then, maybe you do understand what I mean. That sort of childhood is restricted. There are all kinds of dos and don'ts. Standards. Shibboleths.' She glanced at him to make sure that he did indeed understand what she was trying to say. He nodded encouragement, and she went on: 'At least, it was like that when I was young. Things may be changing now, I don't know. It's just that, sometimes, I feel like two people. . . Am I making any sense to you at all?'

'Oh, yes, I think so.' Spiros Georgiadis gestured with one of his beautiful hands. 'I was born in the slums of Athens, eight years before the outbreak of the First World War.' He must be fifty-nine, then, some time this year, Harriet thought, doing a couple of lightning calculations in her head. Younger than she had imagined him to be. He continued: 'I knew what real poverty was; what crime was. That it was necessary to be absolutely ruthless to survive. So I have no inhibitions about being a very rich man. You, on the other hand, the daughter of a priest, brought up to embrace certain morals and values. . . Yes, you would be bound to have this dichotomy of feeling, even more so because you are a woman. Women are not expected to be ruthless or successful or to use people.' His eyes twinkled. 'Especially not after we men have trained you for centuries to be soft and gentle and clinging.'

'You're an exceptional man,' Harriet said warmly. 'And you speak beautiful English. You make me ashamed. My Greek is confined to "ochi" and "né", and even those I get mixed up. I'm always saying "yes" when I mean "no".'

'A dangerous practice,' her companion answered lightly. 'Perhaps it might help you to remember which is which, if I tell you that on the twenty-eighth of October every year we Greeks celebrate Ochi Day. It commemorates the day in nineteen forty when General Metaxas said "no" to the Italian troops who wanted to cross the border into Greece from Albania. . . And here is our charming hostess, coming to rescue you from my clutches.'

Madame Papidopolou was bearing down on them like a small but determined tug, her podgy arms loaded with bracelets, a diamond choker set with stones of an almost unbelievable size and brilliance clasped about her short fat neck. Spiros Georgiadis rose at her approach and gallantly kissed her hand. He spoke rapidly in Greek, then turned and made a bow to Harriet.

'Good night, Mrs Cavendish. It has been a very great pleasure to talk to you.'

'You're surely not going already?' Harriet asked, then blushed, realizing that in her disappointment she was usurping her hostess's role.

'Alas, yes. I have, most unfortunately, another engagement. But I sincerely trust that we shall meet again very soon. Don't come with me, Melina.' He patted Madame Papidopolou's plump cheek affectionately. 'I'll find Dimitri on my way out.'

He was gone, swallowed up by the press of bodies, which was denser than ever.

'Who is he? I mean, what does he do?' Harriet asked. For the past half-hour, she had enjoyed herself more than she had done in years at this sort of gathering. Spiros Georgiadis was the first man since her father and Edmund who had really understood her. Perhaps he had understood her even better than Edmund because he was older; much nearer her father's generation in age.

Madame Papidopolou looked astounded at Harriet's question. Her three chins wobbled in united disbelief.

'You don't know who zat was?' She emitted an incredulous ear-splitting shriek of dismay, which had every head in the vicinity bobbing round to see what was happening. 'Spiros Georgiadis is one of richest men in world. He is shipping millionaire. Multi-multi-millionaire.' The hands

261

gesticulated wildly, two dimpled butterflies performing some exotic mating ritual. 'He able to buy up everyone in zis room.'

Considering the assembled company, Harriet was inclined to think this a wild exaggeration. She was to learn her mistake.

'Spiros Georgiadis?' Ken Lambert breathed reverently. 'Dear sweet God in heaven!'

He, June and Harriet were having breakfast in Harriet's suite the following morning. June was looking her usual cool and businesslike self in a white linen shirtwaist dress, with an antique silver brooch set with turquoises pinned to one of the lapels. Harriet had not seen it before, and guessed that it was a present from Ken, an assumption she considered justified by her secretary's air of quiet satisfaction, and the way in which she unconsciously fingered the jewel from time to time. In spite of all Ken's protestations, he must like June Grazini quite a lot. Last night must have gone very well indeed.

Harriet, however, had had no chance, as yet, to ask. Ken's enquiries about her own evening had elicited the fact of her meeting with Spiros Georgiadis; and mention of the Greek's name appeared to have sent her chief accountant into a catatonic trance. He kept saying 'Oh my! Oh my!' until Harriet requested him, with some asperity, to stop behaving like Mr Toad catching his first sight of a motor-car.

'He's rich, Harriet,' Ken Lambert said, awe-struck. 'And when I say rich, do I mean rich! Like Croesus! Like Midas! Like the pair of them rolled into one! Aristotle Onassis? Forget him! Peanuts compared with this guy.'

The two women looked at one another, each vainly trying to visualize the sort of wealth which reduced the Onassis fortune to peanuts. Their minds boggled. In the end, they gave it up.

The brilliant spring sunshine flooded through the open windows, and a faint breeze ruffled the long white curtains. The light was transparent, completely different from anything Harriet had experienced before. Its clarity was dazzling. She loved it, but at the same time it made her homesick for the valleys of the Windrush and the Evenlode, and the first soft flush of green which, even now, would be starting to blur the view. Through the window, she caught a glimpse of the library and tower – the Tower of the Winds – built by the Emperor Hadrian nearly two hundred years before Christ was born; but in her mind's eye she saw the grey huddled roofs of Winterbourn Green. Two people; always she was two people. Spiros Georgiadis had understood. Just for a moment, yesterday evening, he had made her whole again.

There was a knock at the door. June got up and went to answer it, returning with a sheaf of deep red roses, wrapped in the silver and grey paper of Athens's most expensive florist.

'For you,' she said, laying them in Harriet's lap.

There was a card with the simple message: 'Thank you for talking to me last night. I should very much like to renew our acquaintance. Will you have dinner with me some time?' It was signed 'Spiros Georgiadis' and there was a telephone number scribbled underneath.

Silently, Harriet passed the card to June, who read it with Ken Lambert looking over her shoulder.

'Spiros Georgiadis has never been married, you know,' Ken said at last, raising his head and staring speculatively at Harriet across the débris of their breakfast. 'Mistresses, yes. One after another. A whole series of them, if the gossip is to be believed. But he's never actually tied the knot. He has the reputation of being something of a misogynist. Although he's noted for his generosity, he's treated his women with a fair amount of contempt. Georgia Tyson, the film star, was one of his floozies before she made the grade in Hollywood. An actress friend of Aileen's, who's worked with her, reckons she can't say anything bad enough about him.'

'You seem remarkably well informed,' Harriet commented waspishly. She was feeling more than a little foolish because she had never even heard of Spiros. He must, she concluded, be a very reclusive man, or she surely would have read something about him at some time during her daily perusals of the newspapers. Ken confirmed this with his next remark.

'Oh, I keep my ear to the ground all the time where men like Spiros are concerned. Especially when they're as publicity-shy as he is. Maybe that's why he's avoided matrimony for so long. He doesn't get all the hassle and notoriety that divorce and alimony settlements and court-cases attract.'

Harriet's eyes narrowed. She was beginning to follow the workings of Ken Lambert's mind.

'Ken,' she said drily, 'I'm a married woman, remember? And I'm not interested in becoming anybody's mistress.' She stood up to go into the bedroom and get dressed. 'Neither am I interested in money, especially not Mr Georgiadis' money, which seems to me to be totally unreal.'

Ken managed to look confused and yet shocked by her final heresy at one and the same time.

'I wasn't suggesting... Honestly, Harriet, I wasn't hinting for a moment... I mean... Hell! It was just some information I thought you'd like to have, particularly if you're dining with the guy. Put you on your guard,' he added, trying to appear ingenuous.

Harriet laughed, asked June to see about putting the roses in water, and went through to her bedroom, shutting the communicating door.

It was a large room, impeccably furnished in shades of grey and a very pale oyster pink, but impersonal, as was all hotel accommodation. A television set stood, unused, in one corner. Greek television programmes left Harriet floundering.

She lifted the receiver of the bedside telephone and asked for the number on Spiros' card. When it rang, a female voice answered, speaking in Greek.

264

'Mr Georgiadis, please,' Harriet said firmly in English. 'This is Harriet Cavendish. My call is expected, I think.'

'It is, indeed,' said Spiros' voice, cutting into the conversation. He gabbled something else rapidly in Greek, and there was a click as the lady, who was presumably his secretary, cleared her line. Spiros went on: 'But I didn't dare hope to hear from you quite so soon.'

'I want to thank you for the beautiful roses,' Harriet said, 'and to apologize for not recognizing your name. You must think me an ignorant fool.'

'On the contrary, I found it refreshing. It is what I should have expected from a daughter of the vicarage.'

Harriet burst out laughing.

'What an odious description! Assure me that you didn't make it up.'

'No, no!' He, too, was laughing. She could hear the rich satisfying chuckle at the other end of the line. 'I read it somewhere. In one of your English newspapers, I think.'

'That figures. There's no one can turn a triter phrase than our gossip columnists. Daughter of the vicarage! It conjures up visions of the Brontës, and I don't think we've anything in common at all.'

'Nothing,' he agreed. 'For a start, you do not have an overheated imagination. You are a very cool and calculating lady.'

'And which sort of woman do you prefer?' she asked in a bantering tone. But, suddenly, she found that his answer mattered to her quite a lot.

'Your sort, of course. Do you really need to ask? I think the Brontës would have been very uncomfortable to live with. They would have expected such impossible things. And I am too old to be a Heathcliffe or a Mr Rochester. So, now we have established that fact, will you have dinner with me this evening, at my apartment? I should very much like to continue the conversation we started yesterday, and which Melina Papidopolou interrupted with such misplaced solicitude for our joint welfare. I, at least, have never been in less need of rescuing.'

'Nor me,' Harriet said. 'And thank you, I should be most pleased to come this evening.'

'Good. Good. My car will pick you up at your hotel at eight o'clock. I obtained your address from my good friend Dimitri Papidopolou, in case you are wondering. I look forward to seeing you again very much indeed.'

The line went dead. Harriet sat staring at the receiver, still clutched in her hand.

28

Spiros' apartment, a block or two away from the Grande
Bretagne Hotel in Constitution Square, was at first sight
rather disappointing. There were no obvious signs of
wealth, except for a signed Paul Klee on one wall of the
main salon. The furniture was modern and could have
been bought in any one of half a dozen well-known department stores in Athens, London or New York.

'You expected more,' Spiros said with amusement, as he
took her thin silk coat.

'No, of course not!' Harriet protested. Then she grinned.
'Well, perhaps. Just a little more.'

'Of course you did. Harriet Chance from the vicarage
expects a multi-millionaire to have Old Masters on every
wall, to eat off gold plate and walk on ancient Persian rugs.
Isn't that so?'

'How well you seem to know this Harriet Chance,' she
countered lightly. She sat down on a long low couch,
upholstered in a beige floral cretonne, facing a window
which ran from floor to ceiling and looked down on the
bustling traffic of the Square. 'Don't forget she's also head
of the Chance Corporation.'

Spiros smiled. He looked older than she remembered
him from the previous evening. The face was heavily
lined, and there was a jaded expression in the dark eyes, as
though he had already lived too long and seen too much.
Harriet found it rather shocking.

'May I offer you a drink?' he asked formally, turning
towards a tray on a small table set back against the wall. 'I

won't offer you brandy. I have only Greek, and although it is Metaxa, the best of a bad bunch, it is still rough compared with Western vintages.' Again, Harriet felt a slight sense of disappointment. Was Spiros mean over small things, like so many millionaires? 'But,' he went on, 'you can have anything else you fancy. Name your poison.'

The outdated phrase was endearing. Harriet said: 'May I just have a fruit juice, please? I'm thirsty.'

He poured her fresh orange juice from a jug which he took out of a small refrigerator beside the table, and added ice from the bucket. It was long, cold and delicious.

He sat beside her on the couch, with a glass of ouzo in his hand.

'I like it,' he said, interpreting her glance, and she blushed.

'Yes, of course. I wasn't criticizing.'

He laughed. 'I have two yachts, a jet and an island in the Aegean,' he offered, quizzing her. 'A whole fleet of Rolls-Royces.'

'If you keep on like this, I'm going back to the hotel,' she threatened. 'I don't care for the way you keep reading my mind.'

'That would be a pity. It would ruin what could be a beautiful friendship.' A knock on the door heralded a waiter with a trolley. 'Ah! Dinner!' Spiros said, rising. 'I have all my meals sent up from the restaurant on the ground floor. I hope you don't mind.' His eyes crinkled at the corners, and suddenly he looked younger. 'I must apologize again for not having my own private chef. OK! OK! From now on I promise to behave.'

They ate on a wide balcony at the back of the apartment, overlooking a flagged courtyard, where a sorry-looking vine fretted against the south-facing wall. To start with, they had the stuffed vine leaves known as dolmathes, then kalamarakia, crisply fried pieces of young squid, accompanied by a green salad sprinkled with olives, followed by a cheeseboard and Greek coffee, very thick and sweet, and served in tiny cups. The wine was a full-bodied Naoussa from Macedonia. And all the time, while the light drained from the sky and the night lights of Athens began to prick the warm darkness, they chatted like old friends about books and films and plays, and about the differences between growing up in the slums of Athens and the vicarage at Winterbourn Green.

'I can talk to you,' Harriet said, leaning back in her chair and smiling at Spiros across the table. 'We only met twenty-four hours ago, and yet I feel I know you almost as well as I know myself. You remind me of my father.'

Spiros grimaced. 'I'm not sure whether to be flattered by that remark or not. There are, after all, only twenty years between us.'

'How do you know that?' she asked curiously. 'I don't recall telling you my age.'

'I'm afraid my secretary automatically checks up on anyone to whom I'm introduced. It is one of the less pleasant aspects of wealth. You have to be very careful who you trust. Shall we go inside now? It is growing chilly.'

They returned to the salon. Spiros flicked a switch, and immediately the room was suffused in a warm pinkish glow from a number of discreetly placed wall-lights. They reseated themselves on the couch, at a decorous distance from one another.

There was silence, during which Harriet remembered the two men, built like stevedores, she had noticed lurking in the entrance-hall of the apartment-block when she first arrived. Spiros had come down in the lift to meet her, and she recollected that he had nodded to them. At the time, she had assumed they were acquaintances of his. Now she realized they were bodyguards. Had they been carrying guns?

'A long way from Winterbourn Green, isn't it?' he asked quietly, and she jumped.

'You're still doing it,' she accused. 'Getting inside my head. It's unnerving, and I wish you'd stop it.'

269

'You're a rich woman yourself now. You must think like one. Accept the power that money gives you.'

Harriet smiled wryly. 'Oh, I do, believe me! But I was raised in a highly religious atmosphere, and the New Testament isn't very encouraging about the acquisition of wealth.'

'It's not only that, is it?' Spiros asked, after a pause. 'You feel guilty about the child you had adopted.'

She gasped and turned her head so that she was looking directly at him. She was no longer smiling.

'Your secretary does a very thorough job, doesn't she? Is it really necessary?'

'You're angry.' He made a movement as though to take one of her hands, but she moved it away. 'I'm sorry if you think I have been – what is the English word? – prying.'

'Well, haven't you?'

He shrugged, suddenly very Greek. She could see the shoulder muscles ripple under the white silk shirt. Beneath the biscuit-coloured trousers, his thighs were those of a powerfully built man. In his youth, she thought, he must have been very impressive. Come to think of it, he still was.

'I repeat, I am sorry,' he said. 'But it is necessary. There have been so many threats to my life, to my family – my mother, my sisters – that I have to make sure you are who you say you are. I have to know everything about you.'

Harriet was slightly mollified. 'OK. I accept that. But where do you get all your information from?'

'I have contacts. It is one of the advantages of my kind of money. I can buy almost anyone. Don't look so disapproving. At your age, you should know that.'

Harriet raised her eyebrows. 'You sound exactly like my husband.'

'I hope not. I do not like your husband, Mrs Cavendish.'

'That's something else we have in common.'

There was a protracted silence, during which Spiros got up and went to the drinks-table. This time, he did not ask

270

her what she wanted, but came back with a whisky, to which he had added water and some ice.

'Drink it,' he ordered, 'it will do you good.' He added abruptly: 'Why did you marry him?'

Harriet laughed shortly. 'It's a long story. I'm sure you don't want to hear it.'

'I should not have asked if I were not interested.' Spiros reached for her hand again, and this time she let him hold it. His long slender fingers were reassuringly strong. 'Why do you not tell me everything from the beginning?' he asked. 'I think you need to talk to someone. Why not me?'

She hesitated. She had known him for so short a time that it seemed all wrong to be burdening him with her problems. But she did need to talk to someone, to an impartial outsider; someone, moreover, who was older and wiser than she was. Spiros Georgiadis admirably fitted the bill.

And so she started and, once started, could not stop. It all came tumbling out: her father, Gerry Canossa, little Hilary, Gus, Michael, Edmund, Seamus Hogan, the Careys, Hallam, Piers; her ambitions, her ruthlessness, her guilt. Above all, her guilt, and the sense she had of having used people simply to further her ends.

It was quite dark by the time she had finished, the uncurtained windows oblongs of black slotted into the pale pinkish glow of the walls. The roar of traffic through Constitution Square was faintly audible, but neither Spiros nor Harriet noticed it. They had moved closer together, to the centre of the couch. He was no longer holding her hand, but had his arm about her shoulders. To Harriet, there was nothing romantic in the embrace. For the moment, Spiros had become a substitute father.

To her disgust, she found that she was crying. Impatiently, she wiped away the tears and blew her nose defiantly on the wisp of lace and cambric which she extracted from her evening bag.

'I'm sorry,' she said. 'I'm being a fool.'

Spiros did not answer immediately. Then he murmured: 'You love him very much, this Edmund Howard.'

'Yes. Yes, I suppose I do.'

'Would you like to be free of your husband?'

'Of course. I hate Hallam more than I ever thought it possible to hate anyone.'

'And then you would marry the Irishman, is that not so?'

'Oh, no!' Harriet put her handkerchief back in her purse and looked round in surprise. 'I told you, Edmund's married.'

'There is such a thing as divorce.'

She shook her head positively. 'I wouldn't break up his marriage, even if I could, and by all accounts it's a reasonably happy one. No, what was between Edmund and me is over. As long as I can keep him free of Hallam's clutches, that's all that matters to me now. And, anyway, this discussion is entirely academic. There's no way I can get rid of Hallam without endangering Edmund and myself. And my company.'

'Ah!' Spiros smiled. 'At last you begin to talk more like the woman who has built up something as big as the Chance Corporation, and less like a lovesick schoolgirl. No, don't fly out at me. I am just a poor Athenian who understands all about business and nothing whatsoever about love. God preserve us all from the sentimentality of the Germanic races!' Spiros removed his arm from around her shoulders and went on briskly: 'If you will leave everything to me, I predict that you will be free of your husband by the end of six months. This is April. In September, therefore, I shall ask you to marry me.'

'Hold on!' Harriet put a hand to her head. 'Mr Georgiadis –'

'You must call me Spiros if we are going to be married.'

'Mr Georgiadis,' she said firmly, 'I should be extremely grateful for your help, if I thought there was anything you could do. But, as I told you, I dare not risk a breach with Hallam. As long as he holds the information I told you about, my hands are tied.'

272

'This husband of yours, would he be prepared to face a long prison sentence, do you suppose? A sentence, say, of ten or twelve years.'

'No. . . I don't know. I shouldn't think so.'

'Not even for the sake of revenge?'

'Twelve years is a long time, and Hallam's no masochist. He likes the good things of life. But he wouldn't get anything like that, surely, for suppressing information?'

Spiros snorted. 'That! No, of course not! Not in England. I doubt if any of you would end up in prison after all these years. No. The damage your husband could do to you and to Mr Howard, as you have so rightly surmised, would be the damage of bad publicity, especially now, just as you are getting ready to open more restaurants in Britain. Yes, I know about that, too. I have done my – er – what is it? Homework? Yes. I have done my homework thoroughly.'

'Then, what are we talking about?' Harriet asked.

Spiros poured himself another whisky. He seemed able to hold his liquor without showing any ill effects. She noticed that he did not offer to replenish her glass. Instead, he offered her a cigarette, but she shook her head.

'No, thank you. I don't. I used to, occasionally, but not any more. I never really liked it. But you were saying,' she added impatiently, 'about Hallam. . .'

Spiros lit a cigar for himself, drawing on it heavily. The smoke rose ceilingwards, like stray wisps of pale blue nylon.

'You told me you saw your husband talking to the King brothers. You said they seemed friendly.'

'Very friendly.'

'Then, your husband, my dear, is bound to be up to his neck in shady dealing. You have a saying in English: "You cannot touch pitch without dirtying your hands." I have no doubt whatsoever that criminal proceedings – is that the correct phrase? – could be instituted against him.'

Harriet frowned. 'I should say that's very likely. But as the police have never succeeded in pinning anything on the Kings I think it highly improbable – forgive me! – that you could.'

Spiros chuckled. 'I have no desire to "pin anything", as you put it, on my very good friends, Albie and Charlie. Now you are looking shocked! But the sad fact is that I number quite a few people you would call criminals among my friends. From many different countries. Not all my money is made honestly.' The chuckle became a full-throated laugh. 'You know, you and I will be good for one another. A daughter of the vicarage and a child from the Athens slums.' He drew again on his cigar and went on: 'Albie King owes me a favour. A big favour. He will be persuaded, I am sure, to let me have all the necessary information regarding his deals with your husband.'

'And incriminate himself?' Harriet was sceptical. 'Hallam wouldn't believe it.'

'My dear, there are ways and means of arranging these things. Leave it to me. You need know nothing about it. Besides, I am not interested in sending your husband to prison. Merely in procuring for you a divorce, and a settlement in which you will not be bled white by that man. In the mean time, may I suggest that you begin to off-load some of that guilt you carry around with you by setting up a trust fund to aid some of your more deserving countrymen who are not in a position to help themselves?'

Harriet turned to him excitedly. 'A charitable trust! The Chance Trust! Spiros' – the name came out so naturally that she did not even notice that she had used it – 'you *are* clever!'

'My dear, I wonder you have not thought of it for yourself! A little philanthropy always makes your standing good in the eyes of the world. And it does wonders for your taxes.'

'What a cynical man you are.' She grinned broadly. 'Oddly enough, it's one of the most endearing things about you.'

'Only one? You mean I have more? I am flattered.'

'There you go again. . . Do you really think you can get Hallam to divorce me?'

'I am positive. And I have a vested interest in doing so, as I intend that you shall marry me instead.'

'We're strangers!' Harriet expostulated. 'We've only known one another for twenty-four hours.'

'I can make up my mind about something I want in twenty-four seconds. In this case, I have had a whole lifetime to decide what it is I am looking for in a woman. As soon as we started to talk last night, I knew that I had found it.'

'But . . . but you can't have fallen in love with me. You haven't had time.'

Spiros threw up his hands, the glowing tip of his cigar describing a fiery arc in the air.

'There speaks the sentimental Teuton again! Anglo-Saxon, Prussian, German, you're all the same! What has a successful marriage to do with love?' He smiled. 'But, if it makes you happier, you don't have to give me your answer now. When you are a free woman will be time enough. Then you can consider my proposal carefully and give me any answer you like, providing it is "yes"!'

Harriet laughed and leaned back in her corner of the couch. 'You really are the most extraordinary man.'

'Yes, I know.' His complacence was tempered by the twinkle in his eyes. 'May I make another suggestion, if you won't think it presumptuous of me?'

'What's that?'

'That you try to trace your adopted child. I do not advise that, when you have found Hilary, you make yourself known. But you can keep an eye open for your child's interests and welfare. It may be that no helping hand from you will ever be needed, but you will be in touch if ever it is.'

Harriet's heart began to beat faster. Locate Hilary? Could she? Dare she?

'I have no idea who the adoptive parents were. Where they lived. Anything.'

'Your father's solicitors would have a record of the agency used. Start with them. But if, as I suspect, they won't reveal the identity of the parents I know of a very

275

good detective agency, not far from Hanover Square. They get results, so I never question their methods.'

Impulsively, Harriet leaned forward and kissed Spiros' cheek. She had no intention of marrying him, whatever he thought, but she liked him. She liked him very much. He understood her better than anyone else had done since her father died. She wanted him for her friend.

29

At the beginning of September, the *New York Times* carried a press dispatch from Saigon, reporting the bombing, by the United States Air Force, of a Buddhist pagoda and a Catholic church, with the loss of many lives. It also described the plight of a woman in one of the delta provinces who had had both her arms and her eyelids burned off by napalm. Two of her children had been killed in the same raid which maimed her.

Some people read it with horror and concern, but most gave it a cursory glance and impatiently turned over the pages until they came to the report of the wedding, two days previously, on the Aegean island of Agios Georgios, of Harriet Cavendish, head of the Chance Corporation, and Spiros Georgiadis, the Greek shipping multi-millionaire. The bride had worn a cream silk Dior gown and the antique cabochon ruby ring given her by the groom.

The press, both American and European, had managed to make capital out of the story for quite a few months. Harriet's divorce from the Honourable Hallam Cavendish had been remarkably quick and painless, and had caught the gossip columnists napping. Afterwards, however, Hallam had set out to cause his ex-wife as much embarrassment as possible by turning himself into the victim of the piece: a loving husband abandoned for an older and far richer man; a desolate father robbed of his son, but nobly refusing to separate Piers from Harriet.

'The little chap isn't two yet,' he was reported as saying.

'A child of that age needs his mother. Besides, she will be able to give him so much more than I can.'

There were other interviews, a lot of them, all equally dignified, equally self-sacrificing.

Harriet was furious.

'Not a word,' she raged, 'about the million-pound settlement.'

Spiros, to whom she had been speaking on the telephone, sounded surprised.

'But what did you expect? You know what the man is like, and you can hardly expect him to be grateful.'

Spiros had never revealed the full details of Hallam's dealings with the King brothers, nor what pressures had been brought to bear; neither had Harriet asked him. She had been content to leave that part of the affair to Spiros. She only knew that, four weeks after her return to New York from Athens, Hallam's solicitors had written to say that he would agree to a divorce provided that certain financial demands were met. Harriet had willingly acceded to the terms set out in the letter and cabled Mossman, Son & May to that effect.

Two days later, Spiros arrived with his entourage, booking himself into the Plaza Hotel on Fifth Avenue, a few blocks away from Harriet's apartment. In the evening, he appeared and dropped a manila envelope into her lap.

'With my compliments,' he said, smiling.

The envelope contained a number of signed statements from members of various Irish political factions and organizations, swearing to Edmund's involvement with the IRA. How Hallam had obtained them, whose arms he had twisted, whose palms he had greased, there was no way of knowing; but certainly it had been no idle boast when he had told her, all those years ago, that he could get Edmund sent to prison. There were also newspaper cuttings, dated July 1958, reporting the attempted break-in at the MP's home near Oxford, and the subsequent attempts to capture the man who had escaped. There was also the *Daily Telegraph* line drawing of Seamus Hogan, surprisingly recognizable. It was easy to see how Hallam had known who he was.

When Harriet had finished going through them, Spiros put everything back in the envelope, took the envelope into the kitchen and set fire to it and its contents in the sink. After that, they went out to dinner at the Times Square Last Chance restaurant.

He was polite, friendly and charming, keeping the conversation on an impersonal level, steering her away from any questions she might have wished to ask about his dealings with Albie and Charlie King. Nor did he mention the word 'marriage' until the very last moment, when he was wishing her a chaste goodnight at the door of her apartment.

Refusing her invitation to go in for a drink, he kissed her cheek paternally and said: 'You should be a free woman by the end of August. I've fixed the fourth of September for our wedding.'

Then he disappeared into the elevator, followed by two of his bodyguards, and she was left standing in the open doorway, not knowing whether to laugh or cry or to stamp her feet in sheer vexation.

'Are you all right, Mrs Cavendish?' Jeanette Baynton asked, helping her off with her wrap, adding, without waiting for a reply: 'Nanny says would you go through to the nursery and see young Piers? He's been an absolute demon this evening.'

Piers had grown from a fractious baby into a fractious toddler. Nothing seemed to please him for long, and Kathleen Tettenburg described him as 'sly'. She even presumed on her old friendship with Harriet to say it to her face.

'He's going to need a firm hand, a man's hand,' she had said more than once. 'And, if you don't mind my saying so, Michael does, too. That boy's getting too big for his boots.'

Harriet found it impossible to maintain her rule of dignified distance with Kathleen. Besides which, Nanny was invariably right. Her opinions were based on sound common sense and close observation. Harriet resented the strictures on her eldest son, but was bound to admit, the

279

next time she saw him, that there was some justification for them.

Michael was now seventeen years old and in his last but one year at Rutherford's Academy. Soon, he would be going on to business school at Harvard. But what he really wanted to do was to step into his mother's shoes. He already had a way of speaking to her about modern business methods and marketing techniques which made her feel redundant. For the first time in her life, Harriet felt in urgent need of someone stronger than she was to help her cope.

The obvious answer was Spiros.

She telephoned him in Athens to say that she was coming over, and he sent his private plane to fetch her. The press got wind of it, their first scent of an affair which, in the ensuing weeks, was to become almost an obsession with the gossip columnists, and which made Athens unbearable for the pair of them. It did not matter where they went, a photographer seemed to be lurking round every corner. The Italians were the worst. Spiros, seeing that Harriet was distressed by a pressure of publicity she had never before encountered, flew her to Agios Georgios, where they were at least sure of their privacy. The trouble was that Harriet still insisted on reading the newspapers each day, and so met with the full blast of hostility from the British press. She was deeply upset.

For several weeks, hardly a day passed without either a photograph of, or an interview with, Hallam appearing in one or another of the popular dailies. The reporters, to a man, to a woman, were all on his side.

'Bastard!' Harriet exclaimed.

'Calm yourself,' Spiros advised her. 'It is a waste of energy to lose your temper over things you can do nothing about. And, in this case, your hands are tied. You cannot reveal your real reasons for divorcing Hallam without divulging so much more. He can vilify you to his heart's content, knowing full well that you will do nothing to prevent him.'

'They're getting at you, too, you know!' she pointed out angrily. 'This rag implies you're no better than a crook.'

'So what?' shrugged Spiros. 'In English, you have a saying about sticks and stones. Besides, they might even be right.'

He made her uncomfortable when he talked like that, but she was becoming increasingly aware that he had many shady friends and underworld connections, both in Europe and in the States. She closed her mind to the knowledge as well as she could because she needed him. He represented power and protection and paternalism at a time in her life when she was feeling exposed and vulnerable. She still had not fully recovered from the beating Hallam had administered six months earlier. The physical scars had vanished, but the mental ones remained.

Spiros treated her with a mixture of old-fashioned courtesy and ruthless high-handedness which exactly suited her present mood. He made no attempt to seduce her and, contrary to all the feverish newspaper speculation, they slept in separate bedrooms. At the same time, Spiros talked about their marriage, once her divorce was absolute, as a foregone conclusion, while Harriet remained adamant that she had no intention of marrying him or anyone.

Not even Edmund Howard, if he were free?

The question rose up to taunt her in unguarded moments. Wasn't most of her revulsion at the newspaper stories a result of knowing that Edmund, too, must be reading them, and imagining his disgust? They would confirm and reinforce his view of her as an unscrupulous woman who used people and then tossed them aside when something better offered. As far as Edmund knew, she had ditched him for Hallam and the prospect of a title, and now she had apparently thrown over Hallam for one of the richest men in the world. She could guess the direction his thoughts must be taking.

So what? as Spiros had said. Edmund was a married man and nothing to her now. What did his opinion matter?

But it did, and she resented the fact. She grew more short-tempered and difficult to live with.

281

Spiros accepted the irritability as he accepted most things, with an amused equanimity. But in the end even his patience snapped.

'Go back to England,' he told her, 'and see about the setting up of that trust. You will have to face the press some time, unless you wish to become a recluse, and it will give them something else to write about you. You might even find that a few of them are on your side.'

'They'll most likely see it as a conscience offering,' she retorted.

Nevertheless, Spiros' advice was, as always, sound. And she wanted to go to England for another reason. The firm of private detectives hired by Spiros had recently informed her that they were hopeful of a new lead on Hilary's identity and present whereabouts. She wanted desperately to know if they had discovered anything further. Suddenly, she could no longer wait passively on Agios Georgios for their next report.

She was, moreover, getting out of the swim of things. She was feeling bored, and it was time she came out of hiding and faced up to any unpleasantness which might be in store. She would regret leaving Agios Georgios, though. In the three weeks she had been there, she had grown to love it, with its stretches of white sand, rocky scrub-studded slopes and the eternal hushing of the sea. She had grown to love the people, too; Spiros' workers and tenants who lived in the solitary one-street village, with its kafenéion and taverna and all-purpose shop; not the conventional Greek village shop, but one stocked with expensive delicacies imported from Athens.

Beyond the huddle of houses lay the airstrip, a ribbon of concrete bordered by bushes of purple sage and dwarf juniper. It was here that she said goodbye to Spiros two days later, as she boarded his private plane which would take her as far as Athens.

'Not all the way to London,' she had insisted. 'It'll make me too conspicuous.'

'Don't forget,' Spiros said as he kissed her, 'we are

getting married at the beginning of September.'

'I haven't made up my mind yet,' she retorted, making a bid for independence.

She mounted the steps. At the top, she glanced back over her shoulder. Spiros blandly returned her gaze. He was at his most enigmatic. There was no way of knowing what he was really thinking.

She managed to avoid the vigilance of the press for twenty-four hours after her arrival in London, during which time she checked in to her usual suite at Claridges and telephoned New York.

'Get on over here right away,' she told June Grazini.

There was a momentary silence at the other end of the line.

Then: 'I'm sorry, Harriet,' June said quietly, 'but I can't. I've just written you a letter. I've resigned. Ken and I were married last week.' She took a deep breath. 'As soon as his divorce came through.'

'But that doesn't stop you working for me,' Harriet protested, before she could stop herself. 'I'm sorry, June. Congratulations, of course. And to Ken. You're certainly both fast movers. I wish you'd told me, though. I wish I'd been there. However, what I said just now still holds good.'

'Yeah, sure.' There was another pause, followed by an embarrassed laugh. 'Truth is, I'm pregnant. Isn't that ridiculous at my age?'

Harriet felt winded. A lot more must have been going on between them in Athens than she had realized. But she rose gallantly to the occasion.

'Of course not. You're younger than I am.'

'But you do see. . .'

'Yes. Yes, of course.'

'I've been in touch with the agencies, looking for a replacement. I should have contacted you sooner, I suppose, but I didn't like to disturb you while you were on the island with Mr Georgiadis.'

'Thanks,' Harriet said, 'but don't worry about it. I'll see

283

to it myself when I come back. And, June, good luck. I'll be sending you a wedding gift as soon as possible.'

Harriet hung up. She had been counting on June. She needed a secretary, a companion, another woman. A friend. Over the past year, June Grazini had become all those things. Now, suddenly, Harriet found herself alone. She would have to get a temporary secretary through one of the London agencies. She telephoned the head offices of Chance Enterprises (UK) Ltd and asked them to arrange it. Then she took a taxi to the offices of Brewer's Detective Agency, near Hanover Square. She was received by the proprietor in person.

Cecil Brewer was like his premises, clean, smart and businesslike, the antithesis of all the seedy and disreputable private eyes depicted in films and books and on television. He beamed at her as he ushered her into a chair and asked his secretary to bring in two cups of tea.

'I have very good news for you, Mrs Cavendish,' he said, sitting down on the opposite side of his curiously uncluttered desk. He produced a file from one of the drawers and opened it. 'Very good news indeed. We have definitely located the former Hilary Canossa. Of course, the person concerned is no longer known by that name, and hasn't been since the age of three.' Mr Brewer's smile grew wider. 'Nor is the person aware of our interest. Everything has been done with the greatest discretion, according to your instructions.' He handed Harriet the file. 'All the information is in there. What you do with it now is up to you. Our part in the affair is ended.'

Harriet opened the file with shaking fingers and flicked through three closely typed pages. There it was in black and white. At last! At last she knew where Hilary was. After eighteen years, she was once again in touch with her eldest child.

She spent the rest of the summer in England, setting up the Chance Corporation Trust, which would provide financial aid for deserving young people. Everywhere she went, she was besieged by reporters, but she had ceased to care about their animosity. Her happiness was apparent to everyone, and if they attributed it to the wrong cause that was not her fault. A few of the less hard-boiled pressmen were even won over by her, and wrote articles suggesting that the Honourable Hallam Cavendish might not be as hard done by as he pretended. But the majority found it better copy to go on casting Harriet and Spiros as the villains of the story.

In her present state of euphoria, however, Harriet hardly noticed. She could not wait for the Trust to grind laboriously into action, and during a visit to Birmingham, to see for herself how the newly opened restaurant was progressing, she met Dick Norris, who washed up in the kitchens by night and worked in a solicitor's office by day, in order to raise enough money to put himself through university and take a law degree. Two days later, he found himself the recipient of a sufficiently large sum of money to enable him to put his plan into action.

Madge Shelton was a chambermaid at Claridges, neat, quick and extremely conscientious. Making Harriet's bed one morning, she was astounded when Harriet herself walked in and asked if she would like to be her personal maid. At first, she thought Mrs Cavendish must be joking, and nearly collapsed with astonishment when she discovered that she was not. The rest of the girls in the hotel were green with envy. They could not believe her luck. Neither could Madge. A salary three times what she had been earning up until then, a glamorous new life and a chance to see the world! It was a dream come true.

Harriet continued in her daze of excitement and well-being, but she could still be difficult when she chose. She rejected every single applicant for the post of temporary secretary until she found exactly the one she wanted. After a long and demanding search, she engaged Bess Holland.

Bess had not in fact been looking for a job, being very happily employed by a firm of travel agents in Holborn;

but the principal of the Four Star Secretarial Agency, on whose books she was registered, had telephoned her personally.

'This job is made for you, Bess. Mrs Cavendish has stipulated very precise requirements, and they fit you like a glove. You've always said you're ambitious and want to see life. Want a job that isn't strictly nine to five. Well, here's your chance.'

'It is temporary, though.' But Bess had demurred only for a moment. Everyone knew the name of Harriet Cavendish. The opportunity to work for her, if only for a few months, was surely one not to be missed.

'If you play your cards right, there might be the chance of a permanent job,' the principal had told her with cautious optimism.

And so Bess had gone for the interview, but without much hope of being selected. There would be literally hundreds of applicants after such a glamorous post. To her astonishment, Harriet engaged her on the spot.

In the middle of August, Spiros arrived at Claridges without any warning.

'We shall be married on the fourth of September on Agios Georgios,' he announced. 'It is all arranged. All you need do is buy your dress.'

Harriet looked at him for a long moment and then began to laugh.

'All right,' she said. 'You win.'

30

There were two wedding ceremonies on Agios Georgios;
one in the tiny onion-domed church at the back of the
house, by Greek Orthodox rites, and a second conducted
American-style in the main salon by an Anglican vicar
flown out especially for the occasion.

A cohort of bodyguards patrolled every beach and
landing-stage, every inlet and bay of the island to make
sure that no uninvited guests arrived to mar the day's
festivities. Two of Spiros' helicopters took to the air to
warn off all others and any enterprising cameramen who
had the idea of being winched down to take unauthorized
photographs of the proceedings. What pictures there were
were issued by Spiros' secretary to selected newspapers
and journalists.

Harriet remarked to Bess Holland that she knew now
how the Maltese must have felt during the war, under
siege. She did not like it, and wondered again if she had
made the right decision. It was too late, however, to
reverse it.

The number of invited guests was relatively small.
There were a dozen or so of Spiros' friends, including one
of his sisters, an elderly woman who closely resembled
him, and who conceded nothing to the occasion by dressing up. She wore the plain black frock of most Greek
peasant women, except that hers was made of silk. A
wooden cross, suspended by a gold chain about her neck,
and small gold hoop earrings were her only adornment.

On Harriet's side, there were Carlo and Sophia, both of

whom had put on weight and could now only be described as fat; Ken and June Lambert; Francis Derham, Pete Zanardi, Jack Dolia and their wives; Kathleen Tettenburg, in charge of Piers. And Michael.

Michael disliked his mother's new marriage and made the fact plain. He had barely had a civil word for Spiros when they met, and had spent most of his time since arriving on the island trying to persuade Harriet to change her mind.

'He's too old for you,' Michael repeated stubbornly, when Harriet patiently tried to discover the real reason for his objections. 'He's old enough to be your father.'

'He's fifty-nine! Twenty years older than me, that's all. Lots of women marry men as old as that.' Harriet tried not to sound as exasperated as she felt.

'He's never been married before,' Michael argued stubbornly. 'Why has he picked on you?'

'Perhaps he cares for me! You didn't make all this fuss when I married Hallam.'

'I was younger then. I wasn't really interested.'

But Harriet knew that it wasn't the real reason for her elder son's antipathy towards Spiros. Michael had not seen Hallam as any sort of threat to his own future position in the business. Hallam had kept his nose out of Chance Corporation affairs as long as he was paid regularly and was happy. Michael had felt contempt for his former step-father, but had written him off as harmless; a man who could be bought.

Spiros, however, was altogether different. Michael suspected him of marrying Harriet in order to acquire the Chance Corporation for himself. When Harriet finally understood this, she tried to explain that Spiros had no need to resort to such measures.

'He isn't the least bit interested in the corporation, Mickey. In Spiros' terms, it's very small beer. If he'd wanted it, he could have bought me out a hundred times over. But he doesn't. You must believe that. The business will be yours and Piers's.'

Michael remained unconvinced, and she resigned herself to the inevitable. She found it difficult, herself, to imagine a fortune so vast that the multi-million-dollar Chance Corporation could be regarded as a pleasant little hobby; something to keep a wife amused while Spiros attended to his own concerns. But that was certainly how her future husband regarded the matter. He had no wish and no intention of doing Michael out of his inheritance.

Harriet's own doubts were of a different nature. At her wedding to Hallam, her feelings had been simple and clear-cut. Fear and hatred were the predominant emotions, but she had been absolutely sure of the necessity of what she was doing. Her marriage to Spiros, however, reminded her of her marriage to Gus. It had in it the same elements of need on her part; the need for affection and protection; the need inherent in most women to be cushioned against life when the going got too tough. And both men were substitutes; Gus for Gerry, Spiros for Edmund. Standing beside Spiros during the two ceremonies, giving and exchanging rings, Harriet wondered if she were not, once again, using another person to further her own ends.

The other thing which struck her forcibly, glancing around during the reception, was how very few friends she had. She had no friends at all in the strict sense of the word. Carlo and Sophia were Gus's relations, and she had let herself drift apart from them. The rest, except for Michael and Piers, were either employees or ex-employees. She had even had to ask Ken Lambert to give her away. She had naturally approached Carlo first, but for some reason, not immediately apparent, he had preferred not to do it. Harriet decided that it was probably pique. He and Sophia had begun to regret letting her buy them out of the business, watching its subsequent growth with envious eyes. And in some obscure way they blamed her for their decision. But at least they had come to the wedding, even if, as Harriet suspected, curiosity was their only motive, and she was grateful to them. She had so few friends and acquaintances to show for her thirty-nine years that, for a moment, she felt deeply depressed.

Then she remembered Hilary. Her heart lifted, and her face broke into a brilliant smile.

They spent two weeks on Agios Georgios before returning to Athens. It had originally been intended that Michael should stay with them, but he excused himself as soon as the wedding was over and returned to New York. Later in the month, he would head north for Maine and the start of his last year at Rutherford's Academy.

'He doesn't like me,' Spiros said.

They were having dinner on the bedroom balcony after all the guests had gone. Piers was tucked up in the nursery, watched over by Kathleen. Earlier, he had been sick from too much food and over-indulgence, and was now sound asleep, worn out by the day's excitements.

Spiros went on: 'It's understandable, of course. Michael's afraid that I have usurped his place in your affections. He did not feel that way about Hallam because you so obviously disliked him and spent so little time with him. Wasn't Michael ever curious as to why you married Hallam?'

'Michael isn't curious about anything except money,' Harriet answered drily. 'Talking of which. . .' She broke off, fingering the necklace of rubies and diamonds at her throat. 'Thank you. I love it. It's fabulous. But you really shouldn't have spent so much. Not after the emeralds you gave me for my birthday.'

Spiros chuckled. 'One of the reasons I married you, my dear, is because you are the only woman I know who isn't after my money. Not because you are a wealthy woman in your own right, but because, from time to time, you still allow yourself to be ruled by the economics of the vicarage. Your Puritan soul is revolted by ostentation.'

She considered the proposition seriously and nodded.

'I guess you're right, at that. When I think of the shifts Dad and I were put to, to survive. . . Incidentally, I must go to Winterbourn Green again. The vicarage conversion must be nearly finished.' She returned his smile. 'I'll take you there some time. But, first, I must go to London. And there's Glasgow. The opening of the new restaurant in October.' She turned her head to stare out over the balcony railing at the wide expanse of beach, cool now after the heat of the day, and swathed in shadow. A rising slip of moon sent a finger of light slithering across the surface of a rock pool, probing the glittering shallows. 'It's beautiful here,' she added. 'Beautiful, peaceful and exotic.'

'I am glad you like it,' Spiros answered quietly. 'It is now your home.' He reached across the table and held one of her hands. 'Harriet, what do you intend doing about Hilary?'

'Nothing more for the present.' She glanced down at their entwined fingers, his palely olive against her fairer skin. 'Maybe later. But for now I'm content to let things remain as they are. When the time comes to make changes, I shall know.'

Spiros nodded, satisfied. 'You're wise to trust your own instincts. I have always trusted mine, and they are invariably right. They were right that evening at the Papidopolous'. As soon as you sat down beside me, I knew that you were the woman I should make my wife.'

She raised her eyebrows in an indignation that was only half-assumed.

'Didn't I have any say in the matter?'

Spiros shook his head. 'None at all. Now, if you have finished, let us go to bed.'

Harriet was not at all sure what she had expected. The fact that Spiros had made no attempt to sleep with her before their marriage had made her wonder if he were as virile as he looked. In one tiny corner of her mind, she had even wondered if he meant their relationship to be platonic. It was not an idea she had entertained seriously; but she certainly had not been prepared for the demands of a strong, healthy and active body which kept her awake the better part of the night.

Her other fantasy about Spiros had been that he was a romantic and tender lover, as carefully considerate for her

291

satisfaction as for his own. This was not true, either, and on reflection she supposed she should have known better. He was not a romantic man. He had sent her flowers only once, the morning after their first meeting, and they had been in the nature of a bribe. The priceless pieces of jewellery he had lavished on her since were – she could see it now – in the nature of investments. Spiros was very down-to-earth.

Strangely enough, Harriet found herself liking him the better for it. It occurred to her, that first night, that she would have been unable to respond to too much tenderness from him. That sort of lovemaking, the giving and accepting without restraint, what seemed like the very mingling of flesh and bone, belonged to her and Edmund. She had tried, in her daydreams, to transfer her feelings for Edmund to Spiros, and, on occasions, believed she had succeeded, but she had been fooling herself. She knew it the moment she and Spiros got into bed together. She was grateful then for his matter-of-fact no-nonsense approach.

What existed between her and her husband, she realized the next day, was friendship; a friendship which included sex, the enjoyment of one another's body, but without the deeper emotional responses which turned love into a cage. The only man she could ever bear to share that cage with was Edmund Howard.

When they returned to Athens, in mid-September, Harriet was relieved to find that the pressure of publicity had eased a little. The fact that she and Spiros were now married made them of less importance in the eyes of the world's press, who were more concerned with scandal than with marital happiness. There was a brief upsurge of interest when she left alone for London, giving rise to the inevitable stories of a rift; but as no corroborative evidence was forthcoming her copy value once more flagged.

She descended on the main offices of Chance Enterprises (UK) Ltd, unannounced and demanding information about the company's current state, which she expected to be supplied within the hour.

'I won't tolerate slackness and inefficiency,' she told the

vice-chairman of the board, deputizing for his superior, who had taken the day off to play golf. 'Where are the turnover figures for the Birmingham restaurant? Simple elementary information of that kind should present no problems. So why the delay?'

'The department concerned is looking them out for you now, Mrs Cavendish,' the poor man mumbled. He caught at the tattered rags of his dignity. 'As you can see from the chart on the wall behind you, business is booming. The fast-food shops and the snackbars are doing exceptionally well, and there are plans, as you know, to open half a dozen more of the latter before Christmas. I cannot be expected to have the details of one particular restaurant at my fingertips.'

'Why not?' Harriet rapped back. 'It's the attention to detail that has made the Last Chance restaurants so successful.' She smiled at him sweetly. 'Like knowing that I am now Mrs Georgiadis, not Mrs Cavendish. Ah! At last!' One of the secretaries had appeared with a sheaf of papers, which she laid respectfully on the desk in front of Harriet.

Harriet had taken over the vice-chairman's desk on entering the room, and gave no sign of moving as she settled down to read. The disgruntled and dispossessed occupant was forced to make shift with a small table near the door.

An hour later, Harriet raised her head. 'There's a report here from the accounts department, signed by someone called Frank Bryan. His analysis of the returns for the Birmingham restaurant suggest to him – or so he says – that there are several things wrong with the general set-up. His conclusion is: Good, but not good enough. I'd like to see this Mr Bryan.'

The vice-chairman buzzed for his secretary again. The woman frowned, puzzled. There was no section head of that name in the accounts department, she was positive of that. Further enquiries, however, elicited the information that Frank Bryan was a clerk who had done the analysis on the Birmingham restaurant in his spare time, submitting it to his boss, who had promised vaguely to look at it one day, then put it aside. In the panic following Harriet's unscheduled appearance, and her demand for facts and figures, the report had accidentally been pushed in with the other papers by someone who had not paused to read beyond the heading.

A nervous Frank Bryan found himself whisked up to the holy of holies on the top floor, to confront the legendary Harriet Chance herself. She came round from the other side of the desk, smiling a welcome.

'Mr Bryan, I'm delighted to meet you. I hope you weren't given the impression that anything is wrong. Quite the contrary, I assure you.'

He rubbed his sweaty palms against the legs of his trousers before grasping her outstretched hand.

'Well, I didn't imagine I was going to be sacked. You could have done that without bothering to see me. I mean. . . You'd hardly have brought me all the way up here just to tell me that.'

Harriet regarded him approvingly. 'You're smart,' she said. 'I like that.'

She saw a young man in his early twenties, small, with fine bones. Not a person one would naturally look at twice, but she was adept at reading signs. The light of ambition burned at the back of the pale grey eyes, and Frank Bryan had already demonstrated that he could stand up for himself when the occasion demanded it. He was not easily overawed. A fighter. And he was shrewd.

Harriet indicated a chair and resumed her own seat on the opposite side of the desk.

'Sit down, Mr Bryan.' She picked up his report. 'Now, tell me how you came to your conclusions.'

'So I made it perfectly plain,' she told Spiros over the telephone that evening, 'that from now on I have a special interest in Frank Bryan. It won't make life easy for him, but if he's half the man I think he is he'll overcome that handicap.'

294

'Be careful,' Spiros warned her, 'that the lad doesn't make too many enemies. Your voice sounds muffled. Do you have a cold?'

'I think I may have one coming. I hope not. I'm off to Scotland at the beginning of next month for the opening of the Glasgow restaurant.'

'Don't go if you're not feeling well.' His voice sounded a note of alarm, and she realized yet again how very fond of her he was.

Why did it surprise her? Why did she still find it hard to accept that she was capable of inspiring genuine affection? The scars left by Gerry Canossa and Hallam went deep. And then there was Edmund. . .

But memories of Edmund were to be avoided at all costs. She had Spiros now.

'I shall be OK,' she reassured him brightly. 'It's only a sniffle.'

'All the same, take care. Promise me you won't go if you feel the slightest bit – what is the phrase? – under the weather! What expressions you English have!'

She laughed. 'If I'm on my deathbed, I promise not to go. But I'm taking my new secretary, Bess Holland, with me. She's very protective and will make sure I don't overdo things. Other than that, nothing will stop me. You know how important this Glasgow trip is to me, Spiros!'

31

Harriet's cold, while it lasted, was severe, confining her to
bed for several days; and when, finally, the fever abated it
left her feeling weak and shaken. She decided to go to
Winterbourn Green to recuperate.

Her appearance at the George and Dragon created even
more of a stir than her last visit. The excitement among the
villagers was intense but, being country folk, they were at
great pains not to show it. Harriet, therefore, found herself
treated with courteous indifference, which suited her very
well. She felt nothing but relief when Mrs Wicks, now in
her seventies, nodded distantly and crossed to the other
side of the street.

The only people to treat Harriet naturally were the
young vicar and his wife, who seemed to find nothing
incongruous about inviting the wife of one of the world's
richest men, and a very wealthy woman in her own right,
to share cauliflower cheese, cold meat and salad or whatever else they were having for supper in their modern
semi-detached vicarage. Harriet was extremely grateful,
and doubled her contributions to the Church Restoration
Fund.

'No, no!' the Reverend Philip Gresham protested, his
plump boyish face puckered up in embarrassment. 'You've
been too generous already. Stella and I didn't. . . What I
mean is, there was no . . . no. . .'

'Ulterior motive?' Harriet suggested with a smile. 'I
know that. I'm not such a poor judge of character as you
seem to think.'

They were taking a short cut through the church-yard, Harriet on her way to the Old Vicarage, where work was almost finished, the vicar to a meeting in one of the vestries. It was a beautiful morning, soft and golden, the path, with its carpet of moss and small plants push-ing bravely between the flags, winding in and out of the ancient gravestones. The yew trees stood like sentinels, their feathery branches thick with the little acorns which would eventually fall and seed again amongst the grasses.

'I wonder why yews are always planted in churchyards,' Harriet said, anxious to change the subject. Any talk of her generosity made her uncomfortable. She felt it was undeserved. She quoted: ' "And mournful, lean Despair brings me yew to deck my grave." '

Philip Gresham chuckled. 'Blake's too pessimistic a poet for a morning such as this. Yew trees in graveyards are a legacy of the Middle Ages, when the Norman overlords grazed their cattle and sheep on common land. In order to protect their burial-grounds, the peasants planted them with the poisonous yew. A few dead animals, and the drovers and shepherds in charge of them made sure they didn't feed there again.'

'Thank you,' Harriet said. 'I never knew that before. What a shocking admission for a vicar's daughter to make.' She paused, looking around her. 'I don't know if it was growing up with the graveyard virtually on the doorstep, but I've never found it at all eerie or frightening. In fact, when I was a little girl, I used to play here a lot, amongst the headstones. And I'd come along this path on the blackest night without thinking twice about it. The names on the gravestones were so familiar that they were like old friends.'

The young vicar nodded. 'I know what you mean. Graveyards give a sense of history.'

'Roots,' Harriet murmured. 'They're important. And now,' she added briskly, 'before we both start quoting from Gray's "Elegy", we'd better get on. I'm so glad we bumped into one another, but I mustn't make you late for your meeting.' She held out her hand. 'Thank Stella again for me, will you? I shall be leaving first thing tomorrow morning. I'm flying up to Scotland in two days' time.'

'We shall miss you,' Philip Gresham said with gentle sincerity, before turning and disappearing through a side-door into the church.

The Old Vicarage, its name proclaimed on a newly painted sign fixed to the gate, was familiar and unfamiliar both at once. It was her childhood home, and yet neat and picturesque in a way that Harriet had never seen it before. The roof had been retiled in Cotswold slate, the walls repaired and, in places, rebuilt with the local grey-coloured stone. The garden had been cleared and restocked by an Oxford nursery, the lawns returfed. New guttering shone in all the glory of a fresh coat of paint. Window-frames had been replaced. The front door was a glittering white, with a huge brass knocker. Harriet pushed open the gate, which no longer creaked, and went in.

At the back of the house, the garden had also been tamed, reduced from the wilderness of her youth to well-ordered flower-beds, islanded in close-cut grass. The old coach-house and gardener's cottage had been refurbished and turned into additional guest-rooms, each with its own bathroom. Harriet looked through the windows, but did not go in. Instead, she returned to the front door, which stood open. Inside, she could hear hammering and cheerful whistling, as the last of what had originally been an army of workmen completed the final jobs.

Everywhere there was the smell of raw wood and new paint. The hallway was already wallpapered in a delicate shade of primrose, and through the open doorway of what had once been her father's study she could see a William Morris print.

A man in blue overalls emerged from the cupboard under the stairs, saw her and jumped.

'Bloody hell!' he said. 'You gave me a turn! You're not supposed to be in 'ere, madam. This is private property.'

'I know. I own it. I'm Harriet Georgiadis. Cavendish that was.'

The man's gaze sharpened, but he made no comment. He knew all about her, though, she could tell.

'Sorry,' he apologized. 'But how was I to know? I'm the electrician. I've just finished the wiring upstairs, so they can get on with the last of the plastering tomorrow.' He indicated the cupboard with an inclination of his head. 'I was switching on at the mains. I'm going up now, to make sure that everything works.'

'Can I do it?' Harriet asked breathlessly.

The man stared at her in surprise.

' 'Course. It's your place, after all.'

He followed her upstairs, the banisters gleaming with smart cream paint. Harriet stood on the landing for a moment, looking at the switches and the power points; then she ran from room to room switching on all the lights. In her own old room, she stopped, fighting the urge to burst into tears.

When she turned round, she saw the electrician watching her, wide-eyed. Plainly, he considered that she was mad.

It was a debatable point whether there were more guests than journalists at the opening of the Last Chance restaurant in Sauchiehall Street, but everyone agreed that it was one of the best first nights ever.

Harriet, together with the chairman and vice-chairman of Chance Enterprises (UK) Ltd, flew up to Glasgow at the beginning of October and booked into the Excelsior Hotel. She had made up her mind that the opening of the first Last Chance in Scotland was to be a glittering affair, and had extracted promises of attendance from every well-known personality who could lay claim to even the smallest drop of Scottish blood, and every civic dignitary she could muster. Bagpipers, dancers and a superb meal all helped to contribute to the success of the evening. Even the celebrities forgot to be jaded.

'Truly a night to remember,' the chairman remarked pompously over lunch the next day. The vice-chairman was quick to agree with him.

'A splendid show, Mrs Georgiadis. My warmest congratulations. Are you flying back to London with us this afternoon?'

Harriet swallowed a forkful of spinach. 'No, I'm staying on for a couple of days. I've never been to Scotland before. I'd like some time to look around. I may visit Edinburgh. I feel there must be possibilities for a Last Chance there. If so, when I get back to Town, I'll discuss it with you.'

The restaurants were still very much her own baby. No other branch of the Chance empire engaged her personal attention – suffered from her personal intervention, her staff might be forgiven for thinking – like the catering side of the business. Reports on the progress of her other interests – the dress shops, the television rental chain, the record company – were submitted to her at bi-monthly board meetings, held in New York, or posted to her wherever she was in the world. But as long as they were doing well and showing a substantial profit she rarely interfered in the running of them. It was much the same with the Take-a-Chance eating houses and the fast-food shops, but the restaurants were different. They were special to her. They were a memorial to Gus and to Harvey Muldoon.

She hired a car and drove to Edinburgh the next day, taking Bess Holland with her. In the short space of time Bess had been her acting secretary, the two women had grown very close, and Harriet had decided to make Bess's appointment a permanent one. For the girl's twenty-first birthday, she had given her a chinchilla coat.

'It'll keep you warm in the winter,' she had said, when Bess had tried to stammer her thanks. 'You'll find New York colder than London. Besides, a woman as attractive as you deserves the best.'

To call Bess Holland attractive was an understatement. A beautiful figure, perfect legs, smooth dark hair and soft brown eyes made her an asset in any company, one of the reasons why Harriet had chosen her from the long list of applicants. Another reason was her shining intelligence. Harriet's main fear now was that Bess, like June, would one day get married and leave her. Bess said absolutely not.

'Once bitten, twice shy,' she had said, then broken off in confusion, recalling that her employer had been married four times.

But Harriet had merely laughed, not in the least offended.

'We'll see,' she remarked. 'I can't believe one year of marriage can have put you off men for life.'

'Oh, not off men.' Bess had grinned cheekily. 'Just off marriage. I don't care for being tied down. It's different for you, Mrs Georgiadis,' she had added hastily. 'You're free to come and go as you choose. You and Mr Georgiadis don't live in one another's pocket. It's the proximity I can't stand.'

'It depends who you share it with,' Harriet answered guardedly, thinking of Edmund.

'Well, Mark Skells and I just weren't suited,' Bess stated flatly. 'We were only eighteen when we married. Far too young. We had nothing in common, as we found out after a couple of months.'

'Didn't your parents try to stop you getting married?' Harriet had asked abruptly, and Bess had laughed.

'They tried all right. But I was always too headstrong for them. They're nice gentle people. They didn't know how to cope with someone as headstrong as me.'

'I know exactly what you mean.' Harriet had smiled conspiratorially. 'You and I are two of a kind.'

On the way back to Glasgow from Edinburgh, Harriet said: 'I wish you'd stop calling me Mrs Georgiadis in that formal way. It's such a mouthful. My friends call me

Harriet, and I hope we're friends, as well as being employer and employee.'

If Bess was astonished, she tried not to show it. She knew some of Harriet's staff were permitted to call her by her first name, but surely not after so short a time! A matter of months, that was all.

'Thank you,' she said as calmly as she could. 'I should be honoured.'

'That's settled, then. You know,' Harriet went on, changing the subject, 'I've been thinking a lot lately about engaging a chauffeur. My husband keeps nagging me about it. He doesn't like the idea of me driving around with no male protection. What do you think of the idea?'

Bess Holland considered the proposition carefully, as she did everything.

'I suppose Mr Georgiadis is right, when you think about it. Kidnapping seems to be on the increase, judging by the stories one reads in the newspapers. As soon as we get back to London, I'll make enquiries.'

'There's no need for that,' Harriet said quickly. 'I have the name of a young man living in Glasgow I'm thinking of hiring.'

'With good references, I hope.'

'Well. . .' Harriet kept her eyes fixed firmly on the road ahead. 'As a matter of fact, he can't even drive.' Bess Holland was mute from astonishment. Harriet went on swiftly: 'I got his name from a charitable organization in London; one that deals with young offenders. This particular young man – his name's Bill Brereton, by the way – comes originally from the south of England. He was sent to a detention centre near Guildford for twelve months when he was only fifteen. Petty larceny. After he was discharged, his parents moved up here, to Glasgow. His father had been offered a job in one of the Clydeside shipyards. The boy works there now as well. An unskilled labourer.'

'But ... but why, for heaven's sake?' Bess Holland sounded thoroughly distressed, as well she might be. 'This young man's a thief!'

'I know. But you see, Bess, my dear, I've had so much to be thankful for in my life.' Harriet made an effort to explain. 'I've been so lucky, and lately I've begun to feel guilty that I haven't done more for other people. My husband would tell you that I'm inhibited by my vicarage upbringing. He may be right, but it isn't only that. Abraham Lincoln, in one of his speeches, talked about "an equal chance". That's why I've set up my own charitable trust, to help deserving cases. But these things take time to get moving. So, in one or two instances, I've jumped the gun.'

'Madge,' Bess murmured.

'Yes, Madge. She's a bright personable youngster who's worth more than just a chambermaid's job.'

Bess hesitated. They were driving through the outskirts of Glasgow.

'Forgive me, but . . . isn't such an arbitrary choice a little bit like playing God?'

Harriet swerved to avoid a stray dog which was leisurely crossing Duke Street, oblivious to the rush of early-evening traffic.

'Perhaps,' she agreed, after a moment's silence. 'But isn't doing *something* preferable to doing nothing whatsoever?'

'Not always,' Bess answered, in some trepidation. She felt she might be laying her whole future on the line.

Harriet laughed, but she sounded displeased. To Bess's surprise, however, she said: 'You may be right. In future, I'll leave all such decisions to the Trust, who will no doubt make dull but entirely worthy choices, entirely on merit.'

'And this young man you've just mentioned?'

'Ah! Well, he's a little special. I think . . . I'm sure that there may have been extenuating circumstances for what he did. I don't believe he's really bad. Anyway, you shall judge for yourself. We'll go visit him this evening.'

Bill Brereton, like Madge Shelton before him, could not

303

believe his luck. It was a fairy-tale come true. Harriet had swept into his life in the role of fairy godmother, waved her magic wand and transported him into another world.

'Why me?' he had asked her.

She said she had seen him on the street and liked his face, but he wasn't sure that he believed her. It was a good enough face as faces went – lean and darkly handsome in a rather Italianate sort of way – but not sufficiently striking to attract the attention of a stranger and persuade her into making this ridiculous offer.

'I can't drive,' he had told her, to which she had replied with a shrug of her shoulders: 'Presumably you can learn.'

He knew who she was, of course. He had read all about her, a fact which made what had happened even more unreal. In a moment of what his father had regarded as lunatic honesty, he had informed Mrs Georgiadis of his criminal record.

'Thank you for telling me,' she said. 'I appreciate that very much. But it makes no difference. The offer is still open if you wish to accept it.'

Wish to accept it? Of course he bloody well wished to accept it. His parents made no move to influence him one way or the other. They never had. They had never really been interested in him, and he wondered sometimes if it was because he was an adopted child. He said goodbye without any regrets, and within a month had found himself – via London and a quick course in driving – in Athens. Then on to Agios Georgios and New York for Christmas. This was life. This was seeing the world. He was part of the Georgiadis circus, in perpetual motion, where money was reckoned in billions of dollars instead of in pounds, shillings and pence. Bill sent part of his salary home every month to his parents; a sop to his conscience, but otherwise he thought no more about them. He abandoned himself to what still seemed like an impossible dream. One day, he felt certain, he would wake up.

Harriet gave up driving when Bill joined her staff. She had never been keen on it, and after her marriage to Spiros his repeated strictures on the dangers of travelling about unaccompanied had eventually begun to have their effect. In a world where violence, epitomized by the escalation of the Vietnam war, was becoming the norm, she felt increasingly vulnerable. There were too many people who envied her, or hated all that she and Spiros represented, to take unnecessary risks.

The British press in particular was never slow to print adverse criticism of her. It was almost, Harriet sometimes thought, as though the whole of Fleet Street was deliberately aiming to stir up resentment against her.

'Why do they dislike me so?' she demanded angrily of Bess Holland, after reading a more than usually scurrilous article about herself in one of the less reputable morning papers. 'I've never done anything to them.'

Bess smiled wisely. 'It's not as personal an attack as it seems,' she consoled. 'You know how we Brits resent success, especially success as obvious and as dazzling as yours. We're a terribly envious nation. Americans might envy you, but they admire you, too. Other people's success only spurs them on to try to emulate it. So just ignore rubbish like this. It's not worthy of your attention.'

Harriet's frown remained for a moment; then her face cleared, and she laughed.

'You're a wonderfully comforting person to have around, my dear. You have a good sound head screwed on those young shoulders of yours. I'm glad I found you. I hope you're equally glad that you accepted the job.'

'I'm very, very happy,' Bess assured her solemnly. 'In fact I've never been so happy in my life before.'

It was true. There had been a rapport between the two women, which both had recognized, from the first moment they had met. Moreover, Bess felt protective towards the older woman. Unobtrusively, she tried to look after Harriet as much as she possibly could.

And In January there was a further reason for taking care. Harriet was still in the States, after the New Year celebrations, when her doctor confirmed what she already suspected, but could not quite believe. At the age of thirty-nine, she was pregnant once more. By the time the baby was born, some time in early October, she would have passed her fortieth birthday.

32

The day after Elena was born, Spiros gave Harriet a string of racehorses, five in all, bought from a bankrupt owner in southern Ireland, together with the stables and paddocks.

'What on earth am I going to do with them?' she demanded, between laughter and tears, sitting up in bed in the big sunny room she shared with Spiros, and flicking through the contents of the folder he had given her. This comprised photographs of the horses, their pedigrees, receipts and all the information she could wish to know about the Malachi stables, near Waterford.

'Race them, of course,' Spiros answered, sitting on the edge of the bed and peering at his daughter in her cradle. There was a light in his eyes, a tenderness in his bearing, which Harriet had never seen before. Fatherhood had come late to Spiros, and the wonder of it had taken him by surprise.

He had insisted that Harriet have the baby at home, on Agios Georgios, attended by a veritable army of doctors and nurses. She had agreed to the former, but rebelled against the latter, eventually losing her temper to such good effect that all but two midwives were paid off and asked to leave the island, with Harriet's own Greek doctor on stand-by in Athens, ready to be flown over the moment she went into labour.

'For heaven's sake, Spiros!' she had exclaimed in exasperation. 'I've had children before!'

In spite of her age, she had found this pregnancy easier than the previous three. She had suffered very little from morning sickness, and experienced almost nothing of the

307

lethargy which had afflicted her in the past. Indeed, after the first three months, she had been bursting with energy, and had been hard put to it to prevent Madge Shelton and Bess Holland turning her into an invalid.

'Stop treating me like a piece of Dresden china!' she had shouted at them on one occasion. 'I'm a normal healthy woman!' And on another: 'Having a baby is not a terminal disease!'

But, if her secretary and her maid were bad enough, Spiros was worse, although Harriet did not delude herself that his main concern was for her. Most of his thoughts were for the baby, to whom he referred throughout the entire nine months as 'my son'.

'It might be a girl,' Harriet warned him, afraid that if it were he would be desperately disappointed.

But she need not have worried. When, the preceding evening, he had at last held his baby daughter in his arms nothing could have exceeded Spiros' wondering delight. The tiny, fragile, pink-and-white creature, with a fuzz of soft blonde hair, had captivated his heart. All regrets that she was not a boy had immediately vanished.

'Elena,' he had said. 'She shall be called Elena, after my mother.'

Again, Harriet experienced a surge of irritation that her wishes had not been consulted, but she shrugged it aside. She was used, by now, to her husband's high-handed actions. And in this particular instance it was understandable. Elena would probably be his only child: she had three others.

The birth had been relatively easy, contrary to all predictions, and Harriet had slept well. She woke early to the ministrations of the midwives and to feed her daughter. After breakfast, Kathleen Tettenburg brought Piers in to see his new sister, and they were closely followed by Spiros, who was temporarily sleeping in one of the guest-rooms, carrying a dark green folder.

'For you, my darling,' he said, placing it on Harriet's lap. 'As a thank-you for my beautiful daughter.'

Twenty minutes later, they were still wrangling amicably over Spiros' totally unexpected gift.

'But I know nothing whatsoever about racing,' Harriet pleaded. 'I don't even like horses very much. They're not animals with whom I feel any affinity. What am I going to do with five of them?'

'You put in a good manager. A trainer. You need never go near the place if you don't want to.' Spiros kissed her gently on her forehead. 'But these horses will win money for you, Harriet. They're a good investment. I've done my homework.'

'Don't you always? But why did the owner go bankrupt and have to sell them?'

'Because he was a fool. He made too many other, unwise investments.'

With that, she had to be content. It was no good arguing with Spiros; once his mind was made up, that was it. She had learned never to expect any say in the things he gave her. Nor would he take them back if he thought they were unwelcome, or condone her getting rid of them. She would just have to get used to being a racehorse-owner.

After he left the bedroom, Harriet went through the contents of the folder once again, wondering uneasily why her husband had made this particular gift. Spiros was no fool, and must know that the combination of horses and southern Ireland was bound to bring thoughts of Edmund Howard to her mind. Was Spiros so sure of her affection and loyalty that he considered it no longer a risk? Or was it some kind of test, like the ones inflicted by Duke Walter on the long-suffering Griselda? She could never be sure with Spiros, finding it increasingly difficult to follow the twists and turns of his devious brain.

The Malachi stables. Presumably called after the Irish high king, Malachi II, who had defeated the Norsemen at Tara in the tenth century. It looked a beautiful place from the photographs. It must have broken the owner's heart to part with it. Harriet leaned back against her pillows and stared into space, conscious only of Elena's gentle breathing. Harriet Chance, the girl from the vicarage, was now a racehorse-owner.

Somehow, she still did not quite believe it.

It was two years later, during Ascot Week, that she met Edmund Howard again. One of her horses, Emerald Isle, was running on Ladies' Day in the three-thirty.

Harriet was with her trainer, Carlin Boyce, a big soft-spoken Irishman, who was her guest for the week at Winterbourn Green. They were in the saddling-up enclosure, and Carlin was speaking to the jockey. Harriet, aware of her shortcomings as an owner, the paucity of her knowledge and, worse still, her lack of any real interest, was standing well back, keeping nervously clear of the restive mount. As she watched, Emerald Isle threw up his head with a whinny, showing the whites of his eyes; and, although in no danger, she automatically stepped back another couple of paces. As she did so, she collided with someone passing behind her. Turning to make apologies, she found herself face to face with Edmund.

'I'm so sorry —' she began, then broke off, the words dying in her throat.

Edmund, too, about to give the usual polite reassurances, stood stock still, unable to speak.

It was seven years since they had last seen one another, under circumstances which were etched in pictures of fire in both their minds. She noted the grey in his hair and the fine lines at the corners of his eyes.

He spoke first.

'Good afternoon, Mrs Georgiadis. I wondered if we should meet, some time or another. I heard, of course, that you are now an owner. Your husband bought the old McCoy stables, near Waterford, for you, didn't he?' The blue eyes were expressionless, but there was a note of contempt in Edmund's voice which flicked her on the raw.

'Is there any law against it?' she snapped childishly.

'I don't know,' he answered levelly. 'You tell me. I'd say

310

there ought to be a law against anything that involves Albie and Charlie King.'

She stared at him helplessly. 'What on earth are you talking about? What have the King brothers to do with my horses?'

Edmund raised his eyebrows. 'Don't play the innocent with me, Mrs Georgiadis. Just remember that I know you better than most people. Don't pretend you weren't aware that Pat McCoy went bankrupt after getting involved with a finance company run by the Kings. That's why your husband was able to buy the Malachi stables at half their market price. I wonder who told him that Pat McCoy was that desperate? I believe Albie and Charlie King are friends of Mr Georgiadis?'

'I know nothing about any of that,' she answered heatedly. 'And, whatever Spiros has or has not done in his life, you, at least, owe him a very big debt of gratitude. You have no cause to speak slightingly of him, believe me!'

It was Edmund's turn to look bewildered, but at that moment a tall, elegantly dressed woman approached and laid a hand familiarly on his arm. Harriet, although they had never met, recognized her as a member of exiled European royalty, and recalled having read somewhere that she had bought several of her horses from Edmund. He nodded curtly at Harriet and moved away towards the mount and jockey sporting the royal colours, but she saw him glance briefly over his shoulder, evidently intrigued and puzzled.

Carlin Boyce had finished briefing the jockey and was now politely waiting to escort her back to her box.

'Can we win, do you think?' she asked, as they walked together across the springy turf, trying to sound excited by the prospect.

Carlin smiled. 'You don't have to come to meetings if you don't want to,' he told her in his lilting Irish brogue. 'I'd be perfectly happy to run things for you.'

She laughed. 'Oh dear, is it that obvious? And I thought I was dissembling so well. But this is Royal Ascot. As much a social event as anything else, wouldn't you agree?'

'I shouldn't have thought that mattered to Harriet Georgiadis. I'm talking, you understand, about seeing and being seen. If you were really interested in the horses, now, that would be different. And, yes, we ought to win if the ground doesn't prove too heavy, which it could well do after all this rain.' He opened the door of her box and ushered her in.

Bess Holland, Ken and June Lambert and the Papido-polous, who were also spending the week with her at Winterbourn Green, were already seated. The two men rose as she entered.

Emerald Isle won his race by a length and a half, to Harriet's great relief, as she knew that both Ken and Dimitri Papidopolou had bet heavily on him. And, while the result made no difference to the Greek, Ken, with his new family and extortionate alimony payments to Aileen, could not afford to lose. He would have been too proud to let her make it up to him.

Bess Holland was more excited than any of them.

'I've won fifty pounds!' she exulted, making Carlin Boyce laugh. He teased her gently, calling her the last of the big spenders.

He's sweet on her, Harriet thought, and felt sorry for her trainer.

Bess would sleep with him for a night or two, make him fall even more in love with her than he already was, and then move on. Harriet had come to realize that when Bess said she would never marry again she meant it. She was glad. She liked the idea that they would always be together.

As she and Carlin waited to congratulate the winner, he said: 'Was that Edmund Howard I saw you talking to earlier on? If you ever think of adding to your stables, I'd advise you to go to him. The best breeder in the whole of Ireland.'

'A pity Spiros could not be here to see you win,' Dimitri Papidopolou said that evening at dinner. 'But I know he is occupied. Things have not been so good in Greece since the coup. None of us finds it easy.'

The previous year, 1967 had seen a bloodless coup d'état, and the establishment of a military government in Athens. King Constantine II had been deposed, and had fled with his family to Rome.

'Me, I am a royalist,' announced Madame Papidopolou, waving her short fat arms, laden with diamond bracelets. 'But sshh!' She laid a podgy, heavily beringed finger against her lips. 'It is not fashionable now to say so.'

Ken Lambert grimaced. 'Things have been really rough in the States as well. Negro riots, Vietnam protests. And now all this crap about a massacre at some place called My Lai. Christ! No one bleated when we bombed the Krauts to hell during the war. People are going soft. No guts any more to stand up for the things they believe in.'

'Perhaps they don't believe in them any more,' Bess Holland suggested, regarding Ken with dislike from the opposite side of the table. 'Perhaps they've come to realize how threadbare those sorts of concepts are.'

Bess, Harriet had discovered, was a woman like herself: a woman of strongly held and strongly expressed opinions. But she could, on occasions, be persuaded she was wrong if the counter-arguments were sufficiently cogent; and this was another aspect of a complex personality which Harriet was growing more and more to admire. She was growing extremely fond of Bess.

She would have continued now with a swingeing attack on the Vietnam war, but Harriet caught her eye and gently shook her head. She was in no mood for political arguments. She was tired after her day at Ascot and the long drive back to Winterbourn Green. Seeing Edmund again had shaken her. The miracle was that they had not run into each other before, during the past two years. She had forced herself to go to enough race meetings. She had even been to Ireland three times, to visit the stables.

Had she, subconsciously, been hoping to see Edmund

again? She had kidded herself that she was merely trying to be a good owner and take an intelligent interest in Spiros' gift. But normally she wasted no time on things which bored her. She was far too busy a woman for that. Yet she had persevered with the race meetings. Until now, she had never really examined her motives.

Harriet had installed a married couple, the MacGregors, as permanent caretakers at the Old Vicarage, the wife as cook-housekeeper, the husband as gardener and odd-job man. Mr MacGregor also, when the occasion demanded it, waited at table. For most of the time, they had the place to themselves, for which they received a handsome salary. Neither fact, however, stopped them from gossiping in the village. Harriet was aware of the fact, but the couple were quiet and efficient, so she kept them on.

As Ewart MacGregor was serving the coffee, the telephone rang in the hall. When he returned from answering it, he bent over Harriet's chair and murmured: 'A Mr Howard on the line for you, madam. He's calling from Ascot. The Royal Foresters' Hotel.'

Harriet tried to behave calmly, but her hand shook and she spilled some of her coffee into the saucer. Cursing inwardly, she excused herself to her guests, closing the dining-room door carefully behind her.

'Hello, Mr Howard, what can I do for you?' Her voice, at least, was steady.

'I want to talk to you. Not on the phone. I want to see you. I want to know what you meant by that remark this afternoon.'

'I see.' She wished her heart would behave normally, instead of jumping around in this ridiculous fashion. 'Will you be at the races tomorrow?'

'Yes, but that's no good. We shan't be able to have any sort of conversation.'

'Why do you want to, after all these years?'

'I told you. Your remark intrigued me.' There was a long pause, which she made no attempt to fill. At last, Edmund went on: 'Incidentally, if you're wondering how I dis-

314

covered your number, it was Hallam who gave it to me. It's not in the book.'

'Hallam was there today? I didn't see him.'

'He saw you, though. He was with his father. The Viscount had a horse running. Blue Diamond. Three o'clock.'

'Did he? I'm afraid I don't read my race-card very carefully.' Harriet added sharply: 'How did you come to be talking to Hallam? I didn't imagine you two were . . . were friends.'

'We're not. I hate the bastard.' Edmund's tone was harsh. 'But it's been difficult to avoid him altogether. We're always bumping into one another at meetings. Besides. . .' His voice tailed away, and there was another silence.

'Besides,' Harriet finished for him tonelessly, 'you blame me for what happened more than you blame Hallam. That's right, isn't it?'

Edmund did not answer immediately. Ewart MacGregor came out of the dining-room, having finished serving the coffee, and vanished in the direction of the kitchen. Harriet watched him go, then spoke again into the receiver.

'That's right, isn't it?' she repeated.

'Yes, I suppose it is. Or was. Lately, I've begun to have my doubts. I want to see you, Harriet. If there is an explanation, I'd like to hear it.'

It was Melina Papidopolou's turn to emerge from the dining-room, opening and closing the door on a cushion of noise. By the sound of things, a full-scale argument was developing between Bess and Ken Lambert. The Vietnam war. Civil rights. Martin Luther King. There was almost nothing that the two of them agreed on. Melina grimaced and waved a chubby hand before chugging upstairs, heading for the bathroom.

Harriet came to a decision.

'I think it would be easier if we met here,' she said. 'I have guests at the moment, but they'll be leaving at the end of the week. Can you stay on for a couple of days, or do

315

you have to get back to Ireland? Is Isabelle with you?'

'No, she's not here. What about Sunday?' he asked. 'Is that OK? You can give me lunch.'

Harriet was still staring at the receiver, which she had just replaced in its cradle, when Bess, too, came out of the dining-room on the same errand as Melina. With one foot already on the bottom stair, she paused, her attention arrested by the look on Harriet's face. After a moment's hesitation, she turned and walked across to her employer.

'Are you all right?'

'What?' Harriet was startled. She had barely noticed Bess. Her thoughts had been miles away, in Ascot. 'Oh! Yes, I'm fine.' She made an effort to speak normally, and smiled. 'You're looking very attractive tonight. I suppose you know you've got poor Carlin Boyce hooked?'

Bess laughed, blushed and disclaimed. But she was looking her best this evening and she was too honest to deny the fact. A short white dress embroidered with crystal and pearl beading enhanced her dark colouring and set off the delicate olive skin to perfection. As she moved away and mounted the stairs, Harriet knew a momentary pang of jealousy for all that youth and elegance, particularly the former. Youth certainly was a stuff that would not endure. Sometimes Harriet wished fervently that she could have hers all over again.

33

By one of those twists of Fate, Harriet did not see Edmund
again for the rest of the week, but one of the first people
she noted, after arriving at the racecourse the following
morning, was Hallam. He was standing near the entrance
to the Members' Enclosure, talking to another man. As
Harriet and her party approached, he glanced in her direction, said something to his companion and headed straight
towards her.

'My dear Harriet, we meet at last! We seem to have
spent the whole week just missing each other. Did you
hear from Eddie? He asked me for your telephone number
at Winterbourn Green, and I took it upon myself to give it
to him. My father told me you're staying there this week.'

They were forced to see one another from time to time,
over matters concerning Piers, but until today Hallam's
attitude had been openly hostile. Now, it seemed, he was
at last prepared to let bygones be bygones. Harriet, however, felt deeply suspicious of these friendly overtures.
They were out of character.

Another thing which nagged at her was the identity
of the man Hallam had been talking to. Although she had
only caught a fleeting glimpse of his profile, there had
been something vaguely familiar about him. And that
glimpse had made her uneasy; she had no idea why.

'Who was that?' she demanded sharply. 'That man you
were speaking to just now?'

Her tone of voice was sufficient to make the two bodyguards, who travelled everywhere with her nowadays, at

317

Spiros' insistence, close in from their position at the edge of the group.

'I've no idea,' Hallam said smoothly. 'Just some chap asking the way to the jockeys' changing-room.'

He was lying, of course. Harriet recognized the shiftiness in his eyes, but there was no way she could prove it, and she had no wish to make a scene in front of her guests. She changed the subject.

'Yes, Edmund telephoned me.' It was her turn to be noncommittal, and she was pleased to see the look of unsatisfied curiosity on Hallam's face. 'Did you want anything in particular? You're holding up my friends. We'd like to get to our box.'

'Merely to confirm, on behalf of my parents, that Piers and the excellent Nanny Tettenburg – thankfully so English, in spite of her name – will be spending August with them at Carey Hall, as usual.'

'Yes, of course.' Harriet indicated her surprise at the question with a lift of her eyebrows. 'I've never prevented them seeing their grandson whenever they've wished. And the August visit is an understood thing.'

'Just checking,' Hallam murmured. 'Wouldn't like the old dears to be disappointed. They're getting rather frail now, and one does what one can to protect their interests. Don't look like that, my dear girl! You know better than anyone that I've done my best to ensure that they have a worry-free old age. It isn't my fault that they've got less than they bargained for. How is dear Spiros, by the way? Not with you?'

'No.' Harriet prepared to move on. 'He's too busy.'

'Making more and more of that lovely, lovely lolly, one presumes.' Hallam smiled bleakly. ' "Unto those that hath, et cetera, et cetera." '

'You did damn well out of me, so don't start whining,' Harriet snapped, finally losing her temper. 'You got a damn sight more than you deserve!' She turned back to Ken and June and the Papidopolous. 'I'm sorry about this interruption. Shall we go? Goodbye, Hallam.'

'Slimy bastard,' Ken Lambert muttered, as they moved away. 'I sure as hell don't know how you can bring yourself to speak to him.'

'He's Piers's father,' she answered shortly. 'Let's talk about something more pleasant, shall we? I hope you've all backed Morning Glory to win. Carlin reckons she's the best in the stables.'

Morning Glory romped home to give Harriet her second win of the week; but while everyone congratulated her, and toasted her in her own champagne, she could not shake off the sense of disquiet which had nagged at her all day, ever since she had glimpsed the man with Hallam. She was certain that she knew him; that they had met some time in the past. But, though she racked her brains, she could not recollect where. If she had been able to see his face properly, it might have helped, but as it was she had nothing to go on except the way he stood and walked.

In the end, she gave it up. There were other things to occupy her mind. Like seeing Edmund Howard on Sunday.

Edmund arrived at the Old Vicarage a little after one-thirty, driving a red Aston Martin sports-car. Harriet greeted him at the door, unable to conceal her nervousness at the meeting.

The Lamberts, Carlin Boyce and the Papidopolous had left Winterbourn Green early the previous morning, and Harriet had spent the rest of Saturday devising ways and means of ridding herself of the remainder of her household. The MacGregors were no problem; she simply told them they could have Sunday off, provided Mrs MacGregor left a cold luncheon ready in the dining-room. Madge Shelton and Bill Brereton had been equally easy to persuade, and on Harriet's recommendation had driven up to Stratford-upon-Avon. Bess Holland had been more difficult to dislodge, and it was only when Harriet told her bluntly that she wanted some time to herself that the secretary had reluctantly agreed to go on the Stratford trip with the others.

That left the two bodyguards, and Harriet knew better than to try to get rid of them. But as they spoke very poor English, and kept mostly out of her way when at home, she felt they were unlikely to intrude unless summoned. She asked the housekeeper to leave a meal for them in the kitchen.

To begin with, she and Edmund were stiffly formal. He obviously had not forgiven her for what he naturally saw as her betrayal, and Harriet felt she could hardly plunge into explanations the moment he set foot inside the door. Instead, she offered him a drink, which he refused, and suggested that they had lunch right away.

Mrs MacGregor had left cold chicken and a variety of salads set out on the sideboard, and they helped themselves, carrying their plates to the table. Neither was hungry, but each made a pretence of eating, until Edmund, cutting through the meaningless small talk, asked abruptly: 'So what did you mean by that remark about your husband? What has Spiros Georgiadis ever done for me?'

So she told him, watching the varying emotions chase one another across his face, from downright incredulity, through dismay and growing anger to, finally, barely containable rage.

'Why the bloody hell didn't you tell me the truth about Hallam?' Edmund shouted, banging his fist impotently on the dining-room table. 'I'd have killed the bastard!'

'And that's why I didn't tell you. Couldn't tell you. And stop pounding the table. You're spilling the wine.'

Edmund slumped back in his chair, putting a hand to his forehead.

'I still can't really believe it,' he said. 'And to think these past few years I've actually felt sorry for the sod, because I thought you'd treated him the same way you treated me.' He stared at her, bewildered. 'For God's sake, *why didn't you tell me the truth*?'

'I repeat, how could I? Your reaction then would have

320

been exactly the same as it is now. Your first instinct would have been to half-kill Hallam, and where would that have left us? In prison, most likely.'

'Do you think I'd have let you go to gaol on my account?' Edmund demanded hotly, his anger rekindling. 'You could have denied your part in the Seamus Hogan episode, and I'd have backed you up. There was only Hallam's word against ours.'

'Oh, for heaven's sake! The adverse publicity wouldn't have done me or the business any good, whatever the outcome. And you'd have ended up in prison. I saw that file before Spiros destroyed it, remember. I don't know what methods Hallam used to obtain his information, but it was all there. Signed statements about your involvement with the IRA. How you'd come to England to set up a safe house. The lot. I couldn't bear the thought of you going to prison.' She added quietly: 'I love you too much.'

Edmund absorbed this in silence for a moment or two. Then he said sullenly: 'If you'd loved me, you'd have taken a chance, and told me what was going on. We'd have worked something out somehow. We'd have got out of England before he could harm us. I'd have gone with you to New York.'

'I had Chance Enterprises to think about as well.' Harriet wondered if she were being a fool, being so honest. He had always been jealous of her commitment to her 'empire' as he scathingly called it. But there seemed no point in only telling half the truth. If he was unable to accept it, that was his loss, not hers. For a second, she felt completely detached from him. Nevertheless, she added: 'I did what seemed best for both of us at the time. Perhaps it was stupid. I don't know. I was terrified of calling Hallam's bluff.'

The room was suddenly very quiet. Through the open window, they could hear the cooing of a dove, calling to its mate. The June sunlight lay in slabs across the thick red carpet, and the pale green curtains stirred in a faint summer breeze. From where Harriet sat, she could see a wide

321

expanse of sky, stencilled with little clouds in thin white lines, like chalk marks on a blackboard. She was reminded sharply of days at the village school, on the other side of the green. She remembered the drone of bees and the smell of honeysuckle outside the classroom window. How uncomplicated life had been then.

She waited resignedly for Edmund's inevitable attack on what he must surely regard as her divided loyalties, but it did not come. Instead, he said quietly: 'All the same, I wish to God you'd trusted me.'

'There wasn't time to think. It all happened so fast. I could see, afterwards, that that was part of Hallam's strategy. There didn't seem anything else to do. And, anyway, it's all so long ago now. You're married to Isabelle. I'm married to Spiros. We can't go back and weave the pattern of our lives anew.'

She spoke wearily, closing her eyes against the sun, watching the hot orange circles roll up inside her lids.

'What a mess,' she heard him say. 'What a bloody awful mess. And it's all my fault. If I hadn't involved you with Seamus Hogan in the first place, as I knew damn well I shouldn't, none of this would have happened. Hallam's suspicions would never have been aroused. If it comes to that, why did I get mixed up with the Army? There's hardly a member who wouldn't sell his grandmother for sixpence. What it really needs,' he added, half to himself, 'is total reorganization from within.'

'Do you have any contact with them any more?' Harriet asked, opening her eyes at his last remark and regarding him suspiciously.

Edmund shook his head.

'No. Not that I've forgiven the English, mind you, for eight hundred years of misrule and oppression, but I've come to accept that you're not all bad.' The blue eyes softened, and the old humour peeped out. 'There are a few of you I wouldn't want to see harmed.' The spurt of amusement vanished as quickly as it had surfaced. 'What in God's name are we going to do?'

322

'Nothing,' she answered. 'There's nothing we can do that won't hurt two people we're fond of. And I have Elena to think of as well.' After a pause, she added: 'Did you and Isabelle never want children?'

Edmund shrugged. 'It just hasn't happened. One of those things, I suppose. Perhaps I'm to blame. Isabelle badly wanted a child when we were first married. I didn't care. All I cared about was losing you.'

'Did it hurt that badly? I hoped you'd hate me too much to have any regrets.'

He absentmindedly crumbled the remains of a bread roll between his fingers, making little pellets of soft grey dough.

'Oh, I hated you all right! But it hurt like hell, all the same. I didn't know whether it was worse then, or later, when you married Spiros. I found that difficult to believe, even of you. That you'd marry a crook like him.'

'Don't say that!' she replied angrily. 'I don't know what I'd've done without Spiros. He saved me from Hallam. He gave me back my self-respect. He saved you, too. Perhaps that's difficult for you to realize, as you've never known that you were under threat. But he's made it possible for me to tell you the truth at last. You owe him that much, at least.'

'Maybe I'd rather not have known.' Edmund raised his head and looked at her across the debris of their half-eaten meal. There was an expression in his eye which she found hard to interpret. 'What does it feel like, being the wife of one of the richest men in the world?'

Harriet propped her elbows on the table and cupped her chin in her hands.

'Cary Grant is reputed to have said: "Everyone wants to be Cary Grant. *I* want to be Cary Grant." And that's exactly how I feel. Everyone wants to be Harriet Georgiadis. *I* want to be Harriet Georgiadis. The trouble is I'm not. Most of the time, I'm Harriet Chance, who grew up in this vicarage with no electric light and no spare cash. Does that answer your question?'

In spite of himself, Edmund smiled. 'Damn you, Harriet! How do you always manage to get under my skin?' He glanced away, trying to alienate himself from her once more, and found inspiration in his surroundings. 'You know, you have absolutely no sense of period! You cram everything in together, just as it takes your fancy. This room's a mess. Chippendale chairs, a modern table, William Morris wallpaper, a Paul Nash and three very cheap copies of what could easily be framed chocolate-box covers.'

'I like it,' she retorted defiantly. 'And Spiros never complains. He says I have a style of my own.' Edmund snorted. 'And that's all that matters.'

'About what I'd expect from a self-made ignoramus like Spiros Georgiadis! He can hardly educate your taste, when he has none of his own.'

'He doesn't presume to educate me! What the hell is the matter with you, Edmund?' Harriet's temper and voice were both rising. 'If you can't be civil, please leave! I will not sit here tamely and listen to you insulting my husband, to whom we owe so much.'

'The man's a crook! He consorts with crooks!' Edmund stood up, his eyes blazing. Harriet rose, too, equally furious. 'Be your age, woman! You can't get as rich as he is on the straight and narrow! Without trampling all over innocent people!'

If Edmund had stopped to analyse his emotions, he would have recognized that he spoke from jealousy; an all-consuming jealousy at the thought of Harriet making love with another man. Now that he could no longer feel contempt and hatred for her, those feelings had transferred themselves automatically to Spiros, who, from what he knew of him, Edmund had always disliked.

Harriet threw herself at him in a rage, battering her fists against his chest.

'Don't ever speak like that of Spiros! He's a good man! A better man than you'll ever be, you bastard! Do you hear

324

me? Don't you ever speak like that of him again!'

It was the language and behaviour of the nursery, but it released the pent-up misery and tension which had been building steadily inside her throughout the morning; a safety-valve suddenly blowing to give off a great head of steam.

Edmund's hands came up to grip her wrists, his fingers biting into her flesh, crushing her bones. Harriet kicked him hard on the shins, and he swore, pushing her into the table, so that she could feel the edge hard against her spine. But she was not afraid, not as she had been with Hallam. This was a different sort of physical violence, she realized, and mutually enjoyable.

She tried to sink her teeth into Edmund's thumb, but he jerked her towards him and his mouth descended savagely on hers, biting her lower lip. She could taste the blood, salt against her tongue. She struggled for a moment, but when he suddenly released her wrists her arms went round him, holding him so closely that their bodies were almost one. She could feel herself melting into him, flesh of his flesh, bone of his bone. . .

Harriet could never remember actually lying on the floor and taking off her clothes. What she could remember was the feeling of ecstasy, like flying, which she had never experienced before, not even with Edmund. She heard someone gasping on a high shrill note, and only realized later that it was herself. Her back arched suddenly under Edmund's weight; she felt him give one final thrust; heard him breath: 'Holy Jesus! Mother of God!' Then they were both lying quietly in one another's arms.

She raised a hand and smoothed his ruffled hair.

'I love you,' she said.

'And I love you. I've always loved you, ever since that first day on the beach.'

'But there's nothing we can do about it, is there?'

Edmund shook his head. 'No, nothing. I can't leave Isabelle. I owe her too much. It wouldn't be fair.'

'And I can't leave Spiros for the same reason.'

'I know.' Edmund pushed her away and sat up, searching around for his scattered clothes.

'But you'll think of me kindly sometimes, now that you know the truth?'

He turned his head at the note of repressed anguish in her voice, and bent to kiss her gently.

'In my heart of hearts, acushla, I've always thought of you kindly. Subconsciously, I suppose, I've known that there had to be a reason for what you did.'

They held one another for a minute, before he pulled himself free.

Twenty minutes later he was gone, the red Aston Martin roaring away down Vicarage Lane, disturbing the villagers' Sunday peace.

When the others returned, late that evening, Harriet was sitting by the open window in the drawing-room, staring into the garden. Everything was beginning to fade and merge together in the gathering dusk.

It was Bess Holland who came in search of her.

'How are things?' she asked, standing anxiously in the doorway.

Harriet stirred and smiled faintly. 'Fine. Why shouldn't they be?'

Bess advanced a few paces inside the room. 'I don't know. I just thought that you seemed a bit unlike yourself this morning.'

'Well, I'm OK now,' Harriet reassured her. She noted how smart Bess was looking, in a pale beige dress with tan accessories. She really was a very handsome woman. 'I told you,' Harriet went on, 'I needed some time to myself, to recharge my batteries.'

Bess's worried expression disappeared, and she nodded. 'Yes, of course you did. It must be very tiring, always being surrounded by people. Do you know that bit in *Emma*, where Jane Fairfax says, "Oh, Miss Woodhouse, the comfort of being sometimes alone!"?'

'*Emma* is my favourite book,' Harriet answered simply. 'Do you like Jane Austen?'

'I read her all the time.' Bess smiled and turned to go. 'Good night, Mrs Georgiadis.'

'Good night, my dear.' The voice of her father echoed back to Harriet down through the years. Softly, she added the ancient benediction: 'God bless you.'

34

Harriet was never to forget Thursday, 21 August 1968.

She was in New York for the bi-monthly board meeting of the Chance Corporation, and had set her alarm for seven-thirty. For a moment or two, after waking, she lay quietly, listening to the clock's shrill insistent note, before reaching out a hand to switch it off. She could hear Jeanette moving about in the neighbouring bedroom; then a door opened, and the housekeeper went across the hall to the kitchen. There was the usual clatter of cups as she prepared the early-morning tea.

Harriet rolled on to her back, staring at the ceiling. The build-up of traffic along Fifth Avenue came to her ears like the lazy droning of bees on a summer's afternoon. The curtains were still drawn, long swaths of heavy pale-green linen, giving the room a subaqueous look. It was rather, Harriet thought drowsily, like being in an underwater cave.

> *Sabrina fair,*
> * Listen where thou art sitting*
> *Under the glassy, cool, translucent*
> *wave. . .*

Her father used to quote that a lot, she remembered. He had always had a partiality for Milton. Her father . . . the vicarage . . . Edmund. . .

She was suddenly wide awake, needing Edmund, wanting Edmund, recalling once again the feel of his body pressed against hers. The longing was sometimes so desperate that she felt she could leave everything and everybody and run away with him. She sat up in bed, arms locked across her chest, rocking to and fro in an agony of loss.

Gradually, she fought down the tide of emotion. In another two days, she would be flying back to Greece; to Agios Georgios, where her husband and daughter were waiting for her. Spiros spent a great deal of his time on the island since Elena's birth, and it bore more resemblance to an armed fortress every time Harriet saw it; bodyguards, dogs, a small arsenal of weapons housed in one of the downstairs rooms. For Spiros was terrified of a kidnap attempt, and was taking no chances with the safety of his only child.

'She'll grow up like Miranda, in *The Tempest*, if you're not careful,' Harriet had protested on her last visit. 'A girl and her father' – she had refrained from saying 'old father', but the thought was in both their minds – 'on an enchanted island. You can't keep her from contact with the world for ever, my dear, just on the offchance that something might happen to her.'

Spiros had shrugged, but not answered. Harriet knew that mood. It meant he had made up his mind on a certain subject and was not open to persuasion. Harriet had shrugged in her turn. The child was very young, not yet two, and she hoped that time would work its own cure.

From Elena and Spiros, Harriet's thoughts flitted to Michael. He was twenty now, and in another year would be joining the Chance Corporation.

'You start at the bottom, learning the catering business in one of the restaurants,' she had told him at the start of the summer vacation.

'What about the corporation's other concerns?' he had asked insolently. 'Or don't they matter?'

'Of course they matter!' She knew very well that he thought himself capable of taking over the entire corporation and its administration tomorrow. Self-doubt had never been one of Michael's weaknesses. She had continued: 'Chance Enterprises is the hub of the Chance Corporation, and the vital heart of Enterprises is the Last Chance restaurants. They are the foundation stone of our reputation, our wealth, our everything. And you can't start at the top. Your fancy Business School theories are no substitute for practical experience. Believe me. I know.'

Michael had looked sceptical and gone off to spend a couple of months with some friends in Maine. Later in the season, he would return the compliment and entertain them at the Connecticut farmhouse. Harriet guessed she would not see him again before he returned to Harvard in the fall. Perhaps it was no great loss, but she would have liked their relationship to be a closer one, if only for the sake of Gus's memory.

And then there was Piers, who would be five next month. He was at Carey Hall with Kathleen Tettenburg until the end of August, being indulged and petted to the top of his bent by the doting viscount and his wife. Harriet always dreaded seeing her younger son again after one of these visits, when even Kathleen found it hard to control him. Naturally self-willed, his grandparents' adoration made Piers more wayward than ever. Punishment had very little effect on him. Young as he was, he simply weighed up whether or not the crime was worth the consequences and, if the answer was affirmative, went ahead with whatever piece of devilry he had in mind. He was the most calculating child Harriet had ever met. Nevertheless, she was fond of him.

Was that the way a mother should think of her child? she wondered guiltily. Was she, as she so often feared, lacking in maternal instinct?

The bedroom door opened, and Jeanette Baynton came in with a cup of strong, hot, sweet tea. 'English tea' she always called it, with a grimace and a shudder.

'Don't mock,' Harriet would reprove, laughing. 'It was on brews such as these that we won the war.'

'You're looking serious,' Jeanette remarked now, putting the cup and saucer down on the bedside table and going across to pull back the curtains. 'Have you heard the news?'

'No. What's happened?'

'The Russians have invaded Czechoslovakia. The newspapers and radio bulletins are full of it.'

'Oh dear,' Harriet sighed. 'I haven't listened to the radio this morning.' She sipped her tea gratefully. 'Lovely. Just as I like it. You've got the knack of it at last. No, I was thinking about children and how damn difficult they can be. They're a problem from the day that they're born.'

'I wouldn't know,' Jeanette said. 'Ted and I never managed to have any. Not for the want of trying, mind you.' She smiled reflectively. 'He was a very passionate man, although you might not have thought it, to look at him. However, children weren't to be, and I often feel there's something missing from my life. Not like yours. You and your three.'

Harriet opened her mouth to say 'Four', but quickly bit back the correction. She thought tenderly of that other child, whom she saw now so often. Dear Hilary! She hugged her secret knowledge to her.

Sometimes Harriet felt guilty that she was not doing more for her eldest child, but Spiros was adamant.

'Wait!' he would advise, whenever they discussed the subject. 'You are not the only person to be considered. There are the adoptive parents. There is Hilary, who, so far as we know, expresses no interest in the past. And there is Michael, who believes himself to be your eldest child. Public acknowledgement would be too disruptive. Too unfair.'

So Harriet said nothing, content, for now, to let the problem slide. Spiros was right: there were so many other people, besides herself, to be considered. And it was too early in her relationship with Hilary to arrive at any major decision.

Jeanette Baynton went through to the bathroom and

331

started to run Harriet's bath. The bedside telephone rang, and Harriet picked it up. It was Spiros.

At the sound of his voice, she knew a moment's panic.

'What – what is it?' she asked haltingly. 'What's the matter?'

He laughed. 'Nothing. Nothing at all. Can't I telephone my own wife without something being wrong? I just called to say' – he hesitated – 'to say that Elena and I are looking forward to seeing you.'

'Oh!' She knew she must sound surprised, but Spiros had never before made anything so closely resembling a romantic gesture, and she was thrown off balance.

'I thought you would like to know,' he said, trying, and failing, to be casual.

'Yes, of course. It's just that . . . that it's not eight o'clock over here yet. I'm still in bed. Still half-asleep.'

'Ah! Well, when you wake up properly you can remember to be pleased.' His tone was gently ironic. 'I shall look for you on Saturday, my dear. *Au revoir* until then.'

He hung up. Harriet sat staring at the receiver for a moment or two, before replacing it in its rest.

Her feelings were in a turmoil. The last thing she had either expected or wanted was that Spiros should fall in love with her. Their relationship, as far as she was concerned, was a satisfactory one, based on mutual respect and a strong physical attraction. But love was something else. That meant emotional ties and a commitment which she could only give to Edmund.

Yet what did her commitment to Edmund amount to? Inchoate daydreams, which had never formed themselves into a plan of action; nebulous schemes; intentions without substance. But in the weeks since she and Edmund had made love she had entertained a vague hope that some day something might happen to change the pattern of their lives. Suddenly, she knew that as long as Isabelle was alive that hope was nonexistent. She wondered why she was so sure of this fact. Edmund had divorced his first wife

332

without any regrets; but she had sensed his underlying affection for Isabelle. And, besides, would she really leave Spiros? She did not know. Everything was a muddle.

Jeanette came back into the room to tell her that her bath was ready.

By the time the meeting, held in the board room of the offices on West 72nd Street, was over, Harriet felt calmer. She managed to smile at Bess Holland as they both returned to her private office.

'That went OK, didn't it?' She dropped wearily into an armchair near the window. 'How about some lunch? You must be as hungry as I am.'

Bess laughed. 'I must admit, I'm starving. Shall I call Times Square? Or would you rather have something sent up?'

'Call Times Square. And you're coming with me. It'll do us both good to get out.'

'Are you feeling well?' Bess asked, moving towards the battery of different-coloured telephones strung along the edge of Harriet's desk. 'I thought once or twice this morning that you were a bit *distraite*.'

'I've a headache,' Harriet answered guardedly. 'My period's been heavy this month.'

Bess was at once all sympathy and concern. 'Why didn't you say? I'll get you some aspirin.' She regarded Harriet affectionately. 'You really ought to take more care of yourself, you know.'

A telephone rang, a little light beneath the dial indicating which one. Bess moved back to the desk and lifted the receiver. Harriet closed her eyes and began to relax. When she felt low, it was good to know that Bess was at hand. The friendship between the two women was steadily ripening. She did not listen to what Bess was saying. It was just a routine enquiry. . .

She opened her eyes again to see her secretary just standing there, staring at her with a horrified expression on her face. Harriet was immediately in full

333

possession of her faculties, every nerve stretched and thrumming.

'What's happened?' she croaked. 'Is it . . . is it my husband?'

'Yes. That is, no. Not Mr Georgiadis.' Bess extended the receiver as though her arm had been pulled by a string, her dark eyes brimming with concern. 'It's Mr Cavendish. He says . . . Piers has been kidnapped.'

Harriet's knees buckled as she got to her feet, but she steadied herself and snatched the telephone from Bess's hand. Without realizing what she was doing, Bess put an arm about her shoulders.

'Hallam?' Harriet's voice was shaking. 'What in God's name is all this nonsense? Bess is saying that Piers has been kidnapped. What's going on over there? What's really happened?'

'It's true!' Hallam's answer was indistinct, blurred by distance and emotion. 'Piers was kidnapped this morning, while he was out with that nanny of his. They were down at the stables, looking at the horses. Two men just appeared out of nowhere and grabbed him. . . Harriet! Are you still there?'

'Yes, I'm still here.' She took Bess Holland's hand and held on to it tightly. The contact comforted her. 'I'm catching the next plane over.'

She hung up and turned to Bess. 'Get me my husband,' she ordered. 'Quickly!'

She reached Carey Hall at four the following morning, jet-lagged and haggard from lack of sleep. Hallam was there to greet her.

Spiros had met her at the airport, furious that she had not waited in New York for his private plane. The number of his bodyguards had increased from two to five, and Harriet could well imagine what things were like on Agios Georgios; the precautions which were being taken to ensure Elena's safety. Two of the bodyguards, Stephanos and Constantine, rode with her, Spiros and Bess Holland in

334

the Daimler, one of a fleet of cars which, nowadays, were kept permanently garaged in London for the Georgiadis' use – another sign of Spiros' growing obsession with the dangers of kidnapping which his daughter's birth had triggered. The other three bodyguards followed in a Rover, one man acting as driver. The Daimler was chauffeured by Bill Brereton, who had accompanied Harriet and Bess from New York.

It was light by the time they reached Carey Wanstead and drove up to the Hall. The journey, through the misty greyness of an English summer dawn, had been accomplished mainly in silence, neither Harriet nor Spiros nor Bess being in any mood for conversation. Harriet had stared bleakly out of the car window, watching the distances change from black to mauve to pale translucent blue. Houses stood like ghosts in the silent villages, with here and there the odd bright eye of a lighted window in the house of some early riser – a milkman, a postman, someone heading for a Reading factory and the day's first shift. All she could think about was Piers and how small he was, and how frightened he must be. Her mind felt trapped, caged in by horror and fear.

Hallam had obviously been listening for the sound of the car, because he came out on to the front steps before Bill Brereton had killed the Daimler's engine. Harriet got out and gripped her ex-husband's arm, unaware that she had even moved.

'What's happened? Where are the police?'

'Police?' Hallam stared at her as though she had taken leave of her senses. 'You don't think I've called in the rozzers, for God's sake, do you? They told me on no account to contact anyone!'

'*They*? Who are *they*? Do you mean the kidnappers have been in touch with you already?'

Spiros was behind her, his steadying hands on her shoulders.

'Let us go inside,' he said gently. 'Come in, Harriet, and sit down. We cannot talk to Mr Cavendish on the doorstep.'

Hallam suddenly became aware of Spiros and his body-guards, who had emerged from the cars and were now standing in a grim-faced row. His voice rose tautly.

'Who asked this lot to come here? Who *are* all these fucking gorillas?'

'Let us go inside,' Spiros repeated quietly, making allowances for the state of Hallam's nerves. 'Did you really think I should not wish to be with my wife at such a time?'

'No . . . I suppose. . . Oh, well! Let's go in, as you say. One of the maids has stayed up to make us coffee and sandwiches. In here.' He led the way into the dining-room.

'Where are your parents?' Harriet asked, making no attempt to remove her coat. In spite of the central heating, which she had had installed at enormous expense, Carey Hall was still cold at this hour of the morning. She sat down on one of the dining-chairs, beside the table.

'They're in bed. My mother's under sedation. This business has hit them hard, as you can imagine.'

'It's hit us all hard,' Harriet answered.

A young girl in a flowered housecoat came through the service door from the kitchens, carrying a tray. When she saw the array of people in the room, she was visibly taken aback.

'You'd better get more cups and cut more sandwiches, Gillian,' Hallam told her resentfully. 'For our unexpected guests. I hope to God,' he added peevishly to Harriet, 'you don't expect us to accommodate all this mob.'

'We are returning to London as soon as we know how matters stand,' Spiros said, holding his temper on a tight rein. This was neither the time nor the place to have a fight with Hallam Cavendish. 'Are we to understand that the kidnappers have contacted you?'

'Last night. About eleven o'clock. Nine hours after the boy disappeared.' Hallam buried his face in his hands. His voice was muffled. 'They want two million pounds by the end of next week. In cash. Unused untraceable notes. No police. Otherwise we won't see Piers again. That's a promise.'

There was silence. Harriet stared at the tapestry on the opposite wall; a seventeenth-century Aubusson, depicting a scene from the story of Judith and Holofernes. She noted, with a kind of wondering detachment, the massive size of Judith's breasts.

Spiros was the first to speak again.

'Perhaps it is just as well, then, that I am here. Finding that sort of money, in cash, in so short a time, is not an easy task. I shall, however, do my best to raise it.'

Harriet gave him a speaking look and squeezed his hand.

The girl called Gillian came back with more cups and saucers, and began to hand round coffee.

'You'll have to wait for the sandwiches, the extra ones, I'm afraid,' she said.

No one took any notice of her. The Greeks and Bill Brereton were stolidly eating their way through those already provided. Nobody else was hungry. Bess Holland was looking sick.

'I still think we should tell the police,' Harriet insisted.

But here Hallam found a powerful ally in Spiros, whose lifelong philosophy had been never to involve the law when he could deal with things himself.

'There is no need for that,' he said. 'We pay the money. We get the boy back. And then we track down the kidnappers and we kill them.'

Harriet and Hallam looked horrified. Bess Holland gasped.

'You can't do that, sir!' she exclaimed, startled into speech.

Spiros stared at her in astonishment, unused to employees, particularly female ones, speaking out of turn. He made a mental note to mention her secretary's lack of deference to Harriet at a more suitable time.

Bess continued, undaunted: 'You just can't kill people in cold blood, no matter what they've done. It's wrong.'

'That'll do, Bess!' Harriet's tone was peremptory. Her head was aching. Nevertheless, the girl was right. She turned to Spiros.

337

'Bess is talking sense,' she protested. 'You'd do well to listen to her.' She began to laugh hysterically. 'For heaven's sake! This is England!'

Before Spiros could express his contempt for such a typically craven Anglo-Saxon outlook, Kathleen Tettenburg burst into the room, tears streaming down her face.

'Mrs Georgiadis! Harriet! Oh, God! Can you ever forgive me?'

35

'There's something . . . well, *odd* about it all,' Kathleen Tettenburg said, frowning.

She, Harriet and Spiros were alone in the dining-room. A few moments after Kathleen's dramatic arrival, the Viscount had appeared, demanding Hallam's immediate attendance on his mother.

'She's awake and asking for you. She wants to know if there's any more news.'

He looked dreadful, the skeletal features paper-white, the thinning hair straggling in untidy strands across his forehead. He was wearing a dressing-gown over an old pair of flannel trousers and a shirt, indicating that he had not been to bed properly. Sitting up with Lady Carey, Harriet thought.

Hallam had gone with his father, and the Greek body-guards had withdrawn to the hall, out of sight but still within earshot if they were needed. Bill Brereton suggested to Bess Holland that they go for a stroll in the park, to clear their heads. The maid had disappeared to the kitchens.

'What do you mean, "odd"?' Harriet asked sharply.

Spiros said nothing, but lit a cigarette, glancing round vaguely for an ashtray. When he was unable to find one, he tapped the ash into a *famille rose* vase, in the middle of the table. His head was tilted back, his eyes fixed on a vast painting of dead game, fruit and vegetables by Franz Snyders over the sideboard; but his attention was focused entirely on what Kathleen Tettenburg was saying.

She was quieter now, her emotions under control, her Gloucestershire accent less pronounced, able to speak rationally. Harriet's assurances that she held the nanny in no way to blame for the kidnapping had calmed her.

'You've been told what happened?' Kathleen asked. She, too, had obviously not slept, and was still in her uniform skirt and blouse, although she had replaced her normal low-heeled court shoes with a pair of bedroom slippers.

'Not exactly. There hasn't been time to get details.'

'He loves horses,' Kathleen explained. 'Piers, I mean. Every day, he has to be taken down to the stables. He never wants to go anywhere else. Just to the stables. So that's what we do. After lunch, every afternoon, as regular as clockwork for the whole month we're here. Rain or shine. The stables.'

'And everyone knows this?' asked Spiros.

'Yes. I suppose so. Everyone in the house, that is. Well, we went down yesterday afternoon, as usual, and we'd just stopped so that Piers could give one of the horses a lump of sugar – I always take some with me – when this car came along the track at the side.' Kathleen turned to Harriet. 'You know, the track that runs down from the main road to the stable-block.' Harriet nodded. Kathleen went on: 'I didn't think anything about it. Lots of people have called at one time or another while we've been there. Owners, the trainer, the vet. Could have been anyone.'

'What make of car was it?' asked Spiros. His eyes never wavered from the heap of dead game.

'I'm not very good at cars.' Kathleen was apologetic. 'They don't interest me much, and those I can recognize are mainly American. It was dark blue, with a paler blue stripe along the side. A saloon, but a bit sporty-looking, if you know what I mean. On second thoughts, it may have had a soft top, but it was up.'

'Sounds like a Triumph Herald,' Harriet said to Spiros.

'Go on Kathleen. What happened then?'

'The car backed into the stable-gate, and a man got out. Not the driver. He stayed at the wheel. The other man, the passenger, came towards me as though he was going to ask a question. He was smiling and had that sort of look of enquiry on his face. Then, when he was close to us, he just grabbed hold of Piers and ran for the car. The engine must still have been running, because he threw Piers on the back seat and the car was away, up the track, before I'd even got my breath back.' Her accent thickened once more as she grew agitated. 'I wasn't expecting it, was I? It all happened so quick!'

'Yes, of course it did,' Harriet soothed. 'What about Piers? Did he cry or struggle?'

'No. Not at the time anyway. He was like me. He was too surprised to be frightened.'

'Did you get the number of the car?' Spiros asked, but Kathleen shook her head. She began to cry again. Spiros at last withdrew his gaze from the still life and handed her his handkerchief. 'Don't worry. The number-plates were probably false.'

Kathleen gave him a grateful, if watery, smile.

'And after that?' Harriet prompted.

'I ran back here as fast as I could to raise the alarm. I thought Mr Cavendish would send for the police, but he didn't. Said if Piers had really been kidnapped, then there'd be a ransom demand, and the kidnappers wouldn't be prepared to do a deal if the police had been called in. Lord and Lady Carey didn't agree with him, but they were both in such a state that, in the end, they let him have his way. Turned out, of course, he was right. According to Mr Cavendish, the first thing the man who phoned him asked was if he had notified the police.'

It was now broad daylight, the sun already high over the trees in the park. Ribbons of pink and gold dispersed the early-morning mist, and the air was alive with birdsong. Everything was normal and peaceful and quiet, thought

341

Harriet. Just another day. Only it wasn't.

'You said earlier that there was something odd about it all,' she reminded Kathleen.

'Yes... Perhaps I'm imagining things, but there does seem something queer about the whole affair.' Kathleen blew her nose on Spiros' handkerchief and sat up straighter. 'Usually, there are people around the stables in the afternoon, but yesterday we didn't see anyone. Not a soul. So, last evening, I made a few enquiries.'

'And?' Spiros dropped the butt of his cigarette into the *famille rose* vase and leaned forward, listening intently.

'The two stable-girls, who are normally there after lunch, had both been given leave by Mr Cavendish. Deirdre had apparently asked for time off to go to a friend's wedding, and Mr Cavendish had told Fiona she might as well go, too.' Kathleen frowned. 'I thought that was funny, because only last week I heard him having a go at them for taking their tea-break together. Quite nasty about it, he was. And the stable-lad, who comes in afternoons, had been called up to the house. That's odd as well, because generally Mr Cavendish comes down to the stables if he wants to speak to anyone.'

'I didn't realize Hallam had so much to do with the stables,' Harriet said. 'I suppose Lord Carey's getting too old to cope on his own.'

'He does seem to run things a fair bit nowadays,' Kathleen agreed. 'Much more than he used to do, when we've been here before.'

Spiros made an impatient gesture.

'These are irrelevancies.' He lit another cigarette. 'What exactly are you implying, Nurse Tettenburg?'

'I'm not implying anything.' Kathleen looked frightened. 'It's just that . . . well, the kidnappers couldn't have picked a better moment. There was no one about except me. It was almost as if they'd known.'

Harriet and Spiros exchanged startled glances. There

was a look of speculation on their faces which gradually hardened into overt suspicion.

'He couldn't have,' Harriet breathed, revolted. 'Oh no! Surely even Hallam wouldn't sink so low.'

Spiros laughed. 'You must be joking, my dear. For two million pounds, your ex-husband would sell his own soul. And to have me pay him the money would be revenge at its sweetest.' He turned again to Kathleen, who had been following their remarks with mounting dismay. 'This man who took Piers, you must be able to describe him.'

'Yes, of course! I had a good look at him. But, Mr Georgiadis, you shouldn't attach too much importance to what I've just said. I'm sure Mr Cavendish wouldn't. . . Oh, bloody hell!' Momentarily, she was once again that Kathleen Mason of the transit camp on Salisbury Plain. 'It could all've been a coincidence, you know!'

'Just describe the man,' Spiros told her firmly.

She hesitated. She obviously had not expected her suspicions to be accepted so readily, and was now beginning to get cold feet in case she was wrong. Reluctantly, she said: 'Average height. About five foot six, I'd reckon. Brown hair, parted on the left-hand side. Short back and sides. None of these fancy new styles the youngsters are wearing nowadays. I think his eyes were blue, but I couldn't be certain. Age, nearer forty than thirty. Tweed sports-jacket and pale beige trousers. And he had one of those red birthmarks – not a very big one – on the right side of his forehead, just below the hairline.'

'Good God!' Harriet looked at Spiros with horrified eyes. 'Of course! That's who Hallam was talking to, that day at Ascot. I knew he was familiar, but I couldn't remember his name.'

'Who are you talking about?' Spiros demanded testily. 'And what is his connection with Hallam?'

Harriet spoke with suppressed excitement, automatically lowering her voice and glancing furtively over her shoulder at the door.

'Kathleen's description fits a man called Richard Pace. He used to manage the Haymarket restaurant until I fired him for incompetence. That was some years ago. I didn't set eyes on him again until last June, when I saw him talking to Hallam outside the Members' Enclosure. As I said, although he seemed familiar, I didn't realize until this moment who he was. He moved away quickly when Hallam spotted me. And, now I come to think of it, when Hallam spoke to me it was to confirm that Piers would definitely be staying at Carey Hall during August. He was anxious to make sure that there hadn't been any last-minute change of plan.' Nobody said anything for a moment or two. Then Harriet added slowly: 'That's it, isn't it? Piers hasn't really been kidnapped. It's a put-up job, organized by Hallam.' Relief flooded through her as the realization dawned that her son was in no physical danger. 'Two million pounds is a hell of a lot of money, but he knew we'd pay up to get Piers back.' Her mouth set in a grim hard line. 'The bastard! Upsetting his parents! Making his mother ill! Right! Now we know the truth, there's no reason not to call the police.'

She got up and moved towards the telephone, but Spiros said: 'No!'

'What?' She half-turned, one hand already reaching for the receiver, and regarded her husband in shocked surprise.

'No,' Spiros repeated calmly. 'No police. First, we find out if our suspicions are correct. And, if they are, we deal with Hallam ourselves.'

By the time they got back to London, after what, in retrospect, seemed one of the longest days of her life, Harriet had been persuaded to play the game according to Spiros' rules. This he had achieved by the simple expedient of threatening to wash his hands of the whole affair if she refused to agree. For a moment, Harriet had nearly decided to go it alone, but in the end it was Spiros' argument that only embarrassment could result from Hallam's arrest and imprisonment that had finally made up her mind.

344

'Think what it would do to the Viscount and his wife,' Spiros had urged. 'The humiliation and shock would probably kill them. And do you want Piers to grow up the son of a common criminal?'

Harriet, against her better judgement, had given in. She felt as though she were moving in a Mad Hatter's tea-party world, where normal rules no longer applied. She tried to hang on to sanity by thinking of her father and her childhood at the vicarage, but it was like trying to wake up from the unreality of a dream.

Hallam, promising to keep them in touch with developments, had encouraged Harriet and Spiros to return to London with a relief and enthusiasm now completely understandable.

'Nothing at all you can do here,' he had told them, smiling bravely. 'And so many people! The Mater's nerves are in shreds already. It would only make her worse.' Filial concern had been etched in every line of his face. Harriet had longed to slap it. 'You'll be much better employed in London, raising the money.'

They went, as always, to Claridges. Within half an hour of their arrival, Spiros was speaking personally to Cecil Brewer, with urgent instructions to track down Richard Pace.

At eight o'clock on Saturday evening the telephone rang. It was the detective agency for Spiros, and Harriet listened in on one of the extensions.

'We've found him, Mr Georgiadis.' Cecil Brewer sounded justifiably pleased with himself. 'A piece of cake. Made no attempt to cover his tracks.' For a split second there was a note of curiosity in the carefully impersonal tones. Clearly, from the little Spiros had told him, Cecil Brewer had anticipated a much more difficult task. 'He used to be the manager of a small café near Paddington Station, and has been living in lodgings in Praed Street. Unmarried. Bit of a loner. Usually short of cash, but recently has seemed a bit flush. Gave in his notice at the café end of last month. Ditto with his lodgings, end of last week. Told his landlady he'd come into a bit of money from an aunt, who'd recently died. Said the old dear had also left him a cottage, and that he was going to stay there for a while before selling it.' Mr Brewer's voice assumed a note of triumph. 'Even left her his address, so she could forward any mail. It's Mill View Cottage, Carey Lane, Ayerst, near Carey Wanstead, Berks.'

The following evening, Cecil Brewer telephoned again.

'I've had one of my men keeping that cottage under surveillance all day, Mr Georgiadis, just as you requested, and he reports sighting a child on two or three occasions at an upstairs window. There's also a two-toned blue Triumph Herald parked near the house. As far as he can ascertain, besides the child, there are only two men in the cottage, one of whom answers to the description you gave me.

'Ayerst itself is a tiny place. Three or four dwellings and a farm. No shop, no pub, no post office, no church. Mill View Cottage is way off the beaten track, at the far end of a lane which used to be the old Carey Wanstead road before a new one was put through in the thirties, ironing out the bends. Carey Lane isn't used any more. The only other building near the cottage is the old water-mill that gives it its name. That's derelict now. Falling to pieces.'

Spiros asked: 'Has there been a visitor during the day? A tall thin man, dark hair, blue eyes, small moustache?'

'No visitors at all, not even the boy from the farm who delivers milk.'

Typical of Hallam, Harriet thought, again listening in on the extension. Protecting his own skin. Staying well away from the cottage until the business was done. Playing safe.

Cecil Brewer's voice resumed: 'But we did find out who owns Mill View Cottage. I rang round the local estate agents myself yesterday as soon as we knew the address. I managed to get the information from a Reading firm, just before they closed, Saturday evening. It belongs to a couple

346

who live somewhere in the Midlands, a Mr and Mrs Smallridge, but it's leased out as holiday accommodation to anyone who really wants to get away from it all. At the beginning of July, it was rented for three months by a Mr Guy Standing.'

Harriet put a hand over the mouthpiece of her receiver and hissed at Spiros: 'Guy is one of Hallam's Christian names, and Standing was Lady Carey's name before she was married.'

Spiros nodded. 'Thank you very much, Mr Brewer,' he said. 'Your firm has done excellently, as always. Please send your account to my secretary in the usual way.'

He hung up, and Harriet replaced her receiver. 'What are you going to do now?' She asked her husband.

He shrugged. 'Stephanos, Constantine and the others will accompany me to this place, this Ayerst, and we shall fetch Piers. We shall bring him straight back here, to you and Nurse Tettenburg, after which it will give me very great pleasure to telephone Carey Hall and tell them all that the child is safe. Hallam can draw his own conclusions.'

Harriet was uneasy. 'I wish to God you'd call the police,' she said. 'Give them all the information you've acquired and let them do the rest.'

'I thought we'd agreed that I can't do that,' Spiros answered gently, 'without involving Hallam.' He walked across the room and kissed her. 'Don't look so troubled. It will be a piece of cake, as you English say. These men are not professionals. They are bungling amateurs. A couple of inept fools recruited by Hallam because one of them, at least, has a grudge against you. We shall be six men to two – seven if you count your precious Bill Brereton. And I've never met a Scotsman yet who didn't enjoy a good fight. Harriet! Harriet! Take that frown off your face. What can possibly go wrong?'

'I don't know,' she admitted. 'Put that way, it sounds easy enough. Much too easy. And Bill isn't really a Scot, by

347

the way. I just don't like it, that's all. But if you're right, and it is going to be such a simple matter, you can't have any objection if I come with you.'

Bill Brereton's sitting-room and bedroom were, like those of the rest of the Georgiadis staff, situated on the same floor of the hotel as his employers' suite. At eleven o'clock that night, he was just thinking of getting ready for bed when there was a knock at his door. When he opened it, he was astonished to find Bess Holland and Madge Shelton outside.

'We want a word,' said the former, walking past him into the sitting-room without waiting for an invitation. Madge followed Bess.

Bill was nettled. 'Please come in. Make yourselves at home,' he urged with heavy sarcasm.

'Never mind that!' Bess was impatient. 'Look! Neither of us knows what's going on tomorrow, and I don't think I particularly want to know. Nor does Madge. But presumably you're involved in whatever Mr Georgiadis has in mind.' Bill made no answer, and Bess seemed satisfied. 'I guessed as much. That's not my business, but we understand that Mrs Georgiadis is insisting on going along, too. She's told Madge to wake her very early and to lay out trousers and a thick sweater.'

Bill looked puzzled. 'So? What's it got to do with me?'

'Just that it's probably going to be dangerous. Mr Georgiadis can be a very dangerous man. So try to keep your eye on Mrs Georgiadis if you possibly can. We don't want any harm to come to her.'

Madge nodded. 'We're very fond of her,' she added.

Bill glanced from one concerned face to the other.

'Strange as it may seem,' he said, 'so am I. I owe Mrs Georgiadis a hell of a lot. But if she insists on coming with us against all advice – and I know for a fact that Mr Georgiadis has done everything he can to dissuade her – I don't really see what I can do.'

348

Bess almost stamped her foot. 'You can do your level best, that's what you can do! So just watch out for her, Bill, or Madge and I will have your guts for garters!'

Five minutes later, Bill closed the door thankfully behind his unwanted visitors. Women! he thought. Why did they always have to get so emotionally involved?

36

They drove down to Ayerst early the next morning, as they had driven to Carey Wanstead seventy-two hours before: Harriet, Spiros and two of the bodyguards in the Daimler with Bill, the other three men following in the Rover. The same silence prevailed, but this time Spiros' disinclination to talk stemmed from anger, not from sympathy. The night before, he and Harriet had had a furious row.

'You are not coming with us! This is man's work. It has nothing to do with you!'

'Piers is my son!' she had yelled. 'It has everything to do with me! And, according to you, it's going to be a piece of cake.'

'Maybe. Maybe not.' Spiros was shouting louder than she was. Bess Holland had fled to her room. 'But, in any case, women do not concern themselves in such matters.'

'You're nothing but a male chauvinist!' Harriet had flung at him. 'When the chips are down, you're as biased as the rest of your sex! Men! You all belong in the Stone Age!'

'And no bad thing, either. At least, in the Stone Age, men and women knew their proper roles!'

'Leave me behind tomorrow,' Harriet had threatened, 'and the moment you're out of that door I call the police!'

He knew her well enough to accept that she meant what she said. Sullenly, Spiros had capitulated.

Ayerst, three miles to the south of Carey Wanstead, was exactly as Cecil Brewer had described it; four cottages clustered along the edge of the Carey Wanstead road, the outhouses of a farm, just visible through the lacework of some trees, and a lane, hardly more than a track, opposite the main farmhouse gate. The track itself was bordered by a stream, and half a mile along its length were the remains of an old water-mill. The wheel had rusted, the roof had fallen in, and the crumbling walls were slowly being torn apart by ivy, which had gained a fingerhold in almost every crevice. In the field behind, purple loosestrife caught the eye in a patch of undisciplined colour, and the last of some yellow irises gleamed in the early-morning light along the further bank.

It was still only five o'clock when the Daimler turned into Carey Lane and Spiros ordered it to stop. A few moments later, the Rover crunched to a halt immediately behind it. Everyone got out, including Harriet. Spiros looked at her, but said nothing, evidently deciding, by her mulish expression, that it would do no good.

There was a chill in the air, and she was glad of her dark grey slacks and all-enveloping Arran jumper. Spiros glanced from one face to another, like Leonidas surveying his troops at Thermopylae, she thought with a nervous inward giggle, and then picked Constantine and Stephanos to go with him to reconnoitre.

Five minutes later, they were back.

'There's no sign of life,' Spiros said. 'No one is awake yet. So, if we can take them by surprise, we should not have any trouble.'

He spoke in English for her and Bill's benefit, then translated his words into Greek. One or two of his bodyguards knew very little English. As they moved forward up the lane, he added something else in his own language, and Harriet saw one of the men reach inside his jacket.

'Oh my God!' she thought. 'The damned fools are armed!'

She had not considered that possibility; she never did when she was in England. But she remembered Spiros once telling her that he kept a couple of revolvers, legally bought and licensed many years ago, in the safe deposit of his London bank. She also recalled Stephanos being sent to the bank on Saturday morning.

She clutched her husband's arm.

'For Christ's sake, Spiros, what are you playing at? Constantine has a gun!'

'So has Lambis. What did you expect? Hasn't it occurred to you, Harriet, that your Mr Pace will probably be armed? A shotgun, most likely, provided by Hallam. Do you mean to tell me that your ex-husband and his father never go out shooting?'

Of course they did! Harriet knew that shotguns and fowling-pieces were kept in the gun-room at Carey Hall. Why, oh, why had she not foreseen this situation? What a fool she was not to have thought it through; considered all the ramifications. If she had, she would never have let Spiros talk her out of sending for the police, whatever the consequences might be for Hallam. Suddenly, she felt very frightened.

They were within a yard or two of Mill View Cottage. 'Cottage' was perhaps, too fancy a name for it. The date, shown in plaster on the pebbledash façade, was '1930', and it was a functional box-like structure of the kind Harriet used to draw at school: four sash windows, two up, two down, and a green-painted front door placed exactly half-way between the latter. There was a long front garden, mostly grass, with a few untended borders, and a concrete path leading from the gate. Just inside the gate was a dusty-leaved overgrown laurel. The Triumph Herald was parked on a patch of rough ground to one side of the house.

Spiros directed three of his men round to the back, ordered Harriet to take cover behind the laurel bush and advanced up the path to the front door with the remaining two bodyguards and Bill Brereton, to whom he was whispering urgently.

352

He's enjoying himself, Harriet thought angrily. The bastard's actually enjoying himself!

The whole episode clearly appealed to some primitive atavistic strain in Spiros' nature; a strain buried deep inside most men, but particularly in those of the old Mediterranean cultures, who were brought up to revere the stirring deeds of their ancestors. The ancient heroes! What place, what hope was there for women in such a world?

Bill Brereton knocked loudly on the front door. The two Greek bodyguards and Spiros disappeared round the corner, out of view.

After a few moments, the right-hand bedroom window was pushed up cautiously, and a man's head appeared – not Richard Pace's – in the gap. Bill had moved back a step, so that he could clearly be seen without the man having to crane his neck.

'What do you want?' a sleepy voice demanded.

'Excuse me.' Bill adopted a thick Glaswegian accent. 'My car's broken down.' He gave a sketchy wave in the opposite direction to the Carey Wanstead road. 'Late last night. I need to get in touch with the AA. Can I use yer phone?'

'We haven't got one,' the man snapped. 'Try one of the houses on the main road.' He made a stabbing movement with his right hand, then drew his head in and slammed the window shut.

Bill hammered on the door again. The other bedroom window went up with a crash. This time, the face that appeared was familiar to Harriet. Richard Pace.

'What the bloody hell is going on?' he shouted.

'Hey, you!' Bill called. 'My car's broken down and I need a telephone. Yer friend tells me ye have na one. But I can see the wires. What sort of a bluidy fool do ye take me for? Typical Sassenach hospitality! I'm not legging it miles down an unknown road at this ungodly hour o' the morning. I'll just stay here and bang on yer door until ye let me in.'

Richard Pace hesitated, but Harriet guessed that he would not wish to arouse suspicion in a stranger.

'Hold on!' he said shortly. 'I'll be down in a minute.'

The window was closed again, and immediately Spiros and the two bodyguards reappeared to range themselves one on either side of the front door. As soon as it opened, they would jump the unsuspecting Richard Pace and overpower him before he could alert the second man. That way, they would be able to get to Piers before he was harmed.

Suddenly, for the first time in days, Harriet found herself thinking clearly. None of what was happening made sense. These two men would not hurt Piers. He was Hallam's son. True, they were part of a con trick, a criminal attempt at extortion, but they were not kidnappers in the true sense of the word. There had been no telephone call to Hallam, threatening the child's life. It had not been necessary. The story was all part of the general plan. So why should these men be armed? If Harriet had insisted on calling in the police in the first place, what would have happened? Hallam would have warned his fellow-conspirators, and they would simply have disappeared, leaving Piers in a prearranged spot near Carey Hall.

And, now she came to think of it, why had she and Spiros not gone to see Hallam and tell him that the game was up? With their promise not to take legal action against him and the other two men involved, the situation could have been resolved without any of this ridiculous charade. Surely Spiros, less emotionally concerned than herself, must have realized. . .

But, of course, Spiros had realized. What was it he had said to her and Hallam?

'We pay the money. We get the boy back. And then we track down the kidnappers and we kill them.'

That was before he had known the truth, but his threat still held good. Hallam might have to go free – for the time being, at least – but there was no reason why the other

354

men should escape. Spiros had come here to kill them! Under that civilized façade, he remained a brigand; the ruthless boy and man who had clawed his way up from abject poverty to become one of the richest men in the world. No one who tried to rob Spiros Georgiadis was allowed to get away with it.

Harriet found that she was shaking, and this time it was not with the cold. She could not possibly let him do this! It was terribly, dreadfully wrong. Whatever distress and anguish these two men had caused her, they did not deserve to pay with their lives. Killing was evil. It was the principle which had kept her father out of the forces during the war.

She moved out from behind the laurel bush just as the front door began to open. She saw Stephanos withdraw his hand from inside his coat. He was holding a gun. Harriet started to run blindly up the path, shouting: 'Look out! Look out! They're going to kill you!'

She could see Richard Pace quite plainly now, framed in the open doorway. There was a dazed uncomprehending expression on his face as he stared at her, his jaw dropping ludicrously. Then the look sharpened into naked fear. Out of the corner of his eye, he saw the shadowy figures of Spiros and his men. At the same moment, there was a crash as the other three bodyguards broke down the back door. He could hear their feet on the stone flags of the passage. Richard Pace half-turned, but terror kept him rooted to the spot, unable even to cry out and warn his partner. Like a slow motion shot in a film, Harriet saw Stephanos raise his gun and level it.

She ran forward yelling, 'No! Don't!' without any clear idea of what she was going to do. She only knew that she must prevent Richard Pace from being murdered. She had some vague notion of pushing him to the ground.

Instead, she felt herself being pushed as Spiros' heavy body lunged against her, sending her flying. He was shouting, but she was unable to make any sense of the words. Her head cracked against one of the door-jambs, momentarily dazing her. She was conscious of a soft plopping noise, which she realized later must have been Stephanos' silenced gun. There was a cry, a sudden hush and then a babel of horrified voices. As her head ceased to buzz and her vision returned to normal, she could see Spiros lying on the ground in a pool of blood.

At the same moment, there was the patter of feet on the cottage stairs, and Piers's voice crying: 'Mummy! Mummy!'

Harriet turned as her son ran towards her, wearing a pair of alien striped cotton pyjamas. She gathered his little body into her arms and held him close.

Closer examination revealed that Spiros had been hit in the shoulder. It was not a serious wound, but it bled copiously and obviously occasioned him a great deal of pain. They got him into the Daimler, while Harriet climbed into the back of the Rover and wrapped Piers in a rug. She had dared any of the Greeks to lay a finger on either Richard Pace or his accomplice, and without any counter-orders from Spiros they had obeyed, although it clearly bewildered and angered them to do so.

To Richard Pace, Harriet had said: 'Get out of my life! Do you understand? I never want to see you again. If I so much as smell you, as God's my witness, I'll make you sorry you were ever born!'

They drove the three miles to Carey Hall and roused the household. Harriet was astonished to discover that it was not yet six o'clock. There was no hope now of concealing the truth from the Viscount, but they did manage to keep it from Lady Carey, who was still in bed, after taking three of her sleeping tablets the night before. The look the Viscount gave his son was one of deep contempt, but whether it was on account of what he had done, or because he had bungled the job, Harriet was not quite sure. Her ex-father-in-law had always been an enigma to her, and she had never really liked him. She had an idea that, in his own quiet way, he was as devious and as unscrupulous as Hallam.

Hallam himself looked both scared and defiant. He expressed no regrets for the anxiety and misery he had caused her and his parents, saying with a shrill laugh: 'You've no one to blame but yourself, my dear. You shouldn't have been so stingy with my settlement. You must admit it was worth a try.'

On one level he seemed to be asking for her commiseration for a neat little scheme gone wrong. Harriet felt she would never understand him. She had no compunction in informing him that he would have a substantial bill for damages at the cottage.

She telephoned Kathleen at Claridges to come and take care of Piers.

'And ask Bess to come as well,' she instructed. 'I don't know how long we'll be staying here.'

She needed Bess. She needed her comforting presence, her stability, her calm. Bess was rapidly becoming indispensable to her. She could not imagine how she had ever managed without her.

The local doctor, who had been told of an accidental shooting while Spiros and Hallam were fooling around in the gun-room during a cleaning session, was content, whatever his private reservations, to go along with the story. He was an elderly man, flattered by the occasional invitation to dine at Carey Hall, and with no intention of forfeiting the Viscount's goodwill. He removed the bullet, dressed the wound and announced that Spiros would be fit enough to travel in three or four days. He did, however, insist on speaking to Harriet alone.

'Mrs Georgiadis, did you know,' he asked gently, 'that your husband has a very bad heart?' Harriet's astonishment must have shown in her face, because he went on: 'No. Obviously not. I don't think Mr Georgiadis realized it himself. I gather he has no time for doctors. Never has medical check-ups. But in future he really must. This accident' – the doctor paused, coughing delicately, then resumed – 'has put him under very great stress. He will have to take care. He must avoid severe physical exertion.'

Spiros, sitting up in bed, in a huge four-poster, ridiculed the whole idea.

'The man is a charlatan!' He regarded Harriet balefully. 'I suppose you know that I should not be in this position if you had not been such a damn bloody fool?'

'You'd be in the dock, accused of murder,' Harriet retorted acidly. 'How on earth did you hope to get away with killing those two men?'

'It could have been arranged. Anything can be arranged if you have enough money.'

She sat on the edge of the bed, taking the hand of his uninjured arm in both of hers.

'Oh, Spiros! What a philosophy!'

'It is true, though.' He leaned towards her; then, as the pain of his wounded shoulder made him wince, fell back against the pillows. She noted that he was breathing heavily. 'Spiritually, my darling, you have never left that vicarage of yours. When will you learn to accept the realities of this world?'

'I know what will work in this country and what won't,' she said, raising his hand and kissing it lightly. 'I haven't thanked you yet for saving my life.'

He smiled. There was an unhealthy blue tinge round his lips.

'I love you.'

She had been half-expecting the declaration, yet dreading it, too. It was still a shock to hear him actually speak the words. She did not know how she felt.

Their eyes met, and then she knew.

'I love you, too,' she answered.

Not in the same way that she loved Edmund Howard; but, then, there were all sorts and degrees of love. The affection she felt for Spiros had ripened and deepened over the three years of their marriage until now, when she realized that she could not bear the thought of losing him.

She squeezed his hand and insisted: 'You have to take care. When we get back to Athens, you must see your own doctor, and you must promise to do everything he tells you.'

She should have known that it was too much to hope for, and she was not always on hand to bully him into submission. Just over a year later, during Elena's third birthday party on Agios Georgios, Spiros suffered a massive heart-attack from which he only just managed to recover. Harriet was at his bedside, day and night, for almost three months.

Without Bess Holland to support her, she could not have coped with the double strain of her husband's illness and running the Chance Corporation, often from a distance. Bess shuttled to and fro across Europe and the Atlantic, but somehow always managed to be there when she was most needed.

One night, when she had returned to the Athens apartment from the hospital more than usually despondent, Harriet's spirits had been lifted by the sight of Bess still waiting up for her. Dropping into an armchair, Harriet held out her hand. Bess went immediately to sit beside her on the floor, handing Harriet the drink that she had poured her. Harriet smoothed the sleek dark hair.

'Don't ever leave me,' she murmured.

It was an appeal she would never have made had she not been so low, and was ashamed of it the moment it was uttered. She, of all people, had no right to ask for total fidelity.

Bess, however, seemed to find nothing untoward in the demand. She lifted her head, mouth and eyes smiling.

'I have no intention of leaving you,' she said, 'unless, of course, you ever feel the urge to get rid of me.'

'That will never happen,' Harriet promised fervently.

She could recognize herself as a young woman in her secretary; a woman with great strength of purpose. Bess was the only member of the female sex whom Harriet had ever wanted as a friend.

359

When Spiros at last left the hospital, in time for Christmas with his family, it was in a wheelchair. The doctors told Harriet that he would never leave it. With the utmost care and attention, they said, he might live a few more years.

Harriet vowed that he should have those years.

PART FIVE

1979–84

Our wisdom and deliberation for the most part follow the lead of chance.

MICHEL DE MONTAIGNE

37

Spiros had those years and more; ten in all, finally dying peacefully in his sleep during the early hours of 3 July 1979, two months to the day after Margaret Thatcher became the first woman political leader of the West, and at the height of a world energy crisis.

For once, Harriet was uninterested in what was happening outside Agios Georgios. The piles of American and British newspapers remained unread, while she came to terms with her loss. And it *was* a loss, she had no illusions on that score. Over the past ten years, she and Spiros had drawn closer together, no longer inhibited by the pitfalls and rivalries of sex: of his desire to prove himself the equal of a younger man, and of her need to subjugate all memories of Edmund Howard. In some ways, Spiros' confinement to a wheelchair had liberated them both. He knew that she would never desert him, while Harriet was freed from the necessity of making an unhappy choice.

If Isabelle Howard were to die tomorrow, she often thought, I couldn't leave Spiros. And Edmund would respect that decision.

In the event, it was not one Harriet was called upon to make, but the freedom from that sort of emotional crisis forever hanging, like Damocles' sword, above their heads had given her unlimited reserves of strength. She and Spiros became friends in a way which would have been impossible had they also been lovers. He grew to rely on her to such an extent that, by the time of his death, she was one of the key figures of the vast Georgiadis empire, as well as being the linchpin of the Chance Corporation, now an even bigger force to be reckoned with than it had been when she married Spiros, fourteen years before. Harriet was now recognized as one of a handful of truly powerful figures in the commercial world, and its only woman. She was among the first people to be invited to lunch at Downing Street by the new British Prime Minister.

Spiros was enormously proud of her and, as his strength ebbed, grew to rely on her more and more. He knew that he could trust her absolutely; a rare and valuable attribute in the world of big business, where a million dollars, or even pounds, was regarded in much the same light as Harriet had looked on her sixpence-a-week pocket money when she was a child. Sometimes, if she let herself stop and think, she was terrified by the amounts of money which she had at her command; her ability to make or break lives by the creation or destruction of jobs, merely by putting a few pencil marks on a piece of paper, or speaking a few words over the telephone.

Spiros, aware of this tendency of hers – a tendency he deplored – to stand periodically outside of herself and assess what she was doing through the eyes of a stranger, kept her constantly employed. The past ten years, Harriet realized, had been years of permanent activity; never still, never in the same country, let alone the same place, for more than a few days running. New York, London, Paris, Rome, Athens could be a single week's itinerary, followed by a day or, on occasions, just a matter of hours snatched to refresh herself on Agios Georgios.

When she protested, he said: 'You love it. You thrive on it. You know you do.'

And Bess Holland would poke her head round the door to remind Harriet that she was attending a hoe-down at the White House, given by President and Mrs Carter, or that she was due in Brussels to meet representatives of the EEC or that she was dining next week in Canberra with the Australian Prime Minister. Sometimes, Harriet felt as though her feet barely touched the ground.

She doubted if she could have survived the pressure without Bess Holland. It was not just that Bess was superbly efficient at her job, always ensuring that Harriet was in the right place at the right time, with all the necessary information at her fingertips; she was also a friend. She was always there when Harriet needed a shoulder to lean on; someone to confide in. Someone she could trust.

She thought of Edmund almost every day of her life. Even if she had tried to forget him, it would have been impossible, with a constant stream of news about Ireland and Irish affairs in the daily papers. The resurgence of the IRA during the 1970s, re-formed and revitalized under dynamic new leadership, had led to an escalation of violence in the northern province and, for a short time, on mainland Britain. In 1974 alone, bombs had exploded in a carpark at Heathrow airport, alongside Westminster Hall, at the Tower of London, at Birmingham, Manchester and Guildford. The troubles this time looked as though they were here to stay.

Harriet could not help wondering what Edmund thought of it all; whether or not he sympathized with the growing violence and the supply of newer and ever more sophisticated weapons from the United States. She suspected that he would be torn between horror at the suffering and injuries caused, and his natural sympathy with the Irish cause. One thing, however, was certain: it was no longer the world of *Odd Man Out*. Confronted today by Seamus Hogan, Harriet had no doubt that her response would be very different.

Wherever her travels took her, she kept in touch with Spiros by telephone. Just knowing he was there, on Agios Georgios, made her feel safe.

Now, suddenly, she was once again on her own.

The one area of disagreement between Harriet and Spiros during the past ten years had been over the raising of Elena. On that subject they were so divided that it could never be mentioned without sparking off a row.

365

As far as the two boys were concerned, it was accepted from the first that they were Harriet's responsibility. Spiros treated them generously, with a great deal of avuncular affection, gave them the run of Agios Georgios and the Athens apartment whenever they wished, and loaded them with presents. When, at the age of twenty-four, Michael had married Julia Colonna, the only daughter of one of New York's wealthiest Italian families, Spiros had not only presented the couple with an apartment over-looking Central Park, but had also given them a flat in London, near Hyde Park Corner, and a Paris house in the fashionable Bois de Boulogne. And when the two boys were born, first Angelo and then Marco, Spiros set up a trust fund of a quarter of a billion pounds for them, just as if they had been his real grandsons.

He treated Piers with the same open-handed generosity; and when the boy went away to school added his own quarterly allowance to that of Harriet's, with the cynical observation that as long as a young man had plenty of money he could always rely on having plenty of friends. But in the all-important area of decision-making Spiros would never interfere.

'They are your sons,' he would tell Harriet, when she asked for advice. 'You must decide.'

Elena, however, was different. She was his child and the apple of his eye. The trouble was that Piers's kidnapping – even though, as Harriet constantly pointed out, it had not been a true kidnap attempt – had badly shaken Spiros. It had reinforced previous fears for the safety of his only child, and brought home to him how easily an abduction could be achieved. Consequently, Elena was educated by a series of governesses, and only allowed off Agios Georgios for an occasional trip to Athens under the strictest super-vision and surrounded by bodyguards.

'You're asking for trouble,' Harriet told her husband. 'A high-spirited strong-willed girl like Elena isn't going to put up with this sort of treatment for ever. It's far too restrict-ing. And when she does start kicking over the traces it will be with a vengeance. One of these days, you're going to find that you've a thoroughly unmanageable daughter on your hands.'

Spiros, however, refused to listen. Nor would he heed the warning signs. A few months before his death, during one of Harriet's brief sojourns on the island, the twelve-year-old Elena had let herself into Bill Brereton's living-quarters one night and climbed into his bed. Nanny Tettenburg, summoned by inter-house telephone to the flat above the garages, had been duly scandalized, and informed her employers of the escapade the following morning.

Bess Holland, with whom Harriet discussed the incident, said bluntly: 'Elena's too old for a nanny and that prunes-and-prisms governess of hers. She needs to be with young people, not kept a virtual prisoner.'

Harriet agreed with Bess's opinions, repeating them to Spiros without revealing their source.

'Elena's growing up ignorant and wild. The more you confine her, the worse she'll get. The damage may be done already. She has a sweet loving nature, but you're crippling it. Let her lead a normal life! Let her meet boys her own age, so that she doesn't have to indulge in erotic fancies about a man nearly three times as old as she is.'

'You're talking nonsense,' was all that Spiros had said, and Harriet had known by the tone of his voice that it was useless to argue.

'He's sowing the wind,' she had remarked bitterly to Bess Holland, later the same day, 'but I shall be the one who reaps the whirlwind.'

Harriet remembered those words now, as she sat on a rock, staring out to sea, trying to come to terms with Spiros' death. She could hear the soft murmuring of the water and see the hot July sunlight sparkling and dancing over the waves, but the sight failed to move her. She felt as though her right arm had been cut off. She felt frightened.

Five days ago she had celebrated her fifty-third birth-day. The realization that she was no longer young – a grandmother – had sent her flying to the nearest mirror. What she had seen had only partly reassured her. She was still a good-looking woman. Age had produced a bloom, laid a patina on Harriet that had defied, to some extent, the passage of time. There was a maturity about her, a self-assurance she had lacked in her youth, which created, in itself, a kind of beauty. Nevertheless, life was slipping away. The young girl who had first met Edmund Howard on a California beach no longer existed.

Yet why should that concern her? There seemed little hope now that she and Edmund would ever marry. Spiros might be dead, but Isabelle was still very much alive. Harriet had seen pictures of her with Edmund only a week or so ago in the *Tatler*, gracing some hunt ball or other in County Wexford. They had looked prosperous and happy. . .

Harriet pulled herself up short. Spiros had been dead less than four hours, and here she was thinking about Edmund. She owed Spiros more loyalty than that. But the truth was that the two men represented separate compartments of her life. She loved both equally, but in different ways. She could grieve for Spiros and think about Edmund at the same time, without detracting from her love for either.

She got up and looked about her. Agios Georgios was unnaturally quiet, a kingdom which had lost its king. Harriet turned and made her way back to the house, now sightless, with blinds drawn in every room. There was so much to do, she would have no time to brood. Apart from everything else, there was the will to unravel. Harriet was one of the executors. It would probably entail years of work.

Michael arrived with Julia for the funeral.

'Didn't you bring the boys?' Harriet asked, kissing her daughter-in-law's cheek.

Julia shook her head. 'I don't agree with young children being brought into contact with death too soon. Michael agrees with me, don't you, dearest?'

Her husband nodded. 'And it's not as though Spiros was

368

their grandfather,' he added. 'Not really family, if you'll forgive me saying so, Momma.'

Harriet compressed her lips.

'He was very good to you, Mickey,' she reminded her elder son.

'That was only to be expected.' He smiled condescendingly. 'And please stop calling me by that baby name. I don't feel it's fitting nowadays.'

They were an exasperatingly complacent pair, Harriet decided. And so middle-aged in their attitude towards life.

She was hurt, because she had looked forward to seeing her grandchildren – an unreasonable sense of injury, she knew, as she could see them any time she cared to in New York. But she suspected that she was being paid back for her neglect of Michael when he was young. There must have been many occasions when he had wanted to see his mother and she had not been there; when she had been too busy, rushing all over the world.

Michael, at thirty-three, had been managing director of Chance Enterprises for the past ten years, and was proving to have all his mother's business acumen. He might be like Gus in appearance, but he had Harriet's brains. She knew that he would not be satisfied with the subsidiary company for long; that he wanted nothing so much as to step into her shoes; to be head of the entire Chance Corporation. She knew, too, that he regarded himself as her natural successor. He despised Piers as he had despised Hallam, although he was ignorant of all the details of her relationship with her third husband. Harriet had never considered it necessary to enlighten him. Michael's dislike of his first step-father was based entirely on the clash of personalities; just as his antipathy towards his half-brother stemmed from the fact that he saw Piers as an interloper. It was Gus who had helped found the Last Chance restaurants. By rights, Michael felt, everything should belong to him.

Piers arrived by one of the Georgiadis private jets later the same day. He was sixteen now, tall and thin like the Cavendishes, with a world-weary air copied from his father, and which concealed a basic unhappiness. He did not like school. He had hated his prep school and found Harrow only marginally better. Too indifferent to all forms of sport to be any good at them, he had learned early on that another sort of popularity could be courted by being slightly eccentric. The Harrow 'bloods' were contemptuous of Piers and his cronies, with their affected ways, drawling voices and throwaway humour; but they were tolerated generally because they were deemed to be amusing.

Although Harriet's two sons had no time for one another, they both, in their different ways, were fond of Elena. She was not a rival for their inheritance. She would succeed to most of her father's wealth when she eventually reached the age of twenty-one; but as neither Michael nor Piers had ever expected a share in the Georgiadis fortune they might envy but did not resent her.

They did, however, find her high spirits, which sometimes bordered on the frenetic, a little overwhelming.

'What she needs,' Piers informed his mother sententiously, 'is some discipline. A decent girls' school would teach her that she can't always get her own way. *Esprit de corps* and all that rot.'

Harriet, torn between amusement and irritation, answered gravely: 'It wasn't possible while her father was alive. He wouldn't hear of her leaving the island. But I mean to do something about it now he's dead, I do assure you.'

But when Dick Norris flew in the next day, to attend the funeral and to read the will, Harriet found that Spiros had forestalled any such move on her part.

'I'm afraid you won't be able to do that, Harriet,' Dick said half-apologetically when she confided her plan to him. 'At least, not until Elena is turned fifteen.'

He hated to disappoint Harriet in anything. But for the Chance Corporation endowment, which had put him through university, he would never be where he was today: senior partner of Hutton, Taylor & Norris since the retirement of Ronald Hutton two years previously and the unexpected death, shortly afterwards, of Jeremy Taylor. It was Harriet who had got him his original place in the firm, and who later, after he had obtained a partnership, persuaded Ronald Hutton to change the firm's name to incorporate Dick's own. He handled all of the Chance Corporation's British affairs, and Spiros had been cajoled by Harriet into entrusting the firm with the drawing up of his will.

Harriet looked into the troubled brown eyes beneath the ever-so-slightly thinning hair, and said: 'Oh, shit! I might have guessed!'

Bess Holland knocked and came in, reminding Harriet that it was almost time to go. She saw the look of perturbation on her employer's face and at once gravitated protectively to her side. Dick Norris was amused. He had heard that the relationship between the two women was close. Bess Holland reminded him of a lioness ready to defend her young.

Spiros was to be buried on Agios Georgios, on a promontory on the far side of the island, away from the village, overlooking the sea. He had requested that it be a quiet ceremony, attended by only family and one or two close friends.

'Something wrong, Momma?' Michael asked, as he and Julia came into the room, ready to leave.

Harriet sighed, 'Maybe. But I shan't know for certain until Dick, here, reads the will. Right! Now, if Piers and Elena are ready, shall we go?'

38

The terms of Spiros' will laid down that Elena would continue to be taught at home, on Agios Georgios, until the age of fifteen, and that his remaining sister, a stern, seemingly indestructible octogenarian, was to be in co-charge of the child with Harriet. After Elena's fifteenth birthday, however, her aunt's guardianship would cease, and all responsibility for her education and welfare devolve upon her mother.

Harriet was furious.

'Isn't there any way at all we can overset that clause?' she asked Dick Norris, but he regretted that there was nothing they could do. Harriet bit her lip. 'It's asking for trouble, you know. When Elena finally gets her freedom, it'll go to her head like half a dozen bottles of champagne. The popping corks are going to be heard from here to Hades.'

'I'm awfully sorry,' Dick Norris said gently. 'I can see that you're in for a very rough ride. Spiros was an extremely wise man, except where Elena was concerned. It was that kidnap attempt on Piers eleven years ago which frightened him so badly.'

'You know about that?' Harriet looked at him sharply. 'I thought we'd kept it a secret. We didn't want the police to find out.'

'Spiros told me about it.' Dick chuckled. 'How typical of him to take the law into his own hands and flush out the kidnappers. You have to admire a man like that. Mr Cavendish must have been very grateful.'

They were in the main salon of the house. Harriet gazed moodily out of the window. The funeral was over, the buffet lunch eaten, the will, a long and involved document, read. The nub of it was that, although Elena would inherit the bulk of Spiros' fortune as soon as she came of age, Harriet would continue to help run the Georgiadis empire, and hold the controlling vote in any major decision until she decided to retire. Spiros had also left her a private income of a million pounds a year and the use of the house on Agios Georgios as long as she wanted it. She was now one of the richest and most powerful women in the world.

She was also a mother, with much the same problems as any other parent; problems where money was a positive hindrance rather than a help. And quite a few of them were directly traceable to Hallam. Damn the man! He had hung like a shadow over her life, ever since the day she first met him.

The afternoon was hot and very still. Nearly everyone, except herself and Dick Norris, had retired to their rooms for a rest. The path to the beach, running between banks of maquis and flecked with the blue of sage, was deserted, powdered almost white under the sun's relentless glare. Harriet had a sudden vivid memory of Sunday-school trips to Weston-super-Mare when she was a child: the wind, howling across sands pitted with rain, shivering donkeys huddled in the lee of a wall, the long arm of Brean Down reaching out into the storm-riven waves. *That* was the sea-side, not this sparkling paradise of sun-drenched sands, hot white rocks and green-blue sea.

She turned and smiled down at Dick Norris, sprawled in an armchair beside her.

'I hear you're getting married,' she said.

His face lit up, relieved at this change of subject.

'Yes. We haven't fixed a date for the wedding yet, but when we do we hope very much that you'll come.'

'Try and stop me! What's your fiancée like? Tell me about her.' Harriet sat down on the couch.

'She's called Melanie,' Dick told her eagerly. 'Melanie

373

Crossland.' He laughed self-consciously. 'She's years younger than I am. Only just twenty-one. Extremely pretty. Blonde. I'm a very lucky man.'

'She sounds wonderful.' Harriet could not help contrasting Dick's starry-eyed description with the one Frank Bryan had given her the last time she had been in London. Frank, now the chief accountant for the whole of Chance Enterprises (UK) Ltd, had come to know Dick Norris well over the years. Quite surprising, Harriet reflected, considering how diverse their two personalities were: Dick extrovert, hail-fellow-well-met with everyone, Frank as dry and humourless as the figures he dealt with daily.

'An empty-headed flibbertigibbet,' was Frank's opinion of the future Mrs Norris.

Harriet recalled how irritated she had been by his staid middle-aged responses. He was thirty-five, the same age as Dick, but in outlook and temperament he might have been another generation.

All the same, she was fond of Frank. She had watched over and nurtured his career, and been repaid a hundredfold by his loyalty and devotion. He had a clear incisive brain, as she had realized all those years ago when she had read his report on the Birmingham Last Chance restaurant.

'Melanie is a wonderful girl,' Dick agreed enthusiastically. He rose, picking up his briefcase. 'I must go, Harriet. One of your pilots is giving me a lift back to the mainland in time for me to catch the evening plane from Athens. I have to be in Town tomorrow for an important meeting.' He kissed her cheek. 'Please accept my most sincere condolences. I know how you must miss Spiros. He was a man I admired very much indeed.'

'Yes, I know you did.' She patted his shoulder. 'Thanks, Dick, for all your support today.'

'I'm just sorry I couldn't be of more assistance over the matter of Elena. But you know Spiros. Thorough. Every clause of that will is absolutely watertight.'

'I never imagined otherwise. I just hadn't realized quite

how obsessive he had become about the possibility of kidnapping.'

Damn you, Hallam! she thought again. *It's all your fault!*

Dick Norris took himself off with a final reminder that he would expect to see her at his wedding, whenever that might be, and left her alone with her thoughts.

Five minutes later, Elena came in. At twelve, she was thin and coltish, all arms and legs, with a mane of long blonde hair caught back in a pony-tail. She was wearing a black frock which Harriet considered both unsuitable and unnecessary; but her sister-in-law had been so scandalized at the prospect of Elena not being properly dressed for the funeral that Harriet had finally agreed. Now, however, she advised: 'I'd take that ugly black thing off as soon as possible, if I were you.'

Elena ignored her, flinging herself into an armchair with a disconsolate expression on her face.

'I'm looking for Bill. Have you any idea where he is?'

'Having his afternoon siesta, I should imagine, like any sensible person.' Harriet regarded her daughter suspiciously. 'Why do you want to know?'

Elena shrugged. 'Dunno,' she lied. English was her first language; Greek, to her aunt's disgust, a very poor second. 'Thought he might want to come down to the beach for a swim.'

'What you mean,' said Piers, who had entered the salon just in time to overhear his half-sister's last remark, 'is that you fancy him. You hope to see his manly torso stripped to the waist. Those bathing-trunks of his don't leave much to the imagination, do they?'

'Oh, shut up!' Elena threw a cushion at Piers.

'But it's true, isn't it?' he demanded triumphantly. 'I heard all about you getting into his bed.'

'You're a pig and I hate you!' Elena stormed, hunting around for some heavier missile to launch at him. 'A sneaky little tell-tale-tit!'

'Be quiet, both of you!' Harriet spoke sternly. 'How dare you behave like this, today of all days!' She looked at

Elena. 'You're to leave Bill Brereton alone, do you hear me? There is to be no repetition of that disgraceful episode in May. I warn you, Ellie! If you don't stop pestering him, I shall make sure he doesn't come to the island in future.'

'You don't have to worry about Bill,' Piers cut in scathingly. 'He thinks she's just an irritating little brat. No tits,' he added, eyeing his half-sister appraisingly.

Elena flew up out of the chair and hurled herself at Piers, nails clawing two long weals across his cheeks before Harriet could separate them.

'Bloody little hell-cat!' Piers dabbed at his wounded face with his handkerchief. 'What she needs,' he told his mother, 'is a damn good hiding. She's as randy as a bitch on heat.'

'That's quite enough of that sort of talk,' Harriet repri-manded him. 'You will both go to your rooms and stay there until dinner-time. And, Ellie, if I hear of you worrying Bill again, I shall be tempted to take your brother's advice. Now, get out of my sight, the pair of you.'

'Trouble?' enquired Bess Holland, coming in with some correspondence which needed Harriet's signature, and passing Elena and Piers on their way out. 'I'm sorry to bother you with these today,' she went on, handing over the letters for Harriet's perusal, 'but time and tide and the Chance Corporation wait for no man, as you know only too well.'

Harriet laughed, flicking through the closely typed sheets and signing where necessary. When she had fin-ished, and Bess was folding them into their respective envelopes, she asked: 'Do you think Ellie's sweet on Bill Brereton?'

' "Sweet on," ' murmured Bess. 'Now, there's a nice old-fashioned phrase. To use another, I think she's probably in the grip of a schoolgirl crush. Bill's quite good-looking, in case you hadn't noticed.'

'I'd noticed. Rather Italianate, wouldn't you say?'

'Definitely. There was a time when I quite fancied him myself. But I got over it. So will Elena, and sooner than you

376

think. Much sooner than she thinks. Nothing wrong with schoolgirl crushes. I suppose we've both suffered from them at one time or another.'

'Yes.' Harriet smiled reminiscently. 'Mine was called Leslie Norman. I see him now and then, when I go home to Winterbourn Green. He married my erstwhile best friend. He's fat and middle-aged and balding. So much for love's young dream.' She hesitated. 'I suppose ... I suppose there's no chance that Bill fancies Elena?'

'Good God, no!' Bess was shocked. 'He's my age: mid-thirties. Elena's a child.'

'Now, yes.' Harriet sighed. 'In three or four years, she'll be a woman. And she's half-Greek, remember. Southern women mature much earlier than we Nordic types.'

'Well, she hasn't matured yet,' Bess pointed out sensibly, 'so stop worrying. Bill will soon give her a flea in her ear if she tries anything again. He was very quick to phone Nanny Tettenburg when it happened before. As I said previously, Elena's really too old for a nanny.'

'I know. The trouble is that Kathleen and I go back a long way. I first met her when she was on her way to the States to marry Eugene Tettenburg. She was Kathleen Mason then. And we both come from the same part of the world. I haven't the heart to ask her to find another post after all these years.'

It was Kathleen herself, however, who resolved the problem a few months later, when she resigned; not because she would admit that Elena had outgrown her services, but on account of her increasing squabbles and disagreements with 'that bloody Miss Georgiadis', as she confided to Madge Shelton when she arrived unexpectedly in London just before Christmas.

Kathleen had also hoped to see Bess Holland, of whom she was surprisingly fond; surprisingly, because the two women had very few interests in common. But Bess had gone to visit her parents, a retired civil servant and his wife, now living in Tunbridge Wells. A duty visit, Kathleen

377

suspected. She had often heard Bess speak of her mother and father with respect, but rarely, now she came to think of it, with any great affection.

Harriet, on the point of leaving London for Ireland to visit Carlin Boyce at the Malachi stables, tried not to let her relief show at Kathleen's decision.

'What will you do?' she asked.

'I've been offered a post in the States,' Kathleen said. 'California.' She named a well-known film star, whose wife had just had a baby. 'I rather fancy Hollywood and all those casting-couch goings-on.'

Harriet laughed and held out her hand. 'Goodbye, Kathy, and good luck. You're a part of my past. I shall miss you.'

'Me, too. That transit camp on Salisbury Plain. . . Oh, well! A lot of water's flowed under a lot of bridges since then. I little thought, when I first clapped eyes on you, what you were going to become.'

'Take care of yourself,' Harriet urged, pressing the other woman's hand.

Since Spiros' death, Harriet had bought a flat in Bruton Street, just off Berkeley Square, suddenly tired, after so many years, of always staying at Claridges. She accompanied Kathleen down in the lift and saw her into a taxi, waving a fond farewell. In spite of her relief, she felt depressed. Kathleen had been the only person close to her who remembered her as a young woman. There were very few people left who could do that. Carlo, who was now a widower, eking out a rich and lonely existence in New York, still embittered because he had pulled out of Chance Enterprises too soon. And, of course, Edmund Howard, whom she had not seen now for many years.

She had given up attending race meetings, the only places where they might have met, and left the running of her string of racehorses entirely in Carlin Boyce's capable hands. She paid flying visits to the stables every now and then, unable to kick the habit of personal supervision, but never stayed long enough to meet any of the Irish racing fraternity.

She flew to Dublin and had Bill Brereton drive her down to Waterford. Although she went rarely to Ireland, she had grown to love it; the lush green countryside, the air of gentle peace. And yet it had such a violent and blood-stained history. Harriet remembered, as a child, her father telling her the story of the battle of Clontarf, when Brian Boru had defeated the Vikings, only to be murdered in his tent as he knelt to give thanks to God for his miraculous victory.

It was late afternoon when they reached the stables. Frost was already hardening the ground, the December sun sinking behind the roof-tops in a ball of fire. Through the still uncurtained windows of the trainer's house, Harriet glimpsed a Christmas tree, strung with coloured lights and shimmering with tinsel.

For once, she had not warned him of her visit. Now and then, she needed to reassure herself that people were doing their jobs properly without prior warning of her arrival. It was never wise, she had found, to take anyone's loyalty and industry for granted.

There was a Peugeot estate wagon parked in the drive of the house, which stood a few hundred yards back from the main road, alongside the stables. Harriet did not recall such a car belonging to Carlin, although it might, she conceded, be a recent acquisition. It was nearly a year since she had last visited Malachi. Bill stopped the Daimler, supplied by the Dublin offices of the Chance Corporation, at the far end of the approach road, and got out to open the white fencing gate. As he did so, two men and a woman emerged from the house.

It was a long time since Harriet had seen Isabelle Howard but, oddly enough, she recognized her before she identified Edmund; probably because Isabelle was standing in the porch, clearly visible in the light from the hall. The two men were a few paces ahead of her, half in shadow.

Carlin Boyce turned his head as Bill pushed open the gate and raised his hand to his peaked chauffeur's hat in salute.

'Hello, Mr Boyce,' he called. 'It's Mrs Georgiadis to see you.'

379

Harriet, her heart beating a suffocating tattoo, got out of the back seat of the Daimler and waved.

'Carlin!' She advanced across the frosty grass, a smile carefully held in place. 'I'm sorry to take you by surprise. I had to come over to our Dublin offices for a meeting,' she lied glibly, 'and I thought I might as well take the opportunity to pay you a visit. I'm going to Agios Georgios for Christmas and then on to New York for a couple of months. So I thought if there were any problems this would be a good chance to get them cleared up. If it's inconvenient, Bill and I can go to a hotel in Waterford for the night, and come back tomorrow morning.'

Carlin grinned and wrung her proffered hand.

'If you're both willing to take pot-luck, supper's no problem. My housekeeper always leaves my fridge well stocked, God bless her! As for the beds, there are clean sheets in plenty. I think you know Mr and Mrs Howard?'

'Yes, of course.' Harriet found herself shaking hands with Edmund and Isabelle as if in a dream. Bill, meanwhile, had parked the Daimler alongside the Peugeot, near the house, and was standing respectfully at a distance, awaiting orders.

'As I wrote to you,' Carlin went on, 'we're adding to the stables this spring and, naturally, we're buying from Eddie. Only the best is good enough for the Malachi. So, as he and Isabelle were in the vicinity for the day, we've been concluding our business. They were just off.' A thought struck him. He turned, beaming, to Edmund and Isabelle. 'As you and Mrs Georgiadis are old friends, why don't you both stop for a bite to eat as well? You can stay for an hour or so, and still be home well before midnight.'

39

They quarrelled violently, all through supper and afterwards, to the embarrassment of Isabelle and Carlin Boyce, and the secret amusement of Bill Brereton, who, as one knowing his place, ate quietly, listening but saying nothing.

The row, ostensibly, was political – that evergreen subject, Anglo-Irish affairs – but, every now and then, Bill caught undertones of other, more personal, emotions. He had noticed Mrs Georgiadis' heightened colour when Mr Howard leaned across the table and squeezed his wife's hand.

The evening had started quietly enough with Carlin Boyce pouring them all liberal measures of Irish whiskey 'to keep out the cold'. After that, with Bill's assistance, he had gone into the kitchen to open tins of soup, grill steaks and take ice cream from the freezer. The other three sat round the fire in the big open-plan living-room and made desultory conversation.

Harriet had not been happy. There was so much she wanted to ask Edmund, to tell him, but Isabelle's presence cramped her style. She was unable to deduce from the other woman's manner whether or not Isabelle knew anything of her relationship with Edmund. Except in appearance, Isabelle had not changed; she still had the same air of cool detachment that Harriet remembered from all those years ago at Carey Hall.

Edmund sat beside his wife on the couch, holding her

hand. The sight of them smiling at one another, obviously comfortable and contented together, irritated Harriet. She knew that she was being stupid and childish and unreasonable, succumbing to a jealousy she had no right to feel, but she could not help herself. By the time Carlin summoned them to table, her temper was at flash point. After some chat about horses, in which Harriet did not join, the trainer applied the match which lit the fuse.

'Terrible thing,' he said, 'those five soldiers being killed in Ulster last Sunday. I don't hold with the Brits being in Ireland, if you'll excuse the frankness, Harriet, but I can't condone violence, either.'

Harriet smiled scornfully. 'Not many of your countrymen would agree with you, Carlin, including Mr Howard. Edmund always had sympathy with the IRA.'

Edmund, too, was feeling frustrated. Harriet's unexpected arrival at Malachi had knocked him sideways. For the past eleven years, ever since he had read in the newspapers of Spiros' heart-attack and subsequent confinement to a wheelchair, he had tried to put Harriet out of his mind. He knew then that he had found her, only to lose her again. She would never abandon her husband now; not as long as Spiros lived.

After leaving her at the Old Vicarage that Sunday, he had toyed with the idea of telling Isabelle the truth; of asking her for a divorce; of presenting himself to Harriet as a free man and waiting to see what happened. But somehow he could never quite bring himself to do it; the moment never seemed propitious. He had meant what he said to Harriet that afternoon: he owed Isabelle too much. She had been a good wife to him. How could he suddenly desert her? He was still dithering a year later, when he read about Spiros and realized that he had, in any case, left it too late.

At first, he had entertained the barely acknowledged hope that Spiros would die quickly, but the years had gone on and he had begun the long painful process of forgetting Harriet. He had devoted himself to Isabelle and had slowly forged a deeper relationship with her, so much so that he had actually begun to fancy himself in love. Then, two hours ago, Harriet had stepped out of her car and all the old feelings for her came flooding back; now, when he could not possibly break up his marriage without burdening himself with a guilt which would follow him to his grave. He wanted to yell aloud with rage and frustration. His anger focused on Harriet. She had no right coming back into his life, upsetting him in this fashion.

Isabelle said, in her quiet English way: 'Oh, I'm sure that's not true, Harriet. Edmund would never sympathize with an organization like the IRA.'

Harriet looked mockingly at Edmund, and he had the grace to blush.

He said sharply: 'Please don't presume to speak for me, Isabelle. I'm quite capable of doing that for myself.' Then, seeing her wounded expression, he leaned across the table and squeezed her hand. 'Sorry, acushla, I didn't mean to snap.'

At the sound of the old familiar endearment, Harriet felt her colour rising, and her temper with it. He had no right to use the word to anyone but her. She ignored the voice inside her which whispered: 'You're fifty-three years old. Try to behave like it, for God's sake!'

'I'm afraid you're being rather naïve, Isabelle,' she could not prevent herself from saying. 'I'm sure you'll find your husband, like most of his compatriots, thoroughly approves of maiming and killing young servicemen and innocent bystanders in the name of freedom. And blowing up MPs. I'm referring, of course, to Airey Neave, who was killed by a car bomb, you may remember, last March, just before the general election.'

It went on from there, Harriet and Edmund getting more and more heated in an argument which dragged in such fruitful topics as Cromwell's massacre at Drogheda, the battle of the Boyne, the Easter Rising, Sir Roger Casement, the potato famine, and finally degenerated into a slanging match which was only ended by Carlin getting to his feet and banging on the table.

'Look,' he said quietly, as they both turned startled faces towards him, 'I don't know what this is about, and I don't mean any disrespect, but I think the rest of us have had enough for one evening. Let's talk about something else, shall we?'

Harriet gave a strained smile. 'Yes, of course, Carlin. I'm sorry. Edmund and I do seem rather to have got . . . well, carried away.' She felt ashamed, aware that she had made a spectacle of herself. She and Edmund had behaved abominably.

'It's time we were going, in any case,' Edmund said, gulping down the remains of his coffee. He, too, sounded subdued. He got to his feet, avoiding Harriet's eyes. 'We've a long drive home.' He smiled shamefacedly at his wife.

Isabelle rose and went round the table, linking one of her arms through his. She looked troubled, sensing, as Carlin and Bill Brereton had done, that something deeper lay beneath the confrontation they had just witnessed than simply two people getting hot under the collar about politics. She was no fool. She had always been deeply in love with Edmund, but had sensed that, for some reason or other, she must not show it. There was another woman in his life, she was convinced of that, and suspected that it might be Harriet. Harriet had been around all those years ago when Edmund had broken off their engagement, although Harriet had been married then to her second husband, and had continued to be so for another two years.

Isabelle was away in London when Harriet had again turned up at Carey Wanstead. Her father had been sure that Harriet and Edmund were about to announce their engagement; instead, she had married Hallam Cavendish. But it was then, Isabelle recollected, that Edmund had suddenly proposed to her again, sweeping her off her feet, insisting that they get married at once by special licence. Unable to believe that her dearest wish had at last come true, she had asked no questions. In any case, she was not the sort of woman who poked and pried; who wanted to own a man body and soul. Later, however, she had been forced to put two and two together. And, finally, there had been that time – ten, eleven years ago? – when Edmund had been so short-tempered and restless. He had been to Ascot, and she had been unable to accompany him. She had heard afterwards, through friends, that Harriet had been staying at Winterbourn Green.

She said now, in her clear unruffled tones: 'Thank you, Carlin, for supper and for a very pleasant evening.' She turned to Harriet, holding out her hand. 'Good night. I've enjoyed meeting you again after all these years. And listening to you and Edmund has been most instructive.'

Harriet eyed her warily. What exactly had she meant by that?

'It's been very nice seeing you again,' she said, equally insincerely and shook hands with as much dignity as she could muster. 'I really must apologize once more for getting so carried away.'

Edmund, releasing his arm from his wife's, began pulling on his coat and scarf.

'That's one thing you can always rely on the English for,' he remarked sardonically. 'They know how to carry off an awkward situation.'

Carlin said sharply: 'That's enough, Eddie! Leave it!' He helped Isabelle on with her fur jacket and accompanied her out to the car.

Bill Brereton gathered up some of the dirty dishes and vanished tactfully into the kitchen. Edmund and Harriet looked at one another. He took a half-pace towards her, then changed his mind. He moved in the direction of the living-room door, but paused to glance back.

'Well, here's to our next meeting in another eleven years' time. Let's hope it's friendlier than this one.' Their eyes met. He smiled wryly. 'Goodbye, acushla!'

Harriet flew to New York early in the new year for a series of meetings with the board of the Chance Corporation and representatives of the Georgiadis Shipping Line (USA). She had spent Christmas on Agios Georgios with Elena and Piers, and had stopped off in London to deal with several matters arising from the Chance Corporation Trust for the Underprivileged. She had always disliked the name: it had a patronizing ring to it, but it had to be called something, and at least it stated the trust's intention in a simple straightforward way. And it had never deterred young people from requesting grants, as was witnessed by the piles of completed application forms for the coming year alone. Harriet liked to consider every one herself, and to make personal recommendations to the trust's co-directors.

As a result, it was nearly the middle of January before she finally arrived in America, but she decided to give her customary New Year party just the same. She instructed Bess Holland to send out all the usual invitations, giving her *carte blanche* to add to the list any new business acquaintances or associates of the past twelve months who might be upset by being excluded.

'You're so much better at remembering these people than I am,' she said, lightly kissing Bess's cheek. 'You see how I rely on you.'

'That's what you pay me for. And pay me very handsomely, I might add. Give my love to the boys, if you're going to see them.'

'I am.' Harriet rose from the breakfast-table. 'I must make the most of my grandsons while I can. It's a damn nuisance always having to spend Christmas on Agios Georgios, but I must put Elena first. And for another two years she's virtually a prisoner on that damned island.' Harriet swallowed the dregs of her coffee as Jeanette Baynton appeared, ready to clear the table. 'I don't think I asked you: how were your parents when you went home in December?'

Bess glanced up from the list she was compiling, her eyes a little troubled.

'Both rather frail. Mother's arthritis is getting worse, and now she's had this cataract operation. Daddy's all right, really, I suppose. It's just that he's worried constantly about Mummy.'

'Do they resent the fact that you don't go home more often? You could, you know. I should understand.'

Bess smiled, the sweet smile which lit her dark eyes. 'I know you would. But I don't have a lot in common with my mother and father. We get on each other's nerves when we're together. We're happiest apart. Perhaps it's common to adopted children and their parents.' The smile deepened as Harriet made an effort to look surprised. 'Now, don't pretend you didn't know. You know everything about all your employees. Besides, I'm fully aware that you have a soft spot for adoptees and orphans. Bill, Dick Norris, Madge and myself are all adopted. It's one of the reasons why you gave us a chance in the first place.'

'You're all excellent at your jobs,' Harriet said defensively, putting her empty cup and saucer down on Jeanette's tray with a snap.

Bess was unperturbed by this hint of anger.

'Of course we are, or you wouldn't have put up with us. But I still maintain that our adopted state was a deciding factor in our favour.'

'You know too damn much!' Harriet retorted briskly, as she prepared to leave. She gave an impish grin, belying the severity of her words. 'I shall expect all those invitations out by this evening. Get some of the typists to help you. I'll see you at the office later this morning.'

'Right. Do you want me to send one to Mr Geraldino?'

Harriet hesitated. Carlo had been invited to last year's party and had cast a blight over the whole evening, not only by getting very drunk, but also by being extremely abusive. In the end, Ken Lambert and Francis Derham had, between them, managed to carry him out and bundle him into a hastily summoned taxi. Harriet, therefore, had not included him among this year's guests; but now that Bess had brought the omission to her attention she began to feel mean. He was Michael's uncle, if only by marriage, and the only person left who could recall the early days with Gus.

387

She nodded curtly. 'OK. Send him an invitation. I just hope he behaves himself, that's all.'

But Carlo, when he arrived the following Wednesday evening, to swell the already formidable numbers crowded into Harriet's Fifth Avenue apartment, seemed to be a changed man. Although well into his sixties, he had the air and bearing of someone much younger. His hitherto grey hair was suddenly restored to a youthful near-jet-black, and he was drenched in a particularly pungent aftershave. He wore tight jeans, a pink silk shirt open to the waist, and a large silver medallion engraved with his Taurean birth sign. When asked what he would like to drink, he chose orange juice.

The cause of this metamorphosis was not hard to find. Clinging to his arm was a very young, very curvaceous blonde – '38–21–36, honey,' as she told anyone who was interested enough to listen – who was introduced to Harriet as 'my friend, Natalie'.

'Hi!' said Natalie, taking a deep breath that threatened to part her magnificent breasts from their skimpy covering. She held out a hand with five scarlet talons and tossed a head of short blonde curls. 'Natalie Schuster. I'm in films. Leastways, that's my ambition. Lots of people say I look like Marilyn.' Her enormous blue eyes, beneath their thick fringe of false lashes, encountered Harriet's startled gaze, and she added impatiently: 'Ya know! Marilyn Monroe.'

'Yes. I do realize who you mean,' Harriet said, unable to stop herself staring at this vision.

'D'ya think I'm like her?' was the next coy question, and Harriet nodded.

'Yes. Yes, I guess you are.'

It was true. Natalie Schuster was exactly like the late Marilyn Monroe. She was sixteen years out of date. No one looked like that any more; certainly not girls with aspirations to make it in the movies. Her short tight black dress and stiletto-heeled shoes made her seem like someone who had peaked in the early sixties and forgotten ever since to move with the times.

With an effort, Harriet at last tore her eyes away.

'I'm glad you could come, Carlo. It's nice to see you.'

'Hell! I didn't come for my own sake. After what happened last year, you're lucky to see me here at all. I don't take kindly to being thrown out. No, I came for Natalie. To advance her career. So where are ya hidin' him, Harry? Where's Rollo?'

'Rollo who?' Harriet glanced around vaguely at the packed and chattering throng.

Natalie Schuster gave a high-pitched giggle.

'Hey! Aren't you priceless? Rollo Wingfield, the movie director. Carlo said, if he brought me, you'd be sure to introduce me.'

'I'd no idea he was here this evening. How did you know he was coming, Carlo?'

'That secretary of yours told me. I called her to know if there were going to be any Hollywood people at this shindig of yours, and she said yes, Rollo Wingfield. Well, when Natalie heard that, she just cried with excitement. Didn't ya, doll?'

'I sure did. You will introduce me, Harriet, won't you?'

'If I knew which one he is, with pleasure.' Anything, Harriet thought, to get rid of this simpering creature. Sophia must be whirling in her grave.

She suddenly heard Bess Holland's incisive English tones cutting through the general hubbub. She called: 'Bess! Come here a moment, please. I want you!'

Bess fought her way to her employer's side.

'My God, what a crush!' she exclaimed. 'I don't think a single invitation was refused.'

She looked, as always, cool and unflustered, with that slight aura of detachment about her which Harriet shared. Often, during functions such as this, the eyes of the two women would meet, and each knew exactly what the other was thinking. What am I doing here, in this Never-Never Land of the beautiful, the famous and the rich? Both Bess and her employer came from the same solid, no-

nonsense and, in Bess's case, Nonconformist background, which kept their feet firmly anchored to the ground.

'I hope you won't go getting ideas above your station, my girl,' had been Mrs Holland's only comment when Bess had entered Harriet's employ.

'You can trust our Bess,' her husband had chided her.

And indeed they could; too much so, Bess sometimes reflected, impatient with her own ability to stand on the outside of things, looking in.

Harriet explained what she wanted, and Bess stood on tiptoe, peering over the heads of the crowd.

'Rollo Wingfield, eh? He'll probably be with the Derhams somewhere. He's come with Francis and Judy's daughter. You know, the actress one. She landed a Hollywood contract with one of the major film companies last year and had a small part in Rollo Wingfield's latest film. Someone told me she'd caught his eye. Not surprising, really. He likes pretty young girls. So far, he's been married to three of them.' Bess craned her neck still further and gave a sudden cry of triumph. 'There he is! I can just see him at the far end of the room, sitting on the arm of the couch. If we can push our way through, I'll get Francis to make the necessary introductions.'

'Right,' Harriet said. 'I must have shaken hands with him when he arrived, but there were so many people I didn't catch all their names. But I have seen a couple of his films, and I think I liked them.' She clapped Bess on the shoulder. 'OK. Lead the way.'

40

Harriet judged Rollo Wingfield to be about her own age, although he was in fact younger. When she first met him in this January of 1980, he was less than two months past his fortieth birthday. His hair, worn unfashionably long, was beginning to turn grey, but was still remarkably thick, sweeping back from a widow's peak in the middle of an impressive forehead. The hazel eyes in the finely boned face darted restlessly from person to person, roving beyond his immediate circle; afraid, Harriet thought, to miss anything of consequence which might be happening elsewhere. He was dressed, like Carlo, in designer jeans, silk shirt open to the waist, heavy gold pendant. But, whereas her quondam brother-in-law was a Bohemian manqué, Rollo Wingfield gave the impression of being the genuine thing.

He was reclining on the broad velvet arm of the couch, one leg hitched nonchalantly over the other, his jeans riding up above his ankles to reveal a pair of leather boots, hand-made exclusively for him by a London firm. His right arm, sporting a gold Cartier identity-bracelet, rested negligently around Patsy Derham's shoulders, while his left hand, a ring on every finger, gestured constantly to underline any point he happened to be making. Judy Derham, seated on the couch next to her daughter, was leaning forward, lips slightly parted, every bit as captivated by this Hollywood legend as Patsy. Francis Derham was standing clutching a glass of chilled white wine and looking ineffably bored. He hailed Harriet's approach with a sigh of relief.

'Harriet! Great party! Hope you didn't mind us bringing Rollo and Patsy. Bess said it would be OK. They're staying with us for a couple of days.'

Patsy Derham, an ethereal waif-like girl in the Mia Farrow mould, smiled and batted her eyelids.

'I wanted Mom and Pops to get to know Rollo,' she said, raising huge worshipful eyes to the man seated beside, and a little above, her.

Harriet looked thoughtful, but made no comment. It was obvious that Patsy already saw herself as the fourth Mrs Wingfield, no doubt deluded into believing that she was *the* one, the love of Rollo's life. The previous three, including his first wife, to whom he had been married for twenty-odd years, before marrying and divorcing in quick succession two nubile young maidens less than half his age, had plainly been mistakes. A genius like Rollo Wingfield, Patsy's expression intimated, must be allowed those sorts of error before finally discovering his soul-mate.

Harriet felt sorry for her. It did not take much percipience to know that there was only one person in the world Rollo Wingfield would ever really be in love with, and that was himself. Nevertheless, Harriet was conscious of his attraction as she introduced Carlo and Natalie Schuster.

'Oh, Mr Wingfield, I've been simply *dying* to meet you,' Natalie murmured throatily, bending forward so that he could get the full glory of her magnificent breasts.

'Hi!' Rollo waved a languid hand, unimpressed. God! Not another Marilyn lookalike, he groaned to himself. Couldn't all these silly simpering cows see that it wasn't enough just to have the wiggle and the tits and the breathy high-pitched voice, when they so palpably lacked that indescribable something – the combination of extreme sexuality and childlike innocence – that had been so peculiarly Marilyn's own?

His eyes flicked to Harriet. So this was the famous Mrs Georgiadis, the great female tycoon. Not a bad-looking woman for her years. In fact, to be fair, very attractive.

The hair was tinted, of course; no grey to be seen, and she was over fifty. But her figure was good; her legs great. Like most Englishwomen, she had a beautiful complexion, although, at her age, it was impossible to disguise the increasingly crêpe-like skin of the neck. She was too old for him, that went without saying. Five years ago, he had realized with all the clarity of a divine revelation that in order to nurture his artistic genius, to give his all to his chosen medium of the cinema, he must be surrounded by youth and beauty.

He had still been fond of his wife, Cora May, with whom he had shared twenty-two years of his life, but at forty-four she could no longer inspire him. So he had divorced her and married a rising young starlet, who had very soon ceased to amuse him, and he had then married his continuity girl. Once again, divorce had followed, after a series of well-publicized quarrels. At the moment, he was unattached and wondering if Patsy Derham was the answer to his prayers. He was tired of big busty blondes. For the time being. . .

Harriet moved away to mingle with her other guests, leaving Carlo and Natalie Schuster with the Derhams, votaries at the shrine of a twentieth-century god. Bess Holland went after her.

'Phew!' she said. 'He thinks a lot of himself. Mind you, that last film of his, *Man in the Moon*, got rave notices from most of the critics.'

'Oh, he's a brilliant director,' Harriet agreed, pausing to grab a glass of champagne from the tray of a passing waiter. 'But difficult to live with, I should imagine. That sort of man usually is. Too much adulation spoils them. Not that I think either of us needs worry. Even you, my dear, at thirty-five, are probably over the hill as far as the Boy Wonder is concerned.' She sipped her drink. 'God! I needed that. Exposure to genius always give me a thirst. Now, where are Michael and Julia? Can you see them anywhere in this crush? I'd better have a word – several

393

words – or I shall be accused of ignoring them in favour of my friends.'

It was two years before Harriet set eyes on Rollo Wingfield again; two years in which dissatisfaction with the life she was leading increased from a vaguely sensed discontent to a nagging daily misery. Sex, she supposed, or the lack of it, had something to do with the way she felt.

While Spiros was alive, Harriet had been content with occasional brief affairs, but even they had been few and far between. Looking back, she realized that they had been strictly business arrangements; no strings attached; a night in bed and an unregretted farewell the following morning. A satisfaction only for the body. Emotionally, she was committed to Spiros and to Edmund. There was no room for any other man. But Spiros had been dead for almost three years, and Edmund had once again dropped out of her life. Mutual friends in the racing world spoke of his and Isabelle's happiness.

'They seem to have grown together, two halves of the same whole,' Carlin Boyce had told her in his poetic Irish way. 'You feel nowadays that they've found that extra something in their relationship which they didn't have before.'

Harriet had said, 'I'm delighted for them,' and changed the subject. But, lying awake at night in her lonely bed, she had forced herself to accept the fact that Edmund had put her out of his mind. It was the only thing to do if he wanted to make his marriage work; and, by all accounts, he was succeeding.

Which was all very fine and noble, but where did that leave her? Fifty-six years old, still attractive, still as capable of love in all its forms as a woman half her age. What she wanted, she supposed, expressed in its crudest form, was a man; but a man to whom she could make an emotional commitment; a full-time lover or husband. She needed someone to share her disappointments along with her 'highs'; her problems as well as her passion.

And not the least of those problems was Elena, now fifteen, soon to be sixteen years old. She was at present at boarding school in Switzerland, where Harriet had sent her as soon as she had celebrated her fifteenth birthday the previous October and the conditional age of Spiros' will legally passed. But Elena at large was proving to be as much of a handful as Elena prisoner.

Three or four times during the past few years, Harriet had been summoned to Agios Georgios because Spiros' sister simply could not cope with her wayward niece. At eighty-five, Harriet thought acidly, it was hardly surprising.

'She is . . . she is. . .' Ariadne Georgiadis had sought for the colloquial English expression. 'She is man mad!'

'If she had been allowed to live a normal life, or as normal a life as possible,' Harriet had retorted, 'something like this would never have happened.'

'Something like this' embraced, on each occasion, involvement with one of the young estate workers who lived in the village – a contingency, Harriet felt, which Spiros should have foreseen. Each time, she had been forced to dismiss the boy concerned from the island, to the great distress of his family, although she had made sure that no one, least of all the young man, suffered financially. Harriet had no doubt at all that it was her headstrong ungovernable daughter who had made all the running. Elena swore every time that 'nothing had happened', and Harriet believed her, largely because Elena still had the indefinable air of innocence which went hand in hand with virginity. But it was only a matter of time, she felt, before Elena found someone less scrupulous than the Georgiadis employees she had so far attempted to seduce.

Harriet had convinced herself that boarding school was the answer and in the late autumn of 1981 had packed her daughter off to the Bernese Oberland, to a well-run, highly recommended school near the exclusive skiing resort of Gstaad. It was a co-educational establishment, and Harriet hoped that normal everyday contact with the opposite sex might persuade Elena to stop regarding boys as forbidden fruit and something, therefore, to be urgently tasted.

As far as the other side of her life, the business half of it, went, Harriet was as occupied as ever. But in her more honest moments she admitted that it was a self-imposed workload. Both the Chance Corporation and the Georgiadis Shipping Lines were now so vast that they had become self-perpetuating; gargantuan automata, grinding out more, and ever more, piles of money. There were no obstacles on which they could founder: they were far too big. Anything in their path was simply gobbled up. If Harriet had been content to make an appearance once or twice a year in their respective boardrooms, it would have been more than was necessary, or, indeed, expected of her. As it was, everyone kept up the pretence that her continual presence was vital to both concerns; and she still made regular visits – 'pilgrimages' some wag sarcastically dubbed them – to the Last Chance restaurants, wherever she happened to be in the world.

Michael resented his mother's refusal to retire.

'You've earned a rest,' he kept urging her. 'After all these years, you must be tired.'

'I am not yet as decrepit as you would like to think,' she would retort, adding maliciously: 'I'm only in my fifties. I can carry on for years. Queen Victoria was still ruling at the age of eighty-one; Elizabeth I at seventy. Generally speaking, women have more staying power than men.'

But she recognized herself in Michael; the desire to do things his own way, not to be subservient. She recalled how, in those early days in Greenwich Village, she had taken over the lead from Gus and Carlo and Sophia. But the fact that she understood her elder son in no way affected her decision not to retire until she was ready to do so.

In early May she went to stay with Francis and Judy Derham on their Kentucky ranch for a long weekend. The other guests were Patsy Derham, her husband of six months, the film star Julius Casey, and Rollo Wingfield.

'How come Patsy and Rollo didn't get married?' Harriet asked Francis curiously.

It was Friday, the evening of her arrival. Dinner was over. Conversation during the meal had centred almost exclusively on the outbreak of hostilities between Britain and Argentina over the Falkland Islands. As the only English person present, Harriet had found herself held responsible for all the decisions of Margaret Thatcher's Cabinet, including the sinking of the *Belgrano*. An act of sheer vandalism, Rollo Wingfield had called it, but the others had been kinder. Ronald Reagan's America was more inclined to approve of violent action than Jimmy Carter's had been.

Nevertheless, Harriet was glad to escape into the open air, and she and Francis left the other four to make up a table for bridge. Card games had never appealed to her. They always seemed such a waste of time, and she was relieved when Francis said there were a couple of business matters he needed to discuss with her.

'Let's take our drinks in the garden.'

Francis Derham had grown both physically and mentally in the twenty-five years since he had been manager of the Times Square restaurant. Success and prosperity had put weight on his slender form, and he now looked as solid and dependable as Harriet had always found him to be; one of the most loyal and able members of the Chance Corporation.

They strolled beside the kidney-shaped swimming-pool, lit by underwater lamps, on grass which was thicker and more resilient than any to be found elsewhere in America. It reminded Harriet of the lush fields around Winterbourn Green. A sprinkler, still playing, sprayed the darkness with a myriad diamond drops. On the far side of the house, she could just make out the contours of the stable-block, the neatly railed paddocks and a high-walled mating-compound.

She and Francis had finished discussing their business, and now, sinking into two pool-side chairs, set one on either side of a white metal table, they could turn to more personal matters.

In answer to her question, Francis shrugged.

'One of those things, I guess. Oh, Patsy was keen enough at one time, but Rollo decided he didn't want to get hitched. They lived together for a while, until she got tired of the arrangement. Then Rollo cast Julius Casey opposite her in *Going Back* – did you see it? It was considered to be his best film to date – and that was it. Last fall, as you know, Judy and I got an urgent summons to go to the Coast for the wedding.'

'And Patsy and Rollo? Apparently they're still good friends.'

'Hell, yes! He was going to give her away if Judy and I hadn't been able to make it to the wedding. And she and Julius asked if they could bring him to stay this weekend.'

'How come Rollo hasn't got married again? I'd have bet my last dollar he's the marrying type.'

'Why don't you ask me that question?' enquired a voice behind them. 'I'd say I'm better-qualified to give you an answer than Frank.'

Harriet turned her head. Rollo Wingfield was standing beside her chair, holding a frosted glass containing Pepsi and soda.

'I thought you were playing bridge,' she accused him.

'I've decided I'm not in the mood. I'd rather sit by a pool in the moonlight – or what passes for moonlight – and talk to a beautiful woman. I'm sorry, Frank, old buddy, but you're wanted indoors to take my place.'

Francis groaned, but got up. 'Judas!' he said good-naturedly, and Rollo Wingfield laughed.

'You could always refuse to go.'

'And deprive Judy of her game? You've gotta be joking. It would be more than my life is worth.'

He wandered off across the lawn and disappeared inside the house. Rollo took his vacated chair, opposite Harriet.

'You were saying?' he asked, lifting an eyebrow.

Tonight he was wearing more formal clothes than at her party two years ago: white tuxedo, ruffled silk shirt. He looked very handsome, and Harriet felt a sudden urge to be taken to bed.

'I was wondering why you hadn't got married again. You strike me as the marrying kind.'

'Whatever that is.' He considered her thoughtfully, a slim figure in the Emmanuel blue satin beaded dress, sapphire and diamond earrings, with matching bracelet clasped around one slender wrist. 'I've grown rather tired of babes-in-arms. I feel I'm ripe for the older woman.'

'You should have stayed with your first wife, then,' Harriet responded acidly. 'She's the same age as you are, I believe.'

Rollo regarded her with a widening of his hazel eyes.

'Don't be bitchy, darling. And haven't you learned by now that it's only women who grow old? Men, particularly Hollywood men, just get more mature.'

'So why are you wasting your time talking to an old woman, when you could be scattering your mature charms among the young?'

'I've told you. I'm in the mood for intelligence and sophistication.'

'In other words, you want to be mothered.'

He waved an admonitory finger. 'Naughty, naughty!' He leaned towards her, across the table. 'Admit it, Harriet Georgiadis, you fancy me.'

'That's an exceedingly presumptuous remark.' She managed to sound cool and detached, but the palms of her hands were sweating. He raised one of them to his lips and smiled knowingly. Harriet felt a shiver of desire, like cold water trickling down her spine. 'Let's stop this nonsense,' she suggested briskly.

But when she attempted to withdraw her hand from his he refused to let it go.

'Ungracious,' he murmured. 'But I forgive you. I have a better proposal to make. Let's get married.'

The following morning, Harriet rang her secretary. Bess had taken a long-overdue holiday to go home to see her parents after a letter from her father had stated that her mother was feeling unwell. Bess had made the visit reluctantly. Mrs Holland was a woman who enjoyed poor health.

'It's her,' she remarked unpleasantly, resuming her seat at the table after answering the telephone. 'Mrs Georgiadis. Doesn't she stop to think that we might be in the middle of lunch?'

'It's early morning in the States, Mother,' Bess explained patiently. 'I don't suppose Harriet realized that we'd be having a meal.'

'And wouldn't have worried if she had,' Mrs Holland muttered under her breath as her daughter left the room.

'Bess!' Harriet's voice carried clearly across the miles of ocean stretching between them. She came straight to the point. 'Rollo Wingfield has asked me to marry him. What do you think?'

It had become a habit to talk over problems and doubts with her secretary. Bess's observations were not always heeded – Bess herself would have said that they made no impact whatsoever – but Harriet valued the younger woman's point of view. It was invariably sound and level-headed.

On this occasion, however, Bess felt disinclined to offer any advice. For some obscure reason, she was disturbed at the thought of Harriet's marriage to Rollo Wingfield. She could see nothing in it for either of them, and suspected that it would prove to be pointless and short-lived.

'Well?' Harriet's voice asked impatiently.

'You know best how you feel about him,' Bess answered guardedly. 'I wouldn't presume to offer an opinion on such a subject.'

'Don't be pompous, Bess. I'm asking you as a friend.'

'Then, as a friend . . . I'd say don't do it.'

'Mmmm. . .' There was a protracted pause before Harriet laughed. 'Thanks for being so honest. I knew I could rely on you. It's what everyone will say. Unfortunately, I find I've already made up my mind.'

41

It was a mistake, of course. She knew that almost as soon as she had married him. People – family, friends, newspaper columnists – said it would never last, and they were right. It was doomed from the start. It was a proposal made and accepted for all the wrong reasons. Rollo was seeking a new image for himself because he was temporarily bored with the old one. The intelligent, high-powered, older woman made a dramatic change from his last two wives and various mistresses. Besides which – something he did not quite admit, even to himself – he needed money to finance his new film. While his more recent efforts had enjoyed great critical acclaim, they had done poorly at the box-office, and backers were becoming harder to find. He had a wonderful idea for a family saga set in Mexico, which he was eager to get off the ground. Harriet and her limitless millions would provide the necessary capital.

Harriet, for her part, was lonely. She needed a permanent man in her life; a stabilizing influence. Like many women, she had found the menopause more traumatic than she had expected. The knowledge that a part of her existence was over for good, that she could never again have children, even if she wanted them, made the approach of age that much more of a reality; a door closing in her face, arbitrarily closed by Nature. She needed to be reassured that she was still attractive, still desirable. The offer of marriage from a man over four years her junior, with a well-publicized taste in much younger women, had proved a temptation she was unable to resist.

As far as her family was concerned, Michael was indifferent to the marriage, Julia thrilled at the prospect of an entrée into the glittering Hollywood world, and Piers, from the safe enclosed distance of the 'dreaming spires', pruriently curious. But Elena was edgy with her step-father from the moment of their first meeting at the wedding.

Harriet had elected to be married on her farm in Connecticut. She had deliberately avoided both Agios Georgios and Hollywood because of the association in her mind with Spiros and Edmund. The run-up to the ceremony on 28 June, her fifty-sixth birthday, promised to be fraught, allowing only six weeks to issue invitations and make all the necessary arrangements. Neither Harriet nor Rollo, having once decided to marry, felt it wise to wait very long. Both were secretly afraid of a change of heart. As a result, Harriet could have done without the peremptory summons to Gstaad at the beginning of the month.

Madame Albertine Serrière, who, with her husband Marc, ran the unoriginally named Académie Edelweiss, received Harriet in her study, a spacious white-walled room overlooking the veranda, which ran the whole length of the front of the house, and the flower-strewn meadow beyond. Madame, who spoke excellent English, motioned Harriet to a chair and offered her coffee.

'No, thank you.' Harriet's tone was brittle. 'I just want to know why I have been asked to come here at such short notice. Is Elena ill?'

'No, not ill.'

'What, then? This is a most inconvenient time for me, madame. I'm getting married at the end of the month.'

Madame Serrière inclined her well-groomed head. 'This I know. Your secretary, Miss Holland, has written to me requesting leave of absence for Elena to attend the ceremony.'

Harriet grimaced to herself. 'Leave of absence' made the Académie Edelweiss sound like a military establishment. And, now she came to look at her more closely,

Madame did have something of the bearing of an army sergeant-major. She suppressed a smile at the thought and raised her eyebrows.

'Then, why . . .?'

'I'm afraid, Mrs Georgiadis, that I must ask you to remove Elena from the school. We find her a subversive influence.'

Harriet's eyebrows rose even further. 'Would you care, madame, to substantiate that statement?'

'Certainly. She is not amenable to discipline herself, and constantly encourages the other pupils to flout the teachers' authority. When she chooses, she can be extremely charming, but mostly she is intractable and insolent. To Elena, rules and regulations are made only to be broken. She plays truant from her classes and goes missing for a whole day at a time. On several occasions, she has got out of school in the evening, after she is supposed to be in bed. Twice, she has been found in hotels in Gstaad, drinking with strange men. Skiing instructors,' Madame pronounced awfully, before going on: 'Three nights ago, she hitched a lift into Montreux and persuaded the young men who owned the car to take her to the Kursaal, where my husband and the German master discovered her at midnight, playing Boule.'

'Was she winning?' Harriet asked with involuntary interest; then, noting Madame's scandalized expression, murmured hurriedly: 'I do realize that all this is very bad, but surely expulsion is a little severe. Couldn't you possibly give her another chance? You see, madame, under the terms of my late husband's will, Elena led a very restricted life until she came here. She's just kicking over the traces, as any girl might. She'll settle down. Just give her time.'

Madame Serrière's lips folded into a thin bloodless line.

'I'm sorry, Mrs Georgiadis, but no! Matters have gone far enough. My husband and I have made allowances for Elena as far as we dare, but we cannot have her disrupting the school. I should be grateful if you would remove her as soon as possible.'

'I see.' Harriet suddenly found herself disliking everything about Madame and the Académie Edelweiss. She

403

knew it was unreasonable of her; her anger should be directed against Elena, but she could understand and sympathize with her daughter. The initial fault lay with Spiros and his obsessive love and fear for his only child. She got up from her chair, eyeing Madame coldly. 'If that's what you want, Elena can come away with me now. Will you see that she's ready to leave in half an hour?'

The wedding was over. Three hundred guests choked the lawns surrounding the farmhouse, pushing their way in and out of the four huge red-and-white striped marquees which had been erected by the catering firm hired to do the buffet. White-coated waiters, mini-skirted waitresses carried round trays of champagne. A temporary bar had been built in the main living-room of the house. Arrangements of red and white roses were everywhere, spilling out of vases, jammed into white plastic disposable garden urns, trained over white plastic trellis-work arches. Threading her way between her guests, aware that her pastel-coloured Bruce Oldfield dress was too young for her, Harriet could imagine Edmund's dour comment.

'You have absolutely no taste, Harriet, that's your trouble.'

But she would not think about Edmund. This day was hers and Rollo's. Incidentally, where *was* Rollo? Then she saw him, standing by one of the buffet-tables, talking to Elena. She hoped to God they were going to be friends.

Bess Holland had also noticed Rollo talking to his new step-daughter, and the closed, set, mulish expression on Elena's face. Bess sighed to herself, guessing how Elena must feel. She didn't like the marriage, either; and although, on better acquaintance, Rollo Wingfield was a less self-opinionated and less spoilt man than she had at first thought him she considered Harriet's reasons for marrying him too flimsy.

Harriet had tried to explain her feelings to Bess when her secretary had caught up with her in New York, shortly before the wedding. Loneliness was her main theme, and

Bess had been hurt, although she would have denied any such accusation vigorously. It was not, after all, part of the role of a secretary, however private and confidential, to offer friendship or expect it in return. Nevertheless, Bess did consider herself Harriet's friend, and thought the relationship should have protected the older woman against the sense of isolation from which she was so obviously suffering. Bess was still too young to appreciate the uncertainties and feelings of vulnerability which came with advancing age.

'Penny for them!' Bill Brereton came up behind her and clapped Bess on the shoulder.

'What? Oh, nothing!' Bess turned and smiled at him. 'I was just watching Elena. She doesn't look happy. I don't think she likes Rollo Wingfield.'

Bill shrugged. 'She'll get over it. Doesn't like the idea of a step-father to keep her in order, I expect.' He eyed Elena speculatively. 'A right handful she's turned out to be. Looks good, though.'

Elena did look good, in a white gaberdine suit with cream silk facings. She left Rollo, with whom she had been exchanging a few stilted pleasantries, and made her way out of the marquee. She was growing bored with the game of Spot the Film Star: she had played that all through the service and the speeches which followed the cutting of the cake. She saw a number of well-known male heads turn in her direction as she passed, and knew that their owners found her attractive. Her mirror told her that she was a very pretty girl. Like her vast wealth, it was something she took for granted. There was no one in all this glittering throng who could offer her anything that she could not return a thousandfold. Or, at least, would be able to, once she was twenty-one. Fame and money held no appeal for Elena Georgiadis. She was looking for something else: the bizarre, the forbidden.

She noticed Bill Brereton dancing with Bess Holland on the specially laid dance-floor on the south-facing lawn. A New Orleans jazz band had been hired for the afternoon.

Later, after Harriet and Rollo had left on their honeymoon, there would be a disco in the farmhouse, the music supplied by a famous pop group. Elena stood for a moment or two, watching Bill and Bess Holland, wondering if it would be amusing to cut in, then deciding that it wouldn't. She had lost interest in Bill. It was a childish infatuation which belonged to her past; to the days when she had surreptitiously read *Lady Chatterley's Lover* under the bedclothes, understanding about one sentence in ten, but enough to associate herself and Bill with the two central characters. It had upset people, including Bill, when she had tried to act out her fantasies. It still would, she supposed, but nowadays she thought him rather staid and boring.

She wondered what the school in England would be like. Much the same as the school in Switzerland, she guessed; deadly dull and terribly respectable. At least she would be able to speak English most of the time, instead of French and German. But she could probably find something to amuse her. It was near Ascot, not too far from London, and she could always visit Piers at Oxford. She quite liked her younger half-brother: he annoyed and teased her, but he also made her laugh. Michael was always snubbing her and lecturing her, as though she were a child. Julia was just stupid, running to fat and wrapped up in her two little boys.

'Enjoying yourself, darling?' Harriet had come up behind Elena and was caressing the long blonde hair. Without waiting for an answer, she went on: 'I'm going to change now. Come with me and give me a hand.'

Harriet had elected not to have bridesmaids, not even Elena. She had been worried in case her other children felt excluded.

'OK.' Her daughter's tone indicated no resentment, as she followed her mother indoors and up the stairs.

There was a babel of voices, the pressure of bodies everywhere. Only in the bedroom, set aside for Harriet's use, was there peace and quiet, once the thick oaken door had been closed. A pale grey Bruce Oldfield suit was laid out on the bed. Blouse, gloves, tights, shoes, jewellery, handbag were also laid ready. Nothing had been forgotten. Madge Shelton had been her usual efficient self, making certain that everything was present and correct before going to join in the festivities outside.

Elena perched on the end of the bed, making no real attempt to help, watching her mother change.

She asked abruptly: 'Why did you marry him? That man.'

Harriet paused, her eyes troubled. The heavy peach-coloured satin slip clung to the contours of her body. She could see her reflection in the long wardrobe mirror, and knew a moment of panic.

I don't want to get old, she thought desperately. Out loud, she asked: 'What's wrong with Rollo? Don't you like him?'

'He's the pits. He gives me the creeps.'

Harriet was shocked. She had not anticipated quite so uncompromising an answer.

'Rollo's all right,' she said, slipping on her blouse and starting to do up the row of tiny velvet-covered buttons. 'He has rather a high opinion of himself, but that's only natural when people are always telling him how wonderful he is. There's nothing venal about him.'

'He likes young girls.'

'Has he made a pass at you?' Harriet scanned her daughter's face anxiously.

'No! No, of course not. But I was watching him today. Tits, bums, legs, he never takes his eyes off them.'

'Him and a hundred thousand other men.'

'Yes, I suppose so. But there are ways and ways of looking.'

'Nonsense!' Harriet spoke briskly as she stepped into the pale grey skirt, feeling for the zip under the floating panel. 'I hope you aren't going to resent the fact that I've married again, Ellie. I want you and Rollo to be friends.'

407

'You didn't answer my question,' Elena reminded her. 'You still haven't told me why you married him.'

'For a lot of different reasons you're much too young to understand.' She saw her daughter's face close like a flower furling its petals, and cursed inwardly. That was a silly tactless thing to have said. Elena had every right to look resentful. 'Look, darling, it would just take too long to explain, and I haven't the time. I'm sorry.'

But it was too late for apologies. Elena had withdrawn behind a brightly smiling mask.

'That's OK. None of my business anyway.' She got off the bed and kissed her mother's cheek. 'I guess your life is your business. You can make any damn mess of it you choose.'

In later years, Harriet realized that the best part of her two-year marriage to Rollo Wingfield was the honeymoon; three short weeks when they had time for one another, without the distractions of outside interests.

Ever since she had read Paul Scott's *The Raj Quartet*, Harriet had wanted to emulate Mildred Layton and have a houseboat on Dal Lake, amid the snow-capped mountains of Kashmir. When she had first mooted the idea, Rollo had been unenthusiastic.

'Kashmir!' he had exclaimed. 'Who wants to go to Kashmir? What is this never-ending love-affair you Brits have with India?'

'Don't call it India when you get to Kashmir,' she had warned him, and from that moment forward it had been taken for granted that Harriet would get her own way.

In the event, Rollo loved it. The huge houseboat, moored to a landing-stage – no longer movable as in Mildred Layton's day – had four bedrooms, each with its own bathroom, dining-room, kitchen, veranda and roof-deck with magnificent views. Glass chandeliers, Kashmiri carpets, heavily carved furniture and no less than four luxuriously upholstered sofas soon reconciled Rollo to what he had scathingly termed 'an outpost of civilization'. To cap it all, there were no staffing problems. A cook, a boat-boy, a house-boy and several guides ensured that they were looked after in true Hollywood fashion.

'Not bad! Not bad, honey,' he approved after his first inspection. 'Why don't you buy one?'

'Why don't you?' she countered lightly. 'I'm sure you're able to afford it quite as well as I am.'

She saw the quick sidelong glance he gave her and wondered, not for the first time, just how much her money had persuaded him that it was time to marry an older woman. A moment later, she rejected the thought as mean and inappropriate to a honeymoon. She might at least give the marriage a chance.

And it really did seem, after their first night together, as though it could work out. Rollo was a skilled and practised lover, using fingers, tongue, lips to give her satisfaction. She made every effort to please him in return. The trouble was, as she tried hard not to acknowledge to herself, their lovemaking was a purely physical thing. There was no emotion, no love, no fondness even. There was no dislike or hatred, either, if it came to that. They might just as well have been two animals copulating, she often reflected, after the marriage had moved to its inevitable end.

But for a time, particularly during those first three weeks, Harriet tried to persuade herself that she felt something for Rollo. They held hands, like a couple of young lovers, beneath the wooden-beamed houses of Srinagar, paused to kiss lingeringly in the Mogul Gardens, made love at midnight on deck under the stars. Ironically, it was the most romantic of all her honeymoons, as she and Rollo wandered the foothills of the Himalayas, among mosques and temples and the bustle of riverside life.

But when the honeymoon was over – so apt a phrase – Harriet knew in her heart of hearts that the marriage was, too. By late July they had left Kashmir and returned to what Rollo called the real world of Europe and America, both of them already going their separate ways. Rollo retired to Hollywood to make plans for his forthcoming film, set in Mexico and financed with Harriet's money. She was in either New York or London or Athens, keeping her finger on the pulse of her ever growing empire.

As a natural corollary, Bess Holland found herself with more work to do than ever; and the following summer Harriet asked her to take over the vacant chairmanship of the Chance Foundation.

'I know it's demanding a hell of a lot from you,' she said, 'but the policy committee only meets two or three times a year, and I need someone in charge of it that I can trust. I want someone close to me who understands my objectives and who knows how my mind works. And this time I want a woman because, although history doesn't always bear me out, I believe our sex has a deeper well of compassion than men. Will you do this for me?'

Bess, taken aback by the proposition, begged for a breathing-space in which to think things over. But she knew, deep down, that she had already accepted. It was not simply that she was flattered to be asked or that she thrived on hard work or that she was inordinately ambitious: all those things were certainly true, but there was more to it than that. As soon as Harriet had broached the subject, Bess realized that she was the right person for the job; that it was something she could be happy to do. The added workload, combined with all her other duties, would be punishing, but she had no doubt that she could cope. There would also be a lot of jealousy at a mere secretary being appointed to such a position, but that, too, Bess knew that she could handle.

And in the mean time Harriet and Rollo's marriage continued to be conducted at long distance.

42

'No,' said Harriet. 'Not Farnworth Bakeries. The business has nothing to recommend it. I've been looking into all the facts and figures. The company will be bankrupt by the end of the year. And apart from that great headquarters building in Chicago, which, admittedly, is a nice piece of real estate, it's not worth the price they're asking. It's gone downhill too far and too fast for my liking. It's not for Chance Enterprises. Forget it, Michael.'

Her elder son, seated on the opposite side of her desk in the office on West 72nd Street, looked furious. The takeover of the Farnworth Bakeries group had been his pet project for some time past. He had expended a lot of time and energy on plans to modernize and rebuild the factories and to revamp the image of the chain of retail shops. And now here was his mother vetoing his proposals without even doing him the courtesy of discussing them with him first. He was head of Chance Enterprises and should be making the decisions. But, as always, when the chips were down it was Harriet who had the final word.

Reading her son's face correctly, she tried to soften the blow.

'I'm sorry, Mickey.' And that was a mistake, she reflected: he quite rightly detested the childhood diminutive with its Walt Disney connotations. She made an attempt to retrieve the situation. 'It's just that, after all these years, I know a bad buy when I see one. I'm older than you.' Her second mistake; she really was being most inept this morning.

411

The truth was she had other things on her mind. Her two-year marriage to Rollo was virtually over. Both knew that it was not working, that each was desperate to go his or her separate way. Yet, perversely, they were both loath to take the first step along the road to divorce, without giving the marriage one final try. It was a form of mutual masochism, Harriet supposed with a sigh, because they were both stubborn people. Or perhaps it was just a natural reluctance to admit that all those Jeremiahs who had prophesied that it would never work out were right after all. Whatever the reason, neither of them had yet suggested to the other that it might be better, legally, to part.

Which was the height of absurdity when they were never together; Rollo shuttling between Hollywood and Mexico, shooting the long-planned film, which had only recently, finally, got off the ground, and always with some young starlet in tow; Harriet leading her own highly charged existence, jetting all over the world in pursuit of her business interests, racked by guilt that she had sacrificed too many other areas of her life to her ambitions. She was nearly fifty-eight years old, had lost the only man she had ever wanted to marry and had been a rotten mother. Perhaps that, more than anything else, preyed on her mind, which was why, when opportunity offered, she tended to be over-protective; like now, when the wisest course would have been to let Michael make his own mistakes. The Chance Corporation, even without the backing of the Georgiadis Shipping Lines, could have withstood the losses the takeover of the Farnworth Bakeries would have brought in its train. Instead, she was putting her foot down and antagonizing Michael more than ever.

'I just don't want you making a fool of yourself,' she told him.

'Old age, Momma,' he answered ponderously, 'does not necessarily mean wisdom.' He rose to his feet, a big heavy man of thirty-six with a rapidly thickening waistline. 'Sometimes it means that you ought to retire and leave matters in the hands of younger people.'

Harriet broke into a peal of laughter.

'If you knew how pompous you sounded, you wouldn't make that sort of remark. It might impress Julia, but it cuts no ice with me.' She handed him the manila folder and its contents, which she had been studying earlier. 'Here. Take this away and have another, closer look at it. You'll discover that I'm right. And now, for goodness' sake, let me get on with some work. I haven't even looked at the papers this morning.' She pressed the buzzer on her desk.

As Michael went out, Bess Holland came in, as discreetly smart as ever in a pale-green woollen suit, necessary warmth on this chilly early-June day.

'He looks distinctly disgruntled,' she remarked, referring to Michael. 'Something wrong?'

'Nothing he won't get over, once he realizes I'm right about Farnworth Bakeries. Anything urgent in the post?'

Bess's smile faded as she laid the morning's correspondence on the desk in front of Harriet. Most of it was already opened, but there were a couple of private letters, still in their envelopes, on top of the pile. Bess indicated the first one, which bore an English stamp and was addressed in a sloping feminine hand.

'That writing is Miss Watling's. You know, Elena's headmistress. I have an uncomfortable feeling that it's another letter of complaint.'

Harriet sighed. 'You hardly need to be a clairvoyant to work that out. She never sends me any other kind. It's only my prompt payment of her extortionate school fees which has prevented her doing what Madame Serrière did: expel Elena.'

Harriet picked up her ivory-handled letter-opener and slit the heavy cream envelope. When she had read the contents, she looked up at Bess with a rueful smile.

'I was wrong,' she said. 'It hasn't prevented our worthy Miss Watling from finally throwing in the towel. She requests that I make arrangements to remove Elena from Aston Court immediately. She and all the staff have had enough.'

'Does she say why exactly?'

413

'Oh, very exactly.' Harriet shrugged. 'All the usual things. Truancy, inattention to studies, insubordination, breaking bounds. You name it, Ellie's done it. As Miss Watling points out, such behaviour has a very adverse effect on the rest of the pupils. I shall have to fly over at once. Check if any of the Georgiadis planes is at Kennedy. If not, book me a seat on one of tomorrow's flights.'

Bess asked: 'Do you want to stay at Bruton Street, or the Old Vicarage, or where?'

'Make it the Vicarage. I'll take Ellie there for a few days while I decide what's to be done. Let the MacGregors know. And let me know as soon as all the arrangements are made. I'll telephone Miss Watling and tell her when to expect me.'

Bess started to leave the room, then paused. It was not her place to ask, but Harriet had always treated her more like a friend than a secretary, and she was fond of Elena.

'What will you do about her?' When Harriet did not answer, she added: 'Sorry. None of my business.'

'No, no!' Harriet smiled. 'My silence didn't imply criticism, just indecision. I was asking myself the same question. There's no point in trying to get her into another school now. It's too near the start of the summer vacation.'

'She'll be eighteen in October,' Bess reminded her employer.

'I know. A woman. But she could still do with a bit of "finishing". I'll probably send her back to Switzerland for a final year. I've heard of a very good place near Berne, with advanced modern ideas. Perhaps they'll manage to knock some sense into her. I'll have to see. And now I must do some work. What with Michael and now this, I've done practically nothing. I'll make a start on the morning papers.'

The photograph was in two British dailies, the *Sun* and the *Daily Mail*, both bearing the previous day's date.

'Elena Georgiadis,' read the caption in the former, 'seen leaving Annabelle's last night with her mother's ex-husband, the Honourable Hallam Cavendish.' Alongside was a short column raking over the ashes of Harriet's marriage to, and divorce from, Hallam, and the fact that their son was one of Elena's two half-brothers. 'Is there any law,' enquired the *Sun*'s reporter, 'which says a girl can't marry her half-brother's daddy? The couple looked remarkably cosy in the club, so I am informed, earlier in the evening, dancing cheek-to-cheek and snuggling up to one another at their table.'

The *Daily Mail* contented itself with stating the bald facts and cutting out the speculation, but its photographer had caught Elena at a slightly different angle, revealing – and 'revealing', fumed Harriet to herself, was the operative word – the extremely low cut of her strapless black dress.

Fortunately, the fortieth anniversary of the D-Day landings had President Reagan and Mrs Thatcher competing for the covers of the world's leading newspapers, and Elena's night out on the town with Hallam had necessarily been relegated to the inside – a fact for which Harriet could only be thankful.

But it did not make her any the less angry. How had Hallam and Elena met? Through Piers, of course. Silly question! Elena had expressed her intention of visiting Piers at Oxford, and he had taken her to Carey Hall. Natural enough, in the circumstances, and blame could hardly be attached to Piers. Indeed, Harriet herself was the more culpable for sending Elena to a school so near to Carey Wanstead in the first place. More important, what was Hallam up to, encouraging the girl to play truant, taking her to nightclubs and passing her off, as he must have done, as over eighteen? What was his game? Only one thing was certain, knowing Hallam. He was up to no good.

Bess came into the inner office at a run, in answer to the desk-buzzer's insistent summons. Harriet thrust the two newspapers at her with a face like thunder.

'Have you seen these?'

Bess looked, then gasped with dismay.

Harriet went on: 'Don't bother locating one of our

415

planes. Just get me a seat – any seat! – on the next available flight to London. Phone the apartment and tell Madge to start packing. Ask Jeanette to give her a hand. Tell them both I'm on my way. Now! This instant! Ring me there and tell me what plane I'm on. Then locate Bill. I think he's at Bruton Street at the moment. He went over to see his father in Glasgow, but he was due back in London yesterday. Tell him to meet me at Heathrow with a car.' While she spoke, Harriet was shrugging on the jacket of her cream woollen suit and grabbing her handbag from its customary drawer in her desk. 'I'll let you know where to join me as soon as I can.' She pulled back the door of her private elevator and stepped inside. 'One of these days, I'll murder Hallam!' she exclaimed fiercely. The elevator door closed again, and she pressed the button for the basement carpark.

'I'm sorry, Mrs Wingfield,' Miss Watling said, 'but there was no way we could stop her. Elena is over the school-leaving age, as you know. She packed her cases three days ago. She has gone to stay at Carey Hall with Mr Cavendish and his father. Lord Carey is very frail, I believe. At ninety-three, I suppose that is to be expected. Elena said she was going to help nurse him.'

The headmistress's face expressed a healthy amount of scepticism, reflecting Harriet's own. Whatever Elena was cut out for, it certainly was not nursing. She had always demonstrated a great aversion to the less pleasant functions of the human body.

Miss Watling's study was a bright sun-filled room with apricot-coloured walls and dazzling white paintwork. Long bay windows, with old-fashioned bay window-seats and shutters looked out over a rose garden. A tall cut-glass vase of delphiniums stood on a marquetry table just inside the door. Irrelevantly, Harriet recalled her father quoting Ruskin: 'Blue colour is everlastingly appointed by the Deity to be a source of delight.'

Her eyes returned to the headmistress. 'I should like to

make a telephone call, Miss Watling, to Hollywood. Or I may have to call Mexico City. I'm not sure which. I need to get hold of my husband, and the unit could be on location. Have I your permission?'

'Of course.' Miss Watling rose from behind her desk, with its smother of silver-framed photographs of teachers and pupils, past and present, and indicated the telephone. 'I have an afternoon roll-call in just a few minutes, so I shall leave you alone.'

'Thank you,' Harriet said. 'Please include the cost of the call in my final bill.'

It took her twenty minutes to locate Rollo, who was on set, directing a scene. He was not in the sunniest of tempers at being dragged away to his office, but Harriet cut his protestations short with a succinct account of what had happened.

'So I'm sending Ellie out to the Coast for the next few months, until I decide what's to be done with her. I'll get Bess to meet her in New York and accompany her to LA.'

'For Christ's sake! The kid doesn't even like me!' Rollo objected. 'Got this idea I'm going to make a pass at her or something.'

'And are you?'

'Hell, no! I tried it once,' he admitted frankly, 'and all I got was a flea in my ear and a reminder that I was married to her mother. And you know my motto. Never go back to an empty well. Jeez! You'd have thought she was a cross between St Bernadette and Little Nell.'

'Never mind that.' Harriet once again cut him short. His revelation had in no way disturbed her. The only emotion she felt was one of elation that her daughter had proved so loyal. 'All you have to do this time is play the role of father. Give her the run of Hollywood. Take her to some parties.'

'Hold on,' Rollo said, 'I don't get it. Letting Elena run loose in Tinsel Town is the equivalent of giving smack to a junkie. What's the thinking behind this mad idea?'

'I want to give her an irresistible alternative to staying at

Carey Hall. She'll be well supervised. I trust to Bess to see to that.'

'You're crazy!' Rollo said with conviction.

'Yes, probably,' Harriet agreed. 'Parent-children relationships are always fraught with dangers. One is continually taking risks. I shall be flying out myself in a week or two, but there are things I have to see to first. For a start, I want to find out if this new school near Berne will take Ellie for a year. Just one last year of schooling in an attempt to settle her down. They have, so I'm told, a high success rate with difficult pupils. Meantime, she'll have had a taste of life which should make her feel less of a prisoner.'

Rollo sighed. 'It won't work that way, Harriet, I'm warning you. However, if you've made up your mind –'

'I have.'

'– then, send her on out and I'll do what I can. Only for God's sake mind you do send Bess Holland with her. That dame's worth her weight in gold. Sensible. Level-headed. Good looker, too. OK! OK!' he added, as Harriet drew in her breath. 'Hands off, I promise. She's not my type anyway. But you couldn't have picked a worse time as far as I'm concerned. We're going back to Mexico in a few weeks' time to do some retakes. Look, Harry, gotta go now. Let my secretary have all the details as soon as you can. I'm on the tenth take of a damn difficult scene.'

'Film not going well?' Harriet enquired with a certain amount of malice.

'So, so.' Rollo sounded tired. 'The real trouble is Ramón Perez. He's playing the grandfather. Strange though it may sound, he's too good an actor. Makes the film top-heavy, if you see what I mean. And the annoying thing is I had to fight to get him. Powers that be wanted Paul Newman for the part.'

'Who's Ramón Perez?'

'A Mexican actor. Big star over the border, but not well known outside Mexico. I saw him about ten years ago, in Mexico City, in Lorca's *Blood Wedding*. He must have been in his early fifties then. When I started to plan this film, I knew he was the man I wanted for Manuel de León. But, as I say, now I've got him I don't quite know what to do about him. He's too heavyweight for the rest of the cast.'

'What's his English like? Fairly fluent?'

'Like a native.' Harriet heard Rollo laugh, but he did not elucidate and she was too anxious to finish the conversation to enquire the reason.

She said: 'I'll let your secretary know when to expect Elena and Bess. Be seeing you. Take care.'

She hung up and went in search of Miss Watling, to make her farewells. The headmistress, she thought, seemed relieved to see her go.

'Elena's taken all her clothes with her to Carey Hall,' Miss Watling told her. 'There's nothing left.'

Harriet nodded and held out her hand. 'I'm sorry things have had to end like this. Send your account for this term's fees to my London office as usual. They'll pass it on. Goodbye.'

'Goodbye, Mrs Wingfield, and good luck.'

The headmistress's expression implied that she would need it.

43

There was no scene, thanks to Harriet's foresight. The promise of a trip to Hollywood immediately overcame any reluctance on Elena's part to leave Carey Hall. She might be on the threshold of womanhood, Harriet reflected, but in some ways her daughter was still very much a child; a child eagerly raiding the candy-jar. Offer her a bigger and gaudier sweetmeat than she already had, and she would at once drop the one that she was holding.

To make matters even easier, Hallam had gone up to London for the day. By the time he returned, later that same evening, Elena was forty miles away in Winterbourn Green.

Harriet had telephoned ahead to the MacGregors, who, already forewarned by Bess, were waiting to greet them, with supper in the oven. Bill ate with the housekeeper and her husband in the kitchen, so there was plenty of time for Harriet and Elena to talk. It was not until the meal was almost finished, however, that Harriet, pushing away her empty plate and sipping her coffee, said coldly: 'Well, Ellie? I'm waiting to hear your explanation.'

Elena gave her mother a sideways glance. 'What sort of an explanation?'

'Oh, for God's sake!' Harriet felt her temper rising. 'An explanation, first and foremost, about your decision to leave Aston Court without my permission and take up residence at Carey Hall.'

Elena pouted and shrugged, knowing that she was in the wrong, and consequently on the defensive.

'I was bored at that place. All girls. It was less fun than at the Académie. At least there were boys there. Not that I like boys much. Older men are much more amusing.'

'How did you meet Hallam?' Harriet asked, ignoring the rider. But she had already guessed the answer.

'Piers introduced us. I went to Oxford a couple of times, to visit him. I hitched lifts in cars. And you needn't look so disapproving, Mamma. I bet you did the same sort of thing when you were my age.'

'Maybe.' Harriet put down her cup, remembering. 'Yes, all right, I did. But things weren't the same in those days, in spite of the war. There weren't so many horrific cases of rape and kidnap as there are now. And I wasn't an heiress. Do you realize, in cash terms, just how valuable you are?'

'Oh, yes,' Elena answered calmly. 'But none of the drivers who gave me a lift knew anything about me.'

'But someone could have discovered about this habit of yours,' Harriet was beginning, then stopped. It was only the elderly who lived with a constant sense of danger. 'Tell me what happened with Hallam,' she commanded abruptly.

The sunshine of the afternoon had vanished, to be replaced by grey skies and a rising wind. It reminded Harriet of so many June evenings of childhood, when she had stared out of this self-same window, in what had then been her father's study, at the miseries of an English summer; a world which seemed to be nothing but greens and greys and browns, all colour draining away into the damp-smelling earth. And yet, tomorrow, it could all be so different: hot white roads, bees blundering from flower to flower, harebells, silver grasses, dandelion and thistle seeds, the chatter of lawnmowers, tangles of wild roses in the hedges. It was that constant change, that never-ending variety, that tugged at her heart-strings and kept calling her home, wherever she happened to be in the world.

God! she thought. I'm getting sentimental. Another sign of advancing years. She raised her eyebrows at Elena. 'Well?' she prompted.

Elena drank her coffee and pushed her cup forward to be refilled.

'Nothing happened with Hallam,' she answered guardedly. 'I suppose you don't like him or you wouldn't have divorced him, but he was kind to me. He understood about me being bored at school. He offered to take me to London and show me the sights.' Elena's tone changed to one of accusation. 'I'd never been to London before I went with Hallam.'

'London's not the centre of the universe,' Harriet retorted drily, picking up the coffee-pot. 'And you have your entire life in front of you. You've plenty of time to do everything that you want. Besides, I'd hardly call an evening at Annabelle's "seeing the sights".' She reflected for a moment, before honesty forced her to admit: 'I don't know, though. I suppose in many ways it could be a damn sight more instructive than the British Museum.' Elena giggled, sensing a lightening of the atmosphere, and Harriet went on quickly: 'That doesn't mean that I approve. You're not old enough to visit night-clubs. And certainly not under the auspices of Hallam Cavendish.' She handed back the refilled cup. 'He may be Piers's father, Ellie, but he is not a nice man.'

She had expected her daughter to argue the point but, to her surprise, Elena said quietly: 'No. I'd begun to realize that for myself.' She saw her mother's horrified questioning look and hurriedly shook her head. 'Oh, he didn't try anything on. Nothing of that sort. Told me to look on him as a father.' She stifled another giggle. 'But these last few days, since I went to stay at Carey Hall, I could see that he wasn't really interested in me. Not as a person. I was just someone he was using to get at you. If you hadn't turned up when you did, I'd have left soon anyway. Although I quite liked the Viscount. He's quite simple now, you know. Like a little child. Hallam says he won't last much longer.'

Harriet got up to switch on the lights, then crossed the room to draw the curtains. She paused for a moment, staring out into the windswept garden. She must not worry so much about Elena. The child had her head screwed on the right way, as Mrs Wicks used to be fond of remarking. She pulled together the long swaths of pale green linen and turned back into the room. She loved Elena and was happy that they seemed to have reached some sort of understanding. She sat down again, beginning to feel more relaxed.

A few minutes later, the mood was shattered. An unguarded reference by Harriet to the new school in Switzerland was met with incredulous anger.

'You're not sending me back to school again?' Elena jerked upright in her chair, her eyes bright with tears. 'You don't mean it! You can't! I thought I'd finished with all that nonsense!'

'One more year,' Harriet said firmly. 'By the time you leave, at the end of next summer, you'll still only be eighteen.'

'Nearly nineteen!' Elena choked over her words. 'I won't be sent back to school again! I won't!'

'You'll do as you're told,' Harriet replied icily. 'I'm not open to argument. You're going to have a wonderful three months in LA with Rollo –'

'I hate Rollo!'

Harriet continued as though Elena had not spoken: 'Then one last year at Berne, if I can persuade Herr München and his wife to accept you.'

'Well, I hope you can't. I hope they say no!' Elena shouted. 'You didn't stay at school. You told me. You left when you were only sixteen.'

'The circumstances were different,' Harriet snapped. But were they really? She had overruled her father and done what she wanted. Now she refused to allow her daughter the same freedom. But there had been a war on and not much money. . . Besides, she had been merely Harriet Chance of the Vicarage, Winterbourn Green, not Elena Georgiadis, one of the richest young women in the world. She suddenly felt very tired; tired and stubborn. 'You are going to Berne, Ellie,' she said, 'if it can possibly be arranged. You'll just have to make up your mind to the fact. I'm sorry, but there it is.'

Elena burst into noisy tears and fled from the room.

Elena travelled to America two days later, in the company of Dick Norris and Frank Bryan, both of whom had business in the States.

'Don't stand any nonsense,' Harriet warned them. 'Bess Holland will meet Ellie in New York and accompany her to LA, where Rollo, I trust, is prepared to take over.'

'She'll be OK with me,' Melanie Norris said. She was going with her husband on this trip and, although Harriet at first thought her statement over-optimistic, it became apparent long before they boarded the plane that Elena had taken an immediate liking to the fluffy, seemingly empty-headed blonde.

But she was still not speaking to her mother. The last forty-eight hours had passed mainly in frozen silence on Elena's part, addressing and answering Harriet only in monosyllables. Harriet was just thankful that her daughter had not decamped back to Carey Hall in a fit of pique. She congratulated herself once more on a diversionary plan whose appeal overrode all others in Elena's mind. Elena was even prepared to tolerate Rollo if it meant a few months among the fleshpots of Hollywood.

On her return to the Old Vicarage from Heathrow, Harriet found a pile of mail awaiting her on the hall table. She picked it up with a sigh. She missed Bess, not just for her quiet efficiency – the opened envelopes, the letters sorted and graded, ready for attention – but also for herself. She liked having Bess around. She would be more than pleased to see her secretary again when she flew out to LA later in the month. But for now there was work to be done at the Chance Corporation headquarters in London. Harriet had already told the MacGregors that she would be leaving for Bruton Street the following morning. She supposed it would have made more sense to go directly from the airport, but she wanted twenty-four hours on her own in Winterbourn Green, to unwind and to visit Philip and Stella Gresham at the vicarage. She wanted some time, too, to stand quietly by her father's grave and think about him; some time in which to unburden herself, if possible, of a little of the guilt she still felt for his death.

Harriet carried her letters into what, in the vicarage's heyday, had been the housekeeper's room, and which, in her childhood, had been used as a store for every damaged and discarded household item. 'The glory-hole', her father had called it, and used to protest that he dreaded opening the door because of the chaos inside. Now Harriet had transformed it into a light and airy study, with eggshell-blue walls and cream paintwork. A Sheraton desk, an early nineteenth-century Canterbury music-stand, used as a magazine-rack, a 'Gothic' bookstand by George Smith and a beautiful little Queen Anne bureau stood cheek by jowl with a green metal filing-cabinet and a wheel-back chair, purchased, among other things, at a local auction. One wall sported a set of delicate watercolours, while another was decorated with a large, heavily framed, secondhand print of a Bellotto painting of the Grand Canal. Edmund Howard would unerringly have stigmatized the room a mess: Harriet was perfectly happy with it.

She drew the wheel-back chair to the desk and began to slit open the envelopes. Two of the letters referred to business and had been sent on from New York by Bess. They were not urgent – all urgent business was dealt with daily by telephone – and Harriet laid them aside. There was a note from Julia, enclosing a drawing done for Harriet by her younger grandson, which made her laugh, and the expected bill from Aston Court for a term's school fees and various other expenses incurred by Elena.

The last envelope in the pile bore Carlin Boyce's writing and had been posted in Waterford over two weeks earlier, reaching her eventually by way of New York.

When Harriet had finished reading the contents, she swore.

'Damn and blast!' she said out loud, addressing the Bellotto.

Carlin had been offered a job in Australia and intended to accept.

'I realize this will come as a shock to you,' he wrote apologetically, 'but I feel in need of a change. And a challenge. Perhaps that, most of all. The Malachi runs like clockwork, and you have always given me a free hand. Only the best bloodstock. No interference. Unlimited money. It sounds like a trainer's dream, and it is – if only I didn't feel this sudden urge to build up something from nothing. I shall, of course, wait until Ascot is over before giving you a firm date for my resignation. I don't intend leaving you in the lurch, and shall remain until you have found another trainer, but I don't think you'll have any trouble on that score.'

Harriet sat staring at the sheet of pale blue notepaper, covered with the big round characters so distinctively Carlin's. She suspected that his unrequited passion for Bess Holland had something to do with this sudden urge to up sticks and go to the other side of the world, but he gave no hint of it in the letter. Still cursing under her breath, Harriet reached for the telephone and dialled her housekeeper at Bruton Street, to say that she would be staying longer than the few days originally intended.

'I'll be there until after Ascot,' she told Mrs Nolan, who received the information in her usual unruffled fashion. 'Bill Brereton and Madge are with me, so please make sure their rooms are ready as well.'

She would have to see Carlin and try reasoning with him, but she felt uneasily that it would do no good. He had so obviously made up his mind.

Her father's grave was in the far corner of the churchyard, next to her mother's; both carefully tended by one of the village boys, who, on Harriet's instructions, had been

426

hired by Philip Gresham to keep them tidy. A plain head-stone bore the even plainer legend: HILARY WILLIAM CHANCE, 1900–1947. At the time of Hilary's death, Gardiner, Son & Phipps had seen to its purchase and erection. Harriet recalled Athelstan Phipps telephoning her in New York to know if she wanted a text of some kind as well as the name and dates.

'Some reference, perhaps,' the solicitor had suggested delicately, 'to your father having been received at last into eternal rest.'

'No, thank you, Mr Phipps,' she had answered firmly. 'I'm not sure I believe in an afterlife.'

Mr Phipps had been shocked. Such heresy from a vicar's daughter!

Did she believe any more now than she had done then? she wondered, glancing up at the church spire, topped by its ancient weathercock, now green with age. And, if not, what did she believe in?

The answer, of course, was the same as it had always been: she believed in herself, in her right to make her own way in the world, unencumbered by the burdens of sex or class. Abraham Lincoln's 'equal chance'; John Ball and Wat Tyler's 'communistic law'. But why, then, did she continue to feel that she had failed? Because her father, her husbands, her children had all, to a greater or lesser degree, been victims of her determination to fight her way to the top of an essentially male-dominated world?

Harriet turned and made her way slowly towards the Old Vicarage. She was almost at the wicket gate which connected the graveyard with the garden, when a voice behind her said: 'Hello, Harriet. How are you?'

It was Susan Norman, standing beside one of the graves, and which Harriet saw from the headstone was Mrs Wyatt's. Susan's hair was grey now, and she wore a cheap print summer frock, with a pair of Marks & Spencer sandals. Her face and arms were already tanned, although the English summer had, so far, not been good. She looked healthy and quietly contented.

'Susan!' Harriet smiled, uncomfortably conscious of her beautifully cut and tinted hair, her pale beige Roland Klein slacks and deeper beige Jan Van Velden blouse. Diamonds gleamed in the lobes of her ears and on her fingers. She suddenly felt expensively overdressed. 'I . . . I didn't realize your mother was dead. I'm sorry.'

'Why should you realize it? You're not here that often, and I don't suppose parochial gossip holds any charms for you anyway. Mum died the winter before last.'

'I'm sorry,' Harriet repeated, but the sentiment sounded phoney, even to her own ears. She made no attempt to rectify matters. 'She made the most delicious shortbread I've ever tasted. I remember, on baking days, always finding an excuse to call at your house on our way home from school.'

Susan smiled faintly. She had been planting some clumps of thrift and pinks on top of the grave. Her hands were covered with earth, and she rubbed them self-consciously down the sides of her skirt. She bent to pick up her discarded trowel and fork.

'That was a long time ago,' she said. 'We're both grandmothers now.'

But that was in another country, and besides, the wench is dead.

And that girl *was* as good as dead, Harriet thought sadly. That Harriet Chance, standing with Susan in the Wyatts' steamy kitchen, watching Mrs Wyatt lift the trays of cakes and shortbread out of the oven, had vanished for ever. There was no going back; only forward. It was one of life's most difficult lessons. She and Susan had once been bosom friends, sharing all their secrets. Now they were strangers.

'You and Leslie must come and have dinner at the Old Vicarage next time I'm here,' Harriet said, and Susan nodded.

'That would be lovely.'

But they both knew that Harriet would not ask, and that Susan would not accept if she did.

'Goodbye, then.' Harriet unlatched the gate and stepped inside the vicarage garden.

428

The ghosts of two young girls, school satchels on their backs, school berets stuffed into mackintosh pockets, laughed and jostled their way through that self-same gate, then vanished for ever.

'Goodbye, Harriet,' Susan Norman said, and stooped once more to her planting.

Bess and Elena spent a night in the New York flat before flying on to Los Angeles the following day.

From the start, Bess could see that her charge was in one of her moods and was prepared to be difficult. She did her best to be understanding without probing too deeply into the cause of Elena's simmering resentment. Remembering her own experience with a too prying mother, Bess preferred to wait a while, hoping that Elena might eventually confide in her, rather than demand an immediate explanation of what was wrong. Instead, she made light conversation about clothes and films and who they were likely to meet once they arrived in Hollywood.

In some ways, she was glad of the excuse not to burden herself with Harriet and Elena's problems: she was finding the chairmanship of the Chance Foundation policy committee more of a strain than she had anticipated. It was all very well for Harriet to say that the actual meetings only took place two or three times a year. This was true enough, but there was a great deal of behind-the-scenes work to be got through if all Harriet's wishes and ideas were to be properly implemented. And Harriet never dreamed of decreasing Bess's normal workload to allow her to cope. And here she was now, saddled with the job of chaperoning the wayward Elena.

Ah, well! She knew she was capable of managing it all, and so did Harriet. That was the trouble. She smiled at Elena across the dining-room table.

'What do you say we go to the movies?' she asked. 'That Shirley Maclaine film is showing. *Terms of Endearment*.'

429

44

'I suppose more money wouldn't tempt you?' Harriet asked wistfully.

Carlin Boyce shook his head.

'I'm afraid not. Look, Harriet, I really have made up my mind to go. I've always liked the idea of Australia. Now is my chance.'

It was Ladies' Day at Ascot; a day when people paid as much attention to fashion as to the horses. Outside Harriet's box, women paraded up and down in a fantastic array of hats and costumes, of every conceivable style and shade. Harriet herself wore a Gina Fratini dress in pale lilac silk, with grey accessories. She hated lilac and wondered what impulse had made her buy it. Was it a subconscious urge for mourning, or half-mourning, because she felt sad at Carlin's departure? Who could tell? Unlikely, she would have thought; but he had been her trainer for eighteen years, and she would miss him. Where else was she going to find anyone half as reliable, half as devoted to her interests, half as willing to take responsibility for producing winners in the face of her avowed uninterest?

Something of the sort seemed to be exercising his mind as well, as they watched the royal procession of carriages drive along the course. He said: 'I've been putting out feelers, trying to find someone suitable as my replacement. I thought I'd ask Edmund Howard if he knows of anyone. I'll be seeing him later this afternoon.'

Harriet turned her head sharply. 'Edmund's here?'

'And Isabelle.' Carlin hesitated, then added, avoiding

430

her eyes: 'They seem very happy together. Happier than I've ever seen them. Their business is booming. They're among the leading breeders in Europe, as you know. And now they're exporting to the US.'

Harriet smiled and laid a hand on her trainer's arm.

'It's all right, Carlin. I get the picture. Consult Edmund by all means. He might know of someone who would do. But I'd much rather you changed your mind and stayed.'

Carlin shook his head resolutely. 'I'm sorry, Harriet.'

She shrugged and withdrew her hand from his arm. 'Oh, well! If you won't, you won't. I can't stop you going, I suppose.'

'You could,' he answered, half to himself, 'if you were in a position to promise me the one thing I want above all others.'

'Marriage to Bess Holland?'

'Marriage to Bess.'

'I'm sorry, Carlin.' It was Harriet's turn to express regret. 'I can't even hold out any hope. Bess seems determined never to marry again.'

'Do you know why?'

Harriet shook her head. 'Bess has never really talked to me about it. She was very young, and I think that marrying Mark Skells was simply a way of escaping from home. She's very fond of her parents, but doesn't have a lot in common with either of them. And she's extremely ambitious. She wouldn't have found domesticity any substitute for a career, and of course some men don't like that. Perhaps Mark Skells didn't. I don't know.'

Carlin said sadly: 'It's ridiculous to love someone for so long with no hope of that love being returned, and with so little for it to feed on. I don't suppose Bess and I have been together in the same room more than a couple of dozen times in all the years that I've known her.'

Harriet shook her head again. 'It's not ridiculous at all. It's something you simply can't help. I understand.'

'Yes,' Carlin said slowly. 'I thought that perhaps you did.'

Harriet sighed. 'I accept your resignation, although I

431

don't mind telling you that I came here today with the express intention of making you change your mind. However, I realize now that it would be the height of selfishness on my part. I'll find someone to replace you, even though I know it won't be easy.' She consulted her race-card. 'Our race is the one after next, I see. I'll come with you to the saddling-up enclosure.'

So she watched while Joyous Morning, her three-year-old filly, was saddled and mounted, and while Carlin gave the jockey some last-minute instructions. She was still not at ease, even after all these years, among horses and the racing fraternity, and she wondered if now was not a golden opportunity to sell up. Yet, somehow, she could not bring herself to get rid of the stables. They had been Spiros' present to celebrate the birth of their child. Selling Malachi would, in some obscure way, be like repudiating her difficult, wayward, headstrong daughter.

Joyous Morning won her race by a length and a half, and as Harriet led her into the Winners' Enclosure a voice said: 'Congratulations, Harriet.'

Edmund was standing beside her, Isabelle – a very smart Isabelle in an apricot-coloured suit that, to Harriet's experienced eye, said Belville Sassoon – clinging to his arm.

'Thank you,' Harriet replied coolly. Their last meeting at Malachi, when they had quarrelled so bitterly, was in everyone's mind. Harriet saw Isabelle's eyelashes flutter nervously. She smiled suddenly, warm and expansive. 'You should congratulate Carlin, not me. I'm still totally ignorant of horses and all their ways.'

'A leg at each corner,' Edmund murmured, and his face relaxed into a grin.

And then they were all laughing. After a moment, Harriet exclaimed ruefully: 'I don't know what I'm so happy about! You've heard that Carlin's leaving me after all this time?'

Edmund nodded. 'Have tea with us and we'll discuss it. Maybe I can come up with one or two names.'

Harriet glanced enquiringly at her trainer, who raised his eyebrows in agreement.

'Thank you,' she said. 'We'd like that.'

Isabelle released her husband's arm. 'You three go on. I'm rather cold and I've left my fur stole in the car. I'll go and get it.'

'I'll come with you,' Edmund said. He explained: 'Belle broke her ankle a couple of months back, and it's still a bit weak. Especially,' he added, with a disparaging glance at his wife's flimsy, extremely high-heeled shoes, 'as today she's walking on stilts.'

Harriet laughed. 'We'll all come,' she said. 'I could do with the exercise.' And because her heels were only minimally lower than Isabelle's she accepted Carlin Boyce's gallantly proffered arm.

Edmund's dark green Peugeot estate wagon was parked on the end of a row, next to a brand-new bright-red Aston Martin. As they approached, a man got out of the latter. Harriet recognized him at once.

It was Hallam.

Harriet wasted no breath on preliminaries, but waded straight in.

'I want a word with you, Hallam! What the bloody hell do you mean by persuading my daughter to leave school, to go to live with you and that father of yours at Carey Hall? And taking her to nightclubs! And getting her name in the papers! What did you think you were doing?' Before he could reply, she went on: 'You do that once more – you try to get at me through Elena – and I'll find some way of stopping your allowance! So help me, I will, if it means dragging you through every court in the kingdom! If it costs a fortune in lawyers' fees! I don't care if Carey Hall falls to pieces. I don't give a damn if Piers has no inheritance from you! I'll buy him something better than that mouldering old pile. Don't you ever dare approach my daughter again!'

While she was speaking, Hallam's features had set in a

433

look of rigid disdain. Only a small vein, throbbing high up, under the thin skin of his forehead, revealed his anger at this humiliatingly public dressing-down.

'My dear Harriet,' he sneered, when finally she paused to draw breath, 'I was introduced to your precious ewe-lamb under the most respectable of circumstances, as I'm sure you know. We both happened to be visiting Piers at Oxford, and he, very naturally, made us known to one another. If you can't control your own daughter, that's not my fault. If you're for ever gallivanting all over the world, and consequently have no time for your children, again, I'm not to blame. Elena struck me as a young girl in need of a little parental affection and care. I simply provided what was lacking.'

'By taking her to Annabelle's?'

'She needed some fun, as you would have realized for yourself if you'd ever bothered to talk to her, instead of dumping her in boarding-schools like an unwanted parcel. All right for boys. Necessary in fact. But not a suitable life for girls.'

'Rubbish!' Harriet snapped. 'And you don't really believe in that old-fashioned claptrap. You just hoped to ingratiate yourself and wheedle some money out of her. I know you, Hallam.'

Hallam raised his thin eyebrows until they almost merged with his greying hair.

'I wasn't aware that Elena had any money of her own at present.'

'She gets a very generous allowance, and it's only just over three years before she inherits her father's millions. You always did lay your evil little schemes well in advance. You're a bastard, Hallam! An absolute bastard!'

Harriet had not bothered to lower her voice. Several people, making for their cars and an early homeward journey, had become interested spectators of the scene, a fact of which Hallam was only too well aware. He was looking murderous, and both Edmund and Carlin took an involuntary step forward to protect Harriet, standing one

434

on either side of her. Until that moment, Hallam's attention had been focused on his ex-wife, and the identity of her companions had not really sunk in. Now the sight of Edmund acted like a red rag to a bull.

'Oh, it's you, is it?' he spat. 'I might have guessed it!' His furious gaze returned to Harriet. 'Still got your lap-dog in tow, I see. Always fancied him, haven't you? Does your present husband know? I've never been able to fathom what it is about our wild Irish bog-man that you find so attractive. Not really good-looking, is he? Not as handsome as I am. Not got the money of Spiros Georgiadis, or the glamour of a Hollywood director. So it must come down to sex. Good in bed, is he? Big? Plenty of cock? Is that it?'

Edmund had hit him a punishing right to the chin, which sent Hallam staggering back against the Peugeot's bonnet, before the others had time to divine his intention. Isabelle ran forward and grabbed her husband's arm.

'No, Edmund! Not again!' She muttered under her breath: 'For God's sake! He could sue you for common assault!'

Harriet and Carlin added their entreaties to hers, and reluctantly Edmund lowered his arm. Hallam, looking white and very sick, was leaning against the estate wagon, fingering his rapidly swelling jaw. His eyes were narrowed, and he was breathing heavily. A group of onlookers had gathered on the other side of the lane which ran between the double rank of cars. One of them gave a high-pitched nervous giggle. Hallam's thin face was suddenly suffused with colour.

'I'll get you, Howard,' he whispered viciously. 'I'm not one of your mates in the IRA to be treated like this. Beat each other up regularly, from all I can gather. Kneecapping and other disgusting practices. You keep your hands off me.'

Harriet saw Isabelle glance at her husband with a puzzled frown, and she stepped in quickly to divert Hallam's attention.

'I don't think you're in any position to threaten anyone,'

she told him hotly. 'I could lay charges against you for taking my seventeen-year-old daughter to nightclubs without my permission. And other things. I'd go home, if I were you, and bathe that chin of yours. It looks as though it's going to be very nasty.' She turned to Edmund. 'Get Isabelle's stole and let's go. I think we could all do with that cup of tea you mentioned.'

Edmund nodded and unlocked the Peugeot. A few moments later, the four of them were walking back towards the course, Isabelle still shivering slightly, in spite of the fur draped round her shoulders. As they reached the carpark entrance, the Aston Martin drew up beside them. Hallam lowered the window and leaned out.

'I'll get you for this, Howard,' he said viciously. 'It's about time you had your comeuppance. You've been asking for it for years.'

When he had driven on, Isabelle asked in a troubled voice: 'Could he really do anything to you, Edmund? Or is it just talk?'

'Just talk,' Edmund assured her cheerfully, and Harriet hastened to support him.

There was no evidence now, that she knew of, linking Edmund with his former friends in the IRA. Spiros had destroyed it. But, she reflected uneasily, Spiros had not destroyed Hallam's links with Albie and Charlie King and the criminal world that they inhabited; a world in which Spiros himself had been, to some degree, at home. Did Hallam still maintain those links, in spite of the King brothers betraying him to Spiros? Knowing him, she guessed that he probably did.

She felt uneasy for the rest of the afternoon, paying only scant attention to Carlin and Edmund's discussion, over tea, of possible candidates for the post of Malachi's trainer. It was not until she realized that her abstraction was making Isabelle unduly anxious that she made an effort to forget her fears and join in.

But she found maintaining her part in the conversation extremely trying, and by the time she arrived back in

Bruton Street, later that same evening, she was worn out and longing for bed.

While Bill garaged the car, Harriet rode up in the lift, thankfully removing her hat and shaking out her hair. There was a mirror on the back wall, and she scrutinized her reflection carefully. Not bad, she supposed, for fifty-eight. Some of it was illusion, of course: capped teeth; tinted hair; cleverly applied, very expensive make-up. But she had worn well in spite of her hectic and eventful life; better than Susan Norman.

She wondered idly why Susan and Leslie had married. She would not have thought, looking back to her youth, that they had anything in common. Susan was always such a homebody, while Leslie had nurtured pretensions and ambitions. She supposed the answer was chance, which had thrown them together at a time of life when they were both looking for partners; ready to settle down. But, then, chance played such a large part in everyone's life. Take this afternoon, for instance, and the chance which had taken them to the carpark at the precise moment when Hallam had arrived. If she had not come face to face with him like that, she would not have lost her temper and Edmund would not have knocked him down . . .

She must stop worrying about it. Hallam had been understandably furious and had made threats which he would not dream of carrying out when his temper had cooled. She was being foolish and unnecessarily nervous, because she felt responsible for the incident. If she had wanted to tackle Hallam on the subject of Elena, she should have picked a less public place. She had intended to let it go: Elena had come to no obvious harm, and Hallam seemed to have conducted himself towards her reasonably well. But the sight of him and that expensive new car, which he had undoubtedly bought with her hard-earned money from the over-generous annual allowance which she made him, had angered her, and she had provoked a scene.

The lift came to halt on the top floor, and Harriet got out.

The housekeeper had heard its whine and came to meet her at the flat's front door.

'Oh, Mrs Wingfield!' she exclaimed thankfully. 'There you are! Mr Wingfield called over an hour ago and said you were to ring him as soon as you came in. Terribly urgent, it sounded. He made me promise to tell you the moment you arrived.'

Harriet sighed. 'Thank you, Mrs Nolan. I'll do it right away. Where was he calling from?'

'The house in Bel Air. Said he'd be sitting right beside the phone until you rang.'

Harriet nodded and went into her bedroom, calling over her shoulder: 'Make me some tea, Mrs Nolan, please. I'm parched. And Bill will be up any minute. I'm sure he'd appreciate a cup.'

Madge was laying out one of Harriet's evening frocks, but she waved her away and, lifting the receiver, dialled the Bel Air number.

At the back of her mind, she knew it was to do with Elena, but she suppressed the thought, concentrating on trivialities, like the tea; telling herself that of course it was nothing, just Rollo panicking, as he was apt to do about almost everything.

The telephone only rang once before it was snatched from its cradle with an urgency which made the line rattle.

'Hello? Harriet?' It was her husband's voice, taut with anxiety and something closely akin to real fear.

'Yes.' She tried to sound calm. 'It's me. What's the matter, Rollo?'

'It's Elena. She's run away.'

Terror began to stir in the pit of Harriet's stomach. She took refuge in repetition, staving off the evil moment of truth.

'What do you mean, she's run away?'

'For *Chrissake*!' The blasphemy exploded in her right ear with the force of a gunshot. 'What I say! Gone, vamoosed, slung her hook! *Eloped* might be a more appropriate description.'

'Eloped?' Once again Harriet found herself repeating his words as if, by doing so, she could render them harmless. But it was no good, and she knew it. In a few moments, she was going to have to hear the worst. She asked: 'Do you mean she's run away with some man?'

'Not with, but *to*! I did warn you what a mad idea it was to send her out here.' Rollo was fairly screaming down the phone.

There was a pause while he took a grip on himself. Harriet could hear him speaking to someone else, in the same room, but his head was turned away from the receiver and she was unable to catch the words. Then she heard Bess's voice, the normally unemotional tones laced with panic, and her own fear increased proportionately. If Bess was afraid, then there was really something to be nervous about. Bess never lost her head. She was the rock on whom, more and more, Harriet was learning to depend.

She shouted into the mouthpiece: 'Bess! Rollo! What's going on? Will one of you please answer me! What, in hell's name, have you let Ellie do?'

'Be quiet, Harriet.' Rollo was speaking again, this time with more restraint. 'It's no good you blaming me or Bess Holland. Neither of us had any idea that this was going to happen.'

'Who has she run away to, and where?' Harriet asked, her own voice rising. 'Some penniless young starlet, I suppose.'

'That's just it!' Rollo exclaimed, frustration in his tone. 'He's neither penniless nor a boy. In fact, he's damn near old enough to be her grandfather. It's the Mexican I told you about. Ramón Perez!'

45

Harriet left London on the first available flight. By the time she reached New York, where Bess Holland was waiting to meet her, the world's press had got wind of the story. The moment she set foot in Kennedy airport, she was besieged by reporters.

'Is it true, Mrs Wingfield, that this Mexican is over sixty?'

'Harriet! Look this way! Just one picture of you looking worried. Please, Harriet!'

'Did she go of her own free will or has she been kidnapped?'

'Is it true that Elena's agreed to make over all her money to this Ramón Perez as soon as she comes of age?'

'Was she raped?'

'Is she expecting a baby?'

'Harriet . . .!'

'Mrs Wingfield!'

'Just one more picture!'

'Please!'

Harriet remained tight-lipped while Bess and Bill Brereton hustled her and Madge Shelton through Customs and out on to the tarmac, where one of the Georgiadis jets was waiting.

Once aboard, Harriet sank thankfully into a seat and demanded a stiff whisky and water.

'Now,' she said grimly, as the take-off was smoothly accomplished, 'tell me what happened.'

Bess sat opposite her. There were dark rings under her eyes, as though she had not slept.

'There's really so little to tell.' The secretary rubbed her forehead with the back of her hand. 'Elena seemed happy enough during the short time we've been in Hollywood. She doesn't like Rollo, but she didn't object when he squired her to parties, and I was always on hand to see he didn't get . . . well, fresh.'

Harriet nodded. She had no illusions about her husband, one of the reasons why she had insisted that Bess play chaperon.

'Go on,' she said.

Bess grimaced. 'As I say, Ellie seemed happy enough. Although. . .' She hesitated, searching for words, before continuing: 'She did appear edgy at times. Something was bugging her. I did a bit of probing, hoping to discover what was wrong, but she kept saying she was fine and thoroughly enjoying herself. So, in the end, I decided it must be my imagination.'

'No,' Harriet told her wearily, 'it wasn't. Ellie doesn't want to go back to school, and I've said she must. Just for another year. I've managed to persuade Herr München and his wife to take her. Running away is Ellie's way of showing her defiance.'

'A clash of wills,' Bess Holland murmured, and Harriet smiled.

'I'm afraid so. But I shall win. It's time Elena realized that she has responsibilities – to herself and to the company which Spiros built up out of nothing. I don't want her turning into nothing but a jet-setting playgirl, and her education has already been far too scrappy, thanks to her father and his ridiculous will. Tell me about this Ramón Perez. What's he like? A fortune-hunter?'

'I wouldn't have said so. Elena and I met him on a number of occasions: twice on the set, when Rollo took us to the studios to watch him filming, and three times at parties. The odd thing is,' Bess continued, furrowing her brow, 'that I liked him. I liked him a lot. He's very charming.'

'Latin men usually are,' Harriet remarked caustically. 'They can turn the charm on and off like a tap.'

'Ah! But Ramón Perez isn't really Mexican,' Bess said. 'Not by birth. He's naturalized. He was born in New York. Went to Mexico as a young man and stayed there. Did a number of jobs, including ranching, before he took up acting. He kept Ellie and me amused at one of the more boring parties with stories about his past. But I shouldn't have guessed for a moment that he was interested in Ellie, except in a very avuncular sort of way. In fact' – Bess smiled for the first time since meeting Harriet at the airport – 'I'd have sworn he preferred me.'

Harriet finished her whisky and set down her empty glass.

'My poor deluded Bess,' she said, 'if it's looks, poise and maturity against unlimited wealth, money will always win hands down. So what else did Ellie get up to with this pseudo-Mexican, apart from the Othello and Desdemona act?'

Madge Shelton passed through on her way to the jet's sleeping-quarters, to unpack and hang up some of the more delicate of Harriet's dresses, until such time as they reached Los Angeles. Bill Brereton's laughter sounded from the cockpit, where he was exchanging a joke with the pilot. Whatever the emergency, Harriet reflected, life went on.

'Nothing really,' Bess answered. 'That's just it. That's what is so puzzling. As far as I could see, he didn't flirt with her, or make a play for her. He treated her as if she were his daughter. Even Rollo said he thought it was rather sweet.'

'He did, did he?' Harriet snorted. 'It seems to me that you two were well and truly hoodwinked. When exactly did they leave? Rollo told me Elena left a note to say she was joining Ramón Perez in Mexico City.'

'That's right. He has an apartment there, in the Avenida Juárez. He left LA last Tuesday, because his part in the film was finished, except for a couple of retakes, which had to be done on location in Mexico anyway. Rollo gave a little farewell party for him on the lot, and that was it.

442

Elena seemed perfectly natural with Ramón. As far as I could tell, he was just a nice elderly man she had grown rather fond of. She didn't find any difficulty in saying goodbye.'

'She wasn't saying goodbye, was she?' Harriet reminded her secretary tersely. 'She was planning to fly out and join him within a very few days. When did you discover she'd gone?'

'Yesterday morning, when she didn't come down to breakfast. I went upstairs to see what was wrong, but she wasn't there. Just this note on her pillow. When I made enquiries, one of the boys who works in the garden said he'd seen her about six o'clock, leaving the garage, driving Rollo's Porsche. I got in touch with Rollo at the studios, and he telephoned the airport police. The Porsche was found in the parking-lot, and one of the booking clerks remembered Elena buying a ticket for the early flight to Mexico City. Then Rollo contacted you. Now you know it all. Or at least as much as we do.'

Harriet sat in silence for a moment or two. Then she asked: 'Do I still detect a favourable bias on your part towards Ramón Perez?'

Bess looked guilty. 'Yes, I'm afraid you do. There was a kind of rapport between us from our very first meeting, which I find it difficult to explain. I don't often take to complete strangers, but he was the exception which proves the rule. Whatever that may, or may not, mean.'

'And he's nearer your age.'

Bess was indignant. 'Have a heart! He's over sixty! A very personable over-sixty, I admit, but I'm only thirty-nine, when all's said and done.'

'Nearly forty,' Harriet reminded her with a touch of malice. 'And you do seem smitten with this fortune-hunter.'

'I just liked him, that was all,' Bess disclaimed angrily, and with a heightened colour. 'I'm just sorry things have turned out this way.'

Harriet leaned forward to pat Bess's hand. 'Forgive me,'

she said. 'I shouldn't be taking my bad temper out on you. Nor on Rollo. It's Ellie I'm mad at, because I know damn well why she's done it. She's no more in love with Ramón Perez, or whatever his real name is, than I am. She's just decided she's going to teach me a lesson.'

Bess looked alarmed. 'You don't think she'll go and marry him out of spite, do you?' she asked.

'If she does, she'll soon find herself unmarried again!' Harriet retorted. 'As soon as we get to LA and I've spoken to Rollo, we're going straight on to Mexico City. Tell the pilot, will you? Get him to make necessary arrangements with the airport authorities. Now I'm going to lie down and try to get some rest, and if you've any sense you'll do the same. You look like I feel. Both of us need to sleep.'

At Los Angeles it was the same story as it had been in New York: scores of pressmen all trying to get pictures and copy. Harriet refused to leave the plane, and Rollo literally had to fight his way aboard. But he had no suitcase with him.

'I can't leave the film at this juncture,' he told Harriet without preamble. 'You'll have to manage this one on your own.'

'Why not?' she said, kissing him lightly on the cheek. 'She's my daughter, after all.' She turned to Bess. 'Find Bill, my dear, please. Tell him to flex a bit of muscle with those people out there. I am not coming out to talk to them, whatever they might think.'

'You won't get rid of them that easy,' Rollo said glumly, as Bess made her way forward to look for Bill. 'I bet half of them have chartered planes ready to follow you down there. I've practically had to throw an armed cordon around the studios to keep them out. But it won't do the film any harm, I guess. As someone once said, there's no such thing as bad publicity.'

Harriet took a deep breath. 'Rollo,' she said gently, 'do you ever get the feeling that you and I are through? All washed up?'

444

He grinned at her sheepishly. 'I didn't mean to be callous about Elena. But now that you mention it. . .'

'Someone else?' Harriet enquired sarcastically. 'Some little girl with very big tits and a very small brain, ready and waiting to be the fifth Mrs Wingfield?'

'Look, Harriet,' he protested uneasily, 'you and I are all wrong for one another. I'm very fond of you. Truly I am. You're a remarkable woman. Probably the most remarkable woman I'm ever likely to meet. But you're not my style. I can't compete, and that bothers me. I gotta be top dog.'

She laughed. 'That's honest anyway. I'm fond of you, Rollo, but you aren't my style, either. I'll go and rescue Elena and then I'll file for divorce. How does that grab you?'

He stood up, smiling. 'Sounds fine. And don't think our marriage has been a complete waste of time, because it hasn't. When we married, we both had something the other one needed at that particular moment. It's served its purpose.'

Harriet stood up, too, and kissed him again, but this time with genuine affection.

'You're very percipient, Rollo, when you put your mind to it. It's why you make such splendid films.'

'Hey! You really think so?'

'Yes, of course. Everyone does.'

'To hell with everyone! It means more to me that you like my work than praise from some bunch of overrated critics.' He grinned. 'That's made my day!'

Harriet was touched. She also felt guilty. Had she been so niggardly with her praise that he had never guessed that she admired him as a director? Did she have a mean and stinting nature where other people were concerned?

The co-pilot knocked and entered the cabin to say that they had refuelled and had been cleared for take-off. Harriet thanked him and turned once more to Rollo. She held out her hand.

'Good luck. We won't lose touch.'

'No, we surely won't. And give that shit Ramón a kick in the ass for me. Bess has got his address. Two-timing snake-in-the-grass! I really am sorry, Harriet. If only I'd guessed. . .'

'I don't suppose for a minute that he made the running. It was Elena. In fact, I'm beginning to feel quite sorry for Señor Perez. Although Bess tells me he's really an American.'

'Yeah. Born in the Bowery. Ah, well! Be seeing you, Harriet. Be hearing about you, for sure. You're always good for headline news.'

'That sounds like the pot calling the kettle black. Bring the new Mrs Wingfield to see me some time. You're welcome to honeymoon on Agios Georgios.'

Rollo grinned. 'I might just take you up on that. It would certainly give the newspapers something to talk about.'

'They work hard for their stories,' Harriet laughed. 'They deserve a little *frisson* now and then. And now, my dear, I must insist that you leave, or we shall miss take-off and be stranded here for hours. And I can't afford the delay.'

'Sure. I'm going. You're a swell kid, Harriet.'

'If only I really were,' she murmured. 'But "Time's wingèd chariot" and all that. . .'

He nodded sympathetically and went. Outside the plane, he was once more surrounded by reporters, all clamouring for news. Cameras flashed. Harriet saw him shaking his head as a couple of studio 'heavies' cleared a path for him through the crowd. At the same moment, the jet began to taxi along the runway, and a few minutes later they were airborne.

She first saw the Avenida Juàrez by night; a river of light running through the heart of Mexico City. It had looked beautiful from the air, and at ground level lost none of its enchantment. The clustering street-lights, each with its five white orbs, the trees in white-painted tubs bordering the pavement, the Latin American Tower, the shops, the cinemas, the fountains made it a setting straight out of fairyland. Undoubtedly, by day it would look shabbier and more mundane, like any street in any capital city, but for now Harriet was bewitched.

'Wonderful,' she breathed to Bess Holland, leaning out of the taxi window.

Bess remained noncommittal. She wanted to get the business over, give Ramón Perez a piece of her mind, not admire the scenery.

'We'll come up with you,' she said, indicating first Bill Brereton and then the apartment-block outside which the taxi was parked.

Harriet shook her head. 'No, thanks, Bess. I'll do this on my own. You and Bill can go on with Madge to the hotel. I'll join you later.'

As she spoke, she got out of the cab and walked briskly across the pavement to the big double glass doors, under a red-and-gold awning. Bess and Bill Brereton knew better than to disobey her instructions, but they exchanged uneasy glances as the driver pulled away from the kerb and headed for the Plaza Santo Domingo. At least they had given the waiting pressmen the slip at the airport. That was something to be thankful for, Bess supposed.

A uniformed commissionaire opened the doors for Harriet, and she went inside, crossing the entrance foyer to a desk, manned – if that were indeed the right word – by a voluptuous young woman.

'Can I help you, señora?' the girl asked, unerringly marking Harriet down as either English or American.

'Will you please ring through to Señor Perez' apartment and tell him that Mrs Wingfield wishes to see him?'

The girl lifted the telephone, pressed a button and spoke into the receiver in voluble Spanish. She smiled at Harriet.

'Will you go straight up, señora? Señor Perez is expecting you.'

'I bet he is!' Harriet said grimly, and headed for the lift.

It bore her effortlessly to an apartment on the top floor,

where a softly lit, deep-carpeted corridor led to the front door of the penthouse suite.

Harriet's knock was answered by a manservant, wearing black trousers and a white coat, and with a pleasantly gnarled face, like weather-beaten oak, which was more Indian than Spanish.

'Please to enter, señora.' He ushered her into a big room with a balcony which overlooked the glittering street. 'Señor Perez will be with you in a moment. Can I pour you a drink?'

'No, thank you,' Harriet rapped sharply. 'I just want to see my daughter. Where is she?'

'The señorita is in bed, señora, asleep.'

Harriet eyed the man suspiciously, but he was already on his way to the door. It opened and closed, and she was alone. She felt her temper rising. How dare Ramón Perez keep her waiting like this?

A horrid thought seized her. Could Elena and this Mexican film star be married already? Was it possible, in this country, to arrange things at such short notice? Did they have the equivalent of the English special licence? Her head began to throb, and she sat down on a long white-brocaded sofa facing the open window. But, after a few moments, she started to fidget, anger and apprehension making it impossible for her to sit still. She got up and began pacing around the room.

The décor was mainly white – upholstery, carpets, curtains, wallpaper – and such wood as there was a very pale oak. A collection of Mexican dancing-masks made a splash of colour on one wall, and a white and gold Charro hat hung beside them. There was a display of brightly coloured Mexican pottery and an arrangement of Mexican painted wooden spoons. The dominating feature of the room was a wall-hanging of the Virgin of Guadalupe; a curiously sexless face beneath a peacock-blue hood, and a red-shadowed dress under a cloak sprinkled with golden stars.

Harriet frowned. It was impossible to tell anything about

the character of their owner from these artefacts. It was rather like a stage set: 'Scene: A room in Mexico City.' She could imagine a conscientious props-buyer ransacking the shops for anything which would supply an authentic Mexican atmosphere, and ending up with something completely artifical. . .

A door opened behind her, and she spun round. Her first impression of Ramón Perez was that, in spite of his shock of white hair, he was really quite young. But as he came forward to greet her, hand courteously extended, she could see the fine network of wrinkles around the mouth and eyes.

The mouth and eyes! She felt a sudden sharp jolt of recognition. She knew him! Like a woman in a dream, she put out her own hand to clasp his. The feel and shape of it were tantalizingly familiar. . .

'Hi, Harriet!' said Gerry Canossa.

46

They talked until it was nearly daylight.

Harriet telephoned the hotel and told Bess Holland not to expect her. She did not elucidate. Bess could draw what conclusions she liked: the true explanation would never occur to her. How should it? It was so unlikely it had not even occurred to Harriet. Who would have supposed Ramón Perez and Gerry Canossa to be one and the same?

But, before explanations and reminiscences, there was the matter of Elena to be cleared up.

'Cross my heart, Harriet,' Gerry said, sitting beside her on the sofa and handing her a Scotch on the rocks, 'I did not encourage her. I swear. Even if I'd fancied her like crazy, even if I was the fortune-hunter you all seem to think me, I would never have done anything to harm your daughter.' He smiled, laying a hand on her arm. 'I've been proud of you, kid. I really have. I've followed your fortunes over the years, and it's given me some comfort for running out on you like that. I keep telling myself it was the best thing I could have done for you, so I hope you're gonna tell me that I'm right.'

'Let's finish talking about Elena first.' Harriet regarded him straitly. 'You really did *not* know that she was going to turn up here yesterday?'

'I'll take my Bible oath on it. When she walked through the door and announced that she'd come to marry me, you could've knocked me cold with the proverbial feather. I broke out in a sweat that would've put Niagara to shame. I told her to take herself and her baggage straight back to the airport and get the next plane home.' Gerry sighed. 'She ain't easy to handle, that one.'

'Stubborn as a mule,' Harriet agreed. She chuckled, all her worries laid to rest. 'What did she do?'

'Just tipped the contents of her cases on to the floor and announced that she was here to stay. She then tried to argue me into marrying her. Can't say that I was flattered, though. She made it quite plain that I was just an alternative to going back to school. A marriage of convenience, she called it. Said she'd make me a generous divorce settlement as soon as she came into her money, in three years' time.'

Harriet rested her head on the back of the sofa and stared at the ceiling.

'What on earth am I going to do with her?' she demanded.

'She reminds me of you,' Gerry answered unhelpfully, 'when you were seventeen. Absolutely determined to get your own way. Your father couldn't control you, any more than you seem able to control Elena.'

Harriet lifted her head, staring at him, suddenly struck by the coincidence.

'Oh God!' she said. 'I was the same age, wasn't I, when *I* forced you to marry me? History repeating itself.'

'Not quite.' He slid an arm around her shoulders. 'You had a far better reason than Elena for insisting we get married.' He paused a moment, before enquiring softly: 'What did become of the kid?'

So Harriet told him. She lay back in the oddly comforting circle of his arm and recounted the whole story.

When she had finished, Gerry said: 'It was all my fault you had to have the kid adopted. Don't blame yourself. I was a coward. I couldn't face up to responsibility in those days, so I ran.' He sighed. 'I guess, deep down, I salved my conscience with the belief that Gus would marry you. He was always in love with you. I didn't really think beyond that. I didn't dare. I didn't consider what might happen to Hilary. . . Hilary! What a godawful name!'

'It was my father's,' Harriet answered, offended. 'I wanted our child to be called after him, and I couldn't get in touch with you. I didn't know,' she added bitterly, 'if you were alive or dead.'

'No.' There was a silence before he went on: 'But you did OK without me. And at least now you have Hilary under your eye. You ever going to tell the kid the truth?'

Harriet raised her eyes to his. 'Do you think I should? There are the feelings of the adoptive parents to consider.'

'Maybe.' He got up and poured them both fresh drinks. With his back to her, he said: 'I guess I'd like to think of our child sharing in the great Chance fortune. Hilary's legally your firstborn. It doesn't seem fair that the kid should be punished because of what I did.' He returned to the sofa and handed her her drink. 'It adds to my burden of guilt, doesn't it? You must see that.'

Harriet raised her eyebrows. 'I can't believe it's been a very heavy burden, Gerry. But for this purely fortuitous meeting, I should never have known how you felt. You haven't made any move to get in touch with me all these years.'

'I didn't suppose my interference would have been welcomed. After what I did, I could hardly start hollerin' about justice for my child.'

'Justice,' Harriet murmured. 'Now you're trying to unload some of that guilt on to me. So let me tell you that I have more than my fair share already.'

'Sorry. But it doesn't alter facts where Hilary is concerned. Whatever guilt we may be forced to carry between us, the kid is innocent.'

'The "kid",' Harriet replied with some asperity, annoyed by his quiet acceptance that they were both equally to blame, 'will be forty in August. And what about my other children? Wouldn't my sudden acknowledgement of Hilary be asking a great deal of them?'

Gerry shrugged. 'That's for you to decide.'

Harriet drew a deep breath. 'Opting out again, are you, Gerry? No, no! I'm sorry! You're quite right. It is my decision, and I'll have to make it some time or another. I promise you that when the moment seems right I'll do it. And now let's talk about other things. How on earth did you become an actor? You were never a great reader when I knew you. You wouldn't have had the patience to learn a part in those days.'

He laughed. 'What you mean is that you weren't even sure that I could read. Hell, don't deny it. It's true. But after I got to Mexico I found myself with time on my hands, just bumming around, and I started reading to keep myself amused. After a while, it began to come easy, and I discovered I could remember whole chunks of the text. Photographic memory, I suppose.'

'How did you get into films?'

'Started out as an extra, earning a few dollars. Got to like it. Studio got to know me and gave me bit parts. I progressed from there. Let's face it! The industry down here ain't that big. There wasn't much competition.' After another silence, he asked: 'What you going to tell Elena? The truth?'

Harriet considered the matter.

'No, I don't think I'll give her that satisfaction. What have you said to her?'

'That I'm not interested in her plans. That I certainly have no intention of marrying her. That as soon as you got here, which you were bound to do pretty soon, she'd have to go home with you. She was furious. I got abuse and a hairbrush thrown at my head.'

'OK. We'll leave it at that. If she knows any more, she'll be making all kinds of false assumptions.' Harriet finished her drink and looked round at Gerry. 'It really is good to see you again.'

'Is it? Truly? No hard feelings?'

'No. It's all too long ago. Although, to be honest, I think if you'd asked me that same question yesterday I might not have been so sure of the answer. But sitting here, next to you, no! No hard feelings.'

453

He smiled at her. 'Remember that place you took me to? An old ruin beside a lot of grass and water.'

'Minster Lovell. Yes. That's where we first made love. I was a virgin.'

'Yeah.' His smile broadened. 'And now look at us. Two senior citizens.'

'You speak for yourself!' she exclaimed in mock indignation. 'I shan't be fifty-eight until the end of this month. It's no age in these days of wonder drugs and heart transplants and hip replacements. Future generations won't consider they're old until they're in their nineties. Look at Joan Collins. A sex symbol at over fifty.'

'You're pretty good yourself,' Gerry said admiringly. 'I wish things had worked out for us. I really do.'

'Hindsight,' Harriet retorted. 'At the time, you couldn't run far enough or fast enough to get away from me.'

'I've already apologized for that. Don't let's quarrel.'

'All right.' She leaned back in her corner of the sofa, feeling suddenly overwhelmingly tired. She grinned sleepily at him. 'You're still a very good-looking man, Señor Perez, but I suppose you know that. I can't say I blame Elena for being attracted to you.' She saw the look in his eyes and made a quick defensive movement with her hands. 'Nothing doing, Gerry. I'm not in the market for another soulmate.'

He laughed and relaxed. 'Me neither, kid. My marriages haven't been as well publicized as yours but, including you, I've had four wives already.'

'I will ask you for a bed for the night, though. I'm dog-tired, now that all the excitement and tension of the past two days are over.'

'Sure. There's a spare bed in Elena's room. I'll show you.'

They stood up, then remained for a moment or two looking at one another. Harriet felt as though, somehow, they had completed an episode. It was like a tapestry where a corner of the canvas had been left unfinished. Now, at last, the loose threads were finally woven into place.

Gerry was right. An equal chance. She owed that to their child.

A sullen Elena confronted her mother later that morning.

She had awakened about six o'clock to find Harriet sleeping in the bed alongside hers, in Ramón's blue and gold guest-room. Her first feeling, which she had quickly suppressed, had been one of relief. Her second was anger.

'I will not go back to school!' she had shouted, bouncing over to Harriet and shaking her by the shoulder.

Opening one bleary eye, Harriet said firmly: 'Oh, yes, you will.' And, turning over, she went back to sleep.

For a moment, Elena considered packing her bags and making another run for it, but common sense had prevailed. A year was not, after all, so long, and it could be more comfortable to have her life organized for a little while longer. Independence wasn't all it was cracked up to be. And she had heard a girl at Aston Court speak of Herr München's school in glowing terms. It might not be too bad.

She did not intend, however, to give her mother the satisfaction of knowing that she had changed her mind, and maintained a sulky silence all through breakfast. Unfortunately, her mother and Ramón Perez seemed not to notice: they were too busy talking to each other.

Harriet was amused to note how easily and consummately Gerry slipped back into his role of Mexican film star. The New York accent disappeared, and he even, every now and then, hesitated for a word as though Spanish, and not English, were indeed his native tongue. Perhaps he had always been an actor. Perhaps, all those years ago, he had just been playing at being the boisterous fun-loving GI. Maybe she and Gus had never known the real Gerry Canossa.

She telephoned Bess at the hotel.

'Elena was asleep when I arrived last night,' she said truthfully, 'so I decided to stay, to minimize any newspaper scandal. Order a cab for ten-thirty and pick us both

455

up at Señor Perez' apartment on your way to the airport. Oh, and, Bess, you were right about Ramón. It was nothing to do with him. All Ellie's doing. He's a very nice man.'

'I'm glad to hear it.' Bess sounded relieved. 'I hate to make mistakes about people. See you in about an hour.'

Elena remained subdued throughout the flight to New York, and on arrival shut herself in her bedroom in Harriet's apartment. But, as Harriet remarked to Bess over a belated supper, the atmosphere was beginning to thaw.

They were all, except Elena, who had insisted on a tray in her room, eating a scratch meal in the kitchen: Harriet, Bess, Madge Shelton, Bill and Jeanette Baynton, the last complaining loudly that she had not been given sufficient notice of their arrival.

'It takes hours to unfreeze a joint,' she kept saying.

'Oh, shut up, Jeanette!' Harriet exclaimed at last. 'What you've given us is more than ample. Even Bill looks fit to explode if he eats another mouthful.'

Bill Brereton grinned. He revelled in these informal moments when Mrs Wingfield treated them all as if they were members of one big family. It was not always possible, of course, and he never minded being relegated to the servants' quarters. These last nineteen years had been the most fabulous of his life. Even after all this time – and he was getting on for forty now – he still could not quite believe his luck. To be plucked from the drab streets of Glasgow and transported around the world, always in luxury, was a fairy-tale come true. Occasionally, he and Madge Shelton would compare notes and wonder how on earth it had happened. Why them? The only thing they had in common was that they were both adopted.

Bill's conscience stirred, as it invariably did, when he thought of his adoptive parents. His mother had died two years ago, and his father was now on his own. His visit to Glasgow, earlier that month, had been the first in years. He did not get on with the old man, and remembered too many childhood beatings. It had been an unhappy upbringing, and he had never felt that he owed Ivy and Bert Brereton anything. Adoption was a gamble. Madge Shelton, it seemed, had been extremely happy.

Madge, sitting opposite, was thinking how odd it was that neither she nor Bess nor Bill had ever married. Or, to be strictly accurate, in Bess's case, remarried. She supposed that the other two, like herself, had had affairs, and would probably continue to do so, but matrimony seemed to be out of the question for all of them. They left that to Mrs Wingfield, who, if rumour could be believed, was on the point of divorcing her fifth husband. Was it her fifth? Madge was never quite sure. She had a feeling that there had been a husband before Mr Contarini, but he was rarely mentioned.

'A penny for them, Madge!' Bess Holland called cheerfully as she went to the sink to refill the kettle. Everyone suddenly wanted more coffee.

'Nothing really.' Madge blushed. 'I was just wondering why you and Bill and I haven't married.'

Bess plugged in the kettle and laughed. 'In two words, my dear, job satisfaction. We like what we're doing, and the life we're leading, far too much to leave it all behind us.'

'I hope to God you do!' Harriet exclaimed fervently. 'I don't want a sudden spate of resignations.'

The ringing of the telephone bell interrupted the conversation. Jeanette Baynton went across and lifted the receiver of the kitchen extension.

'Mrs Wingfield's apartment. . . Who? . . . Hold the line a moment, please, and I'll see if she's in.' She placed a hand over the mouthpiece and turned to Harriet. 'Carlin Boyce, calling from Ireland.'

Harriet looked surprised and consulted her watch. It must be getting on for one in the morning over there.

She said: 'I'll take it in the study.'

As soon as she heard Carlin's voice, Harriet knew that something was wrong. He sounded choked with emotion.

'Harriet? There's been a dreadful fire at the Howard stables. The whole place has been burned to the ground.'

457

She started to say something, but he went on: 'Wait a minute! There's worse to come. Isabelle was killed while trying to rescue two of the horses.'

Harriet sat perfectly still, staring unseeingly at the pool of light thrown by the desk-lamp. Her hand felt as though it were welded to the receiver. She knew she ought to be horrified, appalled, express grief. Something! And yet all she could think of was that Edmund was once more a free man.

'How . . .? How did it happen?' She forced herself to ask at last. 'The fire, I mean.'

'No one knows. I only heard, myself, half an hour ago. The fire started earlier this evening. They only got back from England this morning. I'm going over there as soon as I can.'

'Yes. Yes, of course you must.' Her emotions felt frozen. She could think of nothing to say.

Fortunately, Carlin was too upset to notice. He said slowly: 'Harriet, I keep thinking. . .'

'What? What do you keep thinking?'

'That scene with Hallam. . . In the carpark, at Ascot, on Thursday. I keep remembering his threat. He said: "I'll get you, Howard." You don't think . . .? I mean, he can't have had anything to do with this, can he?'

'Oh, for God's sake!' Harriet was beginning, then stopped, her hands as cold as ice. 'Oh, no!' she whispered. 'He wouldn't go to those lengths, surely!'

But, of course, he would. She knew he would. And he was friendly with so many dubious characters, like Albie and Charlie King, who would arrange to have his dirty work done for him, provided the payment was right. And, whatever the truth of the matter, the police would never be able to pin anything on Hallam. They would not even suspect him. He would be in England with the perfect alibi.

She said to Carlin: 'I'm coming over.'

47

When she got to the Malachi stables, she found Edmund there.

'I thought you wouldn't object,' Carlin Boyce said quietly, as he welcomed her into the house. 'There's nowhere else for him to go, except a hotel. And in his present state. . .' He broke off, letting the sentence hang.

'Of course I don't object,' Harriet reassured him. 'Good God! Why should you think I'd mind?'

She had flown to Dublin where a company car had been waiting for her. Bill had accompanied her and driven her down. She had told Bess and Madge to remain in New York for the time being, with Elena. New York would be more fun for her volatile daughter than Agios Georgios.

'But keep your eye on her,' Harriet had warned them.

Carlin said: 'Eddie's in the sitting-room,' adding tactfully: 'I'll help Bill garage the car.'

It was the flimsiest of excuses, but Harriet was grateful for Carlin's absence, as he had known she would be. She pushed open the living-room door and went in.

It was almost dusk. The day had been cold and damp, but at last the rain had stopped, and the sun, edging out from behind a cloud, was setting in a blaze of glory. One of the small windows was open, and the smell of wood-smoke drifted in, thin and acrid. Edmund was seated in an armchair by the empty grate, staring into space.

Harriet was shocked by his appearance. He looked thin and haggard, the flesh beneath his eyes bruised from lack of sleep. His hair, still as thick as ever, seemed to have

459

turned from grey to snow-white almost overnight. His hands were clasped together in his lap. She went to kneel beside him.

'Edmund.' She murmured his name so softly it was like a caress, and she laid both her hands over his. 'Edmund, it's all right. I'm here.'

It did not strike her until afterwards, what an arrogant thing it was to say. It seemed perfectly natural at the time to assume that her presence, the fact that they were together, would begin the healing process.

For a moment, she was afraid that he was not going to respond; then his hands stirred under hers, and he turned dazed eyes towards her.

'She went back for the horses,' he mumbled. 'Two of them were still trapped in the stables. We could hear them screaming.' His voice became a little more animated. 'I told her not to go. The place was well and truly alight. I could see that there was nothing we could do. We'd never get them out of there alive. I didn't think Belle would be so foolish as to try. And then, when I wasn't looking, while I was leading some of the other horses to safety, she ran back in.' The blank look drained from Edmund's eyes, and they were suddenly full of a terrible pain. He began rocking to and fro, tears streaming down his cheeks. 'She died in there, in that awful blazing inferno, with the horses. Two seconds after she got inside, the roof fell in.' His swaying stopped as abruptly as it had started, and he sat staring into some unimaginable pit of hell.

Harriet rose from her knees and perched on the arm of his chair, putting her arms around him and pillowing his head against her breast. Once again, her thoughts betrayed her with the suggestion that Isabelle's death had left the way open for her and Edmund to be reunited; and once again she was horrified by the idea, shooing it back into the dark corners of her mind, where it continued to lurk like some predatory malformed animal. She could almost see its tiny evil red eyes glowing in the dark.

Edmund was crying again, his tears soaking the front of

her thin silk dress, his muffled voice repeating over and over: 'It was my fault. I should have stopped her. It was my fault.'

Harriet's arms tightened around him, and she let him cry himself out, like a child. When his grief had abated, she said fiercely: 'It was *not* your fault! Edmund! Are you listening to me? You were not to blame. You couldn't possibly have foreseen that Isabelle would do anything so foolish. And you were right. It was dangerous to try to rescue the horses. If Isabelle had listened to you, she would be alive today.'

There was a tentative tap on the door, and Carlin appeared. He hesitated when he saw them together, but Harriet motioned with her head for him to come in.

'He's shivering,' she said, glancing down at Edmund. 'He ought to be in bed.'

Carlin nodded. 'The doctor was here this morning and gave him some pills, but Eddie refused to take them. He was up all last night, pacing his room. Each time I woke up, I could hear him. I went in a couple of times, but he just told me to go away.'

'Get me two of the pills now,' Harriet said, 'and some water. I'll see that he takes them.' She released Edmund and stood up, holding out both her hands. 'Come along!' she ordered. 'I'm taking you up to bed. You're going to get a decent night's sleep.' She turned to Carlin. 'Which room is he in?'

'The front spare bedroom. The one next to mine. Do you want any help?'

'I don't think so.' Her voice assumed a more imperious tone. 'Come along! You're going to bed.'

And, to Carlin's surprise, Edmund went – rather in the manner of a sleepwalker, it was true, but, nevertheless, he did as he was told. By the time Carlin followed them upstairs, with the bottle of sedatives and a glass of water, Harriet had removed Edmund's jacket and shoes. She then got him to swallow the pills, forced him to lie down and covered him with the duvet. A few minutes later, he was sound asleep.

461

Harriet and Carlin descended to the kitchen, where Bill Brereton was taking cold ham and salad from the refrigerator, on Carlin's instructions. The trainer busied himself with making a brew of strong tea. Harriet helped Bill lay the table.

'Have the police come to any conclusion about the fire?' she asked Carlin.

He shook his head. 'Too early. And the insurance company's investigators haven't got over here yet. They'll want to poke around. But I'll be very surprised if they don't find it's arson.'

'Ah! Now you're back to Hallam. But they won't be able to prove anything against him, even if you're right.'

Carlin frowned, a little put out, as he always was, by the uninhibited way in which Harriet spoke in front of Bill Brereton. True, the man had been her chauffeur-cum-bodyguard for many years now, and she obviously felt that she could trust him. But Carlin had never really taken to Bill, who, in his opinion, had all the dourness of a Lowland Scot without the distinction of actually being one. Bill had been born and brought up in London, if Carlin remembered rightly. He had also been in trouble with the juvenile courts, although Harriet had never imparted that particular piece of information. Bess Holland had let it drop once, without realizing that she had done so.

He said defensively: 'Perhaps I was a bit hasty in jumping to conclusions. I'm not really sure that the fire wasn't accidental.'

'Oh, I'm certain you're right,' Harriet said, sitting down at the table and pouring out the tea. Bill handed round plates of ham and salad. 'I'm just trying to warn you that you'll never pin it on him. I doubt if the police will even be able to bring the actual perpetrators to book. They're probably safely back in England by now.'

Harriet was correct. Arson was proved, but no suspects ever arrested. The people who might have pointed the police in the right direction remained silent, for Piers's sake.

'My Achilles' heel, where Hallam is concerned,' Harriet said to Carlin.

In September she took Edmund to Agios Georgios to recover. Elena was away at Herr München's school, near Berne, and loving it, so she wrote home to her mother. Piers was still up at Oxford, Michael in New York. So, in Harriet's words, they had the place to themselves.

Edmund was amused at her idea of solitariness. As well as Bess Holland, Bill Brereton and Madge Shelton, there were at least half a dozen servants, in addition to Maria, the housekeeper, and Dimitri, the chef.

'I don't think,' he expostulated with a weak laugh, 'that I'd care for your idea of a crowd.'

She smiled. They were sunning themselves on the balcony of the house, looking out towards the sea, the red and white sun-loungers decorously separated by a small table on which reposed tumblers and a tall jug of iced lemonade. She had hardly left Edmund's side throughout the past three months, supporting him through the trauma of the inquest and Isabelle's funeral, the police inquiry and the questioning, rigorous at times, connected with the insurance claim. The fact that arson had been proved had made things doubly difficult for Edmund. It was only natural that suspicion, at first, should have been directed at him. But his healthy bank balance had finally convinced everyone that he was the loser by the fire, and that even substantial compensation could not reimburse him for the loss of a thriving and prestigious business.

'I don't know,' he said now, out of the blue, 'what I should have done without you. It's times like these that you need a friend.'

'And we've been friends for such a very long time.' She added slyly: 'On and off, that is.'

'That wasn't my fault!' Edmund exclaimed. 'Blame Hallam for that.'

Neither Harriet nor Carlin Boyce had mentioned their suspicions of Hallam's involvement in the fire to Edmund. He seemed to have forgotten their set-to in the carpark at

Ascot – or, at least, had not connected the two incidents – and it was pointless adding to his distress when there was no hope of a conviction.

'It doesn't matter whose fault it was,' she answered gently. 'It's all behind us now.' She hesitated before asking: 'What do you intend to do? Start up as a breeder all over again? You know I'll back you financially, if it's a question of money.'

Edmund shook his head. 'No. I couldn't do it without Isabelle. I shouldn't want to try.'

Harriet felt a stab of jealousy, but she managed to say calmly: 'She meant a lot to you, didn't she?'

There was silence for a moment, broken only by the distant hushing of the sea. Beyond the shadow cast by the balcony's awning, the air was hot and still. Harriet could smell the sage.

Finally, Edmund said: 'She came to mean a lot to me, yes. I wouldn't be honest if I pretended otherwise.'

'Did you love her?' Harriet was forced to ask the question against her will.

Again there was a pause. Maria could be heard, from somewhere in the back of the house, scolding one of the kitchen girls.

'Yes,' he admitted at last. 'But not in the same way that I loved you.'

Harriet steadied her voice. 'Loved!' she exclaimed with a shaky laugh. 'The past tense. I suppose I know now where I stand.'

He gestured towards her with one of his hands.

'I'm sorry,' he said. 'It's just that my emotions are a bit blunted right now. And you're still married to Rollo.'

'Not for much longer. The decree absolute will be through before Christmas.'

Edmund made no comment.

Damn it! thought Harriet. Stop rushing your fences. He was not yet over his grief and horror at Isabelle's death, and here she was, trying to prise a declaration of love from him. She would have to be patient and bide her time.

464

'I was wondering,' she said, 'if . . . well, if you'd consider becoming my trainer when Carlin leaves me. He's off to Australia, as you know, at the end of this month.'

She had anticipated some resistance to the idea, and had been ready with counter-arguments and all her powers of persuasion. But they were unnecessary. Edmund smiled and answered sleepily: 'Thank you. I'd like that very much. I've always loved the old Malachi stables.'

'Good.' She watched his eyelids droop. 'That's settled, then.'

He still looked very unwell at times; crushed and vulnerable. But the various doctors she had consulted all assured her that his weakness was merely temporary, induced by shock, and that time would restore him to health. She wanted to lean across and touch him, smooth his hair and face, but she restrained the impulse. He was not yet ready to receive any demonstration of love.

Later in the day, as they strolled along the beach, after dinner, she said abruptly: 'I saw Gerry again on my trip to Mexico City. Gerry Canossa. My first husband.'

She linked her arm companionably through his, making absolutely sure that there was nothing which could be construed as lover-like in the action, and told him the whole story. When she had finished, she waited for a moment or two before demanding: 'What do you think? Should I tell Hilary and the others the truth?'

Edmund's steps were beginning to flag, so they sat on a rock, arms still linked, staring out to sea. It was growing dark, the warmth of the Aegean night wrapping itself about them like a cloak. Gently, Edmund disengaged himself and stooped to pick a flat pebble out of the sand, sending it skimming across the calm water in a flurry of little waves.

'Was that meant to be symbolic?' Harriet asked.

He laughed. 'No. But, now I come to think of it, it could be.'

'You don't think I should say anything, then? But Gerry has a point of view, you know; one that I've considered many times, myself. It's not as though Hilary is illegitimate. And I am a very rich woman.'

Edmund raised his head, looking towards the horizon, now fast merging into the general darkness of sea and sky.

'I think you'll have to say something some time, or your conscience won't let you rest. But you must do it only when you're good and ready. Don't let this encounter with Gerry stampede you. It's his fault the child was adopted in the first place. It's for you to make up your mind.'

She nodded slowly. 'That's what I feel. I must pick the right moment.'

'Will you know it, when it arrives?'

'I hope so.'

'Woman's intuition?'

'Don't mock! It works more often than men care to give it credit for.' Harriet stood up. 'Come on. Let's go back. There's a chill in the air, and you look as though you could do with an early night.'

A fortnight later, she flew with him to Ireland and saw him installed at the Malachi stables, in the house recently vacated by Carlin Boyce.

'I'd like to stay with you,' she said wistfully, 'but I can't. There's a Corporation board meeting in New York in three days' time, and then I have to go to Istanbul. We're opening our very first Turkish Last Chance restaurant. After that, on to Athens for a Georgiadis Shipping Lines conference. There's another multi-million-pound takeover in the offing.' Harriet sighed. 'I shall be glad when Elena's old enough to run her own affairs.'

Edmund regarded her quizzically. 'Will you? I'm not so sure. You thrive on hard work. You love being the big tycoon. It was your dream when I first knew you. All you needed was the chance afforded you by Harvey Muldoon.'

They were standing by the gate of the small garden which surrounded the trainer's house and separated it from the stables. Bill Brereton, at the wheel of a Daimler, was waiting a little way up the track.

'Do you resent what I've become?' Harriet asked, tracing imaginary patterns with her fingertip on top of the gate, and not looking up.

'I think I did, once,' Edmund replied quietly, 'but not any more. Life's too short and uncertain to spend it trying to change people. Like Oliver Cromwell, as you once had the gall to remind me, they have to be accepted "warts and all".' Harriet still kept her eyes fixed on the gates, so he put a hand under her chin and forced up her head. 'I love you,' he said, 'I've always loved you and, deep down, I still do. You're the only woman I've ever really wanted. But you'll have to give me time. Isabelle's death, the way it happened, has frozen something inside me. Can you wait?'

Harriet slid her arms around his neck and gently kissed his lips. 'As long as I have to. But remember, I'm not as young as I was. Neither are you.' She turned and opened the gate, pausing with her hand on the latch. 'You can reach me whenever you want, day or night, through any of the Chance Corporation offices. I shall leave instructions that you are to be informed of my whereabouts immediately. And, of course, I shall be in touch regularly with the stables.' She lifted a hand and smoothed his lean weather-beaten cheek. 'Don't let it be too long.'

He smiled. 'I won't. I promise.'

Harriet walked swiftly up the track to the waiting Daimler and got in the back. She did not look round. But as Bill revved the engine into life and the car moved forward she had the sudden, unshakable conviction that she and Edmund would soon be together. For always.

PART SIX

1986

Our wisdom and deliberation for the most part follow the lead of chance.

MICHEL DE MONTAIGNE

48

When Harriet had finished speaking, there was a long silence, during which the only sound to be heard in the room was the distant lapping of the waves. Nobody moved for a full minute, all of them frozen in their seats, like the old game of statues, which Harriet remembered playing so often at school.

The echo of her own voice still reverberated inside her head. She seemed to have been talking for ever. In fact, a glance at her wrist-watch showed that it was only something over an hour since she had begun. She had expected interruptions, questions; instead, they had all listened without uttering a word. How much had she actually told them, and how much had been in her mind; her own private gallery of memories, springing up automatically to form a background to the narrative? A great deal, she imagined. But she had informed them of all the salient facts.

Had that been wise? Had it been fair to Piers? Hallam had inevitably emerged as the villain of the piece. She glanced anxiously at Edmund for confirmation that she had done the right thing, and in reply to her unspoken question he nodded, smiling, his encircling arm giving her shoulders an encouraging squeeze. And Michael had been right, reflected Harriet: if she was going to cause a major disruption in her children's lives, they were entitled to know exactly why.

It was Piers who broke the spell. Some time during Harriet's story, he had moved away from the window and

471

perched himself on the arm of Julia's chair. Now he sprang up and began pacing about the room.

Michael rose, too, and helped himself to whisky and soda from the drinks-table. Julia stirred and shifted her position, pleating the folds of her pink silk skirt between unquiet fingers. Elena straightened her back, while continuing to stare at her mother, whom she plainly regarded in a new light. But whether the light was for good or ill Harriet had, as yet, no way of knowing.

Michael returned to his seat and sipped his whisky, frowning at his half-brother.

'For God's sake, sit down, Piers! You're giving me the jitters, walking up and down like that!'

'Oh, I'm sorry!' Piers was heavily sarcastic. 'Your feelings must naturally be of paramount importance.' He thumped his chest. 'What about mine? You're not the one who's been forced to listen for the past hour to a recital of the very peculiar exploits of his father. It wasn't your revered papa who kidnapped you to make a few fast bucks, who blackmailed Mother into marrying him, who burned down Edmund's stables.' Piers ceased his prowling and came to stand behind Harriet, where she sat with Edmund on the couch. 'Although, now I come to think of it, that accusation seems to be a piece of pure speculation without substantive proof. Perhaps the rest of the story is equally questionable.'

Harriet slewed round to face him. 'Are you accusing me of lying?' she demanded hotly.

For a brief moment, mother and son glared at one another; then Piers shrugged and turned away.

'You're letting yourself get side-tracked, Piers,' Michael said harshly. 'Whether or not your father is all Momma makes him out to be is beside the point. The main issue here is this new half-brother of ours. Hilary Canossa, or whatever name he's known by nowadays.' He shifted his gaze to Harriet. 'You still haven't explained to my satisfaction, Momma, why you've suddenly decided to acknowledge him after all these years. Why now? According to you, you've known who he is, had him under your wing for a very long time. So, I repeat, why now?'

'I should have thought that was obvious,' Elena chipped in. 'It was meeting Ramón – Gerry – again, and what he said to her about their child.' The blue eyes widened as they rested once more on Harriet. 'Mamma, why on earth didn't you tell me the truth? It's so romantic!'

'It may seem romantic to you,' Piers snapped, 'but, then, you're not being asked to share your inheritance, are you, Elena dear? Your billions are quite safe from our unknown half-brother's marauding hands.'

Ignoring this exchange, Harriet said quietly to Michael: 'Ellie's right. It was partly meeting Gerry again and realizing that he did care about his child. Perhaps that was what finally decided me, after years of vacillation, that I had a duty to make the acknowledgement. Both Hilary's adoptive parents now being dead, there is no longer anyone to feel that I am trying to steal their child away from them.'

'Don't you mean *buy* their child from them?' Piers asked viciously.

Edmund, who, until that moment, had deliberately kept out of the conversation, decided it was time to take a hand.

'That'll do, Piers,' he said. 'Your mother hasn't taken this step lightly, or without a great deal of heart-searching.'

'Oh, for Christ's sake!' Piers rounded on Edmund. 'Don't start coming the heavy step-father before you're even married to Mother! And I'm too old to be lectured.'

'In that case,' Edmund retorted, 'you're old enough to know that what I'm saying is the truth. Harriet would never do anything to harm either you or your brother.'

'Nothing to harm us!' Piers was spluttering with rage. 'You see losing a third of our inheritance as doing nothing to harm us?'

'Not when the inheritance in question is as large as yours.'

Before Piers could find his voice again, Michael said in his dogmatic fashion: 'You don't know what you're talking

473

about, Edmund. But, then, how could you?' he added fair-mindedly. 'You've never known what real money is.' He looked again at Harriet. 'Well, Momma, I think it's time you told us the identity of this half-brother of ours. Do we know him?'

'Oh, yes!' Harriet smiled serenely. 'Most certainly. You've all known Hilary well for a long time. I thought I'd made that clear. But for the moment the secret remains mine. Hilary knows nothing at all of the story I've just told you, and I think it's only fair that we have a heart-to-heart first.'

'And when are you going to tell him?'

'Tomorrow, after Dick Norris has drawn up the new will. I shall make the official announcement at the party in the evening.'

'Well, I think it's disgraceful!' Julia burst out hysterically, very close to tears. 'I wouldn't have believed you could do this to us, Momma! What about Angelo? What about Marco? Robbing your own grandsons of their rightful inheritance!'

Michael nodded solemnly, leaning across the intervening space to pat his wife's hand.

'Julia's right, Momma. You're not doing right by the boys.'

Harriet got up wearily.

'I'm sorry you're taking it like this. I had hoped that you and Piers and Julia would try to see it from my point of view, but I realize now that I was expecting too much of you. But Hilary is my child. My legitimate child, who deserves an equal chance with the rest of you. Angelo and Marco are amply provided for under the terms of my present will – provisions which will not be altered in any way tomorrow. As for what, in due course, they inherit from you, Michael, they will still be two extremely wealthy young men. There is only so much money even the most profligate of us can spend in a lifetime.'

Michael regarded his mother dourly. 'Spiros was right about you, Momma,' he remarked after a moment's silence. 'He always said you had a *petit bourgeois* attitude towards money.'

'Well, that's hardly surprising!' Harriet snapped. 'I had a *petit bourgeois* upbringing! "Child of the vicarage", that's me!' She took a deep breath. 'I'm going to bed,' she continued in a steadier voice, 'and I suggest you all do the same. It's nearly eleven o'clock, and we have a very busy day ahead of us tomorrow. Sleep on it. You might see things differently in the morning.'

Half an hour later, only Piers and Michael remained in the salon.

Elena had followed her mother and Edmund out of the room, announcing that she found it all extremely exciting and terribly romantic, provoking Piers into the comment that she was a 'stupid cow'! She had almost stuck out her tongue at him, before recollecting that she was now nineteen, going on twenty, and therefore far too grown-up for such childish retaliation. Instead, she had blown her half-brothers a kiss and swept regally through the open doorway.

Julia, persuaded by her husband, had gone to bed soon afterwards, complaining of a sick headache and still sniffing dolefully over the wrong being done to her two 'dear little lambs'. At any other time, these sentiments would have received scant sympathy from Piers, who normally looked upon his half-nephews as an unmitigated menace. Now, however, he merely grunted and grudgingly agreed that it was 'a damn shame'.

When the door had finally closed behind Julia, the two men were left regarding each other across the width of the room. An armed truce had replaced the open hostility which usually existed between them. Michael poured them both drinks, and they moved, by common consent, away from the french windows which gave on to the balcony immediately below the one outside Harriet's bedroom. After a moment's hesitation, Piers retraced his steps and, in spite of the warmth of the night, closed them. Michael nodded approvingly.

'All right,' Piers said, taking a seat next to his half-brother's, 'what's to be done?'

Michael sipped his whisky. 'As I see it, Momma isn't going to change her mind between now and tomorrow morning, and there's nothing we can do to stop her altering her will. It's her goddam money, and she can do what she likes with it.'

Piers lay back in his chair and stretched his long legs out in front of him.

'My reading of the situation exactly. So? Where does that leave us?'

Once again the two men looked at each other. Once again Michael nodded.

In answer to his unspoken comment, Piers said: 'Quite. Operation Eliminate Hilary. But, before we can decide when and how, we have to find out just who the hell Hilary is!'

Michael stared unseeingly at the collection of Atkinson Grimshaws on the opposite wall.

'It has to be one of the "lame ducks",' he said at last. 'It must be.'

'Agreed. And, by my calculations, brother Hilary must be getting on for forty-two. Year of birth, nineteen forty-four. I heard the Mater say so quite distinctly.'

Michael looked thoughtful. 'So who does that give us?'

Piers ticked them off on his fingers. 'Dick Norris, Bill Brereton, Frank Bryan. They're all roughly the right age. Who's the likeliest?'

Michael swallowed some more whisky while he considered the problem. After a pause, he said slowly: 'Not Dick Norris. He's coming tomorrow to draw up the new will. If it was him, Momma'd have asked one of the other partners to do it for her.'

Piers stroked his chin. 'Good thinking. OK. It's not Dick Norris. Frank Bryan?'

Michael wrinkled his nose. 'Gut reaction says not. What do you think?'

'Same here.' Piers reached for his glass on the table

beside him. 'All the same, I suppose he might be.' He took a mouthful of whisky. 'As he works for the company, there's bound to be some way of checking on his date of birth. If it's not nineteen forty-four, we can rule him out. Trouble is, it's eleven-thirty on a Saturday night, and by Monday morning it'll be too damn late.'

Michael gave him a pitying look and crossed the room to the telephone. He lifted the receiver and dialled a number.

Piers asked: 'Who are you calling?'

'Chairman of Chance Enterprises (UK) Ltd. He'll get me the information we need.'

'But it's late!' Piers protested. 'He'll be in bed, or out at a party.'

'It's earlier over there,' Michael, reminded him. 'And it wouldn't matter if it was four in the morning, he'd still make sure I got whatever I asked for. I'm head of Chance Enterprises, and one day I'll be head of the Chance Corporation.' He spoke into the mouthpiece. 'Jeremy? This is Michael Contarini. There's something I want you to do for me. . .'

'Co-head,' Piers murmured to himself, and smiled, dazzled by the promise of future power.

Michael replaced the receiver. 'He'll be back to me as soon as he knows anything. He's getting in touch with his secretary, who'll contact the necessary head of section. In this case, Staff. Someone will find out what we want to know.' He glanced at his watch. 'It shouldn't take too long. Maybe an hour or so. Two, perhaps, if we're unlucky and their lines of communication get fouled up because some goddam fool hasn't left an off-duty number.'

Their luck, however, was in, and the well-oiled wheels of Chance Enterprises (UK) Ltd running smoothly. It was just before twelve-thirty when the telephone rang.

As he hung up, two minutes later, Michael said: 'Frank Bryan's date of birth is the second of April, nineteen forty-five. By my reckoning, eight months too young.'

Piers, nibbling the broken quick of one of his nails, raised speculative eyes to his half-brother's.

'That leaves Bill Brereton.'

477

Michael grunted assent as he lowered himself once more into his chair. 'Always the likeliest of the lot, I'd say.'

'Oh, absolutely,' agreed Piers.

The longer they thought about it, the more inevitable it appeared that Bill Brereton was really Hilary Canossa. His dark Italian good-looks, the way he travelled almost continuously in their mother's company seemed reasons in themselves for considering him the most promising candidate.

'And unlike the other two,' Piers recalled, 'he had no qualifications at all for the job that was offered him. He had a criminal record. He couldn't even drive! Yet Mother was determined to find a place for him. Create a place, one might say.'

'Yeah.' Michael rubbed his nose thoughtfully. 'Couldn't really be anyone else, when you weigh up all the evidence.'

'No. Still, it was just as well to check on Frank Bryan.' Piers grinned suddenly. They were both in a mood for self-congratulation. Their mother was not as clever as she supposed. It had not been too difficult to work out Hilary's identity. Women were never as good at concealing things as they thought themselves. Power, both of reasoning and the ability to get things done, were what counted when the chips were down.

But the moment of celebration was short-lived. They had to come up with a scheme to rid themselves of Bill Brereton before tomorrow evening. Once public recognition of his true identity had been made, any attempt by either of his half-brothers to discredit him could only backfire. People were bound to smell a rat. Piers smiled wryly to himself, as a moment of honesty compelled him to acknowledge the aptness of the phrase.

'Why the hell are you sitting there grinning?' Michael asked, with a return of the old animosity. 'We have to come up with an idea, and pronto! So let's see the result of some of that fancy education you received. Start thinking!'

'No need to be like that.' Piers picked up his glass again,

then put it down, vaguely surprised to find that it was empty. He half-rose to pour himself another drink, but Michael shot out a hand and gripped his wrist.

'Leave it. You've had enough. We've both had enough. Any more, and we shan't be able to keep our wits about us.'

Piers sank back in his chair, the ugly look fading from his face. Michael was right: they had to think, and think fast.

'It'll have to be something good, to turn the Mater against him. He's always been a cocky bastard. It'll be a pleasure to serve him a backhander.'

'Shut up and concentrate!' Michael said violently.

Piers relapsed into silence. After a moment, he remarked: 'What we need to find is his Achilles heel.' He saw the expression on his half-brother's face and waved a deprecatory hand. 'OK. OK. Just thinking aloud, that's all. . .' His voice tailed away. Then he sat up straight, leaned forward and slapped Michael's knee. 'Got it! Elena!'

'Elena?'

'Our little half-sister, as ever was. Bill fancies her like crazy.'

Michael frowned. 'You certain?' To him, Elena was still a schoolgirl. He had never looked beyond the child, to see the woman, fully grown.

'Positive,' Piers grinned. 'I've watched him watching her.'

'She used to have the hots for him.' Michael was unconvinced. 'I remember hearing about the fuss there was the time she got into his bed.'

'That was years ago,' Piers said. 'The boot's on the other foot now, you take it from me. Ellie doesn't give a rush about Bill any more, but he mentally undresses her every time he looks her way.'

'So where does that get us?'

Piers sucked his underlip. 'I'm not sure at the moment, but let me think some more.'

The salon was very quiet. The two men sat close together, in the pool of light thrown by a single lamp. The rest of the room was in shadow, the pearled oblongs of the windows long since merged into the general darkness.

Piers stirred suddenly, glancing at his watch.

'One o'clock. With luck, Bill won't be asleep. If he is, I'll have to wake him.'

'What are you going to do?' Michael asked.

Piers smiled. 'I'm going to employ all my considerable charm and powers of persuasion in order to convince Bill that I'm acting as a go-between for Ellie.'

Michael shook his head. 'Won't work,' he grunted. 'Bill's too shrewd an operator to risk his job and his entire future just for the chance of laying Ellie. Besides, he knows you too well. He's bound to be suspicious.'

Piers rose and took a full bottle of whisky from the drinks-tray.

'Not if he's pie-eyed, stoned out of his skull, completely and utterly smashed. And you know how Mother hates drunkenness. I think our grandmother must have been frightened by a Methodist lay preacher while she was pregnant.'

Michael frowned. He disliked that sort of talk. He regarded his half-brother cynically.

'Mind it isn't Bill who drinks *you* under the table.'

Piers gave him a pitying glance. 'Dear boy, when I was up, I was renowned for having the hardest head in the whole of Oxford.' He drifted towards the door. 'All you have to do is keep your fingers crossed and wish me luck. I'm sure you can manage that.'

49

Edmund opened his eyes, wondering what had woken him. He felt for Harriet, but the place beside him in the big double bed was empty. He sat up and switched on the bedside lamp.

Harriet was standing by the open window. She turned, blinking, in the sudden beam of light.

'I couldn't sleep,' she said. 'I'm all right. You can put that thing off. I like the darkness. It helps me think.'

Edmund slid out of bed and padded across to her, his bare feet making no sound on the deep pile of the carpet. His naked body looked ghostly in the blackness.

Harriet snuggled against him as he put his arms round her.

'You'll get a chill,' she warned him, laughing. 'We're both too old to go prowling around in the buff.'

He chuckled softly. 'You mean this diaphanous garment you're wearing makes the slightest bit of difference?'

'No. But it prevents you noticing all the wrinkles and the flab.'

'You don't have either.'

She raised her face and kissed his cheek. 'Thank you kindly, sir, but I'd be a walking miracle if I didn't. Men don't seem to age as fast as women. Something to do with the hormones.' Harriet moved restlessly. 'I *am* doing the right thing, aren't I?'

'I think you are. Don't you?'

'Yes.'

'Then, stop worrying about other people's reactions.

They are predictable and understandable. But you have to stick to your guns.'

'I've asked Gerry over for the celebrations tomorrow. Today. It must be gone midnight. I heard he was in England to make a new film with Rollo, so . . . I've asked them both to come.'

'And are they?'

'Yes. Gerry telephoned me just before we went into dinner. You don't mind, darling, do you?'

Edmund hugged her, then let her go. 'Not in the least. Since the success of *The House of León*, and Gerry's rise to international stardom, your paths were bound to cross every now and then. Besides, he ought to be here tomorrow. He and Hilary ought to get to know one another.'

'That's what I thought.' Harriet sighed. 'Let's hope that Hilary feels the same way. Oh God, Edmund, I'm so nervous! Tonight, telling Michael and Piers was bad enough, but it wasn't the worst part. That comes this morning. Telling Hilary.'

'It'll be all right,' he comforted. 'You'll see. Now, come back to bed and get a good night's sleep. It's going to be a very long day.'

Harriet nodded. 'In a minute,' she said. 'I promise. I just want to get a breath of fresh air.'

She stepped out on to the balcony. Everything was very quiet and very black. There was no moon tonight to silver a path across the distant water. She could smell the verbena and the sage.

Something moved, to her right. She turned her head, but it was too dark to see anything properly. She moved across to the side-railing of the balcony.

For a moment, she thought she must have been mistaken. Then she saw again the flicker of movement and heard the faint but unmistakable scrunch of feet on gravel. Someone else could not sleep, either, and was out for a late-night walk. As far as she could see, whoever it was was moving in the direction of the garages and Bill Brereton's quarters. Or away from them; it was difficult to tell. Harriet shrugged. Either way it did not really matter. No stranger would find it easy to breach the defences of Agios Georgios. There were too many guards and their dogs patrolling the shoreline at all hours of the day and night.

Piers trod, soft-footed, across the gravel space in front of the garages and mounted the outside stairs to the door at the top. On the small landing, a stone píthoi, crammed with flowers, gave off a pungent scent. Was Bill asleep? It would make things a damn sight easier if he were not.

Piers's luck was in. A streak of orange light beneath the door indicated that the chauffeur, late as it was, was still awake. Piers lifted a hand and knocked.

The door swung inward, and Bill stood silhouetted against the glow from the room. He was wearing a short towelling robe and a pair of heelless slippers.

'Who is it?' he demanded.

Piers moved forward so that he was clearly visible in the stream of light.

'Can I come in?' When Bill hesitated, plainly at a loss, he added: 'Couldn't sleep. Was out walking and wondered if you might be awake.' He held up the bottle. 'Brought you a present. Thought we might crack it together.'

Bill raised his eyebrows. 'You were out walking with a bottle of whisky?'

Piers smiled blandly. 'Going to have a quiet drink down on the beach. Sort of midnight feast, like we used to have at my old prep school. Except that this one is strictly liquid. Then I thought, no fun getting sloshed on one's own, so I came to see if you were still up. And you are. Aren't you going to invite me in?'

Bill reluctantly moved to one side. He was plainly suspicious of Piers's sudden friendliness, but could see no reason for any ulterior motive.

Piers stepped inside and glanced appraisingly round him. It was a Spartan room. What furniture there was was purely functional: a bed, a washbasin, a couple of chairs, a bedside table and a lamp. Another door, set in the far wall, stood ajar to give a glimpse of a white-tiled bathroom. A large cupboard in one corner presumably served as a wardrobe. What struck Piers almost immediately was the absence of books, although a stack of girlie magazines and another of the *Autocar* were piled within easy reach of the bed.

Bill closed the door and looked at his unwelcome visitor with a slightly nonplussed air. Piers smiled winningly and once more held up the bottle.

'Glasses,' he suggested. 'May I sit down?'

Bill flushed and pulled forward the two cane-seated chairs. A folding table, which Piers had not previously noticed, was dragged into the centre of the room, and while Bill went in search of something to hold the whisky Piers unlatched its leaves. Bill returned after a couple of minutes with two mugs and filled a jug with water at the basin.

'You know, you really deserve better quarters than this,' Piers said. 'You ought to kick up a fuss with Mater about it.'

Bill grimaced. 'I like it.' He sat down on the opposite side of the table. 'I hate clutter and, anyway, I spend most of my time up at the house. We're only here a couple of months of the year, when all's said and done.'

Piers poured a generous measure of whisky into each mug and topped up with water.

'Cheers.'

'Cheers.'

There was a momentary silence. Then Piers asked: 'You're not a real Scot, are you?'

'Nope.' Bill took a swig of the whisky. 'Born and brought up in London. Why?'

'Oh . . . nothing. Just that everyone thinks of you as being a Scot because you lived in Glasgow. You were actually born in London, were you?' Piers refilled the mugs, this time putting a little more water than whisky in his own.

'I don't really know where I was born,' Bill answered. 'I was adopted while I was still quite young.'

'Not a babe-in-arms then?' Piers saw the other's look of incomprehension and added: 'You weren't, so to speak, adopted straight out of the cradle?'

'Oh, I see. No. Must've been about two or three years old. I've a vague recollection of some woman I think must have been my mother, but my parents – my adopted parents, that is – just said she died young. They never wanted to talk about her, so I let the subject alone.'

'Very wise, dear old boy.' Piers leaned forward and poured more whisky. His hand was unsteady, and he spilled a few drops. He must be out of practice. The fumes were beginning to go to his head, and he recollected uneasily that he had already had a fair bit to drink that evening. He raised his mug and chinked it against Bill's. More whisky slopped on to the table.

'What . . . what d'you want exshactly?' Bill asked. 'I mean . . . what you doing here?' His words, Piers noted with satisfaction, were becoming a little slurred.

'Told you. Explained all that when I first came in.' Piers was speaking carefully now because he, too, was having trouble making his lips obey him. He went on: 'You fancy Ellie, don't you?'

Bill blinked stupidly. 'What business that of yours?' he demanded belligerently.

Piers hiccuped and topped up the liquid in both their mugs. The whisky was more than halfway down the bottle.

'Fact is, she rather fancies you.'

'Crap!' Bill could manage that without too much difficulty.

Piers shook his head with slow deliberation.

'Not at all, dear old boy. De-fin-itely not crap. Told me so herself, 's morning.'

'Doeshn't care a shtraw for me!' Bill expostulated. The room was beginning to circle around him.

'Can assure you she does. Had a crush on you when she was young, now didn't she?'

'That was years ago.' Bill was also trying to speak

carefully, as though his words had a life of their own and might run away with him.

Piers tilted the bottle once again into their mugs. He was beyond the effort of keeping sober himself. He felt euphoric.

'Don't b'lieve me? Calling me a liar? OK! Let's go find out, then!'

'When?'

'Now, of course! Now. This minute. No time like the preshent.' Piers rose unsteadily to his feet, supporting himself against the edge of the table. 'Come with me. To the house. You can ask Ellie yourself.'

Bill was drunk, but not yet that drunk. His sense of self-preservation was still operating.

'You're pissed,' he informed Piers bluntly.

Piers giggled. 'Have some more whisky,' he offered.

It took all Piers's powers of persuasion and the remainder of the bottle to convince Bill that a visit to Elena's room at two o'clock in the morning would be a perfectly normal occurrence. Piers, whose head was beginning to clear a little, was only concerned that Bill might not make the journey without passing out, or that his own legs might fail to support him. With their arms locked firmly about one another's waist, the pair of them wove a circuitous route to the door, which Piers opened.

The night air, when it hit them, was almost the undoing of both. They staggered down the flight of steps to land in an undignified heap at the bottom. Bill was laughing inanely as a cursing Piers tried to haul him to his feet. Eventually, when they were both upright again, they tottered across the gravel in a lover-like embrace. Bill began to sing in a tuneless baritone.

'Oh, ye'll tak' the high road an' I'll tak' the low road,
An' I'll be in Scotland afore ye. . .'

Piers, feeling vaguely that Bill shouldn't be allowed to have it all his own way, countered with his old school song.

'Forty years on when far and asunder
Parted are those who are singing today. . .'

As they neared the house, however, set between
tamarisk trees, quiet at last, now that the cicadas had
finished their endless daytime chirping, he broke off,
placing a finger to his lips with an exaggerated gesture.

'Ssh! We're nearly there. Quiet, while I get this door
open.'

They went in by the side-entrance and up the two flights
of stairs leading to the bedroom landing. The long row of
white-painted doors remained closed and silent. Miracu-
lously, no one seemed to have heard them approaching.

Piers hesitated, unsure for a moment which door was
Elena's, and Bill slid out of his grasp, sitting on the floor,
still quietly singing.

'Think I'll stop here for the night,' he muttered, grinning
up affectionately at his companion.

'Oh, for Chrissake!' Piers stooped and once more managed to pull Bill upright. 'You chicken or something? Ellie's
'viting you to her room. . . Roll between the sheets.
Come on, upsh-a-daisy! Tha's right. This the door . . .
fifth one 'long. Brashe yourself, Hil'ry, m' boy! We're going
in.'

'You are drunk!' Harriet fumed. 'The pair of you are blind
drunk! How dare you go roaming around the house at this
time of the morning in this disgusting condition!'

She had been sound asleep when her daughter's alarm-
bell, part of a system installed by Spiros in every room in
the house, had shattered her dreams and jerked her wide
awake. At first, she refused to believe her ears; then she
had recalled, with panic, the shadowy figure she had seen
earlier, near the garages. Had someone, somehow, managed to evade the guards and their dogs?

Edmund was already out of bed and struggling into his
dressing-gown. A row of small coloured bulbs on a panel
beside the bed showed the blue one to be lit.

'It's Ellie!' he flung over his shoulder, as he wrenched furiously at the door-handle.

Harriet overtook him on the landing, jostling him aside and bursting into Elena's room. Her daughter was sitting up in bed, her long fair hair tumbled about her shoulders, a strap of her white satin nightdress slipping provocatively down one arm, more angry than frightened. Bill Brereton had fallen, face downwards, across the quilt and was loudly snoring. Piers had collapsed into a pale pink armchair, grinning vacantly.

The room began to fill up as Bess Holland, Madge Shelton, Michael, Julia, Maria and Dimitri arrived on the scene in varying states of undress. Three of the night guards and their dogs had converged outside, on the landing, and Harriet was forced to repress a smile. The situation had, she felt, all the trappings of a Whitehall farce.

She turned to her daughter. 'Are you all right, Ellie? What happened?'

Elena was also beginning to see the funny side of the incident.

'Nothing happened,' she giggled, 'but naturally I was a bit scared when I woke up to find these two morons lumbering around my bedroom. I didn't realize who they were, at first. I'm afraid I panicked and pressed the button.'

'As anyone would,' Harriet agreed, glaring at her son and her sleeping chauffeur. She called two of the guards and instructed them to carry Bill back to his quarters. 'I'll see him and you, Piers, in the morning when you've both had time to sober up. I've never known such disgraceful behaviour!'

'Led sheltered life, Mater dear,' Piers murmured dulcetly, 'tha'sh your trouble.' He focused his eyes with difficulty on Michael. 'Shorry, ol' man. Blew it. F'gotten how mush . . . drunk already.'

Michael sent his half-brother a glance from beneath frowning brows. He knew how astute their mother was.

488

She rarely missed anything, and all the little bits of information which came her way would be hoarded until she could piece them together to make a whole picture. Luckily, at the moment, she was giving all her attention to Ellie.

'Mamma, for heaven's sake stop fussing!' Elena protested. 'I've told you, I'm perfectly OK. Just a momentary panic. And now, if you'll all get out of my room, perhaps I can get back to sleep.'

Harriet kissed her and smoothed her hair. Then she turned to Edmund.

'Darling, will you see Piers back to his room, please? I'm afraid you'll have to undress him, the state he's in.' She began shepherding everyone else out on to the landing. 'Bed,' she went on firmly. 'The show's over and we all need some rest. We have a big day ahead of us. We must really try to get some sleep.'

But, once back in her room, Harriet found it difficult to take her own advice. The incident had unsettled her. When Edmund returned, fifteen minutes later, he discovered her pacing up and down the floor.

'Acushla! Come to bed.' He got in and held out his hand. 'It's gone two o'clock. I know it's an irritating thing to have happened, but people drink too much every day of the week. Bill and Piers were so pie-eyed they didn't know what they were doing. It was just unlucky that they ended up in Ellie's bedroom.'

'That's not what's bothering me,' Harriet answered, but she shed her dressing-gown and climbed in beside him. As Edmund switched off the bedside lamp, she went on: 'What were Bill and Piers doing together in the first place? I'd have sworn they didn't even like one another. And then what did Piers mean by that remark he made to Michael?'

'What remark?' Edmund's voice was fading as sleep overtook him.

Harriet, however, continued to lie wakeful, staring into the darkness.

'I got the distinct impression that he was apologizing to

him for something or other that he hadn't been able to do. I wasn't really taking that much notice, but I'm sure I heard Piers use the words "blew it". Blew what? That's what I'd like to know. And, now that I come to think of it, I sensed a kind of undercurrent between him and Michael. There's a mystery here that needs investigating.'

50

At six-thirty the following morning, Madge Shelton wandered into the salon to find Bess already busily arranging flowers.

'I feel like a piece of chewed string,' she announced, dropping wearily into a chair. 'Couldn't you sleep, either?'

Bess shook her head. 'What a night! Don't get too comfortable. The maids'll be in here in a minute to start cleaning.'

'Whatever got into Bill?' Madge asked, ignoring Bess's strictures. 'I've never known him get as drunk as that before, although I admit he likes a drop. Do you think he'll get the bullet?'

'I shouldn't think so.' Bess finished her arrangement and stood back to admire the effect. 'But he'll certainly get a blasting. You know how Mrs Wingfield hates that sort of self-indulgence. I wonder if Maria's made any coffee yet?'

'I don't know, but I could use a cup.' Madge levered herself to her feet. 'Let's go down to the kitchen and find out. You know, I can't make out what those two were doing together at that time of night. I thought Bill had absolutely no time for Piers.'

'And vice versa.' Bess regarded her colleague thoughtfully. 'Mmm. You have a point there, Madge. I wonder what Piers was up to.'

Madge stifled a yawn. 'Why should he be up to anything?'

'Because the Honourable Piers Cavendish is his father's son,' Bess answered tartly. 'Which is a good enough reason, as far as I'm concerned, not to trust him further than I could throw him.'

'Aren't you being a bit hard on the poor lad?' Madge protested. 'He always seems pretty harmless to me.'

Bess snorted. Then she conceded: 'Perhaps he isn't quite as venal as the Viscount, but I'm not sure I'd bet on it. What I would bet on, heavily, is that Bill's getting drunk last night was at Piers's instigation. But why? What was his object?'

Madge shrugged. 'No idea. But one thing's certain. Mrs Wingfield won't like having to bawl out her favourite. Bill, I mean, not Piers.'

Bess smiled, arranging three more long-stemmed roses in a tall green vase.

'She *is* fond of him, isn't she? I remember when she took him on. Everyone advised her against it, including me, but for some reason or another she was determined to employ him. And she was right of course. She always is. Until last night, his conduct has been exemplary.' Bess sighed. 'Oh God! There's so much to do today. I must try to concentrate and put this other business out of my mind. Dick and Melanie Norris are arriving at nine-thirty on the yacht, and also the man from Sarantopolou's with the extra TV sets. World Cup Final,' she explained, in reply to Madge's puzzled frown. 'Then, as soon as lunch is over, the first guests will start arriving. I must make certain that Dimitri serves lunch early today. No later than twelve-thirty. I must be at the airstrip by two. I'd better check again with Athens about the departure times of the private planes. There was a bit of doubt about one of them yesterday.'

Madge looked at Bess admiringly. 'Thank God I've only Mrs Wingfield's clothes to worry about. That's bad enough. I don't know how you cope, plus all the business side of things as well.'

Bess grimaced. 'I wonder myself, sometimes. But I love it really. I love the feeling of power it gives me.'

'The responsibility would frighten me to death,' Madge shuddered.

Bess laughed and moved towards the door. 'I find it

stimulating. I wonder, now and then, who I get it from, this love of authority and power. Must have been my real parents. My mother and father were two of the most self-effacing people I've ever known.' She looked at her watch again. 'Quarter to seven. Maria's bound to be up and about by now. Let's go and get that coffee.'

Harriet propped her chin on one hand and regarded Bill Brereton, who, looking ill and nervous, was sitting on the other side of the desk.

The room which she used as an office, on the ground floor of the house, was already flooded with sunshine. Through the window, she could see a white vapour-trail, high in the cloudless blue sky. The cement-hard mud of the road leading to the beach snaked between patches of purple daphne. There had been silence for the past few moments, since Bill had finished speaking.

At last, Harriet said: 'So that's your story, is it, Bill? Piers turns up, out of the blue, at one o'clock in the morning, and suggests a drinking session. You let him in because he's the boss's son and you're afraid to antagonize him. Have I got that right so far?'

Bill nodded mutely. The light from the window was hurting his eyes.

'I'm disappointed in you, Bill,' Harriet went on. 'Do you really think, after all these years, that I could be turned against any of my employees by my children? I form my own judgements, Bill, as you very well know. I never listen to spiteful tittle-tattle and gossip.'

Bill murmured shamefacedly: 'I didn't stop to think. I'm sorry.' He added defensively: 'It was gone one. I was tired and ready for bed. I wasn't thinking very clearly.'

'And you were surprised to see Piers, I guess. You and he aren't usually that friendly. Or am I mistaken?'

Bill shook his head. Immediately, a million hammers started banging away inside his skull. He winced.

Harriet tried not to smile.

'It won't happen again,' Bill mumbled.

'I hope very much that it won't. What you do in your spare time is your business. Get drunk if you must. But I don't want you ending up in Elena's bedroom.'

Bill blinked. 'I don't know how I got there,' he said. 'I remember Piers – Mr Piers – telling me that Elena fancied me and I said he must be mistaken, because that was all a very long time ago. After that, I don't recall very much.'

Harriet raised her eyebrows. 'Piers told you that, did he? Did you think, at the time, that he was suggesting you went to her bedroom?'

'I don't know. I didn't know what to think.' He dropped his eyes to his hands, tightly clasped in his lap. 'Are you . . .? Are you going to sack me?'

'No, of course not. I think you've been foolish. I'm *sure* you've been foolish. But I'm equally sure that you regret it and that it won't happen again.' Harriet broke into a laugh. 'When I arrived on the scene last night, you were lying face down on Elena's bed, snoring very loudly.'

'Oh God!' Bill buried his face in his hands. When he raised it again, he asked: 'How does she feel, Miss Elena, about me being kept on?'

'I haven't consulted her. But I'm sure she regards the whole episode as a tremendous joke. Something to be laughed about with her friends.' Harriet saw the blood suffuse Bill's face and felt a certain satisfaction at having flicked him on the raw. He deserved some punishment for being so silly. She continued on a more serious note: 'I do have to be able to trust my employees, you know, Bill, particularly my private staff, who mix with my family. If I can't, that makes those nearest to me extremely vulnerable.'

'I realize that.'

Harriet nodded. 'Right!' she said. 'We'll try to forget that last night ever happened. You'd better resume your duties straight away. There will be a lot of people to meet shortly, both at the airstrip and at the harbour. And tell the rest of the staff that I don't want any gossip about this incident, and I shall be very displeased if I find there is any. Now, you'd better see about meeting Dick and Melanie Norris. They're due to arrive in, I think, fifteen minutes.'

As the office door shut behind Bill, Harriet slumped back in her chair and closed her eyes. A whole twenty-four hours of exertion stretched before her, and already she was feeling tired. Damn Piers! Damn Michael! Damn their conniving little schemes!

It had been early that morning, opening her eyes after a few hours unrefreshing sleep, that the truth had suddenly dawned on Harriet. Piers and Michael had deliberately set out to try to discredit Bill because they thought he was Hilary. It was so obvious that the more she thought about it the less she could understand why she had not seen it from the start. And Edmund, when she put it to him, agreed.

'Of course,' he had said. 'It's so simple really.'

'I feel partly to blame.' Harriet had sat up in bed, hugging her knees. 'If I hadn't made a secret of the business, this would never have happened. Piers and Michael could only hope to get away with something of the sort as long as I presumed them ignorant of Hilary's true identity. They thought they'd worked it out. I wonder why they hit on Bill?'

Edmund had laughed. 'Be fair, Harry! At least you know damn well why they didn't hit on the truth.'

She had nodded and, after a moment or two, had turned to him and grinned.

But she was no longer amused, as she sat at her desk, thinking back over the events of the past night. She might, she felt, have expected some sort of scheme, however botched, to thwart her plans, from Hallam's son, but not from Gus's. But, then, they were her sons as well, and it was unfair to attribute all Piers's low cunning to his father.

She resolutely opened her eyes again and reached for the house telephone, pressing the intercom button for Michael and Julia's room. When Michael answered, Harriet said coldly: 'I want you and Piers in the office, now! Within the next five minutes.' She rang off before he had time to reply.

But her sons must have been expecting the summons,

because it was in fact less than five minutes before they put in an appearance, Michael looking slightly red in the face, Piers as defiant as his hangover allowed. They were both fully dressed and, in addition, Piers was wearing a pair of dark glasses. Without being bidden, he sank into Bill's recently vacated chair.

'Can we have that window shut?' he asked his mother fretfully. 'In my present delicate state of health, those bloody cicadas are like the LSO getting to grips with the "1812"!'

'Serve you right,' Harriet responded unsympathetically. 'Poor Bill is having to work under the same conditions.'

'Poor Bill!' Michael blustered loudly, ignoring his half-brother's gesture of protest. 'How can you say that, Momma? You found him dead drunk last night in Elena's bedroom.'

'Having been helped there by Piers.' Harriet glanced contemptuously at her younger son. 'You know damn well, both of you, that it was a put-up job. An attempt to discredit Bill in my eyes.'

'Why on earth should we want to do that?' Michael demanded, with an unconvincing laugh.

'Because you think he's Hilary. Well, he's not.' Harriet smiled at the look of consternation on her sons' faces. Even Piers had momentarily forgotten his hangover.

'I don't believe you, Momma,' Michael said slowly. 'You're only saying that to protect him until you're ready to make the announcement tonight.'

'Protect him from what?' Harriet asked grimly. 'Another attempt on his credibility? Don't try anything, Michael. Or you, Piers. Anyway, I'm telling you the truth. I must admit I can see why you thought Bill might have been Hilary. His age, his rather Italianate good looks, the fact that he was an adopted child. But, then, all my lame ducks, as I've heard them rather unkindly referred to, were that. I guess it was a sop to my conscience. Something I felt I had to do. Something which made me feel easier in my mind.'

Piers leaned an elbow on the desk and supported his throbbing head in one unsteady hand.

'Well, Mickey, my old chum, we seem to have made a right

balls-up of that,' he said, and grinned mirthlessly. He removed his dark glasses and looked at his mother with a pair of very bloodshot eyes. 'So who is Hilary, Mater dear?' he asked her.

Harriet smiled benignly. 'There's one little point you and Michael seem to have overlooked, Piers. I told you that Hilary was named after my father, and you both jumped to the same conclusion; namely that the child was a boy. What you forgot, the pair of you, is that Hilary can be a girl's name, too.'

It was nearly midday before Dick Norris finished drawing up the new will and handed it to Harriet for signature. Maria and Dimitri had been called in to act as witnesses. When they had appended their names and gone, Maria muttering darkly about the hundred and one jobs she still had to do, Harriet gave a great sigh of relief and smiled across the office desk at the solicitor.

'Well, now you know,' she said. 'About Hilary, I mean. Are you shocked?'

'Why should I be shocked?' Dick Norris raised his eyebrows. 'Surprised, perhaps, but nothing more.'

'I meant, were you shocked by the facts? At my letting Hilary be adopted when she was so small; at my not acknowledging her properly until today.'

'My dear Harriet, it's not my place to sit in judgement on anyone, least of all you, to whom I owe so much. And, from what you've seen fit to tell me, I don't see how anyone could blame you.'

'You mean that?'

He looked at her and laughed. 'Boy Scout's honour. See this wet, see this dry, across my heart and hope to die.'

Harriet joined in his laughter, relaxing visibly. 'I hope everyone is as charitable as you are. Particularly my own children.'

'Ah.' Dick began stowing the documents away in his briefcase. 'How have Michael and Piers taken the news? Elena, obviously, isn't so closely involved.'

497

'The initial response was bad. Worse than I had expected.' Harriet did not elaborate. 'But I'm hoping that they'll become reconciled to the idea in time. If I were a religious woman, I'd probably offer up a few prayers or light the odd candle.'

'That's an unexpected confession from a "child of the vicarage".'

'Yes. My father would have been hurt, but not surprised. He always said I was a pagan. If he hadn't been such a benevolent man, he'd have said that my god was Mammon.'

'Rubbish!' Dick Norris got up. 'You've done a lot of good with your money.'

'Maybe. Not as much as I ought to have done. The truth is I always liked the idea of power. I believed in myself; in my own destiny. I also believed in grabbing any and every chance that was offered me.'

'And now you're offering Hilary a chance. Do you think she'll want to take it?'

'I believe so. I truly hope so. If she has anything of me in her, she will. And she's very like me in a lot of ways.'

'She doesn't know yet?'

'No. I'm sending for her now. Thanks for coming early, Dick. Go up and have a shower and a rest before lunch. There will be a cold buffet in the salon at twelve-thirty.' As Dick Norris moved towards the door, Harriet added: 'Will you give Melanie my excuses and apologies for not being there? I'm having a tray sent in here for me and Hilary. There won't be another opportunity to tell her, once the other guests start arriving.'

'Good luck.' Dick came back and lightly kissed Harriet's cheek. 'Can I tell Melanie the truth?'

'Of course.'

When Dick had gone, Harriet sat down again behind her desk and tried to calm herself. She had never felt so nervous in her life as she did now, at the prospect of the confrontation ahead of her. How would Hilary react to the news that she was Harriet Chance's daughter? Would she be angry, frightened, resentful? Would she blame her

498

mother for having had her adopted? Harriet jumped to her feet and began wandering nervously about the room, trying to postpone the fateful moment. Was she wise to admit the truth at all? But the new will was drawn up now. The die was cast. There was no going back. And there was no one she could call on for support, not even Edmund. This was something she had to do alone.

Harriet moved to resume her seat behind the desk, then stopped abruptly. This was no formal interview. It had to be cosy intimate. The only reason she was forced to use the office was because there would be no privacy today in any of the other rooms. She glanced round her, before dragging a small tan leather-upholstered chair from its corner near the door to a position on one side of the window. After that, she manhandled her own swivel armchair from behind the desk, placing it a few feet away from the other one. She removed a vase of pink carnations from an early seventeenth-century gate-legged table, and arranged the table close at hand, so that Maria would be able to put the tray of coffee and sandwiches where she and Hilary could reach it. That done, she stood back and studied the effect.

So now there was nothing left for her to do but send for Hilary. Harriet could procrastinate no longer. She lifted the telephone receiver on her desk, pressed the inter-house button and sent for Bess Holland.

51

By ten o'clock that evening, the party was in full swing; looking all set, as Frank Bryan remarked to Madge Shelton, with whom he was dancing, to go on well past breakfast-time the following morning. Madge replied absentmindedly that that was the whole idea, and returned to the topic which was absorbing her attention. Hers and everyone else's, if it came to that, except for a small handful of football devotees, who were more concerned with Argentina's victory over West Germany in the World Cup Final.

'Bess!' Madge exclaimed for what seemed to Frank like the hundredth time that evening. 'Bess Holland! Mrs Wingfield's daughter! My God! The press'll have a field-day when this story gets out. As it's bound to after tomorrow.'

Frank stared stolidly over his partner's shoulder, concentrating on his feet. He had never been any good at dancing, and never would be. He devoutly wished he had not come, but Mrs Wingfield had made such a point of him accepting the invitation. Now he was here, he couldn't think why. The house was packed: she would never have missed him, not with all these famous people to talk to. And while Frank remained unimpressed by the celebrities all around him – the Hollywood stars, the politicans, the television names, a sprinkling of the more well-known actresses and actors – he was under no illusion that he could in any way compete in the interest stakes. He might be chief accountant of Chance Enterprises (UK) Ltd, with the prospect of one day becoming head of the entire

Chance Corporation accountancy department, but the job would never have the same charisma as that attached to being a 'personality'.

He had been relieved to note a few familiar faces: Dick Norris and his wife, even though the latter was an empty-headed fluffy little thing; Madge Shelton, of course; Bill Brereton, unusually subdued; Carlin Boyce, come all the way from Australia, just for the party. Madge had pointed out other people – ordinary people, as Frank designated them in his own mind – like Ken and June Lambert, Jeanette Baynton, Mrs Wingfield's quondam brother-in-law, Carlo Geraldino, with his second wife, Natalie, a big dissatisfied-looking blonde.

Others, such as Francis and Judy Derham, Frau and Herr München from Berne, Pete Zanardi, Jack Dolia, Cecil Brewer, who apparently ran a London detective agency, and the MacGregors from Winterbourn Green, meant nothing at all to Frank Bryan, and he had forgotten them almost as soon as Madge had finished speaking their names. Bess Holland's was a recognizable face, however, although it now appeared, to Frank's bewilderment, that she was Harriet Wingfield's long-lost daughter, Hilary Canossa.

'Well, she's not really called Hilary Canossa,' Madge burbled on, confusing him even further. 'I mean, her name was legally changed to Holland when she was adopted, of course, although Elizabeth is her real second name. Mr and Mrs Holland preferred it to Hilary. And then, when she was married, years and years ago, she was Elizabeth Skells, but after the divorce she resorted to her maiden name. To Holland, that is. Frank! Are you listening to me?'

But Frank had lost interest; it was all far too complicated. Give him figures any day; so much simpler to understand, and they never did the unexpected. You always knew exactly where you were with figures. Frank continued to concentrate on his feet.

Bess was dancing with Edmund Howard. She was a good

501

dancer, swaying evenly and rhythmically to the music of the famous American band, but tonight her movements were entirely instinctive. She was still in the daze which had held her in thrall since being sent for by Harriet, early that afternoon.

She had gone, all unsuspecting of the revelation which was in store for her; which would change her life and its direction so dramatically. She had, in fact, been rather annoyed by the summons. Lunch was nearly ready, and she needed to eat hers quickly and get away. There were so many people she had to meet and welcome to the island in the next few hours.

In the event, she met none of them. Who deputized for her she had no idea; nor, after Harriet's first few halting sentences, did she care. Had she been asked, she would probably have found it difficult to recall the guests' names. Piloted skilfully by Edmund around the huge open-air dance-floor at the back of the house, under the shade of the ghostly tamarisk trees, Bess still felt as though she were moving in a dream.

'Am I awake?' she said, raising her face to Edmund's, a little blurred now in the gathering dusk.

'Wide awake,' he assured her, smiling.

'And I really am Harriet's daughter? It's not just something I imagined?'

'No. You really are her daughter. Can I ask you how you feel about the idea?'

'I'm not sure. For almost forty-two years now, I've been Bess Holland. Now, suddenly, I'm Hilary Canossa. It's unnerving, to say the least.'

'Do you think you might get used to the notion? And to having me for a step-father?'

Bess smiled faintly. She was looking particularly beautiful tonight, in a white Roland Klein dress which set off her dark colouring to perfection. Small ruby and diamond studs flashed in her ears, and pinned to the left shoulder of her gown was a matching ruby and diamond brooch. Edmund remembered Harriet giving Bess both pieces last Christmas.

'Oh, I think I'd quite like that,' she answered.

Edmund hesitated. 'And Harriet?' he asked. 'Do you think you can get used to the idea of being her daughter?'

The smile faded. 'I don't know,' Bess said seriously. 'I don't know just at the moment what I do feel.'

The waltz drew smoothly to its close, and everyone clapped. A moment later, the band swung into a quickstep, and Edmund looked at Bess and raised his brows.

'Can I monopolize you for a second dance?' He sensed that their conversation was not finished; that there were questions Bess still wanted to ask him.

'Shouldn't you be partnering Mrs Wingf –?' She broke off, uncertain how to continue; then, like someone tentatively exploring uncharted territory, asked: 'Shouldn't you be partnering my mother? You and she are engaged, after all. Isn't she going to announce it, later this evening?'

'At midnight. The witching hour. She wants to introduce you as her daughter at the same time.'

'Yes, she told me. At least, she asked my permission to do so.'

'And have you given it?'

'I asked her to wait. Until I've had more time to get accustomed to the idea myself.' They took another couple of turns around the floor, the overhead lamps striking sparks from the women's jewels and sequined dresses. Some people were leaving the floor to stroll down to the beach to bathe. Swimming costumes and trunks, of all colours, shapes and sizes, were available for those guests who wanted them. Bess knew, because she had arranged for their delivery from one of Athens's biggest stores. Remembering, it seemed like an action from a different existence, instead of something she had done only three days previously.

Bess demanded abruptly: 'Why did she wait so long?' And then, when Edmund did not immediately answer, went on: 'To acknowledge me, I mean. She's known who I was for more than twenty years.'

Edmund did his best to explain.

503

'Harriet has had to make absolutely certain in her own mind that she is doing the right thing, not just for you, but for her other children. It hasn't been an easy decision, even now, to disrupt all your lives, especially Michael's and Piers's. And there were your parents – your legal parents – to be considered. People who had brought you up and lavished on you the love and care which Harriet had been unable to provide. While even one of them was still alive, the last thing she wanted was to look as though she were trying to buy you back. So she did what she could. She took you under her wing and treated you like a daughter in everything but name. Didn't you ever feel that you were privileged, even for a confidential secretary and friend?'

Bess nodded slowly. 'I suppose so. Now and then, it did cross my mind to wonder why.' The music was once more coming to an end. As they circled the floor for the last time, Bess said: 'So why did she decide to acknowledge me now?'

'Your parents are both dead, for a start.'

'That still leaves Michael and Piers. From the way they've both been looking at me all evening, I can tell they're hardly reconciled to the idea, and probably never will be.'

The musicians crashed out the final chord and laid aside their instruments for a ten-minute break. The dancers dispersed to the tables set out under the trees or wandered off to the beach. Edmund linked one of Bess's arms through his and said: 'Let's find Harriet. I think she's somewhere inside.'

The house was crowded, people milling up and down stairs, chatting to friends and acquaintances, besieging the two bars, or fighting their way into the office to pick out swimming costumes from the pile strewn over the top of the desk. A few fanatics were still lingering around the television sets, watching replays of replays of Argentina's winning goals. The rooms were banked with flowers, mainly Harriet's favourite roses, and the scent was almost overpowering. Coloured lights were strung across the front of the house and looped around the balconies. Edmund gallantly suppressed a shudder.

They found Harriet on the balcony of the main salon, talking to Carlo and Natalie and drinking Buck's Fizz. She was wearing an elegant understated dress in heavy ribbed straw-coloured silk, with a single strand of matched emeralds. Diamond and emerald drops glistened in her ears. When she saw Bess, she broke off her conversation with Carlo and went forward, pausing a foot or so away, as though unsure of her welcome.

Edmund said heartily, 'Carlo! Natalie! Let me freshen your drinks,' and deftly ushered them inside the room before they quite knew what was happening. Edmund pulled the long window shut behind him and positioned himself where he could keep guard over Harriet's privacy.

Tables and chairs had been placed on the balcony. Harriet motioned Bess to sit down and took a seat opposite her. Floodlights were being turned on in the garden and on the beach, and lights were springing up all over the house. The band had started playing again; muted strains of music came in a steady beat from the back of the house.

The two women looked at one another in silence. Then Bess said: 'Michael and Piers aren't going to make life easy for me. If you take me into the company, I'm going to meet an awful lot of opposition.'

'Yes.' Harriet was pulling no punches. 'You are. You're going to have quite a battle on your hands. Do you think you can handle it?'

Bess sat motionless, staring out over the balcony towards the sea, her strong profile outlined against the light flooding through the uncurtained window behind her. After a moment, she turned her head and smiled.

'I think so. In fact, I'm beginning to look forward to the fray. I always wondered where I got my combative spirit from. Now, at last, I know.'

Harriet tried to return the smile, but found that her lips

505

were trembling. It was a few seconds before she could steady her voice.

'You . . . you accept me, then? As your mother? You forgive me for . . . for not acknowledging you sooner?'

There was another silence, while Bess fiddled with the clasp of her evening bag, snapping it open and shut, open and shut, until Harriet wanted to scream. She clenched her hands together.

The clicking stopped, and Bess raised her head. 'I've been talking to Edmund,' she said. 'He explained things to me. Made me see them clearer, at any rate. And you could have left matters as they were. You need never have told anyone that I'm your daughter.'

'But you *are* my daughter, and you deserve an equal chance with my other children. There's no one else to claim you now that your parents – Mr and Mrs Holland – are dead. Except, of course, your father. Your real father, I mean.'

'My father?' Bess looked dazed. 'Don't tell me you know where he is!'

'I'm sorry. I shouldn't have sprung it on you like that. You've had enough to cope with for one day.'

'You mean you *do* know where he is!' Bess pressed a hand to her forehead. 'He's . . . he's not *here*? In this house?'

Before Harriet could reply, the french window burst open and Elena swept on to the balcony, more beautiful than ever in a shimmering white-beaded 'twenties' dress, a sequined band tied round her long blonde hair. She seemed to be arguing with Edmund.

'Of course Mamma wants to see us. What's the matter with you, Eddie? Mamma! Look who I've found. Ramón. You didn't tell me you'd invited him.' Elena, typically, felt no constraint in the company of the man she had once tried to force into marrying her. Then she saw Bess and her voice faltered. 'Oh! I'm sorry. . . I didn't realize. . .' Suddenly she shrugged, enjoying the piquancy of the situation. Her eyes sparkled. 'Ramón,' she went on, 'you remember Bess Holland, Mamma's secretary. Only she isn't a secretary any more. She's my very own sister. Isn't it exciting?'

'Yes.' Gerry smiled, his eyes fixed on his daughter. 'I remember Bess.'

'Ellie,' Harriet said, 'you're incorrigible. I was planning to do the introduction myself, later on.'

'How stuffy and formal,' Elena protested. 'Ramón was jolly nearly family before, weren't you, *querido*? Now you'll be so in earnest.'

'That'll do, Ellie!' Harriet frowned. 'Go away now and deputize for me with the guests. It's time you began acquiring some of the social graces, young lady.'

Elena made a moue of disgust, but vanished obediently. Harriet glanced at Gerry.

'I haven't told her yet,' she said apologetically. 'I was going to suggest you stay the night and break the news tomorrow morning. I felt Bess had had enough surprises for one day.'

Bess was on her feet, staring in growing comprehension at her father. Harriet decided to slip tactfully away. Edmund was waiting for her just inside the salon.

'I need a drink,' Harriet said, clasping his hand for comfort. 'Scotch, a stiff one.'

Edmund gave her fingers a sympathetic squeeze.

'Everything OK? I'm sorry. I guessed you weren't ready for Gerry, but Elena had pushed him through before I could stop her.'

'It doesn't matter,' Harriet assured him. 'Perhaps it's all for the best. Get me that drink, then we'll go downstairs and dance. I need to keep moving. My nerves are all on edge.'

'Hardly surprising,' Edmund responded drily. 'You've had one hell of a day.'

'And it isn't over yet. Oh, Edmund, I hope Bess lets me make that announcement at the same time that I tell everyone about our engagement. It'll mean she's halfway to accepting who she is. Half-way to forgiving Gerry and me for what we've done.'

*   *   *

It was almost midnight. In a few minutes it would be time for the pre-supper speeches: tributes to Harriet from colleagues and friends, which she had done her best to dissuade them from making, but which she knew she could not avoid. And then would come her speech of thanks, the disclosure of her impending marriage. And the announcement of Bess's true identity? She did not know. Harriet had neither seen nor heard from her elder daughter since she left her on the balcony with Gerry.

The band had started to play 'Happy Birthday to You'. People were crowding back from the beach and out of the house. Edmund was urging Harriet towards the rostrum, where the band's conductor was genially making room for her. The family were pushing to the front: Julia with the boys, who had been allowed to stay up late for the occasion; Elena heroically letting herself be escorted by Rollo Wingfield and his new young wife; Carlo and Natalie, the latter dressed – or overdressed, as Angelo giggled to Marco – in yards of primrose-yellow chiffon; Michael and Piers, linked in uneasy alliance by their determination to fight their mother every step of the way. Looking at her sons' faces, Harriet knew she might have won the battle, but the war was far from over. She would have to watch her back from here on in. And Bess's. But her daughter was a fighter, like herself. She had recognized it from the very first moment of seeing her.

But where was Bess? Why didn't she come? The speeches were nearly finished, and it would soon be Harriet's turn. Had Bess, after all, decided to repudiate her inheritance? To go on being Bess Holland? To run away?

Harriet was aware of the sudden silence. The clapping and cheering had died. All eyes were focused in her direction. It was her turn to get up and speak.

She glanced in panic at Edmund, who shrugged and shook his head. Harriet saw the look of hope on both her sons' faces. Perhaps things were going their way. . . .

'My lords, ladies and gentlemen,' Harriet began, but her voice was subdued, barely audible above the crackling of the microphone. People were straining to hear what she had to say. She paused, unable to proceed, so bitter and so overwhelming was her disappointment.

Edmund touched her arm. He was smiling broadly. Harriet turned her head. Bess, holding Gerry's arm, was pushing her way to the front of the assembled guests to stand beside the other members of the family. She looked up at Harriet, her mouth breaking into a wide, almost uncontrollable grin. For a long moment, mother and daughter stared at one another, then Harriet turned backed to the microphone. This time, her voice was strong and confident.

'My lords, ladies and gentlemen! Thank you all so much for coming to my sixtieth birthday party, and for the wonderful things which some of you have seen fit to say about me this evening.' She took a deep breath. 'Not all of them are deserved, I may say, but I'm willing to let that pass, if you are. And now, before you go into supper, I have two very important announcements that I'd like to make . . .'

THE END

UNDER HEAVEN
by Brenda Clarke

It was 1946 when the young American Henry Lynton came to England to take his place in the family's chemical empire. It was then that he realised he wanted two things – to be the owner of the firm, and to possess Katherine Grey, his uncle's cool and beautiful secretary, who was already engaged to someone else.

Henry was ruthless, ambitious, totally male in every way, and shamelessly and sexually attracted to women of all kinds.

Katherine, whose outward composure masked a wildly passionate, wildly emotional nature, was intelligent and capable not only of love, but also of running a business empire as successfully as Henry Lynton.

Their union – over more than thirty years – was to be a stormy and passionate one.

0 552 132292

THREE WOMEN
by Brenda Clarke

'Her work has that rare quality of being difficult to put down'
British Book News

When Joseph Gordon – owner of Gordon's Quality Chocolate factory – married a girl from the factory floor he made it quite plain that her two young nieces were no responsibility of his. Elizabeth and Mary, born to a humbler walk of life, could expect no handouts from their Uncle Joe and their lot was not to be compared with their beautiful pampered cousin, Joe's treasured only daughter, Helen.

But these three girls, Elizabeth and Mary, and the delicate Helen, were to form a bond that all Joe's venom could not break. The passage of two world wars and the years between were to see violent and dramatic changes in their lives and it was Elizabeth, strong, vibrant, working-class and beautiful, who was to be the saviour of the family.

0 552 132608

A SELECTED LIST OF FINE NOVELS
AVAILABLE FROM CORGI BOOKS

THE PRICES SHOWN BELOW WERE CORRECT AT THE TIME OF GOING TO PRESS. HOWEVER TRANSWORLD PUBLISHERS RESERVE THE RIGHT TO SHOW NEW RETAIL PRICES ON COVERS WHICH MAY DIFFER FROM THOSE PREVIOUSLY ADVERTISED IN THE TEXT OR ELSEWHERE.

☐	13289 6	MOVING AWAY	*Louise Brindley*	£2.99
☐	12811 2	OUR SUMMER FACES	*Louise Brindley*	£3.95
☐	12564 4	TANQUILLAN	*Louise Brindley*	£2.95
☐	13260 8	THREE WOMEN	*Brenda Clarke*	£2.95
☐	13229 2	UNDER HEAVEN	*Brenda Clarke*	£3.50
☐	13261 6	WINTER LANDSCAPE	*Brenda Clarke*	£2.95
☐	12887 2	SHAKE DOWN THE STARS	*Frances Donnelly*	£3.99
☐	12387 0	COPPER KINGDOM	*Iris Gower*	£2.95
☐	12637 3	PROUD MARY	*Iris Gower*	£3.50
☐	12638 1	SPINNERS WHARF	*Iris Gower*	£3.99
☐	13138 5	MORGAN'S WOMAN	*Iris Gower*	£3.50
☐	13315 9	FIDDLER'S FERRY	*Iris Gower*	£3.50
☐	13384 1	A WHISPER TO THE LIVING	*Ruth Hamilton*	£2.99
☐	10249 0	BRIDE OF TANCRED	*Diane Pearson*	£1.95
☐	10375 6	CSARDAS	*Diane Pearson*	£3.95
☐	10271 7	THE MARIGOLD FIELD	*Diane Pearson*	£2.99
☐	09140 5	SARAH WHITMAN	*Diane Pearson*	£2.95
☐	12641 1	THE SUMMER OF THE BARSHINSKEYS	*Diane Pearson*	£2.95
☐	12607 1	DOCTOR ROSE	*Elvi Rhodes*	£2.99
☐	13185 7	THE GOLDEN GIRLS	*Elvi Rhodes*	£3.95
☐	12367 6	OPAL	*Elvi Rhodes*	£2.50
☐	12803 1	RUTH APPLEBY	*Elvi Rhodes*	£3.99
☐	12375 7	A SCATTERING OF DAISIES	*Susan Sallis*	£2.99
☐	12579 2	THE DAFFODILS OF NEWENT	*Susan Sallis*	£2.99
☐	12880 5	BLUEBELL WINDOWS	*Susan Sallis*	£2.99
☐	13136 9	ROSEMARY FOR REMEMBRANCE	*Susan Sallis*	£2.99
☐	13346 9	SUMMER VISITORS	*Susan Sallis*	£2.95

All Corgi/Bantam Books are available at your bookshop or newsagent, or can be ordered from the following address:

Corgi/Bantam Books,
Cash Sales Department,
P.O. Box 11, Falmouth, Cornwall TR10 9EN

Please send a cheque or postal order (no currency) and allow 60p for postage and packing for the first book plus 25p for the second book and 15p for each additional book ordered up to a maximum charge of £1.90 in UK.

B.F.P.O. customers please allow 60p for the first book, 25p for the second book plus 15p per copy for the next 7 books, thereafter 9p per book.

Overseas customers, including Eire, please allow £1.25 for postage and packing for the first book, 75p for the second book, and 28p for each subsequent title ordered.